Dear Reader:

I'm delighted to present to you the first books in the HarperMonogram imprint. This is a new imprint dedicated to publishing quality women's fiction and we believe it has all the makings of a surefire hit. From contemporary fiction to historical tales, to page-turning suspense thrillers, our goal at HarperMonogram is to publish romantic stories that will have you coming back for more.

Each month HarperMonogram will feature some of your favorite bestselling authors and introduce you to the most talented new writers around. We hope you enjoy this Monogram and all the HarperMonograms to come.

We'd love to know what you think. If you have any comments or suggestions please write to me at the address below:

HarperMonogram
10 East 53rd Street
New York, NY 10022

Karen Solem
Editor-in-chief

Many Men Coveted
The Basket Bride.

Chevalier Hector de Pombiers—From the moment the dissolute King's deputy laid eyes on the beautiful orphan, he vowed to bed her, by fair means or foul.

Prosper de la Fosse—Snatched from the very jaws of death by Minette's petal-soft hands, the New Orleans aristocrat pledged that his humble angel of mercy would soon be mother to a glorious new dynasty: his.

Alain Gerard—Embarked on colonial conquest, his life in peril, his future uncertain, the handsome, penniless lieutenant had nothing to offer Minette but his body and soul.

Harper Monogram

The Basket Bride

Phyllis Coe

HarperPaperbacks
A Division of HarperCollinsPublishers

This is a work of fiction. The characters, incidents, and dialogues are products of the author's imagination and are not to be construed as real. Any resemblance to actual events or persons, living or dead, is entirely coincidental.

HarperPaperbacks   *A Division of* HarperCollins*Publishers*
10 East 53rd Street, New York, N.Y. 10022

Cover illustration by Jim Griffin

First printing: December 1992

Printed in the United States of America

HarperPaperbacks, HarperMonogram, and colophon are trademarks of HarperCollins*Publishers*

❖ 10 9 8 7 6 5 4 3 2 1

1

The birds sang of summer to come and the Paris sky was a milky, opaline blue, but the halls within the Convent of the Blessed Saint Ursula still held the previous months' chill, Minette thought as she scrubbed the flagstones, a pail of soapy water beside her. She had wadded her winter tweed petticoat with extra rags but still the April cold bit at her knees with the fierceness of February. The thing to do was to go on counting the stones in the wide, flagged hall; one hundred scrubbed with the cornhusk brush and she would rise and ease her body. Ninety-eight, ninety-nine . . .

"Mademoiselle?"

Minette looked first at his boots, high and scarlet, of soft, rich-smelling leather. Then, higher, was a brocaded tunic—covering such a stomach! Above that, a red face, carefully curled chestnut hair and, yes, a plumed hat.

"Did you hear me, mademoiselle? You do speak?"

"Oh, sir, watch out. . . . Oh!"

He slipped on the wet stones, and his hand closed

hard on her shoulder to break his descent. His stomach hit her as hard as a cannonball, and she had to endure his weight until he regained his balance.

He made all apologies, begged a thousand pardons, inquired whether she was hurt.

Minette shook her head.

"I am the chevalier Hector de Pombiers, mademoiselle."

"And I am Minette."

"Are you a postulant?"

"No, sir, I am an orphan. The convent is my home."

"Sad for one so young. Did you know your parents?"

"No, sir. The sisters found me at the gate."

She didn't mind speaking the truth, Minette thought, but wasn't it rude of a stranger to ask?

A foundling, mused de Pombiers. But no peasant, not with that face. The poor tended to clutch at their wretched children, hoping to be cared for in old age; only the well-born had nuns dispose of their inconvenient mishaps. And what a little beauty this one was! The blond hair and bright blue eyes of northern France, but that skin had sun-gold washed into it—the legacy of some southern misalliance, he concluded. Most extraordinary. Firm-fleshed piece she was, too, with a nice rounded shoulder under his hand.

"Sir, how may I be of help to you?" She wished he wouldn't stare so.

"I have an appointment with your mother superior. But this place"—he looked down the branching halls—"is a true maze. I doubt I'd find my way alone."

"Well, in every hall you'll find an orphan scrubbing, sir. It's what we do in spring."

"Would you guide me yourself?"

"I would be most happy to, sir. Please come with me, but mind the stones."

Down the hall they went, her work sabots clattering. "That way leads to the library. We have a wonderful collection, they say. And that passage goes to the kitchen, which is Mother Clotilde's domain. She's the subprioress, of course. And out there is the passage to the garden. Would you like to see the garden? We've planted cauliflowers and cabbages and lettuces already; soon it will be time for the haricot beans. I like to crunch those beans right off the vines if the sisters don't catch me. No, I don't suppose you would be interested in the garden."

Minette knew that she was chattering, but the gentleman didn't seem to mind. Why did she keep thinking about food? It must be that stomach. How many plump fowls, galantines, and fruit tartlets had brought it to that noble curve! Fowl she ate at Christmas; galantines and fruit tartlets she had never tasted. Minette began to imagine a table covered with all the wonderful foods she had never eaten and felt slightly dizzy.

"And this is your chapel, Minette?" He stopped at its tessellated threshold. The red light winked as always in the sanctuary of the Blessed Mother and Infant Jesus, but the true heart of the place was the niche for St. Ursula, teacher and reformer, who stood among small gifts left by her worshipers.

"Yes, Chevalier. See St. Ursula. She's the patroness of girls. She believes in education for women and the common people."

"Who told you that?"

"Why, Mother Catherine, of course. She's a famous scholar herself and corresponds with bishops. Just ask her."

"I shall, when we meet. You are a delightful guide, Minette."

"Thank you, sir. We go upstairs here."

Why was the chevalier visiting their convent? Perhaps he was an ambassador for some grand lady who, disappointed in love, would join the Ursulines for the contemplative life and calm of soul. She might bring a great dowry, money sufficient to put in bigger baking ovens and make altar bread, decorated with crucifixes and holy symbols, to sell to the outside world. Or perhaps even cakes.

Cakes. Oh, she was still thinking of her stomach! She glanced again at the chevalier. How he must have feasted! But greed was an excess of desire, and excess in anything was to be avoided, so Mother Catherine said. Cleanse the mind of greedy thoughts, Minette. Make it pure and open to the Lord.

"Minette?"

"Yes, Chevalier?"

"Is there an end to this most instructive tour?"

"Oh, we are here, sir, unless you would like to walk on a little farther and see the reliquary with the saint's hair?"

"I think not."

Minette hesitated. At this time, the hour of *nones*, the sisters might be reading in the library, and Mother Catherine would certainly be at her meditations, not wishing to be disturbed. Beside her, the chevalier cleared his throat impatiently. As Minette was about to knock on the door of the mother superior's office, the chevalier simply put his leather-gauntleted hand against the heavy portal and pushed.

Mother Catherine, kneeling at her prie-dieu, looked up, then rose with the hesitancy of age. The mother superior of the Ursuline convent in Paris was a small woman, almost lost in her black habit with its full sleeves and veil. Silver-rimmed spectacles enlarged her shrewd eyes.

The chevalier swept the plumed hat off his head and

made a surprisingly graceful bow. "I am honored, Mother Catherine."

"And I have been expecting you, chevalier." With a gentle motion, she dismissed Minette. "Do not gossip about this visit, child. It does not concern you." The chevalier gave her a lingering smile as she left.

After offering him tea and the convent's coarse bread—hastily declined—Mother Catherine seated the chevalier in her best chair, a curving Renaissance seat with the only unfrayed velvet cushion in the room. The life of the mind and the diminishment of the senses illumined the austere room: whitewashed walls, an absence of pictures, many books and charts piled on a table, the prie-dieu, and very little else. The progressive Ursulines might believe in women's education, but, judging from the mother superior's domain, it hadn't made them rich.

"And now, Chevalier de Pombiers?"

"Yes, to our business." Hector de Pombiers had a set speech to make at this point in his interviews, and he rather liked the sound of it. "I come," he said, ceremoniously, "on behalf of the sieur de Bienville, the founder in New Orleans of our French empire over the seas, in the year of Our Lord 1699."

Outside, in the hall, Minette was disappointed; she could overhear nothing. She moved off as quietly as her sabots would permit. Despite Mother Catherine's injunction against gossip, she could at least test her theory about the fine lady coming to the convent with Seraphine and Berenice.

"In the ensuing thirty-five years," de Pombiers continued, "the sieur de Bienville has tried to maintain French dominancy, *bien sûr*, but there are many other races and cultures who live there: black slaves from the West Indies, freed people of mixed blood,

Spaniards, a ragtag of Americans—"

"Americans? Surely you mean British colonists."

"Not quite, Mother Catherine, but that is another story. To continue, all these groups in Louisiana grow in numbers. Unless we have a stabilizing core of French families, an artisan class to maintain our interest, Louisiana will gradually cease to be French. So what is the solution?"

"Our men must marry French, eh?"

"Yes, but who is there to marry unless the French government sends over girls of good character and modest expectations?"

Mother Catherine began to search her desk for a particular piece of paper. Annoyed, he declined to notice the distraction.

"The sieur de Bienville," he continued, "has worked out an excellent plan. I am one of his agents—as well as a personal friend, of course—sent out to gather prospective brides from the population of female orphans. *Naturellement,* they must be of blameless character, such as the girls you shelter here. Your girls are, I assume, trained in the domestic arts?"

"Trained and educated, according to the discipline of our order."

"Excellent. The government of France will provide each of the chosen brides with a *cassette* of linen articles as a dowry, and they will be sent to Louisiana to marry our workers and artisans. If they do not find a husband within two months, they will be returned to France, so as not to be a charge on the colony. But I assure you, they will find husbands! They have a special mission, Mother Catherine: to be reminders of France to men so far away from it, to stitch the rough, loose fabric of colonial life with French seams—neat, small stitches of loyalism, tradition, and *l'esprit français!*"

He looked up expectantly. It was a pretty speech, and at this point other convent superiors, ladies of fine family, had made graceful replies to his eloquence. But Mother Catherine remained unmoved. Her pinched face, withered cheeks, and work-roughened fingertips began to disgust him. This was no rosy, fashionable *religieuse;* he had quite wasted his fire here.

This great, red-faced whale has finally ended his spouting, Mother Catherine thought. Accustomed to working with quick, efficient women, she'd forgotten the nature of male bombast. His request was no surprise. She had told him when they made the appointment that she was ready to proceed. As if she hadn't been in correspondence on this very matter for months with the Ursuline house in Quebec! The man liked to hear himself talk. What a waste of valuable time!

She assumed an air of patience. "How many of these basket brides, these *filles à la cassette*, do you require from us?"

"Your apportionment is five. You understand that this is a new idea. If it is successful, as I am sure it will be, the numbers will be greatly increased."

"Yes, Chevalier."

"Well, then, shall we choose?"

She found the missing piece of paper in her sleeve. "I have the five names on this list."

Obstinacy seized Hector de Pombiers. "Who are these young women? What do they look like?"

"I assure you that they meet the requirements."

"Pardon me, but virtue alone cannot insure a young woman her place. Each must be of presentable appearance—in fact, the prettier, the better. We want quick, successful unions."

"Prettier?"

"For instance, the young woman who brought me to your door. She is most attractive, with a commendable country freshness, innocence, and obvious intelligence. I would want her on the list."

"You mean Minette Marsan?"

"Her surname is Marsan? I understood that she was a foundling."

"Yes, yes, Marsan happened to be the birthplace of the nun who found her at our gate."

"Was there anything found with her?"

"I suppose you mean a blanket with a ducal coronet?" Mother Catherine smiled bleakly. "No. As I recall, the swaddling cloth was of good quality but quite anonymous. We count her as a daughter of the people."

But I do not, thought de Pombiers. He knew women and horseflesh, and there was definitely aristocracy in that filly's bloodline.

"At any rate, Minette will not do, Chevalier. She is only a child."

"Surely she is fifteen years old."

"Sixteen, in fact, but a very young sixteen. Chronology is not the only measure of maturity."

"Sixteen is of full age to start a family, with many more years to breed."

"Breed, Chevalier?"

"Be fruitful and multiply then, as our Lord instructs."

"Quite true, Chevalier, but Minette is far from ready to take up those responsibilities. She is a dear child, but she has a light and frivolous temperament. However, we hope in time that she—"

The chevalier cut into her hopes. "If she is as you say, Mother Catherine, then she has very little future as a ward of the convent and should try her luck elsewhere. She is for Louisiana; I will have her name on the list. Please write it at the top."

With a barely perceptible sigh, Mother Catherine scratched out the first candidate's name—a pet of hers, were all things known—and substituted Minette's.

Hector de Pombiers enjoyed his victory. He had rescued Minette, that orphan charmer, from a bleak and dreary future. What an innocent flirt she was. How she had looked him over, her eyes lingering for a long time on his belt buckle. Lucky the husband who would instruct her, the golden Minette. How her eyes would open wide when—

The convent bell chimed four times, and Mother Catherine rose. "I am needed in the chapel, chevalier. Now that I understand your inclination, will you trust me on the selection of the other prospective brides?"

"I believe I have made my point, Mother Catherine. Please proceed." To tell the truth, he'd rather lost interest in the other four girls. Minette was the only one who mattered.

"Please excuse me. I will find someone to show you out."

"If the orphans are still scrubbing the halls," said the chevalier with a smile, "I will not lack for guides."

Alone for a few moments, the chevalier continued to occupy himself with thoughts of Minette. Golden child, a dazzle of sun in her hair and skin, a warmth . . . No, the warmth was his, a teasing warmth in the groin, a touch of sun's heat awakening. *Bon Dieu,* was it possible, could that be a rush of hot blood to his cold, dead parts? For years the chevalier had been impotent, but now, as the heat mounted, awakening the dead, filling him with strength and youth, he knew it was Minette's magic; somehow, she had done it for him. And he must find her, at this moment.

Dizzy with hope after all these years, he all but staggered down the halls, scarcely noticing his surroundings.

There she was, bent over the flagstones, her adorable rump twitching. This child had brought him back to life!

With only the vaguest of plans to ease his pressing need, he said, "Walk with me to the front door, Minette. I have some wonderful news for you." His hands were clenched protectively against his tunic, even though this innocent child should notice nothing. Never, he thought, even when he was nineteen and rutting like a rabbit, had he felt so ready.

"Chevalier? What news have you for me?"

"You will be leaving the convent, my child. You have been chosen by Mother Catherine to go to a land across the sea, called Louisiana."

"I have been chosen? But why?"

Keep walking, man, keep walking, hold her interest, get her out the front door.

Like someone enchanted, Minette followed. The chevalier looked so strange and red-faced, but his flow of words described a land of tropical flowers, a mighty river many times the size of the Seine, people of many colors. And, for some reason, she was to travel there. The possibility was outlandish.

They passed down the short *allée* of lime trees and out the front gate. His coach was waiting. Did he mean to take her to Louisiana this moment, without even a good-bye to Mother Catherine or—

"Oof!"

With a grunt of effort, the chevalier tumbled her into the coach. He held her down, her face pressed into the plum-colored upholstery, dust in her nostrils, his hands hard on her back.

"Driver!" he shouted. "Away from the center of town. Find me some quiet place!" The coach clattered down the street, picking up speed.

Minette struggled to raise her head, but he pressed harder, whispering into her ear.

"It is a very small favor I ask of you, sweet Minette. You cannot understand, but I beg you, you will be doing a most merciful good deed, and you will be rewarded, oh yes. I will give you three gold écus. Just think, starting your life in the New World with gold in your pocket!"

Now she was truly frightened. Three gold écus—surely for mortal sin and her soul's damnation.

"I don't want the money," she whispered. "Only let me go, please let me go."

"Later, child, later. But now, come to me, golden Minette!"

"No!"

She drove her elbows backward into the bulk of him. He gasped. She kicked upward, and he shifted his weight, but not enough; he was still holding her down.

"Don't make me hurt you."

"You *are* hurting me!"

She shook her head violently, hitting his chin and freeing one of her arms.

It didn't help. He was turning her over, handling her as easily as a toy despite his age and bulk. And his eyes!

"Chevalier, for the love of God . . ."

Now he was searching for the fastenings of her dress, and he ripped it in his impatience.

When she felt his fingers on her bare skin, Minette bit his hand as hard as she could.

"*Putain!*" There were bright drops of blood on the injured hand. "For that you shall have nothing!"

The carriage swayed dementedly as the horses rushed down a narrow wooded lane. The chevalier, snorting like a boar, pushed Minette against its door and yanked up her skirts. When he held her pinned, he began to work at his breeches. When she saw the blind red tip of what came thrusting out, Minette screamed and bucked hard against the door behind her.

Suddenly she was flying through the air, trees spinning as she was thrown clear of the coach. She did not, however, smash her head on the waiting cobblestones, but fell, miraculously, into flowering shrubbery, hard bits of twigs raking her face and arms as she sank into its depths.

Up came her arms, and she kicked out strongly with her legs, finding that they answered her, that she could struggle out of the encircling green. The coach was some distance away, the horses rearing in their traces as the coachman attempted to turn in the too-narrow space. As she looked, the chevalier, breeches flapping, climbed out of the coach and started toward her.

Minette, barefoot and free, began to run across the fields. Let him try to catch her now, the fat old man, without his coach and horses. She saw over her shoulder how the distance widened between them. He was calling hoarsely, and she turned her head slightly to catch his words.

"No one will believe you, Minette. No one!"

When she finally reached home, the heavy door of the Ursuline convent swung open to reveal Minette's friend and fellow orphan, Berenice.

"Holy Mary, where were you? We've all been looking. What happened? Oh, Minette!"

Sister Immaculata, fierce-eyed as a hawk, appeared behind Berenice. "You! Come with me!"

Limping, her bare feet bleeding from sharp stones encountered in her flight, Minette followed. All the convent's occupants were waiting in the main hall but not to welcome or comfort her. She could see the white gowns of the novices and lay sisters, the black habits of professed nuns, could feel the weight of their anger and disapproval, so heavy that she dared not raise her eyes. Whispering and rustling followed her to the door of the chapel.

"Inside, and pray for mercy from Our Lady!"

"Sister Immaculata, does Mother Catherine know?" Minette faltered.

"I am on my way to tell her. You have broken her heart."

"But I've done nothing, Sister. It was done to me."

"Silence. I've no wish to hear your lies. If you were a nun, you would pray for the thrashing cord's discipline across your back. As it is, I do not know what punishment Mother Catherine will mete out to you. But I ask you not to address me again!"

Sister Immaculata had been one of Minette's favorite teachers, but there was no encouragement in her eyes today. Alone with her shame, Minette looked toward the altar. The face of the Virgin swam through a mist of stinging tears. She raised her head in pleading and saw herself reflected in a crystal globe: an apparition stared back, its face bruised and scratched, hair hanging frowsily, full of twigs and leaves, and, most horrible of all, the dress torn at its neck, fluttering scraps revealing white flesh and a rounding of breast. The lowest, dirtiest woman of the streets could look no worse.

The eyes of Our Lady, which often in the candlelight seemed to gleam with sparks of wisdom and tenderness, were cold bits of glass today. Minette turned toward the valiant Saint Ursula, martyred at Cologne. "You believed in the intelligence of women, so you must listen. Blessed Saint Ursula, *mea culpa, mea maxima culpa*. I followed that man right out of the convent, trotting along beside him like a silly little dog, never thinking . . . Can you forgive me for stupidity but not dishonor?"

She waited for the warmth and peace that so often enveloped her when she talked to St. Ursula. But there was nothing, only the cold gray censuring of the chapel stones, rejecting her pleas, rejecting her.

"Minette," said Mother Catherine from behind her. "I want you to go to the dispensary. Sister Josefa will wash those scratches and apply a healing balm. And get another dress from the robe room."

"Mother, you must believe me, if no one else does, for you have spoken to that man and seen the evil in his eyes, which I did nothing to provoke, I swear. . . ." Minette's voice trailed off as Mother Catherine raised a warning hand.

"But the harm has been done, Minette. *Le scandale* is upon us, here in our own motherhouse."

"There need be no scandal. I saved my honor. With the help of God, I fell out of the coach before he could—"

"Look at yourself. We cannot afford even the appearance of scandal. Do you think that the Ursulines have ever recovered from that shameful business of so-called demonic possession at Loudun? We are terribly vulnerable, my child."

"You mean to the world outside the motherhouse?"

"Only in part. To our world within as well. Our community of souls. Though we strive to receive the Holy Spirit and emulate Our Savior, we are all too human. There are those who may believe in your innocence, but there are also those who will be mortally certain of your guilt. I cannot compel them to change their thoughts. Only God has that power. You will be a focus of dissension in our community, a distraction from the plane of life we hope to achieve."

"But surely *you* believe me, Mother?"

"Poor child, you haven't been listening. It matters little whether I believe you or not. You must leave."

"Leave my home because of a lustful old man?"

"You always knew that you would leave someday."

"But now, in disgrace? Where can I go that it will not be known?"

"Nowhere in France, certainly. But you can go to Louisiana. You have already been chosen to be one of the *filles à la cassette*."

"*He* chose me. I will not go."

"And I did not want to send you. But perhaps there is a divine pattern here. Perhaps you were meant to go and find a husband in that faraway place."

"Husband? I want nothing to do with men!"

Mother Catherine permitted herself a small smile. "Minette, you are formed as a flower, to bloom and attract and then be gathered."

"But the chevalier de Pombiers? Suppose he is in Louisiana?"

"It's a large country, I have heard, and you will certainly find a husband to protect you."

"You ask me to leave you, Mother, and everything I have known. I don't think I am ready for that."

"Nor do I, my child. But you must go. Try to compose yourself. Cherish the memories of this, your home."

Alone again, Minette tried for serenity. Cherish the memory of the silvery bells that ruled the convent day from matins to vespers and evening compline, now never to be heard again. Cherish calm and candlelight and lessons learned. She had been taught by many mothers here, in a world complete and ordered, lit by flashes of inspiration as joyously piercing as the blue of the stained glass windows. Sometimes rebellious, unbelieving, and thoughtless, she had meant no harm, never loved this place so much as now, when she had to leave it.

Good-bye, my home.

The medieval walls surrounding the city were topped with guns aimed across the Gulf of Saint Malo at the English Channel and the old enemy. The English knew this belligerent posture well; out of Saint Malo port came cannonballs and small, swift raiders, the Saint Malo privateers.

A brisk sea wind blew gusts of spray into the streets and made Sister Immaculata's bones ache as she struggled to herd her five charges along. It always seemed to threaten rain in this old town of gray streets, gray houses, gray scum on the cobblestones, made even more slippery by the clacking of the country people's Breton sabots.

That was what the nun saw. The five young basket brides were in paradise; they had never been so close to so many young men! A fortified town like Saint Malo had a handsome complement of soldiers, and a month of Atlantic storms had crowded the town with even more of them waiting for overdue ships. For the girls, the streets were dizzying: muscular, uniformed shoulders brushing by; heads turning to stare; hot, bright eyes and lewd whispers after the nun had passed. It was a feast, a feast of excitement and deprivation, look but never sample. The girls shivered and giggled. Their minds were abysmally ignorant of sex, but their bodies continually prompted them. Each night, as Sister snored comfortably, they exchanged fevered misinformation.

But Sister Immaculata had assessed the peril. "Foolish virgins attract stragglers," she muttered, moving hers like a sergeant drilling troops. "Keep walking at a brisk pace, girls, eyes to the front. We must guard our health in this damp and chilly place. Three circuits of Saint Malo for today—quickly, quickly—and if anyone speaks to you, do not answer."

What went on behind her? Was it the silent language of flirtation that she had never learned? These forced marches were exhausting for Immaculata; she was working as hard as the sheepdogs on her father's farm, for she felt that only by walking out their animal spirits, by the authority of her presence and by force of the habitual obedience of their past, could she keep four of the five girls in line. That left Minette.

Mother Catherine, she thought, *what a burden you have placed on my faithful heart.* Once Immaculata herself had preferred the chit for her bright disposition and aptitude for learning, rejoicing in her intelligence. In that, the devil had laid her a fine snare. But how could she have imagined that he would catch Mother Catherine in it, too? How could it be that the mother superior of the Ursuline convent, the sun around whom the small, toiling spheres of nuns revolved as in an orrery of the planets in the design of Our Lord's world, how could it be that the sun would deign to notice one insignificant orphan and single her out, more, take up her cause? Three times Minette had been in Mother Catherine's office for private consultation! She herself, Immaculata, had never had that privilege even once, after so many years of devoted service. Didn't it argue something more than mere coincidence, some malign influence operating on the girl's behalf to make the mother superior excuse her crime and send her, nevertheless, to La Louisiane?

"Why, I am jealous!" she muttered to herself, dragging out that rusty emotion for inspection. "Jealous of the favor shown Minette. Jealous of Minette herself, who breaks all the rules and is not punished." Once she had said it, she felt better, even though no one had heard the confession.

With the exception of Minette, Mother Catherine had composed this virginal bouquet shrewdly. It was bound to please; Immaculata saw it in the eyes of the men who tried to press ever closer to her girls. There was Celeste, a white rose, fair and plump with soft flesh and petal-pink lips; then Eulalie, a neat little daisy with wide blue eyes, the picture of innocence; for contrast, Seraphine, whose lazy eyes and silken black hair made her an exotic lily; and Berenice. What was Berenice? Ah, a sturdy, copper-headed flowering that would produce many children. Well done, Mother Catherine. They each have admirers on the streets of Saint Malo.

Of course, Minette outshone them all. That was always the problem. "But I will redouble my vigilance," vowed the nun. "There will be no repetition of yesterday."

Yesterday the devil's snare had seemed to be just another café in another stone house, its doorway covered by a frayed red curtain. As they went by, however, a soldier, not young or handsome but certainly drunken, had stumbled out to be sick in an alleyway. The curtain had stayed open, releasing a fog of tobacco smoke into the street. As it did so, the room cleared sufficiently to reveal a raised platform at its far end. On it, a luscious, dusky-skinned woman was dancing—naked or nearly so, wrapped only in her cascade of inky hair, some net and shiny stuff. She was barefoot. The girls stopped dead. Thin, piping music accompanied this indecent display—how she moved!—and there was supreme grace in her dancer's body as she dipped and swayed, turned and turned, spun the shiny bits on her net into a shimmering blur. As she whirled to a stop and raised her arms triumphantly, the net over her breasts parted, and she held the pose in brazen glory.

"Hera!" cried the watching men who crowded that room. "Hera!" Over and over, they cried her name.

Coins were thrown at the stage. A soldier rushed forward to offer himself, but he was pulled back before he could touch her. The others were shouting, thumping the tables. "Hera!"

Watching, Minette shuddered. The urgency of the men brought back the voice of the Chevalier de Pombiers as he pressed her down on the seat of the coach. And their eyes must hold the same fevered glare . . .

The nun's arm flung her back. "Shame, Minette! Shame on all of you. All will say penance for this tonight. Shame! You couldn't stop looking. You wouldn't have moved if I'd struck you with a whip!"

Sister had a right to be angry. Seraphine's face had held a dreamy, catlike raptness, and Eulalie's blue eyes had bulged with avid interest.

"So many sins in such a short time, mesdemoiselles. You are in need of a confessor!" True, Saint Malo had many churches, but to use one for this purpose was to advertise her failure and loss of control. She reconsidered. "Penances and no supper. All of us will fast tonight for the good of our souls."

The indignation in her voice brought catcalls from Hera's audience. The men shouted, "Girls, pretty girls, come in and dance with Hera. Show us what you have, darlings, pretty pigeons. Come in, but leave the crow outside!"

As Sister shook her Ursuline black robes, one man in that place turned and looked directly at Minette. A soldier. His face froze her to the spot, because she knew it. This face had been in her mind for a long time: she knew how the bones modeled the smooth contours of his cheeks, how his wide gray eyes were set, the shape of his long, generous mouth. She knew without knowing that there was more to him than a young man joining others in debauch before a naked dancer. Those gray eyes could be tender and compassionate. He looked a poet, or as a poet should.

Ah, that was the answer to the mystery. As Sister Immaculata hurried them away, Minette's mind flew back to the library of the Ursuline convent in Paris. . . . So fortunate that the nuns, adhering to strict routine, were always where they should be. They would not come in, for it was not the proper hour. And the other girls, the orphans, would never think of looking for her in this room. If it was not expressly forbidden for an orphan to be in the library alone, it was only because no one had imagined the problem would occur.

But Minette crept in whenever she could, dustcloth in hand for convenient camouflage. She did dust the books, but she read them, too. Such riches! Together with the proper historical and devotional works, the convent library had a small, select reference collection of philosophy and poetry. But the poetry—though praising heaven, to be sure—used classical imagery. The unfamiliar words challenged Minette's reading skills, but eventually she mastered them. In the process, certain formulations cast a spell over her imagination. There was *adamantine* and *marble-browed, Olympian, strong-thewed*, and especially, *the sun-bright Apollo*. Out of these, and others, she had fashioned in her mind a face, a handsome poet's face of perfection.

Had she dreamed it into life? This soldier in Saint Malo was wearing it. He existed. That was enough. She wasn't bored anymore with the daily walking; he might be on the streets. She didn't care if she missed the chunks of pork in the thin soup that composed the evening meal in the high, narrow, church-owned house where they waited for the coming of their ship; she had no appetite now. Any time not spent in looking was wasted. What if he was looking for her too, as his eyes had seemed to promise before Sister had seized the red curtain to the café and pulled it shut?

And if he found her, what then? She only wanted to study him, Minette told herself. No man should look so much like her private dream.

But consider where you saw him, prompted her conscience. Since when do poets go soldiering? He's just a man, a common lustful man, and where else would he take his pleasures but in a place like that? Out of nowhere, the thought came to her that she hated the dancer Hera.

Wherever he was, he was not on the streets, nor on the waterfront. They spent much time watching the tides come and go. The outgoing tide uncovered huge, sandy runways, and the long black rocks in the Bay of Saint Malo looked like hulls of sunken ships. When the tide thundered in again, a wall of water, it pounded the edges of the seawall and splashed at the top. You could hear the waves sounding from any part of town, and the raucous, jeering calls of the sea gulls.

When they became connoisseurs of the tidal timetables, Sister Immaculata began to badger the harbor master about the arrival of their ship, the *Baleine*. He was a thickset, pipe-puffing man, as solid as the crenellated towers of the town's famous ramparts.

"How do I know, Sister? Ask the winds, ask the weather."

"Surely some fishing boat gone far out to sea might have sighted the *Baleine?*"

He sucked his pipe in silent exasperation. "Have you ever traveled far on a sailing ship, Sister?"

"Thanks to God, I have not. Only to cross the Channel."

"I thought as much. And these young ladies?"

"Never off land in their lives."

"Well, what a treat they've got in store for them. And with the spring tides, too."

"All you Malouins are so cheerful," said Sister sarcastically.

"Comes from drinking our famous Breton cider. Have you tried it, Sister?"

She sniffed.

"I thought as much. A sip now and then might make your waiting easier."

"But for how long? Perhaps our ship has been sunk. Isn't there some way you can find out?"

He laughed finally, his face spreading into a net of wrinkles.

"The town is full of travelers waiting for the *Baleine* and the *Bourgogne* and the *Artemis* and all the others that are overdue. They will come when they come. Meanwhile, Sister, it's market day. Go and see the fun."

Every weekend a large, cleared field near the center of town became a marketplace. As soon as the city gates were opened, the peasants came in with squawking chickens and noisy carts piled high with potatoes, beets, turnips, cabbages, and cauliflowers. The onion sellers wore huge garlands of their stock; women carried livestock in cages—brown hares, young squabs and ducks. Everything was for sale—fabrics, wheels of cheese, honey, spoons, rugs woven of rags. The farmers set up rickety booths in the morning chill on ground that would soon be churned into mud.

Each market day the girls had asked permission to attend, and each time Sister refused. "I cannot protect you"—she meant from fondling and pinches—"in the press of that crowd." But this time, after the harbor master had been so indifferent to their hopes, she was inclined to give the diversion consideration. And when she saw medicinal roots and dried herbs set out for sale, it was decided. She had been the convent's nurse for all but the most serious of illnesses, and there was sure to be something in this display to be added to the black satchel she had brought from Paris. She led her wards in.

It was like swimming in a sea of people. As Sister bargained combatively for what she wanted, Minette could detect in her the capable farm girl she had been so many years ago. Why, Sister must have had sisters of her own, and brothers; there might still be doddering old parents who proudly remembered the daughter who'd become a nun. Her name would be in the family Bible, her yellowing communion dress still packed away in an old humpbacked family trunk. Sister Immaculata had been someone else before she chose the Ursulines.

But as for Minette, her life had begun at the convent gate. She was alone in the world. Even the other orphan girls had only scorn for her.

All the way from Paris to Saint Malo on that jolting coach, they had ignored her. Even now, she trailed last on their walks. Berenice had been her avowed friend in the convent and clearly still wanted to be, but the others held her back. Seraphine's green eyes turned sly and nasty when they rested on Minette. Celeste and Eulalie nervously avoided her—and all because she had been forcibly tumbled into a coach by the evil Chevalier de Pombiers. Well, she'd ignore them, too. She had better things to think about. For instance, the soldier might be here in the market crowd, if he was waiting for a ship and as bored as they'd been.

There was a cockfight in the market that afternoon, and a pig escaped, and squalling children became separated from their mothers, and a woman made a great scene that she was cheated by a peasant who had sold her a sick cockerel. Everyone in Saint Malo appeared to be there, except for a certain poet-soldier. Perhaps he was in a little room with a bed and the dancer Hera, Minette thought miserably.

The next morning, soon after they had set out for their usual dreary walk, Minette had the strongest impression of energy and presence to her right. And there he was, his eyes asking, *Where have you been?* Before she obeyed Sister's command to walk on, she saw his soft black hair, tied back in a peruke but without the stiff, rolled side curls so many of the soldiers in the streets were wearing. Black hair for her golden, "sun-bright Apollo?" Minette's imagination made it right in an instant: "raven" locks were equally well suited to a poet with a storm at the heart of his nature.

"Minette, please. Sister will be angry!" Berenice was still trying to help.

But Minette couldn't move. It was too wonderful. He stood there, tall and muscular, wearing a uniform of dark marine blue, the red facings of the coat turned back and decorated with gilt buttons. There were a great many bright buttons with no apparent use, including those on the pocket flaps. A blue waistcoat could be seen, and under that, a white shirt and a high stock. The blue knee breeches, short and tight—oh, those thighs—were met by high black boots. He was an officer; she saw a gilt emblem and a flutter of regimental color in the epaulet on his left shoulder. As she watched, he took off the black cocked hat trimmed in white and slowly tucked it under his right arm. The gesture was not a bow but an acknowledgment that their eyes had met, met and held until Minette became afraid that he would speak.

Oh, please don't, she thought, *and don't come any nearer or Sister will lock me in a room till the ship comes.* She concentrated fiercely on this message, willing him to understand. Don't come closer, but don't go away, now that you've found me.

Was that the flicker of a smile? He seemed to have received her heartfelt silent message; he fell back to a distance at which Sister Immaculata could not be absolutely sure that he wasn't merely strolling in the same direction. The performance was repeated the next day as well. He seemed endlessly patient.

But Seraphine cornered Minette as they were undressing for bed in the style of the convent, night-gown pulled on underneath and then the outer clothes removed. "What tricks do you use, Minette? I've been watching, and I can't see anything. Yet he's always there."

"You are finally speaking to me, Seraphine?"

"Don't play the innocent. I want to know about the handsome officer who follows you."

"Why do you say he follows me? Ow! Pinch me again, Seraphine, and you'll be sorry."

"Minette, what have you done this time?" It was Sister Immaculata, who had not seen the pinch.

"What have I done this time, Sister? You must tell me my past offenses, for I do not know."

"Impertinence is certainly one of them."

"Sister, I was only asking. Seraphine makes accusations—"

"Flirting, Sister." Seraphine was ever eager to put the charge before the judge. "She keeps a soldier following us on our walks. He does it only for her. Move her up in line, put her in my place."

"So that you may walk last and take your chances with this soldier? I think not, Seraphine. And I've heard enough of this petty quarreling. It's time to remember who you are and why we are here. Mesdemoiselles, your baskets, please."

They hurried to oblige, since clearly only a lecture was in store, not a punishment. Sister looked at the split-rush baskets, touched their shiny wooden tops with something like reverence.

"There's a reason you may not open these lids until after the marriage ceremony, *mes petites*. They are more than your dowries. They are your contracts with the government of France and our good king Louis the fifteenth. These baskets are articles of faith: When you took them, you promised the king and Our Savior to be

good French wives and mothers, to carry out the highest traditions of our country, to bring the light of French
civilization into a dark, distant land."

"All that with linens?" asked the literal-minded
Celeste.

The nun was briefly amused. "They are the best
quality of linens, far better than your future husbands
would be able to buy for many years. And they are symbols, heirlooms to be handed down to your many
descendants."

"If our children don't wear them out first," remarked
Berenice. She looked and was a practical girl, sole sur-
vivor of a large family wiped out by the typhus fever.

"These linens are not for daily use, Berenice."

"But, Sister, since we're orphans with nothing but the
clothes we stand up in and those baskets, it's not likely
we'll be marrying people who can afford *not* to use them.
If the linens are of such good quality, they'll endure."

There was no immediate answer to that.

"Sister," Berenice pursued, "speaking of children,
can you show us something practical? Are there reme-
dies in your black bag that will keep our children
healthy?"

"You may look." Out came the satchel with its contents of neat, glass-stoppered vials. "Most of this is not
for you. There are things in here that are poisons in the
hands of the inexperienced. This is antimony, and this
is mercury—no, don't touch—but you may learn to
dose your family with sulphur and volatile salts."

"Surely they're not meant for children?" Berenice
was horrified.

"Extreme conditions necessitate extreme treatment.
But the secret of children's health is always cleanliness,
outside and in, and by that I mean good bowels."

Eulalie, the prissiest of them all, made a small, repulsed sound. As a nurse, Sister had her special enthusiasms. She would never discuss the process through which children were obtained, but she was profoundly interested in their interiors.

"There are many emetics and diuretics. Cascara is my favorite. See, these are cascara seeds in my hand. You can trust them. Children tolerate their effects well. But sometimes a good drench of warm water will do the job. Put a funnel in your child's mouth, pour down two or three gallons *et, voila!*"

"And what for fever?" asked Berenice, thinking of her vanished family.

"Call the physician or the surgeon."

"Surgeon! I would not have one of those men bleed my child."

"Then there is only folk medicine. There are healing plants everywhere, even in La Louisiane, I imagine."

"How will we know them?"

"*Zut*, girl, you will ask. Here's feverfew, for instance. I bought some on market day. It's effective when boiled into a tea."

"May I have some, Sister?"

"*La*, Berenice, you don't even have a man yet, and you're planning children!" Seraphine was tired of this conversation and eager to bring it back to Minette's soldier.

"I know I will have children," said Berenice calmly.

"First you need a husband," said Seraphine. "And if you want to know how to get a man, why not ask Minette? She has succeeded already. Find out how she did it. She won't tell me."

Sister turned the eye of suspicion on the miscreant but aloud said only, "Mesdemoiselles, I extinguish the candle. Sleep well."

But Minette could not sleep for thinking of tomorrow. Would he be there tomorrow? Or would he have become bored with their stupid walks and his pursuit of a girl not allowed to speak to him? What if, heaven forbid, he was married? Or simply amusing himself with this wordless romance? She needed to consider her situation. She knew nothing—*rien*—about this beautiful man, but she did know Sister Immaculata. If the nun decided she had encouraged the soldier's attention, if he dared to speak to her, she might well contrive to send her back to the convent, even at the very last moment. And then what? She couldn't stay with the Ursulines; Mother Catherine had made that quite plain. It was La Louisiane . . . or the streets. No, not even for a word from him was it worth the risk.

The even breathing of the girls around her told Minette that they were asleep, while she was alone with this heartbreak. "I must renounce you, my poet," she whispered to the air. "But I will cherish the memory of your face and form forever, even after I am married to some strange husband and have children who require cascara and warm-water drenches. You will be my heart's secret." Perhaps it would be enough, knowing that her imaginings actually existed in the perfection of one young officer whom she must renounce in actuality. There was nothing else to do if she wanted to save herself.

The next morning, she did not look for her poet on the street, but he suddenly walked into her line of vision, then went directly past her and straight up to Sister Immaculata. He bowed politely.

"What is it, Lieutenant?" demanded the nun.

"*Ma soeur*, permit me, I have something to tell you."

Minette felt suddenly weak. He could not be so reckless as to expose their unspoken romance!

"I do not know you, sir," said the nun.

"But you have seen me, often."

"That is not an introduction."

"Let me amend that. I am Lieutenant Alain Gerard of His Majesty's Royal Marine Infantry, I have the honor to inform you that your ship, the *Baleine*, will tie up at the quay by midafternoon. I am so informed by the harbor master."

"*Merci mille fois*, but why, Lieutenant, are you so concerned with our passage on the *Baleine*?"

"Because, *ma soeur*, I am your fellow passenger, traveling on detached duty with a number of my men. Since we have all been waiting so long for the *Baleine*—waiting together—I thought to give you the news so that you might make ready."

Again he bowed and then walked swiftly away. Minette felt Seraphine watching her and kept her face expressionless. But she knew the whole exchange had been for her benefit, a promise and a reassurance. By speaking to the nun, he had given her a message. "Waiting together," he had said. Oh, surely that was meant for her. And now, sailing together, for weeks and weeks, however long it took to reach the other side of the world. How clever he had been to think of this irreproachable means of addressing her. He did care. And his voice, heard for the first time, was all she could have expected. The sound had warmed her, crept into her very bones.

3

The three masts and upper skysails of the *Baleine* swayed gently above the horizon for an hour before the rest of the ship could be seen from Saint Malo. The *Baleine,* a merchantman shuttling among France, the West Indies, and America, was almost as big as a warship and carried a row of cannon behind its closed gunports. At sea, against pirates as well as wind and weather, the captain had to rely on himself.

"*La baleine,*" murmured Sister Immaculata. "The whale is the largest of the sea creatures."

"Larger even than the sea serpents?" Celeste asked anxiously. "The ones drawn on the maps?"

"And that's where they remain, Celeste, a product of the artist's imagination."

The girl looked distinctly relieved.

Coming into port, the *Baleine* was majestic but ugly, rising high and bulky above the water. Six leaded glass windows marked the location of the sterncastle, which clung to the ship's far end like a carved and gilded blister.

There lived the captain, officers, pilots, and a few important passengers, and from it the captain's gaze could sweep the decks as he directed his ship. On a merchantman, the sterncastle was the only spot of comfort, on a man-of-war the most dangerous place to be. Immediately below was housed the steering apparatus and, in a man-of-war, the gunpowder magazine. One well-placed shot from an enemy blasted everything.

This arrangement was an inheritance from the cumbersome Spanish galleons of the 1600s, as were the three-tiered poop decks just beneath the sterncastle. Below, down the main deck, were goats and chickens kept as fresh food supply. On extended voyages it could contain a whole pen of sheep.

"How long will the voyage be?" Sister had asked the harbor master.

He'd laughed at her. "Who can tell? The weather may blow you all over the North Atlantic, or you could be stuck in the calms near the Indies and have to send out the longboats to row for wind. Blow or row, take your choice."

"He's trying to frighten us," Eulalie decided.

Sister wasn't sure. Her sea voyaging had been limited to one crossing of la Manche, the English Channel, and *that* she preferred to forget.

The next morning, they joined the passengers boarding a reprovisioned *Baleine*. The detachment of Royal Marine Infantry—and Alain Gerard—was nowhere to be seen. It was notable how many passengers brought their own food. One well-dressed group carried trunks and feather pillows as well and shied away nervously from Sister Immaculata's Ursuline habit.

"Huguenots," she pronounced. "Protestants. It's a wonder they didn't embark from the port of La Rochelle instead of here. They're thick as fleas down there in the Charente."

"Protestants?" The girls were fascinated, but Sister had no intention of discussing the social and economic persecution that sent these Huguenots out of France. She did not entirely approve of it. Why add to the problems of those whose beliefs already condemned them to eternal hellfire?

For the most part, the passengers were peasant families indentured for labor in La Louisiane, exchanging three years of their lives for eventual citizenship in the French colony. Hard conditions awaited them, but hope, too. Ragged women, pinch-faced with hunger, held their listless children. Whatever happened—*ça s'y va*—they would endure.

For the rest, a mixed lot: merchants searching for business opportunities overseas, slightly seedy gentlemen, a few teachers, some raffish types anxious to escape their creditors. And last, a troupe of women with painted faces and rouged lips.

"Hera!" cried Minette. "There's Hera."

In the sunlight, the dancer looked much older, olive-skinned as a Marseillaise but with an even darker bloom to her cheeks. The face was all sensuality—lips almost too full, and long-lashed almond eyes that quickly surveyed Minette and glanced away.

"She won't be allowed to do that dance on this ship, will she?" asked Eulalie.

"This is a Christian place. There are families here," said Celeste.

"And sailors," added Seraphine slyly, "and soldiers. What about them?"

"Soldiers? Where?" Minette followed Seraphine's pointing finger.

Down the quay strode the detachment of the Royal Marine Infantry, packrolls on their backs, white crossed belts holding ammunition bags, muskets shining in the sun. There were three officers wearing swords. And just behind a small fellow with fierce pepper-pot mustaches curling over his cheeks was Lieutenant Alain Gerard.

How splendid he looked! *Turn to me*, Minette begged silently. *Here I am, ready to begin our voyage together*. But he did not turn.

"Where do you suppose the soldiers will stay?" she asked Sister carefully.

"On the gun deck, I am sure," was the dry response. "But don't concern yourself with that, Minette. You will not see them."

What she meant was soon obvious. The girls were sent to a small windowless cabin on the lowest deck, far from temptation and the other passengers. It was musty yet more spacious than the lean-to arrangements, little bigger than dog kennels, which most passengers used for sleeping space wherever they could. It was certainly more private than the rolls of canvas used to separate families packed into the cargo holds.

But privacy would prove to be an unlucky choice. For every sailing ship, under way, had certain areas that defied all known laws of motion when buffeted by the long ocean rollers. This former ship's storeroom was such a spot. When the *Baleine* stood out from Saint Malo and sailed southward to escape pirates from the Channel Islands, its potential for disaster became all too clear. The cabin shuddered dramatically as the ship dipped into troughs between the waves, then went into crazy vibrations that rattled the teeth.

Celeste was the first to go down, moaning and clutching her blankets. Then Seraphine turned an ill-favored shade of green, while Eulalie whimpered pitifully. Berenice gritted her teeth, fighting the nausea as long as she could, and Sister Immaculata, remembering her trip across the English Channel, reached immediately for the slop jar.

Minette alone was unaffected. Outside, the winds roared as the weather changed, but she lay peacefully on her straw pallet, watching the planks above her heave dizzyingly. She felt nothing but a longing for fresh sea air.

The weather, which had been good enough to provide them with an immediate favorable wind so that they could clear port without waiting, now began to test them. The *Baleine* was running through a line of fierce, wind-lashed squalls, and the captain ordered all passengers belowdecks. The ship would heel suddenly as a heavy gust hit, and the rigging would come alive with sailors swarming up to the yards as fast as their legs would take them. As they trimmed the sails, the ship righted itself with reluctance and ominous creaking, only to plunge again in a terrifying swoop toward the waves.

Nevertheless, Minette was hungry. With Sister's muttered permission, she went out into the passage and struggled up the ladder to the mess that served their part of the ship. Here a huge iron kettle awaited, filled with something cold and congealed, since the cook had not been able to light his fires. She took spoonfuls of whatever it was, a sort of stew, and ate absently from her wooden plate. How was Alain Gerard taking this? How was he feeling up there on the gun deck? She could not imagine him in less than shining health. But how would she speak to him? Where would they find each other? Sister had clearly planned efficiently to keep them apart.

The cook's helper, a wizened fellow, watched her eat. The stew was heavily salted, since the only way to preserve food was to salt it down and pack it into barrels.

"Could I have some water, please?" she soon asked.

"The dipper is there."

"Have you something I can use to carry water to my friends? There are five of them, all sick."

"And why aren't you?"

Minette shrugged and smiled agreeably. "Could I have some biscuits too?"

"You'll have to worry the edges first. They're hard enough to break your teeth if you bite down at once," he warned her. "But when your friends can eat again, dry biscuit's the thing to give them, nothing else."

So began Minette's introduction to the business of nursing. She moistened five pairs of cracked lips with a damp cloth, sponged aching heads, then squeezed the precious drops of water out again for later use. Against Sister's feeble protests about draughts, she opened the door and let the icy air of the passage outside dispel the nauseating buildup of odors from the sick. The slop jar had to be emptied again and again; she found the reeking barrel set aside for that purpose. Sponge, soothe, and slop, on and on, while the candle burned through day and night, on and on until their yellow faces gradually brightened and they could move from their rigid positions without instant nausea. Minette was drowsy with fatigue when Berenice, first to recover, raised herself on one elbow to thank her.

"Minette, I will never forget this. I am your true friend for life. If there is ever any way in which I can be of help to you, you have only to let me know."

"She has indeed performed her Christian obligation," said Sister, adding, "I'm sure each of you would have done the same."

Minette laughed. "Not for me, you wouldn't. I'd have been left in my own vomit. But I forgive you."

"You forgive *us?*" Seraphine's voice was full of venom. "You went off on a coach ride with a man and came back as scratched and dirty as if you'd been rolling in the street. You damaged our reputations as well as your own."

"Have you ever fallen out of a moving carriage into a nest of bushes, Seraphine?"

"The bodice of your dress was ripped," added Celeste. "I suppose you're going to say the bushes did that too?"

"Do you want to know what happened, really?"

"Of course not," lied Celeste. They'd been especially infuriated by Minette's refusal to say one word about her encounter with the chevalier, except to Mother Catherine. Their imaginations had given them no rest.

"Well, then, I shall not tell you," she said, enjoying their disappointment. "But this I will say: Saint Ursula protected me during that terrible time, and I know she is protecting me now. I have prayed often for a sign that she understood. And it has come. I am guiltless, so I am well. You, with all your uncharitable thoughts about me, have been puking and coughing up your guts. Now, why am I spared? It's because Saint Ursula knows I am innocent and wishes to punish you for the way you have treated me!"

"Peace, peace among you," said Sister Immaculata hoarsely. "Mother Catherine has vindicated Minette, and we must follow her example."

"I cannot," began Seraphine.

"You will do exactly as I tell you," Sister corrected her. "You will behave in normal, friendly fashion to Minette."

"And if I don't?"

"You have rebellion in your voice, Seraphine. Do I hear you challenging the motherhouse, you ungrateful chit? Don't think you are beyond the reach of the Ursulines because we are at sea. When we land at New Orleans in Louisiana, you will be working in the Ursuline hospital there."

The girls looked at each other.

"Well, what did you expect, mesdemoiselles? To run free? I have told you that you are representatives of French government policy. You will make yourselves useful, and we will see to it that you meet clean, Christian young men. If you refuse to cooperate, remember the rest of the agreement; if you don't find a husband in two months, you will be sent back to France."

They fell into the familiar pattern of obedience. Sister Immaculata went on, "Get me some water, Minette, for the love of Saint Ursula."

"The water's still fresh, Sister. I'll get it now."

As relations between Minette and the others improved, so did the weather. Fearsome waves became long, oily looking swells, the sun appeared daily, and passengers were allowed abovedecks. Minette searched for Alain but saw no soldiers at all, and as the days went on, she grew desperate. Where were the soldiers? Did they drill on the gun deck all day, clean their weapons and do makework jobs like those Sister Immaculata imposed? At night the nun had her charges sewing by candlelight, making repairs to their meager wardrobes. The weather grew steadily warmer, the cabin more confining, but she did not relent.

"We are prisoners," Berenice muttered.

"And for what reason? What have we done?"

Minette thought she might be the reason. Could this all be part of Sister's plan to keep her away from Alain? But if so, why involve the others? Did Sister fear that they'd all fall in love with soldiers?

The word *love* slipped shyly into her thinking, but once there, it seemed natural. Though reason might dictate that she could not love a man to whom she had never spoken, they had had a common language in Saint Malo. They had felt each other's presence and acknowledged it without words. He'd walked the ground she'd just left, perhaps putting his feet precisely where he'd seen her step. She believed she knew his heart and had to speak to him. She must.

Her chance to find him came when she was least prepared. One night after Sister had blown out the candle and they were settling into sleep, there was urgent knocking at their door. After a short exchange with the woman standing there, Sister dressed in the dark, then relit the candle and took her bag of medicines.

"One of the peasant women needs me for her birthing. If I am not back by the morning meal, girls, go to breakfast and return here." The door closed without its customary click, and she was gone.

"We're not locked in," said Seraphine. "When the cat's away, shouldn't the mice enjoy themselves?"

But no one moved—except Minette. She dressed hurriedly, the others watching. No time for modesty now.

"Wouldn't you know," muttered Seraphine. "It's always Minette! She takes any opportunity to break the rules."

"You can come if you like, Seraphine."

"Well, I—"

"You're right, of course," said Minette quickly. "If you stay here, you have nothing to lose. I have everything to lose, but tonight is my only chance."

From the deck, the sea was a sparkling calm, the moon bright, the night murmurous. She saw soldiers, sailors, women. Several times she almost stumbled over couples making love! So this was why they were forbidden to leave the cabin after dark. The women who had come aboard with Hera were busy; the moon shone on heedless bare flesh.

Her mouth dry, Minette watched a young soldier complete the act the chevalier had begun with her. It looked like a game: the woman was willing, and they rocked against each other with spasms of sound, the slap of flesh mating with flesh, gurgling laughter. There were other couples as well—here a hand rummaging a breast, there a gartered knee in the air, petticoats tumbled, lips nuzzling at throats—and from one such union came a deep, muffled cry of satisfaction. Despite her shock, Minette could not look away.

"Quite a night for it, eh?" said a sultry voice at her shoulder. "In the sea the fishes mate when the full moon shines. Here we roll and bump on the deck, answering the moon in our own way. Why are you alone, pretty girl?"

It was the dancer, Hera. Moonlight gave her back the magic daylight had stolen. It put a silver gleam in her inky hair and made her eyes and teeth glisten. She wore only a light wrapper; evidently she'd been coupling with the soldiers. Now she was loose, easy, mocking as she took Minette's reluctant hand.

"You're afraid of me."

Minette would not answer.

"Good little girl. Shall I tell your fortune?"

"I have no money for that," said Minette stiffly. Fortune-telling was a blasphemy.

"No money is needed. Let me see your palm. Or are you afraid to know the future?"

Hera's finger tracing the lines of her palm created a curious, invasive sensation, as if once Hera touched you, she knew more than you might want her to know.

"You're a baby, golden-hair. You've just begun to live. A baby and a virgin."

Minette tried to pull her hand away.

"Don't be angry. We must all begin somewhere. And there will be men for you. In fact, men will be all-important to you. They'll bring you riches and power—and trouble." She laughed. "Men always bring trouble."

Minette hesitated, curious despite herself. "Do you see love?"

"Love? That's harder. But riches certainly. No bad bargain, eh?"

"Can you see the past?"

"Who would want to?"

"I would like to know to whom I was born."

"Ah." Hera dropped her hand. "Little foundling, eh? Me too. If people don't want you, you don't want to know about them. But there was a man in your life not long ago, wasn't there? It did not go well. You did not let him love you."

"You must be a witch!"

"It's enough that I am Hera."

"That man brought me nothing but shame. I never want to see him again!"

"I cannot promise you that. But I'll tell you this: your luck is about to change."

With another laugh she slipped away.

"Minette?" Someone stood close in the darkness. It was Alain Gerard. Like a conjuring trick, Hera was gone, and suddenly her poet-soldier was there. She could scarcely believe it.

"My sweet Minette." He took her hands, linking their fingers.

Now that he was actually here, she was suddenly shy. "I . . . I've been hoping to see you, Alain."

"I was with my men. But I knew where you were, down below in a hellhole, guarded by a black-robed dragon. How did you escape?"

"Sister was needed for a birthing."

"What do you know of birthing, Minette-from-the-convent?"

"I imagine," she said seriously. "We all do. It's our destiny, too."

"Yes, tell me about your destiny. And let us walk a little."

Without the slightest unsavory reference to the love-making couples around them, he led her away to the stern, where, sheltered by the tiered decks, they could watch the phosphorescent foam in the ship's wake. Here the moon seemed private, shining for an audience of two. The quiet, the soft sighing of night winds, liberated Minette. Talk bubbled out of her, laughter and apologies for her small experience of the world. He listened, smiling.

"Are you laughing at me, Alain? Do I sound so foolish?"

"I am memorizing the sound of your voice. It's beautiful."

"Now I am embarrassed. Please tell me about you."

"I'm what you see, a soldier. My family is Acadian, from Canada, so I'm a son of the New World."

"What were you doing in France?"

"I ran away to join the French army."

"And your family?"

"Still trying to farm stones in Nova Scotia, still waiting for the English to throw them off their land."

"Don't they miss you?"

"I wasn't very close to my parents. And there are three strong older brothers to do what must be done."

"You must have sisters, too."

"Why must I?"

"Because you're so easy with women."

He laughed delightedly. "You are a marvel, my Minette. As straight to the point as a child."

"Tonight, someone told me that I was a baby who had just begun to live."

"And who was that?"

"Hera, the dancer. You know her. I saw you watching her perform."

"Minette, I don't deny that I saw her. But I don't *know* her. Knowing her would be quite another thing, and I've no desire to try."

"She told my fortune. Would you like to hear it?"

"I'd rather not waste our precious time talking of Hera."

Clouds blew over their private moon, and a chill breeze sprang up. His arm came around her shoulders easily, and just as easily she fitted into the warm, snug space he'd created. There was a companionable silence, and something she hadn't meant to say, not now, popped out.

"Do you like poetry, Alain?"

"What a curious question."

"But important to me. Have you ever written poems?"

"Yes, some doggerel verse. It seemed fine to me at the time. Why do you ask?"

"One day, I shall explain. Alain, are we flirting?"

Once again he laughed with pleasure at her directness.

"No, it's much more real than that. If we were flirting, you would find ways to make me tell you how beautiful you are."

"Other girls can do that?"

"Yes, and with far less reason. Don't learn to flirt, Minette. Don't be like other girls."

"Why did you follow me in Saint Malo?" Another direct shot.

"I wanted to know you."

"The town was full of girls."

"But you were a golden flower sprung from the cobblestones. I saw a face of innocent beauty, a spirit free and natural, someone unspoiled in this wicked world. It drew me irresistibly."

"Alain, this is love talk. Please don't tell me such things if you don't believe them."

He kissed her, so sweetly, gently, with a warm flutter of breath on her mouth. It was not demanding; instead, it coaxed a parting of her lips, a gradual yielding of her body, and she did not even know when she began to tremble.

"I thought I was a free man, Minette, until I saw you."

Dizzy, dreamy, she murmured between soft nibblings at his lips, "Do you think you could love me enough to marry me?"

"My sweet girl, you take my breath away."

"You see, I must know. I had a future before you took me in your arms. I was prepared to marry a *habitant* in La Louisiane and have a big French family."

"And now?"

"I am not prepared if the man is not you. Oh, please

don't laugh at me, Alain. I don't know what to say next. I've done something wrong, haven't I? I suppose no other girl does this."

"You are like no other girl, Minette."

"And you haven't answered me, not even with a no!" By now, she hated her romantic impulse. "Well, that's it. I've proposed to a soldier, knowing what they say about soldiers!"

"Much of which is true. But don't you think I could learn another trade, an honest bourgeois occupation?"

"You're teasing me."

"I am not. As a matter of fact, his majesty King Louis has a special arrangement for soldiers who want to become settlers in La Louisiane. He grants each man fourteen arpents—"

"Fourteen!"

"I agree, it's a kingdom. He guarantees to supply adequate food for a year, and he furnishes a rifle, a half pound of powder and lead each month, an ax, a pick, a cow, chickens—"

"*C'est incroyable!* The king does this for soldiers?"

"Only for soldiers."

"Then how can he keep men in his army? Why would—" She paused because Alain's face had changed.

"Soldiers are a special breed. And perhaps, my innocent, La Louisiane is not the paradise you imagine."

"But—"

"Minette Marsan!" It was hissed, but it carried. The moon, out of the clouds again, showed Sister Immaculata bearing down on them, her black robes blowing. "Minette, come here!"

Oh, Mother Mary, Minette thought miserably. Why now?

"Stand your ground, sweet," Alain whispered. Stepping protectively in front of Minette, he said, "Good evening, Sister. I am your fellow passenger from Saint Malo, Lieutenant Alain Gerard."

"I know you, sir. But you can have no business with this young woman. She is not available to you. Leave us."

"If that is an order, Sister, I accept orders only from my superior officers."

"Very well. I ask you to leave as a gentleman."

"As a gentleman, I shall comply. Until we meet again, Mademoiselle Minette."

"You shall not meet her, Lieutenant."

"Who can say, Sister? We might meet here tomorrow night, for example."

He made a courtly bow, during which he managed, ever so slightly, a warm pressure on Minette's arm just before the nun hurried the girl away.

All the way down to the cabin, Sister was silent, frighteningly so. Minette shivered. When would the storm break? As they entered their tiny living space, hot, stale air surrounded them, and the others, unable to sleep, stirred restlessly on their tiered bunks as Sister lit the candle.

"Was she with the soldiers?" Seraphine's voice evinced pure malice.

"Be quiet, Seraphine!" said Immaculata, as she would reprimand a child.

Minette, who had a lower bunk, lay down warily.

"What of the birthing?" asked Berenice as the nun bent to remove her heavy shoes. "Was it a boy or a girl?"

"A boy, and he is dead."

"Oh, Sister. Oh, the poor mother!"

"But the Lord sent me in time so that I might consign his soul to heaven instead of it wandering in limbo. The mother was grateful for that."

The girls murmured piously.

"Especially since she had lost three other children, without benefit of clergy."

"What—what went wrong?" Berenice stammered.

"This one was being choked by the umbilical cord," Sister began matter-of-factly. The sudden fright on the girls' faces made her remember to whom she was talking. It was inadvisable to reveal the dangers of childbed now. "Don't worry your heads about medical matters, girls." Briskly, Sister set her black bag down on her bunk and opened it. The sweetish smell of blood from the instruments inside added to the cabin's oppressive air.

"Minette, go and fetch me a dipperful of water."

"You want me to go out, Sister?"

"You know the way." Her sarcasm was evident.

As soon as Minette had gone, Sister asked, "When did she go up on the main deck?"

"Not long ago," said Berenice. "You left the door unlocked."

Seraphine was glad to help. "She was looking for the officer who followed us in Saint Malo. We couldn't stop her, Sister. We argued with her about committing a mortal sin, but—"

"Liar," Berenice cut in. "None of us said anything like that to her."

Sister took out her old leather slippers, her sole personal possession apart from convent issue, and eased her feet into them. She reached for her missal and rosary.

"Aren't you going to do something about Minette and the lieutenant?" It was Seraphine again. "Won't you punish her?"

"I won't have to," said the nun. "And, Seraphine . . ."

"Yes, Sister?"

"Ten Hail Marys for the lustful curiosity behind that question. You may start now."

She knelt to her own prayers.

"My sweet girl, you take my breath away." That didn't sound like no, did it? Making her way back from the water butt, Minette held the dipper away from the arm Alain had pressed so lightly. It still tingled. *She* tingled. The kiss still fluttered against her lips. That a man could be so gentle! And serious. Talking about the king's gifts to soldiers who wanted to settle in Louisiana, saying, right in the nun's teeth, that he would meet her again tomorrow night. She would have to be as bold and get out somehow. She could do it. She could do anything, because she loved this man. And he seemed to love her. And if that was true, she would finally, finally, belong to someone!

They awoke to a gray morning. The newborn awaited burial, its body sewn into a scrap of sail canvas and weighted with small shot so that it should not float. The tiny bundle was placed on a sloping plank above the gunwale as the passengers gathered to hear the captain read the last rites of burial at sea. The mother stood, gray-faced, clutching her two remaining daughters. The father had stayed in the hold, drunk and despairing, unable to watch his son slide into the waves.

Just before the captain picked up his Bible, the Royal Marine Infantry detachment appeared, wheeling smartly into place. Minette spotted Alain; he seemed strained and pale, as if he hadn't slept.

A white seabird circled the foremast as the baby was tipped into the deep. Passengers crossed themselves and murmured prayers, for a white bird was a symbol of the Holy Spirit.

Her head uplifted to watch the bird spiral into the clouds, Minette scented a change in the wind. It carried something else besides its usual cargo of salt. There was a faint presence of green growth and mud, like spring-time at home.

"Land!" said a man standing near her. "Land, and not far away!"

Minette was puzzled. Yes, she had lost track of time, hoping for a chance to find Alain. There had been fair days and foul, dead calms as the harbor master in Saint Malo had predicted, and days when the ship rolled so heavily that they had to tie themselves to their bunks. But this could not be La Louisiane, not even if the ship had wings as well as sails!

"Sister Immaculata, what is this land we're approaching?"

The nun looked at her with lofty patience. "An island in the West Indies, Santo Domingo. Think, Minette, what is it you know about Santo Domingo?"

Minette couldn't think.

"We have a colony there. Our grandest colony, Saint Dominique, the Pearl of the Antilles. If you would stop thinking of that soldier, you might remember your geography."

Minette winced. She had once been Sister Immaculata's best student in geography. Well, *tant pis*, the nun would be even more disappointed in her after tonight. But by then her life would be decided.

The tempo on shipboard quickened. Minette learned that the *Baleine* was to stop at Cap François, the harbor of the Saint Dominique colony, to take on provisions and water and put off some of the passengers. Now, as the sun grew stronger and the rush of water beneath the bow turned leaf green, the sailors put out nets to trawl for fresh fish. They brought in something called a coconut, looking like a monk's head without the tonsure. It was to be cracked and eaten, a delicacy meant for the captain. And then the reconditioning of the ship got under way as the crew, armed with swabs and buckets of sticky, tarlike oakum, began to caulk the seams of the *Baleine*'s planking, section by section.

Still with a feeling of strange unease, Minette approached one of these work parties and spoke to a grizzled old sailor.

"Grandpère?"

He showed her a snaggle-toothed grin. "What is it, *ma petite?*"

"How far away are we from Cap François?"

"Just a day out."

"Does the *Baleine* always go in there?"

"Not always."

"Why now then?"

"Oh, this time the rich colonists don't want to pay their taxes. Fat, lazy bastards, getting rich while their black slaves do all the work. Now the sons of bitches don't want to pay their share to Mother France. But the Royal Marines will choke it out of them. If the rich get away without paying, the king will have to wring his money out of the poor—so get the stinking rich, I say."

"The Royal Marines are leaving the ship? All of them?"

His grin was knowing. "Found yourself a sweetheart there, did you? Well, kiss him good-bye tonight. I don't envy him his mission. You couldn't pay me enough to fight on these islands. It's hot enough to boil a white man's blood!"

His cheerful profanity flowed on, a soliloquy now, because Minette was walking, almost running, away.

It was impossible! Alain would have told her. The old sailor was mistaken. It could not be. Alain was not the sort to lie to her.

But had he? Had he said he would be debarking with them in La Louisiane? No. She had simply assumed as much. Yet he had certainly implied—oh, she couldn't remember! In confusion, she fled to the cabin, luckily empty, and threw herself facedown on her bunk.

That night the cabin door was left unlocked again, and Minette now recognized the unwonted freedom as Sister's punishment. The nun, a natural teacher, was inviting Minette to learn life's lessons the hard way. By all means, go up on deck and wait for your faithless soldier. When you've had enough, you will accept the moral lesson.

After a stubborn, lonely hour on the main deck, Minette's bewilderment turned to anger.

Doubtless Alain was below on the gun deck with the others, making preparations, because, obviously, there was no more sport to be had from her. Even the most naïve idiot would have guessed as much by now. Oh, he was probably even passing the tale around. She could almost hear his voice triumphant: "*Croyez-vous, mes amis,* believe it or not, she proposed to me, offered herself to a stranger! A convent girl!" And she could imagine the laughter as he described his campaign, his seduction of her emotions. First the ardent attention in Saint Malo, then the sweet words, the bait of the king's offer to soldier-settlers that would give her hope for the future, then the tender approach, the gentle, sheltering kiss, the last touch on the arm meant to keep her yearning for him. Oh, cruel, savage, deliberate behavior, more humiliating than the chevalier's attempt on her virtue. The chevalier had offered her gold to become his whore; Alain Gerard had needed only golden words. And he'd succeeded utterly in plundering her emotions.

How could she face the others—Seraphine's spite, Berenice's sympathy, the knowing eyes of Sister Immaculata?

After another agonized hour, she forced herself to return to the cabin and found her companions asleep. At least she was to be spared until morning.

First light found her out of the cabin. The *Baleine*, sails furled, was entering the harbor of Cap François. Minette stationed herself where she could hear the Royal Marines leave the ship, but she could not see them. An apt self-punishment, which Sister might have approved. Because, in spite of everything, she desperately wanted one last look at Alain Gerard. To deny herself that was surely the beginning of wisdom.

The enchanting fragrance of fresh coffee betrayed her resolve and made her turn shoreward. Fresh, roasting *café*, so strong that the steam of it was almost visible in the morning air. Twice in her life Minette had tasted this grand luxury. Was everyone in Cap François taking it for breakfast? The old sailor had said they were rich here. Oh, how rich, how civilized they must be!

Cap François, she saw as she squinted into the sunlight, was snuggled into the shoreline below a towering hill fortified with cannon pointing out to sea. The town was blazingly white, vibrating in the hot morning light. It was large and sprawling, with houses rising, tier on tier, up the sides of the hill. Each house seemed to float above the ground on wooden posts.

Then she heard the sound of a barrel organ across the water, a French thing, a French tune, straight from the streets of Paris. Why, she wondered suddenly, go on to the unknown La Louisiane? Why not stay here on this unmistakably French island?

There was life and bustle on the streets, early risers here. Then two boatloads of rowers coming out to the ship at its anchorage startled her. They were black like the third Wise Man who came to the manger of the Infant Jesus, but a rich, deep black with a purple sheen. They wore blazing yellow, violent green, crimson red, and they called to the ship, waved and chattered, their speech, although it must be French, so soft and liquid that she understood not one word.

The sun poured down, the people smiled—where was the rebellion in this amiable scene? Minette looked beyond the brilliant town to the mountains above, waves of mountains with peculiar, sharp-edged silhouettes extending into the distance. Was the fighting to be there? How could men accustomed to battle on the plains of Europe fight in those mountains unless they could climb like goats? Unwillingly, she thought of Alain, climbing walls of rock, losing his hold—

A hand closed around her shoulder. She whirled to confront her errant soldier, but it wasn't he. It was the wiry, sallow fellow with the ridiculous mustaches who had marched beside Alain.

"What do you want of me, sir?"

"I have come to speak for my friend. There is not much time."

"I don't want to hear any—"

"Please listen. In spite of what you probably think, Alain was deeply affected by you. *Ce fut le coup de foudre*—he was struck by the lightning. You must know what I mean."

"Yes, he was so affected that he lied to me."

"Not precisely. We will be in La Louisiane when we have finished with the colonists here."

"And when will that be?"

"Ask God—you must have better connections with heaven than I do. But it's not much of a rebellion, just a handful of planters. We can manage them."

"I wish you luck in your campaign, monsieur. And your friend also. Now good-bye."

"Look at me, please. I am a plain military man, Lieutenant Guillaume Cernaux, from an honorable Gascon family that has always sent its sons to fight for France. And I would like to be your friend."

"Why? You come on a dishonorable errand for a man who will not speak for himself."

"He is ashamed."

"So he should be!"

"It began as a harmless flirtation. He said that you were so beautiful, he couldn't resist."

"So he followed me in Saint Malo to help to pass the time there."

"However it began, it's different now."

"How, different? How can I believe you if he won't come himself?"

"Because I know him." With a shrug, he changed tactics. "Don't believe me. See for yourself. He will tell you of his love if you wait for him."

"I won't listen."

"If you tell me you have no feeling for my friend Alain . . ." He watched her redden unwillingly.

"*Bon!* It's as I thought, Mademoiselle Minette. The two of you are in the soup together. You're angry now, and rightly so. I acknowledge his fault and present his apologies. But believe that he loves—"

A trumpet sounded, short, imperative notes, a call to waiting boats.

"Ah, we leave now," said Cernaux. "Don't watch us go. I always think that's bad luck. Just remember Alain, and wait for him."

"Does he—will he know where to find me?"

"Good girl!" Cernaux squeezed her hand. "If you stay with the nuns in New Orleans, he'll look for you there. Only wait!"

4

The fallen tree trunk moved. It slid off the bank and into the coffee-colored water. Then, powerfully, it began swimming against the river current directly toward their boats. It had gleaming eyes, a scaly skin, a long, lifted snout with enormous teeth.

Whack! One of their oarsmen hit the water with the flat of his paddle, sending up a great drenching splash. The swimming thing changed course and moved past them, then suddenly slipped beneath the surface of the river.

"It will come up under the boat!" Celeste was choking with fear. "A sea serpent! Oh, Mother Mary, save us!"

Heavily loaded, low in the water, the boats called pirogues were little more than hollowed-out logs. Those great scaly jaws could easily rise above the gunwales and the teeth click open to devour them all. Celeste promptly fainted.

Unconcerned, the Indian paddler in the bow slapped the water again.

"Gator," he announced. "Gone now. But you can smell him for a while. Mississippi alligator stinks."

A heavy, musky odor like things left to rot lingered in the air. No one moved to revive Celeste. First, it was too precarious to reach her, and, second, she'd fainted often during their trip upstream from the mouth of the river. Sympathy itself only seemed to encourage her to roll back her eyes and flop over like a dying fish.

They had come, Minette thought, from the open sea to a sea of grass, where land and water intermingled in endless marshes on either side of them. It was hard to draw a full breath because the low sky pressed down as if it would push them underwater with the drowned trees. The Mississippi—Distant Old Man, the Indians called it—was deep, swift, and treacherous. It was almost at flood now, and here they were in these wooden dugouts because the ship that had met the *Baleine* at the river's mouth had sustained some damage to its hull. Sister had decided not to wait for its repair, so they were traveling upstream in these frail crafts, mere inches above the swimming monsters, open to the things from hell that flew above.

"*Maringouins*," the paddlers told them—the word for *mosquitoes* in their strange dialect. But like no mosquitoes Minette had ever known. They stung like fire and never stopped biting. Clouds of them came out to do battle from the overgrown banks, swirling around their heads, which were shrouded in the netting called *baires*.

The *baires* were the passengers' only protection against going mad. While the mosquitoes whined their war songs, Minette sweated miserably inside her netting, certain that the blazing sun would burn her face and hands into its grid pattern. Her clothing had long since plastered itself to her skin. How could Sister

Immaculata manage in those heavy Ursuline robes? But the nun, as usual, was setting an example. She balanced on some of their baggage and, clutching the sides of the pirogue, suffered in silence.

This was their world: rushing brown water, steaming clothes, shrilling mosquitoes. After a few days, Minette sometimes had the illusion that they were moving backward. The scenery along the banks was always the same and the pull of the water so fierce that it obviously meant to drag them back again to the sand spit at the river's mouth. Her spirits would lift only at the occasional flash of a blue heron, a bird with gorgeous azure feathers, fishing in the shallows on its long, storklike legs.

Day after day, in heat-haunted wilderness, the brown river unwound itself from one curve into another. Somewhere, the marsh grass gave way to mangrove scrub but so gradually that no one could say exactly when the transformation had occurred. Now they were truly traveling on a jungle river. The unchanging view of the paddlers' sweat-soaked backs, their occasional grunted conversation, emphasized the primitive isolation. Could this land ever be tamed by man?

Each night they moored, the oarsmen set up the women's pallets on the high banks of the river and immediately drove stakes into the crumbling earth to drape the mosquito netting over the makeshift beds. The ground was never quite dry. One could imagine the tropical downpours that created this climate.

Each night the nun and her charges crawled under the nets and onto their pallets fully dressed, sunburned and unwashed, for they'd been warned that at flood, as the river was now, the waters could carry infection. Listening to the night calls of hidden birds and animals or the light patter of moisture on the leaves of the trees, they prayed both for sleep and for the postponement of natural needs. A call that could not be ignored meant leaving the safety of the *baires* to crouch in bushes, where every rustle conjured up visions of snakes and scorpions. Celeste, in an unavoidable expedition to the bushes, had seen large, hairy spiders in the wavering firelight.

"As big as dinner plates! Oh, why couldn't we have waited for another proper boat to come for us?"

"Because we'd still be waiting on La Balize island, that red-hot dot of sand! At least we are moving."

Sister did not want to be reminded of the accident that had deprived them of cabin space and put them into these pirogues. She snapped at Celeste for whining in order to forestall the others' complaints. Celeste whimpered in her sleep. She was doing badly, her pale face and arms a favored target of the demon mosquitoes.

They ate coarse bread and dried fish, lost count of the days, and were thankful when the blistering sun went down. Minette found consolation in the stars, their nighttime glory reminding her of the massed candle flames in the convent chapel at home. She tried to fight the homesickness, however, reminding herself firmly that she could never return there. She must go forward, always forward. And surely there was something new to be seen on this first journey. Each morning, she told herself, might bring something she had never seen before.

One morning, when they were far upstream, it did. Astonishing long gray beards drooped from the trees onshore, rippling in stray breezes.

The girls laughed and speculated. How could trees grow beards? The paddlers called them Spanish moss. A few hours after sighting these oddities, there came a miracle. They saw a house.

"It looks to be crooked," Seraphine complained.

"Not at all," said Immaculata. "It's raised on posts. Very sensible with this wet ground."

The house was of rough wooden construction, unpainted, little more than a cabin, but as they watched, three people came out and stood on its square porch. Three actual people who waved and cheered! A little girl ran down to the riverbank and held up her doll to see them pass. The travelers shouted with delight. At last, at last, they were out of the silent wilderness, no longer alone on the river.

Other houses now appeared at each bend of the river, sometimes very large and rambling, built perilously close to the banks. They saw chickens scratching in the yards and smelled the savory contents of iron cookpots. A woman boiling clothes at one spot laughed to see them, beckoning them ashore. As more houses came into view, they saw small fishing boats and men holding up their strings of catches. A boat scarcely larger than their pirogue darted from bank to bank, defying the river currents by the most skillful of maneuvers. People on the shore tossed things aboard this boat. But what?

They drew closer and saw that it was bundles of mail. Letters held in deeply cleft sticks flew through the air and landed on the mail boat's deck. If they fell short, a man scooped them in with a boat hook and set them to dry. Sometimes a stick flew shoreward: mail delivered. A crowd formed at once, people hurrying to hear news of the outside world. A great event, such a letter, and great prestige for those who could read it.

As the river swept around into a final bend, the paddlers shouted, "Nouvelle-Orléans!"

There it stood, the sieur de Bienville's city, capital of La Louisiane since 1722, curved between the Mississippi and Lake Pontchartrain. Their first sight of the city was utterly confusing. They were suddenly in a forest of ships' spars, boats of every description anchored around them in the watery basin, and the paddlers had to "thread the needle" to bring them safely to the steps of the high embankments that seemed to be the sole separation between city and river. To the south and west, the silent swamps stretched back toward the Gulf of Mexico.

But here, in the middle of nowhere, city people shook their ruffles and promenaded on the levee. There were street vendors and shouting and music. What could be seen of the streets and buildings, laid out on a formal grid plan, looked very grand, but the city tapered off at its edges toward encircling walls whose gunports opened on the river. The center of town had many buildings of handsomely timbered brick and stucco, but the outlying parts had a makeshift, thrown-together look, and its structures were of wood, a strange sight to girls from the stone avenues of Paris.

Sister spoke immediately in the unusual city's defense. "You don't know what a swamp, what a pest hole, this was in the beginning. More alligators and poisonous snakes than colonists. The people had to live in little huts. And they were always fighting Indians. But see now, in ten years, how many fine streets and houses!"

Still the girls were silent.

"Well, what did you expect, mesdemoiselles? Paris?"

"At least," said Minette reflectively, "something like Cap François." She had lost her heart to that white city on the island. "Someone told me that Cap François has a theater and a concert hall."

"That's on a mere island. This place is the key to an entire continent," answered Sister in her best classroom manner. "I understand that everything you can get in France is available here."

"There are soldiers, certainly." Seraphine pointed to uniformed men strolling along the levee. She looked sidelong at Minette. "Perhaps you'll have better luck here."

"Seraphine . . ." Minette began.

"You two can scratch each other's eyes out, but do it later." Celeste was bright red with anger. "I want to land, I want to walk on something that doesn't rock, I want a bath!"

"Celeste," warned Sister Immaculata, but the girl went barreling on.

"Look at us. We smell, we're caked with mud, all bitten by those flying things. Pray God that no one remembers what we look like now!"

She was right, of course. Amazingly, there were no accidents disembarking themselves and their cargo from the pirogues. The paddlers pocketed their money and without good-byes disappeared, after tossing their baggage to rough-looking men who at least did not run off with it.

"Is there no one sent to meet us in this crowd?" Seraphine pouted. "After all, we were asked to come."

"Ah, the grand duchesse," Berenice's tone was scathing. "Pardon me for not recognizing you, Your Highness. I suppose you've never gotten down on your knees to scrub a hall or some other things I could mention!"

"We walk," said Sister Immaculata, ending the exchange. She turned to the black men holding their baggage. "Take us to the Ursuline convent, please?"

The panorama of New Orleans was far more impressive from the water than from its grimy streets. The main boulevards were wooden-planked and wide but crisscrossed by narrow, none-too-clean alleys. Since space within the city walls was limited, few houses had landscaping, and they were built right down to the edge of the street, where they shouldered each other for light and air. Shops among the houses added to the congestion. The buildings revealed very little; overhanging roofs were favored, and shuttered jalousie windows protected against the sun. Yet an occasional door stood open, and flashes of green suggested cool courtyards within.

The streets were busy with the strangest mixture of people the girls had ever seen. Bearded men, unkempt in clothes of tanned animal skins, padded along in moccasins. Jesuit priests were much in evidence, resolutely ignoring the equally numerous women with painted faces and beauty patches who showed enough décolletage even in the daytime to leave no doubt about their profession. Lounging dandies eyed their obvious wares. Then there were more respectable combinations— aproned women with market baskets, tamed husbands beside them. Men of business haggled over numbers. Schoolchildren walked in correct files. Mothers with children jostled black women balancing baskets of produce on their heads. Black men hurried by on silent errands. In fact, a good part of the street crowd was black—and apparently invisible to those who were not.

The streets of New Orleans seemed made for enjoyment—eating, smoking, talking expansively, laughing. After so long in the wilderness, Minette found the excitement dizzying. This place could not yet be compared to a large city in France, but it was devilishly proud, and the street signs blazoned French glory. There was Bourbon Street, Toulouse, Conti, Dauphine, Chartres, Orleans, Burgundy, DuMaine. Other streets bore the names of saints: Louis, Philippe, Anne, Peter—on and on went the heavenly roster. Very grand indeed for a city built on a swamp.

Looking everywhere at once, Minette stumbled and collided with someone. She looked into the face of a well-dressed black woman. With no actual idea of the cost of clothes, Minette felt instinctively that the woman's dark dress was expensive, that the necklace of gold nuggets and coral beads was real, as were the earrings, crucifix, and finger rings. Gold, all of them. The snowy scarf wrapped about the woman's head was perfectly laundered and exquisitely starched so that its ends stood out like the wings of butterflies.

"Pardon, madame."

A slight lift of the woman's eyebrows told Minette she had made some mistake in addressing her. She had never been acquainted with such an expensively dressed black person before, and she was suddenly at a loss for words.

The woman stood aside for Minette to pass. But where were Sister and the girls? The crowd had swallowed them!

There was a light pressure on her arm. Smiling, still not speaking, the woman pointed ahead and to her right. Yes, there they were, with Berenice just turning around to look for Minette. An encouraging pat from her silent companion sent Minette off after them. Only belatedly did she realize that the intelligent pale green eyes must have been studying her, or how else would the woman have known her friends? Why, it was as if someone she did not know had been expecting her in New Orleans.

5

For the first time in their lives—and possibly the last, considering a double-bedded future and a houseful of children—the orphans had privacy. The Ursuline convent at the juncture of Bienville and Chartres streets was a fine, large cedar-timbered building, its spacious three stories affording each of the basket brides a room of her own. The supply of glass in the colony was so limited that mirrors were a luxury, but the girls had grown up without and didn't miss them in their neat little whitewashed cubicles.

How quickly the convent had established itself since its founding in 1727! It was complete with chapel, kitchen, washhouse, dairy, classrooms for the Ursuline school, and vegetable gardens, where the nuns tried mightily to coax French seeds to grow in Louisiana soil.

With the nuns as chaperons, the girls explored that portion of Nouvelle-Orléans necessary to the day-to-day functioning of the convent. In the markets, where fresh fish and game were sold, they marveled at oysters, shrimp, venison, wild turkeys, grouse, quail, and things utterly unfamiliar. "*Trop cher*," said the thrifty sisters, who bought only basics. The vegetable stalls boasted strange round orange gourds, odd nuts and berries, tough-skinned grapes for wine, and a lesson in caution. A rosy thing that was sweet at first bite turned very bitter at the last—wild persimmon, a favorite of the Indians.

The *habitants* were forever eating or sipping chocolate or taking café au lait, the strong chicory-scented coffee served with a pitcher of hot, foaming milk. Convent-bred Minette quickly became addicted to the abundance of New Orleans.

Each night in her imaginary letter to Alain, whispered into the darkness, she told him how much she wanted them to live here and send their children to the Ursuline school. King Louis paid the nuns fifty gold crowns per year for each pupil's education—imagine! The children would learn proper wisdom and manners there.

She wasn't at all embarrassed about mentioning their children-to-be. In her mind, Alain was already her fiancé. She'd made the leap of faith on Cernaux's assurances that Alain loved her as she loved him. But how she needed some word of him! Information about the Saint Dominique rebellion arrived only sporadically with incoming ships, already old news. At such times a notice and a casualty list would be placed on the wall of the soldiers' barracks in the Place d'Armes, the true heart and center of the city. Drums would roll to bring in the crowd, and a crier would announce the casualties for those citizens who could not read.

After one tense visit to the Place d'Armes, Minette did not return. Her faith that Alain would be spared was absolute.

However, as the days ran into weeks, time became a

problem. Minette finally decided that she would not go back to France when her months had passed even if Alain still lingered in the Indies. She had a fiancé, didn't she? Surely that fulfilled the contract.

As for the other girls, it was only a matter of their choosing. Celeste had a particularly ardent follower, a big, burly German with a fine golden beard. He farmed, with other redemptioners paying off their passage here, in a section outside the city coming to be known as the German Coast. True, technically, Celeste's admirer was not French, but he was a citizen of Louisiana. Perhaps Celeste could convince him of the superiority of French culture, especially since he surveyed her plump, pink-and-white blondness with such loud appreciation. Nothing daunted this Otto. He didn't even mind doing his courting in the convent parlor, showing his deep respect even as she was driving him out of his mind with longing.

Eulalie was a great surprise. The Royal Hospital, where they all worked, had become a vast hunting ground for her. No longer a meek blue-eyed mouse, she was now a vixen spoiled by too many possible choices.

Berenice, as directly as she did most things, had already found the man destined for her in one convalescing patient, a sail fitter named Arnaud Robillas. They were alike in temperament and looks, both rangy and redheaded—no doubt whatsoever about the coppery curls their children would inherit.

And Seraphine? A problem there. Seraphine was fishing for a rich husband and didn't find him among the hospital's patients. Men adored her beauty, but she left a trail of disappointments in her wake.

The men in New Orleans had a ravenous appetite for girls from France. They could not believe Minette's disinterest, and simply walking down the street unnoticed could be a problem for her. Unfamiliar voices called her name as patients who were discharged from the Royal Hospital passed it along to their friends. She had nicknames—The Golden Statue, The One Who Won't, even *La Belle Dame Sans Merci*. But none of that dubious fame mattered. Each night she told Alain in her thoughts, "I walk with my eyes cast down and speak to no one. I come back to the convent directly from the hospital and spend my time with the nuns." Even the nuns urged her to do otherwise, to attend the public dances or show more interest in the hospital's male patients.

The work that the girls performed at the Royal Hospital was a nice calculation between their modesty as virgins and what was unavoidably necessary. Sponging down naked men was allocated to the nuns—brides of Christ beyond temptation. *Les filles à la cassette* rolled bandages, brewed medicinal teas, and acted as hospital housewives, cleaning the huge building with its long arched windows that could be thrown open, like doors, to catch the breeze. Their unofficial mission was to raise the spirits of patients suffering from congestions, rheumatics, and wounds acquired in tavern brawls, typical complaints of spring and early summer. These young men were not too sick to propose marriage. They did it often.

"In France, we would close every window against the night air," Minette told Alain in her next nightly monologue. "That's impossible in the Royal Hospital here. We'd die of the heat. And without the mosquito netting over each bed, I think our patients would not want to live."

Minette took pride in her growing familiarity with the hospital, especially the new wing, which contained a pharmacy and laboratory as well as offices for the surgeons, doctors, and chaplain. New Orleans's Royal Hospital embodied the very latest ideas in eighteenth-century medicine. Doctors now diagnosed bodily humors by palpation and the color of a patient's urine and could treat many ills by the practice of bleeding. Pain was greatly eased with laudanum, a tincture of opium. Prayer was dispensed freely.

Unfortunately, the transmission of the great plagues that had decimated Europe was still not understood, leaving the great plagues of the New World, with their added climatic factors, yet insurmountable. An annual fury of disease descended on New Orleans in the summer, and the *habitants* of La Louisiane, with its pestilential tropics climate, held their breath awaiting the winds of autumn, which blew the dread miasma away.

The first yellow-faced shaking man was brought in on a stretcher in June. The girls had never seen anything like his case: sweat pouring from him, eyes rolled back in his head, limbs twitching, making him jerk like a marionette on strings. He recognized no one, saw only phantoms, raved and mumbled intermittently. Soon there were others, too many others, their fevered, calling voices creating a din in the once-quiet wards. The nuns forbade the girls to tend these patients.

"You have had no exposure to it. You are at terrible risk."

"But what is it, Sister Immaculata?"

"A plague of tropical places. They call it the shaking sickness. And it often kills."

"Women and children, too?"

"It can strike anyone. Some live, some die, but all suffer in the same way. They seem to recover, but then the sickness returns. Each summer it returns."

"*Nom de Dieu!*" said Seraphine violently. "I did not

come here for this. I won't work in the wards. Sister, you must ask the Ursulines to find me another job."

"Scrubbing pots at the convent?"

Seraphine didn't even hear the sarcasm. "Anything, anything. But I will not stay here."

Sister's answer surprised them all. "You have that right, all of you. You were brought here to produce new life, not to be taken by sickness before that can be done."

"You mean we don't have to stay now?" That was Eulalie.

"What have I just been saying? You have the right to protect yourselves for the sake of your mission here. You're not nuns. You're not even nurses."

"But I will stay and become a nurse, if you will teach me," said Minette. "I will do whatever is necessary."

"Listen to Saint Minette," Seraphine announced. "But don't fall down and worship her. She's doing it because she's afraid her soldier may be sick with this thing in the Indies, and that's the reason she has no letters from him. I suppose it's better to think that than to imagine he has no intention of writing, or even that he's dead." With all her spite, Seraphine had an uncanny gift of perception. This was exactly what Minette had been thinking.

"I could slap you, Seraphine!"

"Try it."

"And I'll knock both your silly heads together," Sister promised. "Have you no sense of what is proper? Men are dying here while you shame the Ursulines who gave you the chance of a lifetime. Seraphine, leave quickly. And anyone else who is of the same mind, go with her."

Eulalie—why had they ever thought her meek?— took off her apron and followed Seraphine. Celeste, the former complainer, and Berenice, who had every reason not to risk her life because Arnaud, her fiancé, had already been discharged from the hospital, stood fast.

"You are all certain?" Sister asked, looking keenly at the three unlikely "nurses."

Minette spoke for them all. "We are, Sister. Show us what we need to know."

"Brave girls." There was maternal pride in her voice. "My brave girls. Now, to work."

Ceiling fans, great swaths of cloth run by pulleys, were brought in to sweep away the dangerous vapors from the sick. More and more patients were brought in suffering varying stages of delirium, and as the cries and groans rose around them, the girls were assigned to follow the surgeons and carry their trays of instruments. A quick incision in a spot above the hand or ankle began the bleeding, with the aim of ridding the body of too much diseased blood. That was standard, followed by poultices to bring the fever down or, if the wracked bodies could endure it, cleansing purges such as ipecac, only lately in general use.

"Is there nothing else?" Minette asked Sister. "Can we do nothing more for them?"

"There is a powder for this sickness. It comes from the bark of a tree. They call it the Jesuits' powder, because those fathers used it first. Many of the surgeons don't believe in it, but I've seen it work."

"Where is it? Don't we have it here?"

"We have some. We brew it into a tea, because there isn't much available."

"May *le bon Dieu* take pity on these men."

"That does you credit, Minette. I have been harsh to you in the past, but I admit that I may have misread your character."

"Does that mean you believe me about the chevalier de Pombiers and you know what happened wasn't my fault?"

"You care so much for my opinion?"

"Oh, yes!" For a moment she had the impulse to embrace this woman who had once called her the best pupil she had ever taught. But Sister stepped away, evidently on guard against the temptation of overfondness.

"Minette," the nun continued, "I don't want you to listen to Seraphine's nonsense. She is a disappointment to us, and she had no right to say what she did about your Lieutenant Gerard."

"You remember his name."

"And his face. He is a very well favored young man, fine-looking in his uniform. Still, he lied to you."

"You seemed to know that he would."

"It's not unheard of. He should have told you that he was leaving the ship at Cap François."

Minette had an overwhelming urge to pour out her anxieties to Sister. It had been a month, at least. Why hadn't she heard something, even an acknowledgment that he knew she was waiting? It was all she asked. And it would be comforting, Minette thought, to have Sister reassure her that soldiers in battle didn't have leisure to write love letters, or some such. But now was not the time for confidences. It was too soon; Sister had just begun to respect her again.

For the next few days, Minette was too busy to think of her own problems. Hot, heavy weather fell on the city, and the windows of the hospital were steamy with humidity. All the cloth fans in Louisiana couldn't sweep the odor of death from the wards. Most of the patients they saw were far gone with the shaking sickness, sometimes too far gone to summon the chaplain. One moment a man was huddled under a heap of blankets, teeth chattering with cold as he blazed with fever, and then, as if his body was exhausted by these contradictions, he died. When he did, the nuns swooped in—like death birds in their robes, Minette could not help thinking—to surround the bed, screen it from the other patients and make the corpse ready for a decent departure from this world to the next. But who were these men, and where were their families? Often they were not from New Orleans and likely not Catholic, delirious in English and other strange languages. How to notify their people of a death so far from home? The nuns kept records in their fine convent-taught hand-writing, listing descriptions of the deceased against the day when someone came seeking a lost husband, brother, or friend.

"I suppose," observed Sister Immaculata, "that the families will think their missing ones were slain by the Indians who surround us. Ah, *les pauvres*. If only we could let them know that their men had Christian burial instead of lying out on a trail somewhere, scalped and waiting to be eaten by the wild things. Yes, we live in a wilderness of savages and cannibals. I will not set one foot out of New Orleans, nor put one toe off the levee!"

But for all her preoccupation with cannibal Indians and their cooking pots, she was tender to the sick and rejoiced whenever there was a recovery. It happened inexplicably; the men on her ward would suddenly awake clear-eyed and lucid. The shaking fits might come again but lessened in strength and duration each time until the patient sat up one day and demanded a shaving bowl of hot water and a razor. None wanted to keep the tangled beard he had grown during his illness.

If some could recover, why not all? Minette fretted. The Jesuits' powder was used in many of these recovered cases, but also with some who died, so no one could credit it completely.

Each night Minette petitioned heaven through her favorite, Saint Ursula, praying that their patients would recover, that all those who tended the sick should continue to be spared, and that some news would come from Saint Dominique. She was so worn out by the harrowing days at the hospital that she sometimes fell asleep during her prayers and didn't send her imaginary letter to Alain.

In the morning she would reproach herself. Why had she ever thought she liked Cap François and its island? She hated the Pearl of the Antilles, hated its discontented planters and its horrible jungles perfect for ambush.

One day, just as the flow of sickness seemed to be slackening off, there was a new patient who needed constant cooling and sponging, so drenched was he in his own pools of sweat. This was a man of a different breed; his clothes and manner set him apart as an aristocrat. This was a man who gave imperious orders even in mortal sickness. Who was he? Ask and he would drift away, mumbling. There was no identification in the fine clothes covered with street mud.

"Robbed," said Sister succinctly. "Set upon and robbed by those bandits from the riverfront taverns."

"Why didn't they finish him off with a knife?" Celeste was acquiring an interest in the sensational to match Sister's.

"Why bother? They saw he had the shaking sickness. They just left him there in the mud to die."

"Who brought him in?"

"Gilles Paignol. He works in the hospital kitchen."

"How lucky he was found."

The patient seemed to realize what had happened to

him. "Robbed, robbed," he would often mutter, trailing off as his voice weakened. "Oh, robbed . . ." Sometimes he shouted it wildly. "Robbed!"

But one day, Minette, sponging his hands and face, thought she heard something else. Was he saying "robbed" or "Robideaux?" Could his name be Robideaux? She bent over him. "Monsieur Robideaux? Is that you? Can you hear me, Monsieur Robideaux?" But he was gone again, drifting off in the fog of sickness.

Minette took the problem to Sister Immaculata. "I am sure he said Robideaux. What shall I do?"

"There is a hall of records, a list of the permanent population of New Orleans. Go and see what you can find."

"Can you spare me here, Sister?"

"Go, before the man dies!"

There were three Robideaux gentlemen listed as permanent residents, one much too old and the other much too young. But the third was a doctor, Emile Robideaux, whose office was on Dauphine Street. With swift intuition Minette sensed that the man in the hospital had been calling for his own private doctor. His whole manner and appearance proclaimed the fact that he could afford such a luxury. The wrong conclusion had led her to the right one.

She hurried to Dauphine Street. Dr. Robideaux, a dry, musty little man, proved to be polite but not at first cooperative.

"My patients are treated at home, young miss, and with a far better rate of success than at the Royal Hospital."

"But he keeps saying your name. Doctor, please think. Since there is such an epidemic of this shaking sickness—"

"It's called malaria. And it comes every summer."

"Then perhaps this man is one of your own patients. He has very fine features, a thin mustache, and an odd little scar on his right temple."

"What has been done for him?"

"Only the usual treatment."

"How much cinchona bark powder?"

"Is that what you call the Jesuits' powder? We have very little of it at the hospital."

"Criminal. The administration of this city is criminal. The doctors are never prepared for epidemics. I shall write a letter denouncing them to the medical society in Paris."

"I think we should hurry, Doctor," said Minette, watching him pack his bag.

"I'll be along after my regular patients."

"The scar, doctor. His scar is shaped like a little sword, hilt and all. And he was wearing a ring when he was brought in, something Sister Immaculata called a bloodstone."

He stared at her. "Why didn't you say so? It's Prosper! I didn't even know he was in New Orleans."

"Prosper? Is that his name?"

"Prosper de la Fosse. *Nom de Dieu*, let us hurry!"

What happened then was a miracle. Not a miracle at one stroke, as when Our Lord multiplied loaves and fishes and transformed water into wine, but a gradual miracle evolving from the first time Doctor Robideaux mixed his cinchona bark powder into a thick paste and forced it between his patient's lips.

"You brewed it into tea. What nonsense. No wonder your poor devils were dying. You weren't giving them enough." His anger included the whole Royal Hospital. "Learn to use what you have!" The doctor did not leave Prosper's bedside for hours. He continually took the pulse, checked the ears, listened to the noises in the chest. More cinchona bark—quinine, as he called it—was given. God be thanked, you could almost see the fever break. Prosper's eyelids fluttered open to reveal deep-set hazel eyes. They fixed not on Dr. Robideaux but on Minette. And he smiled.

"Prosper, you could have died, *mon vieux*. Why didn't you call me? Why did you come to a public hospital?" asked the doctor.

"Emile, I was brought in unconscious."

"No one understood what you were saying, sir," said Minette. "It sounded like 'robbed.'"

"But not to you, my dear girl. You found out the truth, eh?"

"They tell me you *were* robbed, Prosper," said Robideaux. "You were found in an alley with your pockets picked."

Lying in bed, Prosper suddenly clasped a hand to his side, seeking a vanished sword hilt. "The dogs took my Spanish blade!"

"Prosper, you're still confused." The doctor spoke gently. "No one wears a sword on the streets now, don't you remember? Duelling has been forbidden for quite a while. I think you should try to sleep."

"Not while this golden vision is standing here. I've missed too much as it is." He gazed hungrily at Minette, who had just turned to leave. He seized her wrist but couldn't maintain the grip. "See how weak I am? Indulge me. Please stay a while."

"You must rest, sir."

"She's right, my stubborn friend." The doctor made Prosper comfortable on the pillow. "The young lady has other duties here. She—*Alors,* look at this."

Prosper had fallen into an instant, healthy sleep.

* * *

Minette walked toward the riverbank in vain search of a breeze. The day had been very long, and the only bright spot was that the new man, Prosper de la Fosse, was mending rapidly. There would be more quinine available to the ward after Dr. Robideaux's impressive tirade on the subject of the hospital staff's incompetence. Still, de la Fosse was a miracle, really; they had had a coffin ready for him. He seemed to gather strength each day, and with it a charming but persistent obstinacy to keep Minette at his side as much as possible. Such a gentleman's notice was flattering, true, but it also made her a little uneasy.

In her nightly "letters" to Alain, she did not mention Prosper; it seemed somehow disloyal.

Two days later, Prosper de la Fosse was strong enough to sit up in bed for Dr. Robideaux's visit.

"Ah, here you are, Minette. Dr. Robideaux has finally deigned to tell me the full details of the story of your persistent efforts to make him come here to see me."

"I wasn't ready to listen until she mentioned your bloodstone ring," admitted Robideaux.

"We all wondered why the robbers didn't take it from you, sir."

"Bloodstones are supposedly unlucky. I'm glad my attackers were the usual superstitious rabble." Again, the curiously magnetic hazel eyes fastened on Minette. "Who are you, exactly, beautiful girl? An angel sent to me in my time of need?"

"*Mais non, monsieur.* I am simply Minette Marsan, from the Ursuline motherhouse in Paris. I'm a convent orphan, and I was chosen to be *une fille à la cassette.*"

"You mean one of the basket brides?" Prosper was

delighted. "But I'd expected only pious ugliness. Your sponsor, whoever he was, had taste."

"Why do you assume it was a man?" Inwardly she shuddered, reminded of the chevalier.

"Mademoiselle Marsan, the nuns' first requirement would not be pleasuring the eye. Are you spoken for as yet, or must I join a long line of hopefuls?"

That an obvious aristocrat would suggest such a thing was beyond belief. It was unkind of him to toy with her. Her response was as cool as she could manage.

"I am not prepared to discuss that." She was quite final.

"Right. It was louche and boorish of me to ask so abruptly. Let me introduce myself properly. I am Prosper de la Fosse, only son of the house of de la Fosse, late of Cap François on Saint Dominique."

"Oh, sir, the rebellion . . .?"

Prosper laughed. "You probably know more about it than I do. I've been out of my head and raving. Ask Dr. Robideaux."

"It's over," the doctor announced. "I have letters from the island. There may be scattered pockets of resistance, but the government has defeated the planters."

"Why don't we have that news here?"

"Again, the administration of this miserable province. Another reason to protest to Paris. We are always sending petitions home, but they continue to ignore us."

"M'sieu Prosper!" A black woman carrying a basket was hurrying toward them. "Ah, Dr. Robideaux, just the person I was hoping to see. Please tell me that M'sieu Prosper can eat solid foods. I have brought rolls and chicken and his favorite, *boeuf en daube glacé*."

"Much too heavy for a convalescent, Ti Manou," pronounced the doctor. "He may have the rolls, but that's all."

"Ignore him, and give me the basket," Prosper commanded.

She smiled. "If you are certain . . ."

"Set things out for me. I suppose there is no wine?"

"Wine, Prosper!" said the irritated physician. "Are you mad?"

"No longer."

The visitor smiled at Minette. "I see that we meet again, mademoiselle."

Minette could think of nothing to say. This was the woman she'd collided with on her very first day in New Orleans, the elegant Negress with the expensive dress and light green eyes who'd left her with the feeling that she'd been expected. And this woman, whose head scarf today was a light, printed material, was somehow connected with Prosper de la Fosse.

"Ti Manou," said the doctor suddenly, "you continue to mystify me. Did you know that Monsieur Prosper was here, and if you did, why didn't you come to me immediately?"

"I did not know," she answered softly. "I had been looking for him without success until today."

"But how did you guess to come here? To bring food?"

"Enough, Emile." Prosper sounded short-tempered. "She has her ways of knowing."

"I have met Madame before, but I do not know her name," said Minette.

"Madame?" Prosper's eyebrows climbed. "Ti Manou?"

Minette reddened at his tone. What had she said?

Could this woman, who spoke like none of the other blacks, be a slave?

"I am a freedwoman." Ti Manou answered Minette's unspoken question with a quiet pride. "I am personal maid to the mother of M'sieu Prosper, Madame Amadée de la Fosse. Madame is at present not in New Orleans.

"Where is my beautiful mother now?"

"In Nachitoches, visiting your aunt Lamballe."

"Ah, to escape the malaria epidemic. But she went without you? That surprises me." He turned his gaze on Minette once more. "My mother has a horror of sickness, Mademoiselle Marsan, especially when its cause is unknown."

Ti Manou looked away from him, but her lips softly formed a word. *Maringouins.* Minette remembered her hellish trip upstream. The Indian paddlers had called the mosquitoes "maringouins." But what could the connection be? Mosquitoes surrounded them in La Louisiane. If their bite had something to do with the shaking disease, then wouldn't everyone here be sick all the time?

"Have you ever had this sickness, Ti Manou?" She could not prevent herself from asking.

"Malaria? No, Mademoiselle Marsan. I have not. I must be immune to it."

You must be many things, Minette thought. You are no ordinary woman.

Ti Manou smiled at her, a pleasant, submissive smile. Minette shivered. Who could tell why? It was far from cold.

6

Fresh news: a new report from Saint Dominique. Minette came as soon as she heard of it and used her elbows to jostle her way into the considerable crowd around the notice board outside the soldiers' barracks on the Place d'Armes.

"Can you read it? What's it say?" A bonneted old woman was plucking at her sleeve.

"Yes, I can read."

"Well, well?"

"The most wonderful thing. The rebellion is over, and the Royal Marine Infantry is coming back to New Orleans. What do you say to that, Auntie?"

The old woman cupped her ear to catch every word. "They're all coming home?"

"All!" Minette swung around. Alain's name was not on the casualty list—that was the first thing she had seen. He was coming home to her with his regiment, and her future was about to begin.

What a shower of good news, she thought, entering the

Royal Hospital. Berenice was getting married, Celeste was about to accept her ardent German, and she herself would be the next bride. There was no reason to wait; Alain could take advantage of the king's offer of land immediately.

"Minette?" Prosper called out as she passed his bed. He was recovering quickly, and if the malaria outbreak had not been slackening, he'd have been asked to go home and free his bed for the next patient. But he lingered, with Dr. Robideaux in attendance, each day announcing small complications that might delay the hospital discharge.

They made the finicky aristocrat as comfortable as possible. No hospital food passed his lips; the enigmatic Ti Manou brought daily dainties from the kitchen of the de la Fosse mansion. He had fresh pillows, alert service—and the almost constant company of Minette, which he brazenly demanded.

Still excited with her news, Minette hurried over, but she decided not to tell him about Alain. Instinct told her that, with his cocksure, self-centered personality, Prosper was sure to be jealous that her life with Alain was beginning, while their association was ending. Of course, it could hardly be otherwise. She was far below Prosper's social class. He'd marry a rich wife with a grand dowry. One day Minette would tell her children, "I once knew the wealthy Monsieur de la Fosse very well."

She thought she understood the basis of their friendship. He favored her because he believed she had saved his life by finding and summoning Dr. Robideaux. Regardless of his imperiousness to others, his manner to her was nearly faultless. He was a man of fine education, but certain of his opinions about patriotism and country shocked her. There was an unpredictable reckless streak in his character; he was an avid gambler, a duelist, a womanizer, a man who wouldn't wait for what he wanted. But as long as she could escape the sting of his demanding personality, she was content to learn from this witty, discursive, oddly charming man for as long as she could.

She did, however, tell Sister about Alain.

"My congratulations, Minette. And none too soon, for your alloted time here is ending."

"I would stay in New Orleans, Sister. I'd find some way."

"It has worked out for the best. But Minette"—she smiled as she surveyed her—"you do need another dress. This one has been worn to rags."

"I don't have another dress."

"*Petite idiote!* Look in your bride's basket."

"But the dress there is to wear at my wedding."

"Perhaps it won't be long until your wedding. You need the dress now."

King Louis's bounty to each bride included a serviceable gray dress woven to last. Despite its austerity, it was still the finest garment that Minette had ever worn. And it did have a pointed bodice, in fashion for several seasons now.

"It has possibilities," said Sister mysteriously, and she turned it over to the skilled needlewomen of the Ursuline convent. They found blue ribbons and sewed them along the seams of the bodice in a way that made Minette's slim waist look almost ethereal. They lowered the neckline in order to fill it in with a "modesty piece" of soft fabric, and a friend of the convent produced a set of hoops, which belled the skirt—all of which made the dress much more fashionable. Shoes? Unfortunately, Minette's feet, though high-arched and shapely, were too large to be fitted among the shoes of the convent's friends.

"So I am not *Cendrillon*, with her tiny foot and glass

slipper," said Minette. "*Tant pis*, so much the worse."

"We will sew a blue ruffle to the bottom of the skirt, and your shoes won't be seen." That was the contribution of Sister Mary Martyr, Immaculata's friend and a favorite of Minette's. "But after the wedding, take the ruffle off, my dear girl. It won't last a week in the mud of these planked streets."

"Do you know what I saw the other night, Sister? A group of young girls, nice girls, all dressed up, as if for a dance. The streets were so muddy that they took off their shoes and held their skirts high, laughing and hurrying along in the mud."

"You say nice girls, Minette? Girls of decent family? Showing their ankles and undergarments?"

"But the mud was—"

"We may be a long way from France, but not so long as to forget the basic decencies," the sister retorted.

Minette secretly admired the girls' resourcefulness—decency was, of course, essential, but, *la*, the price of shoes!—she'd have to be more circumspect next time.

It was more difficult to keep secret her private joy at Alain's imminent return in the Royal Hospital. Still the young men on the wards, recovering from sickness but not infatuation, sensed that their "golden untouchable" had somehow changed, that something, someone, had reached her. Prosper himself sometimes lapsed into sullenness at her air of mystery, and she had to pamper him back to smiles.

While Minette waited, Eulalie announced her engagement to a prosperous carter, not young, but the master of many teams and horses. It was by far the most prestigious match to date, this Monsieur Alphonse. Eulalie was heartily congratulated. As for Seraphine, she continued to disappoint the nuns. She had left the convent, and no one knew her whereabouts, but the stories about her and the rich young Creole blades of the town were lurid. "The one rotten apple in a sound bushel," said Sister Immaculata, reaching back into her country past.

The town was ready to fête the returning heroes from Saint Dominique. New Orleans, for all its close trading connections with the colony, had not been sympathetic to the rich planters' attempts to evade taxes. In fact, the *habitants* of La Louisiane were glad to see their West Indian cousins' arrogance put down. Even Prosper, who still had property there, said the insubordination was a futile, stupid attempt to avoid the inevitable.

"La Louisiane is a disappointment to the French treasury," he told Minette, "and Louis is bound to try to wring more money out of Saint Dominique."

"Why do you always say such things, Prosper? Look at all the people who have come here. And this territory is very big, isn't it?"

"Big? It's enormous. Here in *bas* Louisiane we're only the toe in the stocking. The territory goes west to Saint Louis and north to Canada. It's six times the size of France itself but provides not one sixth the return."

"Why not?"

"Do you see any gold here, such as the Spaniards found in Mexico? Are there any diamonds or precious jewels to be mined? Is there land waiting for the plough, or must it be hacked from a fever-ridden jungle? And so many die of the fevers that the king must find more and more people to come here and keep the place from going under—which, by the way, it very nearly is. We're below sea level here, did you know that?"

She hadn't.

"If the Mississippi floods and the levee doesn't hold, we shall drown," he continued.

"Surely it will hold!"

"Even if it does, there are the hurricanes that come in from the Gulf of Mexico."

"Prosper, I think you enjoy my ignorance and are trying to frighten me. But even I can see that the trade in furs that comes down the river to New Orleans is a very valuable thing."

"True."

"And it seems to me that there are enough fine, strong cedar trees to build masts for all the ships in Europe."

"True again."

"So why is La Louisiane considered such a loss?"

"You've put your finger on it, *mon ange*. Discerning the profit takes a bit of imagination. The potential is there. My family knows it, other nations like Spain and England realize it and covet us, but—"

"But what?"

"The king of France, especially a stupid Bourbon king, can't see beyond what *isn't* in his treasury. He doesn't think about the future."

"Prosper, you shouldn't speak that way about His Majesty!"

"Why not, my little *royaliste?* We all do. This must be the most disrespectful colony in French history. We double-damn the king and his policies."

"Prosper, not so loud!"

"Ah, you're afraid for me. You think I'll be packed off to jail. You must care for me after all. I find that very sweet."

What Minette truly cared about as the carefully counted days went by was Alain's arrival. Surely it couldn't take more than two weeks to sail from Cap François to New Orleans. Where was he? He should be here by now. She attended to her hair and nails with homemade creams, took frequent baths in the tub behind the screen, sewed a small sachet of fragrant bergamot from France into the neckline of her gown. She bought strawberries in the market to crush and use their juice to color her lips and cheeks. When the strawberries went rotten, waiting, she bought more. Her gown was finished. She took down the coronet of braids she wore and washed her hair several times in camomile tea, letting the waist-length mass sun dry to make its natural gold glisten. She left it down, braided flowers into the waves that fell around her face. Finally there was nothing to do but clean and reclean the convent parlor, which would be the scene of their reunion. Nervous energy gathered into a tightness at the pit of her stomach and would not dissolve.

All New Orleans knew when the Royal Marine Infantry arrived. Minette heard the guns go off in salute and thought that she too might explode. Music blared, the swinging martial cadence that accompanied the regiment on its victory parade through town. Cheering and clapping, crowds followed the soldiers as they marched down Chartres Street. Unfortunately, Minette's window did not face in that direction.

Hold on and wait, hold on and wait. Into her fervent concentration came the sound of Sister Mary Martyr, running full tilt upstairs in her haste to reach Minette. She was much more demonstrative than Sister Immaculata and fairly pinched Minette's arm in her eagerness to unite the lovers in the convent parlor.

"Quickly, quickly, he's here!"

Minette shook out her hair and let it float behind her as she skimmed down the wide convent staircase with its wrought-iron torchères. She hurried into the parlor, only to stop abruptly. On the sofa, his tricorne hat and cuffed gloves beside him, sat her Cupid in this love affair, Lieutenant Guillaume Cernaux.

"Guillaume? Where is Alain?"

And then she saw the expression on Cernaux's face.

Moments later she was doubled over in pain wailing like a wounded animal. *Non!* No, no, no, no!

Sister Mary hovered, making small gestures intended to comfort.

Minette scarcely saw her. "I don't believe you! It isn't true! I won't believe you!"

Cernaux sat tired and spent. She was taking it all very badly.

"Oh, oh, dear God, it can't be so!" She sank to the floor. He thought that she had fainted, but when he went to help her, the white, tear-stained face turned up to his was not piteous but angry.

"You left him there! You didn't even bring home his body."

"We were in the thick of battle. I couldn't stop to help him. And when I went back afterward, he wasn't there."

"Then why do you tell me that he's dead?"

"Minette, I saw him shot in the chest at close range. I saw him fall. I saw the blood."

"He couldn't have gotten up?"

"I don't see how it would be possible."

"Then where was the body? Bodies don't move. Where was Alain?"

"The enemy could have taken him."

"A dead body? Why? Oh, God, don't tell me you were fighting cannibals!"

"No, Minette. Frenchmen. We were fighting our own people."

"All the more reason to go back for him!"

"Minette, try to imagine how it was. We were

ambushed, crowded together, perfect targets, hardly able to draw our swords. It was hopeless."

"Yet you survived."

"I don't know how."

"But you did. And so could he. Listen, Guillaume Cernaux, he could be staggering about in the jungle, alone and tortured by mosquitoes and fever and pain. Our Lord on the Cross! He could be all alone, abandoned and forgotten by those he had trusted."

"And going where?" Cernaux cut in. "Tell me that!"

"Go back! Go back and find him!" Her certainty grew until she was screaming at Cernaux.

"I cannot."

"You must. Get permission. It shouldn't be hard, the rebellion is over. There's nothing to be afraid of now."

"I am not afraid."

"You were then."

"Ah," he admitted, "we all were, even Alain. We'd never fought on such terrain before, against an invisible enemy who knew how to melt into the jungle and send bullets from seemingly nowhere."

"Yes, it sounds frightful. But you won."

"At what cost? I have lost my dear friend."

"Go back and find him." She clutched his sleeve. "Please!"

"I cannot."

"You will not. I would have died myself before I left such a dear friend alone in the jungle."

"Ah, *zut alors*, you will not understand!"

"Perhaps I am too stupid. You come and tell me Alain is dead, and—"

"He *is* dead. Last rites have been said for him."

"Last rites over an empty coffin."

"You are so fierce, Minette!"

"Bring me a lock of his hair, a button, something I can properly mourn!"

"And then would you believe the truth?"

"Why wasn't his name on the casualty lists?"

Cernaux sighed. "That was my doing. I persuaded my colonel that I should give you the news myself."

"And you think you have discharged your duty by bringing me this story?"

"Have I not?"

"You put us together, you spoke for Alain and persuaded me of his love, you gave me a future to dream on, and now you've smashed it. Am I to thank you?"

"You have changed, Minette."

"I'm sorry if you do not approve. But I don't care! Alain has been betrayed."

"What can I do, Minette?"

"Why was he alone? Why was he abandoned?"

"Woman, you do not understand the nature of war!"

"May I never do so."

As Cernaux watched her in miserable uncertainty, she calmed herself enough to remember her manners. "I . . . I thank you for coming, Guillaume."

He nodded sadly—and fled.

She could feel the presence of the nuns hovering nearby. They would certainly urge her to pray. Pray! She was not ready to resign herself to the will of the Everlasting. She wanted to keep the coals of her anger burning, fan them with her lost hopes, because while they burned, she could doubt the logic of Cernaux's story, and Alain was still alive to her. She went out of the building without a word to anyone and ran down the street.

New Orleans was too absorbed in its own affairs to spare more than curious glances for the young woman sobbing as she hurried along. A lovers' quarrel, *évidem-*

ment, a misstep in the courtship dance.

Today, there were no friendly faces. No one spoke to her, and soon she was beyond the gloriously named streets and into the muddy maze of the city's unplanned growth, where necessity had taken over from architects and created a narrow, shabby reality. Here, near the city wall, unable to draw another breath, she came to a halt. The new dress, with all the nuns' loving work, was splashed with street debris. Her hair hung in wet strings, soaked with perspiration. She stood, exhausted, irresolute, with no idea of what to do.

"Minette?" From a little distance, someone had spoken her name.

She turned slowly.

"Minette Marsan."

A man was standing there, breathing with some difficulty himself. A few times during her flight she'd thought she'd heard the footsteps of a pursuer but had been too sunk in misery to let it register with any degree of alarm. Now here he was, tanned rather than wine-ruddy, somewhat leaner around the waist . . . the chevalier de Pombiers.

He let his eyes roam over her. Silence grew and he was easy in it, a lazy cat at a mouse hole who had only to wait.

She wasn't afraid at first. After all, how had she seen him last? With his breeches flapping around his ankles, red-faced and humiliated. But this was not the same man. This was a predator, a hunter with a fixity of purpose. How long had he been following her? How had he chosen the precise moment when she was without the protection of the nuns? She looked around her; to one side was a cul-de-sac, to the other, an alley that led into a wider street. She would watch for her chance to run that way.

"Well, Minette?"

"Chevalier, I want nothing to do with you."

"Then you must return to France, you know. Your time here is up."

"I intend to stay."

"In that case you must marry at once. I'm sure you've had offers."

"Yes, I—"

"Forget them," he said pleasantly. "You'll make a far grander match than the other girls. You were never destined for the common man, and now you will marry into the nobility of France."

"And who is this dashing bridegroom?"

"Not so dashing, perhaps, but ardent enough. You will marry me."

She began to edge away with small, almost imperceptible steps.

"You never mentioned marriage to me before, Chevalier."

"Much has changed. You are very lovely, and I am a wiser man. The bit of life you've tasted suits you well, Minette. I mean the soldier, of course."

"How can you know about him?"

"I told you I was a powerful man—in France and in New Orleans. Such a high-minded romance, wasn't it? You, bravely waiting, still a virgin, while he died in the Indies. It was much more convenient for me that way. Otherwise, I might have been forced to arrange for his death here."

"You couldn't do that!"

"Ah, you'd be surprised how simple it would have been. But to return to the subject of our marriage . . ."

She shook her head violently. "Never. Never!"

"Minette!" For a moment the old foolish urgency broke through. Then it was coldly restrained. "I offer you the chance of your lifetime. What have you now? Nothing. Admit it."

She did not answer. He went on.

"You are without protection. I offer you the shelter of my family name, a high position in a world you never dreamed of entering. You will grace society as Madame de Pombiers. No one will remember your origins. And our children—"

"You're too old to have children!"

"I will show you that you are much mistaken. Our children will be among the most privileged in New France."

"If your family is so illustrious," she improvised frantically, "you can't marry me, Chevalier. I don't know who I am. I'm certainly a bastard—who else is left at a convent gate? I may also be the child of thieves or murderers."

"You are the love child of an aristocrat. Don't you think I can tell the difference between a purebred filly and a plowhorse? In such matters I am infallible."

And mad, thought Minette. More than a little mad. She had edged into a position from which she could see the other end of the alley and, beyond it, the street. Surely she could outrun this man again. But if his influence was as significant as he said, where would she hide from him in New Orleans? Could she stay in the convent forever?

A thought came to her. Prosper was a gentleman of means and influence. Could he protect her? Prosper de la Fosse, her champion against Hector de Pombiers, aristocrat against aristocrat? She knew that Prosper was grateful to her. Yes, she would run straight to him.

"You have not yet answered me, Minette."

"How can I? She hedged. "It's hardly an hour since I heard that Alain—"

"You hardly knew this Lieutenant Gerard!" His interruption was testy, his patience wearing thin. "Your soldier was little more than a stranger to you. What did he do, kiss you once? For that matter, so did I!"

She shuddered, remembering.

"I was wrong not to offer you marriage in France, Minette."

"You offered me money! I am not a whore, Chevalier—not then, not now."

"Bravely spoken. But I assure you that now you will be my wife."

He seemed to think that something had been settled. Madman! She estimated the distance she needed to cover, straight down the alley and into the beckoning street. Alain, she prayed, help me escape.

To mislead the chevalier, she glanced in the other direction.

"Don't look for help, Minette. No one saw you run in here."

Now! She pivoted and ran for her life. Was he following? She could not risk a backward glance, but she thought not. The wide street was closer. Don't trip. Don't—The breath went out of her as she collided with a squat, powerful man.

"Help me, sir. Help me!"

He grinned at her and twisted her hair so that her head was forced back. Another man stepped out from behind and pinioned her arms. She kicked out and felt her foot connect with a shinbone.

"*Merde!* Hold her."

"Get the bag!"

A burlap sack came down over her head, blotting out the world. She felt herself being folded into a blanket.

"Well done," said the chevalier cheerfully. "And

there's no one on the street just now. Sling her over your shoulder like a rug and take her to the cart."

"And our payment?"

"Immediately!" answered the chevalier. Minette heard the clink of coins. "Just to the cart. I have help of my own waiting."

Oh, well and fully planned on his part. Twice in her life, thought Minette as she struggled against the suffocating pressure. Twice in her life this evil man had trapped her. And now she was utterly helpless.

7

Minette awoke in a splendid bed, a four-poster of glossy mahogany with a damask tester. The mosquito netting protecting her was draped high and caught at ceiling level with a silver ring. The pillows and sheets caressed her skin, and the ivory comforter, artfully puffed, was of cool silk.

For a moment she was afraid to turn her head. Would he be lying there triumphant? She had no memory of the last few hours. But when she finally forced herself to look, no one was beside her, and the lack of indentation on the pillows convinced her that she'd slept alone.

Light, the slumbrous light of late afternoon, filtered in through the jalousies and showed her a magnificent bedroom in an antique style. She saw graceful chairs, a planked cedar floor with a precious oriental rug, a dressing table with crystal flacons and a rosewood mirror, a long cheval glass that picked up reflections of silver and gilt, porcelain and crystal, and set them shimmering in its mirrored depths. On the mantel above the fireplace, a mantel covered with French tiles garlanded in yellow, an ormolu clock worthy of Versailles chimed four times.

Tentatively, she slipped her feet out of the bed, aware for the first time of her batiste nightgown, light and luxurious as a cloud and trimmed with white satin ribbons. A slight bitter taste in her mouth made her reach for the crystal carafe of water beside her. But wait. Did her inability to remember the past few hours mean that she'd been given some drug? And if so, did she dare drink the water? No, he wouldn't get much pleasure out of her unconscious body, the old goat. He'd want her to be awake. The water, still cool, trickled down a grateful throat.

She tried the door. Locked. She listened but heard nothing in the hall outside. Except for the hum of insects and the plaintive call of a mourning dove, the afternoon was absolutely quiet. Padding over to the window, she tried to move the jalousies but couldn't. Peering through the slats, she saw only a sun-dazzle of light over green fields. She discovered the fragrance of hay on the breeze and a sharp scent something like mustard blossoms.

God alone knew where she was. No one else would. How could she escape? This was a luxurious prison, but a prison nevertheless, and with a mad jailer obsessed by her body. Ah, Alain, where are you? But, no, she could not begin to think of him now. She sent up a quick prayer to direct her away from sorrow and make her ready and strong, like a soldier, to win her freedom.

Minette paced off the limits of the room to which she was confined. How Seraphine would love this opulent place. The indolent, pleasure-seeking girl might even learn to love the chevalier himself; he was certainly rich enough. Perhaps she could persuade him to trade her for Seraphine. She was beautiful, graceful. But, no, Seraphine knew her parents before they died; they were farmers. She was not the "love child of an aristocrat," as de Pombiers had said with such delight. What nonsense! But since he set such store on genteel blood, could she disgust him in some way and make him reconsider? Well, but short of body lice, what would do? And how would she acquire them in this clean and beautiful place? Besides, the "ardent" chevalier would probably have her deloused and scrubbed, then brought back for his pleasure.

It was hard not to give in to terror when she thought of his determination and lust. Was it the last obsessive drive of a failing body? His last virgin before old age closed in? If it were virginity he prized, suppose she told him that she'd been unfaithful to Alain and had several lovers in New Orleans? Would it make her less desirable? Would he believe her? Or would he see through the *cocotte* act immediately?

What was the key to this man's wicked obsession?

As days passed and Minette did not return to the convent, the nuns feared that her despair over Alain's death had led her to drown herself. Immaculata thought otherwise.

"Convent orphans are not so careless with life. They're abandoned at birth, and it's only by luck and perseverance that each survives. Would such a girl throw away life so easily?"

"You did not see her face. I did. She was devastated as she rushed past me," said Sister Mary Martyr. "All hope was gone."

"At her age? She's not even eighteen."

"Nevertheless—"

"Nevertheless, it's romantic twaddle. I've never

known anyone more tenacious of life and grateful for its blessings than this girl."

"Does Minette know that you were the one who found her as an infant and gave her the name of your village?" Mary Martyr asked, curious.

Immaculata shook her head.

"Why not, Sister?"

"I could not encourage her to overfondness, to think of me as a substitute mother," said Immaculata. "Especially if one day she joined the order."

"Minette?"

"She has a good, rational intelligence and strongly developed instincts, which I hope are protecting her now."

"Still, I cannot see her as a nun."

"Nor could I," sighed Immaculata, "once she grew up. Her kind of beauty is a curse. Men won't let her alone."

"Do you think a man has taken her?"

"A man, or men—what else can it be? New Orleans is a licentious city."

"Yes, and there are those . . . places, too."

"What places?"

"The houses. You know."

"Sister Mary Martyr!"

"One must be realistic."

"I prefer your romantic twaddle. But for your information, we have alerted the police. It was done yesterday with the cooperation of the Jesuit fathers. Those . . . houses are being searched."

"Let us hope she isn't found there."

"Make up your mind where you want her found! But be assured that whatever has happened to Minette will leave her soul intact."

She said the same thing to Prosper de la Fosse, who still lingered in the hospital. After three days of missing Minette, he answered, "Don't speak to me of her soul! Let us find her alive and breathing. I want to leave this hospital and help in the search!"

"Now that she's not here, you are suddenly strong enough to leave?"

"Do you accuse me of malingering?"

"On the contrary. You are still too weak."

"Aha! A sign from above!" Prosper looked elated as Ti Manou, with her usual basket of delicacies, entered the ward and approached his bed. "Eggs in aspic today," she began. "Chicken, *petit pain*—"

"Stop. Put down the food. I require something else from you." Prosper was sitting up in bed, his face flushed. "Look at me. Now I call you, Ti Manou, three times in your name, and each time you will answer, 'I am here.' Do you know what I need from you now?"

As she put down the basket and began the ritual response, she underwent an almost physical change: tall into taller, dignified into almost frightening, the planes of her face becoming stern and angular, the cool eyes glittering like a cat's at night. Even the voice she used now was deeper, older, and full of confidence.

"What do you require of Mambo Ti Manou?"

"Mademoiselle Marsan has disappeared. She's been gone for three days now, but I don't believe that she is dead. I think she has been taken. Kidnapped. There is a good chance that she's still in New Orleans or in the country around here. Bring me something with which I can sketch her face."

A piece of charcoal was found. Prosper, an accomplished amateur artist, produced several good likenesses of Minette.

"Show these to your followers, Ti Manou. Let them cast a great net for miles around. And find her."

"I will intercede with the powers," said Ti Manou cryptically.

"You are the power!"

"I am its servant. There is a limit to—"

"There is no limit. Do you think I am a fool? Go and do whatever must be done."

With a small, gratified smile, Ti Manou slipped away.

"What is this talk, Prosper?" Sister Immaculata demanded. "What power are you speaking of? That woman is a Catholic. She wears a crucifix."

"Oh, yes, and she can probably say her prayers even faster than you and I. She's a Catholic, all right. They all are. But it changes nothing."

"What do you mean?"

"In the slave trade we tried to—"

"Slavery is an abomination."

"I know your point of view. Do you want to hear my story?"

"Proceed."

"When we imported slaves from West Africa to work in the cane fields of the Indies, we tried to get men from different tribes. Can you imagine why?"

"No."

"Because they all spoke different dialects, and we thought that not understanding each other's languages would prevent them from uniting to plot against their masters."

"With all the slave rebellions, that doesn't seem to have done the trick."

"Precisely. And you know why? Their religion united

them. Regardless of which tribe they came from, they all practiced some form of voodoo."

"Voodoo? Pagan worship? How can you call that a religion?"

"My dear Sister Immaculata, I do. In fact, you have just been talking to a *mambo*, a voodoo priestess."

"Impossible! She is a Catholic."

"We had them all forcibly baptized as Catholics, all the slaves. We thought that might make a difference."

"But it must have."

"Oh, yes? Do you know what they did? Do you know the revenge of the weak upon the strong?"

"I don't understand."

"You will. They have taken over the Catholic ritual to use in their true religion. Our Mass and our prayers bless their voodoo practices. Their gods go hand in hand with our saints. The Church has not been forsaken, not at all neglected, but it has been well and truly used."

"That's heresy!"

"That's their revenge, at least until they're strong enough to fight us with our own weapons."

"Isn't voodoo illegal here?"

"It is, but still you hear the drums in the evening, I never thought—"

"Think about it now. It's fascinating. Combined with whatever they've taken from Christianity, voodoo is twice as powerful as it ever was."

She was silent. Then she said, "That woman, Ti Manou. What will she do now?"

"She will pray to Erzulie."

"Who is Erzulie?"

"One of the friendly gods, luckily. Erzulie wears white, is pretty, wealthy, and hung with gold jewelry.

She is kind, and she often intercedes for lovers. They call her the Great Mother."

"Mother? But that's—"

"Exactly," Prosper cut in. "Now you understand. Erzulie is the image, in the voodoo mirror, of the Virgin Mary."

"Blasphemy!" Sister exclaimed.

"Not for voodoo's true believers," Prosper answered.

That night in her room, which was quite neat and tasteful, Ti Manou was making preparations. Her table, spread with a clean white cloth, would serve as the altar. Colored pictures of the Virgin Mary adorned the wall behind it, as did a crucifix. Ti Manou laid out fresh flowers and a plate of fruit as a food offering and lit a candle. She considered making a voodoo design on the floor with sand—this was a great undertaking, calling for much strength—but in the end, she set out only the Mother's symbol, a paper heart with a paper sword pasted to it. Then, because of her own special powers, and following her private intuition, she added a large bowl of water in which to see the future. At last she was ready. But she must be sure to invoke Erzulie and only Erzulie, not the other, more sinister gods. She must dismiss them in advance, all except for Legba.

"I call on Legba Avarda, guardian of doors, highways, crossroads, paths. Legba, open the way."

She cast flowers on the floor.

"I do not summon Ogun, god of war, whose color is blood red, or Damballa, the snake god, or Baron Samedi from the graveyards, or Gede, the clown. I do not call Hevioso or Agassu, none from the pantheon, except Papa Legba. He will lead me to Erzulie."

In her mind, she saw the tiny image of an old man, poorly dressed, limping, a tramp on the road, a fitting intermediary for the poor and for slaves. This was Legba. As he drew nearer, she explained the need to search each path and crossroads, to penetrate each door in search of the hidden one, the young white woman. The sketch of Minette was offered high, then pressed against her forehead. "This is the one who must be found, Papa Legba. All your powers are needed."

The trance began to overtake her, the trance of the priestess, and soon the *loa*, the intermediary spirit to the gods, would assume control. "Papa Legba!" she intoned. "Take me to the Great Mother, take me to Erzulie so that her faithful daughter may receive her blessing and favor for this thing that is to be done!" She began to move, sinuously and gracefully at first, then more and more wildly, her arms whipping the air, leg muscles quivering, head thrown back, hair, escaped from her tignon, uncoiling down her back. Ti Manou, the cool and orderly, now became a maenad, a wild creature, all spirit, all convulsive motion. And then she suddenly slipped to the floor, murmuring prayers, filled with the essence of what she worshiped. When she awoke from this self-induced trance, she might be able to peer for a while into the future. "And, oh, Mother, your Ti Manou has many questions about this young white girl."

Minette, quite elegantly dressed, sat opposite the chevalier de Pombiers at dinner. She had found the clothes in the armoire, obviously placed there for her. They were beautiful and becoming and thoughtfully chosen, even to peach satin slippers that perfectly fit her generous feet. But the implications were frightening. Such clothes were not easily come by. They'd been ordered from Europe, which required time and fore-thought. The chevalier had been planning on this abduction. She knew that suddenly. She knew every-thing but why.

There he sat, the very picture of a noble gentleman in the prime—or somewhat past the prime—of his life. He looked healthier than when he had come to the Ursuline convent, and he barely touched the wine he urged on her. She only pretended to sip it. He made inconsequential conversation, and, cautiously, she responded. Then he began to talk about his honors and decorations in battle as a famous swordsman, about his noble pedigree and genealogical connections with the finest families in France. On and on he went, seeming to expect no answer from her, only dazed acquiescence. That's what she gave him, hoping to keep him in this civilized mood, hoping to hear something she could use as leverage to help her escape.

Her polite attitude backfired over dessert, which was a luscious *île flottante*, a soft pudding in clouds of meringue served with hazelnut wafers.

"Shall we have the priest in the morning?" he asked suddenly. "I have a woman who can come in and dress your hair, if you like."

"The priest?"

"He's a friendly padre who asks no questions. Why do you look so startled? Haven't I given you my word that I'd marry you?"

She stammered excuses. "We've—we've spent so lit-tle time together. I—I don't know yet if we'd get along."

He laughed hugely. "We've just proved that we can spend the evening in polite conversation, which is a sta-

ple of most marriages in good society. As for the rest . . .
I have no doubt. Ah, don't tempt me, Minette, or I
won't be able to hold out until the morning."

Her nerve broke. "You don't want to marry me!"

"But I will. I will do anything to have you as my own.
I thought I'd made that clear."

"You don't love me!"

"Love? What has that to do with it? But you might
say that I worship you as the goddess of my rebirth, the
fountain from which I am replenished as a man."

"Me?"

"You, only you. That's the joke of it, Minette.
Nature is fond of such jokes. You, a chit of a girl with no
experience. A virgin. Pah! I've never cared for virgins;
they're still too frightened of everything. No sense of
adventure."

She was completely confused. "I thought—"

"You thought it was your virginity I valued?" He
laughed. "Quite the reverse. It's a troublesome state.
There are too many things to teach a virgin, too many
tears and regrets that no sensible woman would
entertain. I'd much prefer you to be an accomplished
courtesan."

"Then you will be disappointed, Chevalier. Why
don't you let me go?"

"Ah, sly boots. You know very well why you are
indispensable to me."

"I swear that I do not!"

"Then let me enlighten you. After our first meeting,
I thought I could look forward to a new life in the arms
of Venus. But I had nothing except disappointment
with other women, however skillful they were. With
your inspiration, I was reborn, just by looking at you!
With them, it was the same old inability."

"Inability?"

"Don't play stupid, Minette. Impotence, if you must have the word. I was unmanned for years. As far as enjoyment of the senses, I had nothing but a flap of skin between my legs. Do you know what that does to a man, especially a man like me, you cold little nun's lamb? Years were stolen from me by impotence. Then I came alive, just looking at you, only to die again in the arms of the very next woman I tried, a trull who really knew what she was doing! Finally, after repeated failures, I realized the joke that Nature intended. I could be potent only with you. So I will have you and your confounded virginity, and no other man will steal you from me."

She made a small muffled sound.

He glared at her. "Crying? I hate tears. Accept the inevitable. I am a rich man, and someday you will be a rich widow. Then you can take your choice of pretty boys. It won't be for many years, my dear. You'll be well saddlebroken and accustomed to my gaits by the time I'm gone. But never fear. If you've lost your youth and freshness, you'll have money enough to buy someone for your bed, I promise you that."

"You look very healthy to me," she said bitterly.

"And I feel it," he said, rising and walking the length of the table to where Minette sat. "I am bursting with health. We might even have a child—though I should not let you nurse it, not with those breasts. No one shall tongue them but me."

He could not resist cupping her. She shivered with fear and repulsion.

"No? Well, I shall titillate myself a few hours longer. I never realized the sweet joys of anticipation before. But in the morning, I shall be your legal husband, and you'll have no right to refuse me your body. Wives are beaten for less than that, you know, all within the law."

In the morning, Ti Manou began to spread her net. From mouth to mouth it passed; the *mambo* of Erzulie wanted such and such a white woman found. Her commands were received by those invisible colonists who would endure as much if not more tenaciously in New Orleans than the whites. In spite of the brutal Black Code of 1726 which provided swift reprisal and death for any aggression against the masters, the slaves in New Orleans itself had more freedom than the many thousands who worked the plantations of La Louisiane. The sieur de Bienville acknowledged that black labor had built his city, and through the same infamous Black Code tried to balance the concerns of white safety and black property by requiring masters to provide for slaves disabled by old age or sickness, or pay the government eight cents a day for the slave's hospitalization. In New Orleans, criminal justice could be brought to bear against masters or overseers who mutilated or killed slaves. Husbands and wives belonging to the same owner could not be sold separately, or children under the age of fourteen sold away from their parents.

Adulthood came early to blacks in New Orleans; it came with hard work and an understanding of their position. They learned to be invisible, inoffensive, useful, and silently watchful. Without realizing it, the white colonists of New Orlean had surrounded themselves with a shadow population of watching eyes, listening ears, and clever hands. All was known to the watchers and servers. And it was to these people that Ti Manou turned: to the street sellers who cried, "*Calas, calas!*" to

advertise their sweet rice cakes; to those who sold strawberries and vegetables and tin pots and pieces of fabric;
to those who served by cleaning chimneys, their brushes
slung over their shoulders, calling "*Raminez, raminez!*"
as they strolled along.

Who better than these unnoticed watchers to find a
missing person?

Yet Minette was not to be found. Gossip at kitchen
doors revealed nothing; neither did a painstaking search
of alleys and corners. Ti Manou gave orders to fan out
into the countryside. The girl was alive; her instinct told
her that. But she had to satisfy the ragingly impatient
Prosper.

Minette awoke in the darkness with the close, musty
smell of vinegar and old condiments enveloping her.
The moon shone dimly through a barred window set
barely above ground. For a moment, she did not remember how she came to be in this damp storeroom.

Oh, yes, the priest. He had come, a convivial toper,
and drunk a good deal of claret with the chevalier. He
was a disgrace to his order and plainly unrepentant; he'd
called her a lucky girl to be taken to wife by a noble
gentleman. Well, she'd shown him how lucky she felt.
First by her frantic crying, then screams, then a faint
that would have done credit to Celeste. They'd poured
cold water on her; she'd held her breath. They'd tickled
her with feathers, held something under her nose; she'd
refused to revive. The chevalier had slapped her, a hard,
bruising slap, and finally the priest had protested. The
bridegroom was not entitled to beat her until after marriage, it seemed.

She could see that she'd managed to put the chevalier in an odd position. The priest had no objection to coming back and performing the wedding "when the young lady has recovered herself," but now he knew that she was there, and he expected a marriage. The chevalier couldn't simply dispose of her in his rage, or lash her like a disobedient slave. The marks would show. Oh, he'd looked at her quite differently after her hysterical performance; there had been a certain wary respect in his eyes.

So he'd set out to break her spirit. This was supposed to do it: this dark little supply closet, the uncomfortable straw mattress, the bread-and-water rations. Hah! She'd had worse. She doubted that he'd let her die. Time was more on her side than on his, if he wanted to make up for all those years of impotent lust. Of course, he could starve her until she was too weak to murmur anything but "yes." And those rustlings in the corner could be rats. She sat up suddenly. She must be active at night and let those rats know she was no easy prey.

Minette turned night into day, pacing and exercising, reciting the catechism, sending special prayers, albeit in vain, to Saint Ursula, reciting all the poetry she remembered, singing occasionally, and willing herself not to think of Alain.

During the weeks of her captivity, she came to terms with the idea that he was truly dead, and, in an odd way, the thought that he was watching from heaven brought her calm comfort rather than despair. It also strengthened her awareness that she could depend only on herself now. No one else could help; she would have no expectations. During the day she was able to sleep, thinking that the rats must be foraging out in the fields. The door was opened briefly when her food came in, but a hefty servant was always there to block any foolhardy dash on her part. She did not see the chevalier at all but thought of him getting older every day.

Minette was still gone, and Prosper had finally left the hospital, retreating to the de la Fosse mansion near Bayou Saint John. His mother was due to return from her lengthy family visit to Aunt Lamballe at any time, and he dreaded making explanations for all that had happened. He had still not recovered his strength; this, his fifth bout of malaria, had been a near thing. Without Minette's help he would probably be resting now aboveground in the marble mausoleum of departed de la Fosses.

Prosper was savage with Ti Manou's lack of progress in finding Minette, and she spent much time anxiously trying to conjure the future. But the waters in her bowl remained cloudy; Erzulie was not ready to help.

The weather changed; the winds blew in torrential rains that turned city gutters into swirling streams and made the country a morass of mud. *Chez* de Pombiers, it was more than ever a battle of wills between the chevalier and Minette. Twice he had cut her meager rations, forbidden her water, left her so alone that she longed for any kind of companionship. She was chilled often, or felt feverish, and talked to herself. Sometimes she sang the nursery songs and rhymes she had learned as a child.

That was what One-Ear Sen heard one night, floating over the fields, and he thought it was a ghost. He whipped up his donkey—curse the delay on repairing the wheel of this cart, or he'd never be out on the roads at night when Baron Samedi walked abroad, clanking his chains. Sen touched his amulet and made a quick voodoo prayer to Saint Expedit.

The high, clear, pure voice followed him for some time, borne on the wind, before he realized the words were in French. Not the *gombo* patois he spoke, but the French of France, like that of his accursed ex-master, M'sieu Beauchamp. He strained to understand. It was nonsense: "*Ron, ron, petit bergeron.*" Something about sheep and shepherds, a song for white children.

White? The white woman was still missing. Could it be she? Ti Manou's anger was hovering over the whole black community. They were failing her, and as a result hens were dying and cows going dry and children falling sick. Who knew what would happen next? Now if he, Sen, could spy out where the woman was hidden, the *mambo* would reward him. On the other hand, to stumble across the dark fields at night looking for a voice was not the act of a sensible man. But of a poor and desperate one whose business as a peddler of household scrap metal had fallen to nothing, yes. For such a one would have nothing to lose and perhaps a new cart to gain. Before he could come to his senses, One-Ear Sen tethered his donkey to a tree and set out across the fields, praying as he went.

He was fortunate; he found the house, a forbidding bulk in the dark. There were no lights showing. He prowled about it as a chilling rain began. The voice was raised again; it seemed to be coming from the ground beneath his feet. Protect me, Saint Expedit! But wait. There was a window down there almost covered by vines. And as he leaned closer, the voice wavered and broke into a series of deep, harsh coughs. It sang no more.

He fled.

8

"*You will show me* exactly where that house is or I will turn you into the donkey you already resemble." Ti Manou regarded this idiot whose right ear had been cropped and branded, more likely for stealing than for rebellion. Could he have managed what all the others had failed to accomplish?

"I marked the place. I made a cairn of stones."

"And how is that cairn different from every other along the roadside?"

"I will show you. I will go with you. But Mambo Ti Manou, it's a long way, and I've had no sleep."

"You'd stop now?"

"It's still dark," he whined.

"I see well in the dark. Do you want a reward, or would you rather have a punishment? We will find that window from which the singing came, and we will find it now. Where is your miserable cart?"

Shortly after dawn, Minette awoke to pain. Tight bands seemed to crisscross her chest, and breathing produced a painful burning. She tried to breathe shallowly, in small gulps, and heard her breath whistle raggedly in her throat. The pressure around her eyes was intense. She raised her hands to ease it and felt them glide through smooth sheets. She was back in the mahogany four-poster in the beautiful room, and a bowl of steaming water beside the bed testified that someone had been giving her treatment.

From the cold pantry to this luxury. How? Why? As she struggled against a swimming weakness, one of the chevalier's silent slaves, an old woman, entered the room and turned back the blankets on the bed. Minette discovered that she was naked. No one had ever seen her thus, never in her life. She felt intense shame.

Small black eyes with the glint of wet pebbles surveyed her.

"Am I dying? Is that why I'm in here again?" she managed to ask.

The woman shook her head. With expert hands she dipped cloths into the steaming water, wrung them out and applied the hot poultices to Minette's throat and chest. The hands kept up a steady, kneading motion, gradually relaxing the congested areas. The woman, as wrinkled as a walnut shell, would not look directly at Minette, but her hands spoke for her, continuing their healing work. Gradually, the breath in Minette's throat grew deeper, and the whistling subsided to a phlegmy fullness. The woman brought another basin and motioned her to spit up the congestion when she could. But Minette was content to drift, eyes closed, enjoying the healing heat and pressure.

Suddenly, she heard the chevalier's unctuous voice. "Such beauties, *ma douce*. Perfect orbs with shell-pink tips."

She was naked and helpless, but a feeble anger came to her rescue. "What? Can't you let me alone, even now? You stand there, enjoying my degradation. Here I am, laid out for your pleasure, but I'm half dead. You are a monster!"

"And you are a monster of stubbornness, my beauty. None of this was necessary. You need not have been closeted down there, and you need not have become sick."

She couldn't stand his greedy gaze on her, following each quiver of her breasts as the woman continued to massage. "I haven't changed my mind. You may put me back down in the dark and this time let me die."

"It is no longer necessary, Madame de Pombiers."

"Madame—? I said I would not marry you!"

"But you already have." He shook open a scroll of paper stamped with the seal of the colony. "Here's your signature."

"I didn't sign it!"

"But you did."

"I have no memory of writing my name there."

"I suppose not, but it makes no difference."

"You've tricked me!"

He shrugged. "The marriage certificate is legitimate enough. Our friend, Père François—surely you remember him?"

"The drunken priest?"

"But still a priest. He had brought it for the marriage ceremony, which you interrupted. What an actress you are, my dear. What a high swoon you produced!"

"The priest said he would not marry us. He said he would wait."

"This certificate proves that he became impatient."

"Let him tell me that to my face. I challenge you to bring him here."

"You challenge me?" He appeared to be delighted.

"I'd accept your challenge, but Père François has been transferred back to France. Our marriage was his last official act in Louisiana."

She let out a cry of anger and despair, followed by a fit of painful coughing. The woman tending Minette looked up reproachfully at the chevalier, who stood very much at ease in a loose robe of printed fabric and fine leather slippers.

"What? I am too hasty, eh, Clou? My bride isn't ready for the taking."

"And never will be," Minette croaked. "But come, let me share my sickness with you. Perhaps it will finish you off!"

He burst out laughing. "How you amuse me, *ma petite!* Each hour, I find new reasons to keep you mine."

"Because I hate you?"

"There's an attraction in that, a delicious irony. But, like most women, you have no sense of humor."

"Oh, I do. The thought of us lying together is completely ridiculous. I'd laugh if I could!"

"Suit yourself. But I am the master."

"I'd rather die than lie with you."

"No, *that* we shall do everything to prevent. Think of the happy years ahead as my wife, Minette. That should sustain you."

He leaned over her, tracing a finger around the tips of her breasts.

"You pig!"

"*Tais-toi,* bride. I am only touching what is mine."

The finger moved from her breasts, passed down her stomach and tugged gently at the nest of small gold curls between her legs.

"All mine in the eyes of the law."

She screamed her revulsion, and it brought on another fit of choking. At a warning glance from the woman Clou, he shrugged and left the room.

Never! Minette thought. *Never!* She'd die first. Overnight, her determination seemed to poison her whole system and she grew sicker, beyond Clou's best efforts. She began to burn with fever.

The chevalier, really alarmed for the first time, knew he should call in a doctor to bleed her and bring down the fever. He shelved his appetites temporarily and began to consider the problem of what Minette might say to any doctor who attended her. Kidnapped, held against her will by the man she'd supposedly freely married? Perhaps delirium would explain that. And wait, suppose he took the doctor aside to apprise him of his young wife's mental instability. Her parents, now returned to France, had entrusted their frail daughter to him because he was so undeniably solid. Yes, that would do it. He would call for a physician. If he sent a slave at first light tomorrow, the doctor should arrive by late afternoon.

The next day, knowing that his appearance at her bedside would only inflame Minette further, he avoided her. This teasing prelude to the sexual act, so similar to a cat's playfulness with a desperate mouse, was surprisingly exciting to him. Even the ache in his groin from postponement was exhilarating, reassuring him of the return of his powers. This anticipation was the ultimate sensation, the frisson, the unexpected thrill for a man who no longer expected any surprises in bed. He had never done this before, never willfully denied himself when the prize was spread out for his taking.

With the experience of an old campaigner, he wondered if anticipation might not surpass realization. The girl knew no tricks; only her fright and distaste would make her lively. She would fight him of course, and there would be pleasure in subduing that. It would be a bumpy ride. He'd overwhelm her—once, twice, as often as he wanted. Still, he'd never had a woman in exactly this situation before. A woman who knew him and hated him—altogether helplessly. It seemed to fuel him, and some part of his male nature wanted to continue this carnal anticipation until the last excruciating moment.

When his servants reported a carriage coming, he dressed himself to receive the doctor. But a shouting and confusion at the door, echoing through the house, made him buckle on his sword and go down to sort it out.

Two of his servants, Cob and Gil, were wounded and cowering before a young Creole gentleman. His drawn rapier had already taken their blood.

"What the devil's the meaning of this?"

Prosper de la Fosse answered with icy ferocity. "Chevalier Hector de Pombiers, I presume? Or so you style yourself."

"I am. And stand where you are, if you are a gentleman, while I see to your helpless victims. You are quite a dashing fighter against unarmed slaves."

The chevalier clapped his hands sharply, bringing two more of his household, Henri and Luc, to assist their wounded comrades. They were idiotically frightened of this Creole popinjay and quickly skittered off to safety.

"Now, sir, I demand to know why you dare to invade my house."

"My name is Prosper de la Fosse, and I have come for Minette."

"Minette?"

"Don't bother to lie. I know she is here."

"Where else should she be? The lady is my wife, Minette de Pombiers."

"I do not believe you!"

"That matters not at all to me. Leave my property, or I will call the city guards."

"I don't think you would welcome an investigation."

"I have told you that the lady is my wife. You must be some former suitor, a bad loser by the look of you. She's mine now."

"Everything you say is a lie."

"Liar? Me, a liar? Are you aware of what you've said, monsieur? There is still time to apologize."

"Never!"

"Then you will take the consequences. I won't be satisfied with first blood. You've insulted me in my own home."

"Do you challenge me, de Pombiers?"

"At your peril, de la Fosse!"

According to the code duello, so dangerously popular in New Orleans that it had been declared illegal by the government, these two strutting roosters of men, social equals, had passed the point of no return, with their insults, challenges, and counterchallenges. And neither could be bothered with the decorous delays of naming seconds and the like. The code's finer points be damned. Each wanted satisfaction now.

"En garde, monsieur!"

No time would be wasted in words either. They took up positions on the broad graveled court in front of the house. It was an odd balance. The chevalier was older, much heavier, and therefore slower but an experienced tactician and swordsman who might well let Prosper bring the fight to him while husbanding his own strength. His blade was heavier than Prosper's slim rapier. But Prosper's wrist would not sustain anything more weighty; he still felt weak from his recent illness. However, Prosper had speed, agility—and determination—

on his side. He must kill de Pombiers, particularly if his lie about Minette was not a lie at all.

A preliminary thrust and parry told each man that he was facing an opponent of experience. They settled down to work, the blades quartering the air between them with an ominous whistling, their feet balanced in the patterns of lunge, thrust, riposte, parry, evade. The strategies of former duels were remembered and attempted. Back and forth they moved across the court before the mansard-roofed dwelling, each man probing for mistakes in the other's technique.

Prosper slipped and recovered himself, but not before the chevalier's blade had slashed his shoulder. At this point, with a show of blood, many a duel would cease.

"Do you yield?" de Pombiers shouted.

Prosper's only answer was a vicious lunge. The sun beat down on them, insects whirred.

To Minette, who had dragged herself to the upstairs window, the two men were toy figures in a strange, mechanical dance. She could not believe that Prosper de la Fosse was actually there and fighting for her. In the carriage, holding the reins of two black horses, Ti Manou was as intent as a hawk on the battling men. Even the horses seemed still, observant.

Though she was watching, Minette didn't see the fatal move, so quickly had the blade flicked in and out. One moment the chevalier was pressing forward, over-whelming Prosper, and the next he had collapsed, clutching his abdomen. Prosper was closing in, prepared to stab the other man in defiance of the code duello.

Enfeebled, the chevalier made a noise of protest. "The devil with it," Prosper answered. "You shall die in your own blood!"

The chevalier fainted.

Immediately servants ran out of the house to gather up their fallen master. Ti Manou secured the horses and descended from the carriage. Prosper, still holding his rapier, dashed up the stairs and hammered on the bedroom doors, calling for Minette. All this seemed to happen at once, and Prosper found Minette still wrapped in her sheet.

He swore. "You are sick!"

"I will be better now. Prosper, did you—"

"Kill him? No, but he's badly wounded somewhere in that tub of guts."

"What if he dies?"

"I should welcome it."

"There is something . . . something I must tell you . . ."

When she staggered, he caught her and placed her on the bed. "Ti Manou!" he bawled. "Come here and help!"

When Minette opened her eyes again, Ti Manou was already searching the armoire for clothes that Minette could wear.

"He said we were married!" Minette whispered. "A priest came to do it, but I pretended to faint. Then they put me in that cold, damp place."

"If he doesn't die, I will kill him!" said Prosper.

"But he had a piece of paper. He said it was our marriage certificate. Oh, please find it."

"Get her ready," Prosper ordered. "I'll be back."

He left the room, sword out, and Ti Manou gently drew petticoats and a gown onto Minette's limp body. When she attempted to stand, Ti Manou protested, "Be still. We will carry you."

"No, I want to walk myself," she said as Ti Manou finished buttoning her dress.

"My hair." Minette turned toward the mirror.

"No, not now." Ti Manou tactfully stepped between her and the glass. "Here, put on this hat. We must hurry."

Leaning on her comforting shoulder, Minette made her way down the hall to the curving staircase. There was no sign of the chevalier, but a spatter of blood on the rugs marked the direction in which he had been carried. The house seemed deserted; the servants had vanished like rabbits. In the still rooms the afternoon sun picked out certain objects, furnishing them with aureoles of gold, and dust specks swam in the brightness. Only Prosper made noise, slamming out of a room with a scroll in his fist.

"Have you read this? I'll have that priest arrested."

"He was sent back to France." The effort of standing wearied Minette. "Please, can we go?"

Outside, he lifted Minette into the carriage, and Ti Manou climbed in to hold and steady her.

"M'sieu Prosper, look at the road."

A drifting cloud of dust announced the approach of another carriage.

"He had called the doctor for me," Minette ventured.

"And here he comes. De Pombiers is one lucky old man."

"Oh, Prosper, I hope the doctor can save him. I don't want you accused of murder."

"There was no murder. We fought honorably."

"So many witnesses," murmured Ti Manou. "Those people may say something else. And the doctor could be troublesome."

Prosper stared at her, and then the whip came down smartly on the black horses' withers. They cut across a field to avoid the other carriage and headed for the town road.

* * *

The de la Fosse mansion was larger than most, virtually a country estate set down intact in New Orleans where, customarily, tight wooden buildings shouldered each other on narrow streets. But the area in which it stood had not yet been developed; a jungle of trees began where its property line ended. The big house of typical white plastered brick was elegantly designed for life in a tropical climate. Green batten blinds protected its windows from the enemy sun. The house was raised off the ground on high stone piles. Its steeply pitched pavilion roof encouraged air currents and, with the aid of slim wooden colonnettes, set over the expansive porches that swept around the house, extended its shade beyond the main walls providing extra rooms and sleeping spaces. The heat and noise of the kitchen was, of course, confined to a separate building.

Amadée de la Fosse, Prosper's mother and the mistress of this sprawling *maison*, was expected home at any time from her lengthy stay with her kin upriver. And that accounted for the servants' absentminded welcome. Normally, the reappearance of Prosper, with Ti Manou and an unknown young woman would have been an excuse for all work to stop. Not today. The servants were vigorously cleaning chandeliers and mirrors with vinegar and water, intent on expunging every flyspeck. They were dusting moldings, beating rugs in the yard, polishing silver, scrubbing floors. The house must meet Madame Amadée's expectations. M'sieu Prosper could be demanding but careless; he was uninterested in details. Not so his mother. The servant who could not perform flawlessly was shipped upriver to the de la Fosse plantation, Sans Pareil.

Minette had a hurried impression of a staircase that curved into two separate wings, a long hall with rich Turkish carpets, and finally a room that seemed afloat in soft white fabric. The walls were covered with it, the ceiling draped in it, the mirrors surrounded in airy netting. The furniture was in perfect scale, French and intimate, upholstered in the blue and champagne colors so flattering to blondes. The dressing table, with its long row of crystal bottles, was covered with sheer, ruffled fabric, the pillows on the wide *bergère* an exquisite melt of pale needlepoint colors, and the insides of the shutters tinted the pearly blue of an early-morning sky. The flowers by the bedside were freesia and anemones, and next to the crystal water carafe a miniature ballerina was frozen in perpetual pirouette atop a gilded porcelain music box.

"Your mother's room?" Minette murmured.

"Hardly," said Prosper. "But it is a room for honored guests."

Then he disappeared, and Minette sank gratefully into the depths of the four-poster.

It was morning when she awoke to find a cheerful-looking young slave girl deftly mixing café au lait in a fine, fitted set of blue-and-gold china. The foaming milk streamed into the coffee, and the savor of cinnamon and sugar rose around her. "Delicious," Minette decided.

After the coffee, she lay back and rested, the relief from her recent ordeal prompting pleasant daydreams. What would it be like to live in a house like this, with a husband like Prosper? Prosper was handsome in his dandified way; even the mustache suited. He was not Alain Gerard; he would never be Alain Gerard. She tried to close her mind to that half-healed pain. Alain was gone. And she must live. And since the rich Monsieur de la Fosse was not about to propose to a penniless convent orphan, she would simply enjoy *la bonne vie* while it lasted. She stretched against the cool, linen-cased down pillows.

As Minette drifted in and out of sleep, Ti Manou came by. The woman seemed distracted. M'sieur Prosper had gone, she said, hours ago, to wait on the levee for the ship that was bringing his mother home. And he had taken several carriages with him. After such a long stay at Nachitoches with her Lamballe connections, Madame Amadée would be bringing back many gifts from her hostess. She loved novelties. Once she had brought back a monkey—a monkey! The beast had fled screaming and chattering to the crystal chandeliers. And the dirt he had made! Ti Manou had grown up with monkeys in Guadeloupe. They were God's mistakes, carrying fleas and lice, which brought disease.

This was a completely novel idea to Minette. "Fleas and lice bring disease? Is that what the doctors say now?"

Ti Manou looked exasperated.

"What happened to the monkey?"

"He ate something that disagreed with him, and he died."

"I thought that animals were very cautious about strange food."

"Some animals, perhaps. This monkey was a very foolish fellow."

The tone was cool and dismissive, and Minette wondered if Ti Manou had had something to do with the creature's exit from this world. Enigmatic Ti Manou, who frightened her with the suggestion of power just beneath the surface, of control upon control, lying in wait.

Ah, but Minette was ashamed of herself! This woman had organized her rescue from the chevalier, as Prosper had explained in the carriage. Without her help,

Minette would probably be buried in some hidden grave by now. Or, worse, buried nightly beneath the weight of the chevalier.

"Don't think of the past," said Ti Manou softly.

"Does it show so much?"

"You haven't learned to dissemble. That face is a mirror of your emotions."

"It's hard to hide my feelings."

"But essential, Mademoiselle Marsan, as you will discover."

"Mademoiselle, pah! My name is Minette, and you will have my gratitude forever."

"Yes? Well, Minette, then. But only when we are alone."

"Ti Manou, I know you are wise. I suspect you have certain powers. Can you tell me what will happen to me?" Rapidly vanishing was the convent girl who once would have shied from such heresy.

"Are you asking me if your life will be easy?"

"Oh, I don't expect that. But will I ever be happy again?"

"You were happy once?"

"Yes, for a short time."

"Your happiness was a man."

"Will I find anything like that again?"

Ti Manou looked at her intently and then smiled. But the smile had no warmth. "I can promise you passion in your life, a great deal of passion."

"And happiness?"

"Isn't passion enough?"

"I don't understand that question," said Minette slowly. "Is there passion without love? Is it possible?"

"Did the chevalier de Pombiers love you?"

Minette shivered. "But—"

"Your future will be very different from your past," said Ti Manou. "That is all I can—"

A racket below interrupted them. The servants of the de la Fosse family were cheering lustily as three carriages swept into the courtyard. The last two were filled with trunks and boxes. In the first, next to Prosper, sat a slim, straight-backed woman whose traveling hat, a dashing tricorne, was enlivened by rose-colored plumes that curled toward her cheek. She graciously acknowledged the servants with a regal tilt of the head. Amadée de la Fosse had come home to resume her reign.

Ti Manou, with an odd smile playing around her lips, had brushed Minette's hair into presentability and supplied her with a pale blue featherlight shawl to cover her shoulders. Finally there was a whisper of silk and unfamiliar footsteps outside Minette's door, and then a knock. Prosper opened it with a proprietary air, standing aside for his mother to enter.

Minette's first reaction was surprise. This woman was so young looking, so lovely, so poised and elegant. Everything Minette could never be.

Amadée de la Fosse's reaction was surprise, also, but mixed with it was a slow, incredulous anger. She saw a beauty in the bed, beauty haggard from sickness but soon to recover its full splendor. Worse, so much worse, its very elements rivaled her *own* beauty! Amadée was blond, or she had been once, her hair the exact shade of new-minted gold. She would never attain that color again, not even with all the contents of all the bottles of bleach in Christendom. This girl's hair was naturally golden, as if kissed by the sun itself. Minette's eyes were her eyes as they had been before the fine lines came; perhaps even bluer and more beautiful. Minette's mouth was her moist rose. Amadée's skin was the marvel of all who saw her, but at what price, only she and Ti Manou knew. Minette had the original velvety sheen without any effort.

Alors, why go on tormenting herself? Minette's face, her very existence, was a reminder of what Amadée had been and would never be again. A most cruel mockery, this mirror into her past. Wait. Had her chin ever had that tiny heartbreaking point? Had her cheekbones, even in her girlhood, been so sculptured? Minette was more beautiful than Amadée had ever been! Put them together, even at the height of her bloom, and Amadée would have been the slightly inferior copy.

What could Prosper be thinking of? Was he a madman like his father, or simply so completely insensitive to his mother's needs, that he had brought this girl into her house? It was not to be borne. She would scream and rage and cow him into submission. No, wait. That was not the way. She must be more clever than that to get rid of the girl. Prosper was infatuated with the chit—anyone could see that. She would suggest, she would insist, that he set her up in a little house of her own, make her his mistress. And once Minette was established as such, there was no chance that Amadée would ever have to see her again. Minette would be *déclassée*, a demimonde, denied a reception in respectable houses, which meant—and this was indeed sweet lagniappe—that none of Amadée's friends would see her either and could not make malicious comparisons between the two of them. *Voilà tout!*

The girl was saying something polite. Amadée bared her teeth in what she hoped was a smile and wished her a speedy recovery. *Speed you out of my house,* she thought. *For I hate you, Minette. I cannot help myself.*

9

The nuns at the Ursuline convent on Chartres Street were gratified to hear that Minette was safe and living at the de la Fosse mansion, one of the finest houses in the city. It would seem that the dear child had finally found some good fortune after her profound disappointment in love.

"You call that love?" Sister Immaculata disagreed. "It was nothing but a shipboard flirtation. You can be sure I allowed nothing more! And what was the man but a handsome soldier in full uniform, any young woman's dream. That's an image, not a man, and only powerful because he isn't here for actual comparison with her fevered imagination."

"You call that kind of romantic love a fever?" Sister Mary Martyr demanded.

"It has all the symptoms, dear Sister," Immaculata answered. "Only consider someone in the throes of it. There's the flush, the giddiness, the lack of judgment, the wild delusions and inability to discern the truth.

You might well compare it to a patient in delirium!" She shook her head. "Alas, unless a couple has established a *spiritual* rapprochement, the unreasonable disappointment that follows infatuation is the secret canker of many an unhappy marriage."

"You speak of love on the physical plane, of course."

"Dear Sisters, we know that the spiritual component of love does not make itself known at once. One must wait for the still small voice. And the brain, the seat of reason is so much harder to satisfy than the heart."

The elder sisters nodded in solemn agreement.

"Do you suppose," said the youngest of the nuns, "that our Minette will have any chance to reach a . . . spiritual rapprochement with Prosper de la Fosse while she is in his home?"

Immaculata was judicious. "She will at least see the young man in his relationships with his family, and that is considerably more insight than most young women are allowed."

"But can you fall in love with a man because he is good to his family?"

"It's a strong indication of character. And Monsieur de la Fosse is already her cavalier, rescuing her from that villain, from the unimaginable!"

"The chevalier should be punished!" Sister Mary Martyr burst out.

"Leave judgment to our Holy Father," said Immaculata righteously.

"He should be made to suffer here on earth as well as in the life hereafter!"

"I dare say he will," said Immaculata dryly.

The young nun persisted. "Do you think that Prosper de la Fosse loves Minette?"

A chime reminded them that it was the hour of ves-

pers. Immaculata rose, moving toward the broad staircase that led to the chapel. "Come, Sisters. Let us go to
our devotions and leave a conversation that has already
become much too worldly."

She was closeted with Ti Manou in her dressing
room, where Ti Manou often practiced the arts that did
such service to Amadée's beauty. Normally, the space
would be clouded by the beneficial vapors of steaming
herbal potions, but now the two women stared into a
china basin of cool water.

"I see nothing," said Amadée. "Why should I believe
you?"

"Of course you see nothing, *maîtresse*. You do not
enjoy the favor of Erzulie."

"Don't talk to me like a voodooienne."

"You compare me to those women with their cheap
tricks? I am a *mambo*, a full priestess of the voodoo religion."

"Then tell me, Priestess," she said in a voice laced
with irony, "am I to put on eternal black and begin to
crochet like all the other old hags? Is that girl to stand
beside me as my daughter-in-law, inviting comparisons
as she blooms and I age? Good God, what punishment!
Why couldn't my son have chosen one of those dark,
luscious Spaniards he used to admire?"

"Perhaps Prosper's choice is an unwitting compliment to you."

"Nonsense. We fight constantly."

"Yet he respects you."

"You mean that I have successfully managed to dom-
inate him. But why do I argue with you? As far as I
know, the girl doesn't dream that he has honorable

intentions. She has no right to expect them."

"Then why hasn't he touched her? Isn't that strange for Prosper?"

"Surely he can't imagine that she's still a virgin after that old hellhound de Pombiers had her?"

"It's exactly what he imagines."

"The fever has weakened his mind."

"Erzulie says that she is still a virgin."

"After weeks in de Pombiers's house? Now I *am* frightened. The girl is dangerous. Can't you help me somehow, Ti Manou?"

"I can tell you this. Though the picture in the water was clear at its center, there was turbulence and mist around the edges. The marriage will have many problems."

"You mean it may not last?"

"I cannot say. I only know that they will marry."

Amadée gave a cry of despair. "Help me! Think of something. I can't bear having her live here."

"Can you stop Prosper if he wishes it? He is the heir."

"Ah! He's the head of the family simply because he's a man. If my twins Aglae and Antoine had not died, at least I'd have three of them to play off against each other. It's not fair. I am finally free of Prosper's insane father and for the first time able to live as I please, and now I fall under the tyranny of my son's whims."

"Not financially, madame. You are rich in your own right. You could leave this house."

"To her, the basket nobody? With all my beautiful things?"

"Take them with you."

"Why should she drive me out? But, God knows, I cannot, I will not live in this house if he marries that girl."

"*When* he marries her. Have you thought of where you'll have the wedding?"

Viciously, Amadée dashed the bowl of water to the floor. The water cascaded out; the heavy china bounced but did not crack. It lay at her feet, intact.

"You are mocking me, Ti Manou. I will have you lashed."

"Me, a freedwoman? It is against the law."

"So confident. You know that I need you, and it makes you brave. But you are still a woman of color. Don't push me too far."

"I don't push you at all, Madame Amadée. I know my place."

"How is it that you never married and had these problems? With all I've paid you over the years, you are a fine catch."

"Men are afraid to marry a *mambo*."

"Probably with good reason. But why don't you marry an equal, a voodoo priest?"

"A *houngan*? It is forbidden. I might lose my powers."

"Ah, you see, you're trapped, just as I am. We women are all slaves, each in our own way."

"You are overwrought, madame."

"I will not be humiliated by Minette Marsan."

"Do not show her open enmity, madame."

"Oh? I am to be denied that last comfort, forced to smile with my ravaged face?"

"Your ravaged face? Hardly that. Though I do see a few red spots, probably due to the fondant candy Madame Lamballe's cook has been making for you all these months."

"How did you know she was making—"

Ti Manou smiled, satisfied at this display of her power.

* * *

In Amadée's garden, Minette walked the graveled paths with Prosper. Though the house was Creole in inspiration and execution, the front garden was defiantly French-from-France, a miniature Parisian park. Here was no rich profusion of iris, sweet peas, daffodils or amaryllis. Amadée had had them all cleared away, and her imported seedlings were trained into strict geometric patterns as a rebuke to the wild exuberance of the region.

Prosper watched for any signs that Minette's strength was waning. She seemed much recovered, very lovely in the white sprigged muslin gown from the chevalier's house. But her face took on an anxious pallor when she learned that her kidnapper was still alive.

"I am afraid I botched the job, my dear. But he recovers slowly."

"Now what will happen? What will he do?"

Prosper shrugged. "What *can* he do? Admit he kidnapped you?"

"Prosper, I am convinced that he had me watched since I came to New Orleans. He made his plans well in advance. Clothes were ready for me, shoes, hats—think of the strategy that took. If I am always under his surveillance, I may not be safe even in the convent or the hospital. And I can't live that way—as a fugitive; always looking over my shoulder!"

"It's true that money and power and connections give him a long reach," Prosper conceded.

She began to nibble her lower lip, and he was charmed.

"Prosper, if you can think of some way to help me . . ."

"I am sure that I can. May I tell you that your luck is about to change?"

Who had said those very words to her? Minette wondered. Ah, yes. It was the dancer Hera, telling her fortune on the moonlit deck of the *Baleine*. Just as she'd said it Alain had come up behind them, and Hera had suddenly left them together. Yes, her luck had indeed changed . . . bringing love and loss. Where would those words take her now?

"Minette," said Prosper. "I'm afraid you are in your past, and I am jealous."

She looked up at him not at all flirtatiously.

"I know that you loved and lost someone. Ti Manou has told me that you spoke his name during your fever."

"It's—"

"Never tell me," he cut in. "I don't want to know. Can you guess why?"

Minette said nothing.

"How can you not know that I love you?"

"I know that you are my rescuer and true friend."

"The devil with that! I want to be your husband."

Could he be serious? Could her daydreams of breakfast in bed, mistress of the manor, be coming true?

"Prosper," she said aloud. "Please don't tease me."

"Shall I drop to one knee and propose properly?"

"You are teasing."

"I am in earnest. I loved you in the hospital with what shreds of strength I had. You were the cool, comforting voice, the face that swam in and out of my vision, the touch that bound me to this world. Please don't tell me that you were only doing your duty, Mademoiselle Marsan."

"Prosper, that is not even my proper name! The nuns gave it to me. I have no name. I am no one. I don't apologize for what is not my fault, but you should know that all I have in the way of pedigree is the king's basket I brought with me."

"I am delighted to hear it."

"I cannot believe that you are serious."

"Here, sit down." He pulled her onto one of Amadée's ornamental benches. "Darling girl, we Creoles are an inbred people, marrying into a small circle of families whose blood grows more languid and self-satisfied with each generation. We do not look beyond the familiar. Oh, the marriage traps that I've sidestepped, here and on Saint Dominique. I had no desire to be caught in such a tiresome alliance, with all the tedious ritual and obligations it entails. I grew up surrounded by my *tantes* and *cousines*, and I prayed for deliverance."

"And I am your deliverance? *Mais non.* I was sent here to marry a man of the people, someone like my friend Berenice's husband, Arnaud, who is a sail fitter. I would be prepared for that, but not to play the piano and sing in foreign languages. I have no such accomplishments. Your family would never accept me."

His dark brows drew down over his eyes. "When my father died, I became the head of the family."

"But your mother—"

"*Maman* will do as I say. She must."

She remembered Prosper's anxiety as he prepared for his mother's return. Perhaps the much-indulged "head of the family" was protesting his freedom from dominance a bit too much, Minette thought.

"Prosper, are you sure that you are doing the right thing?"

"Look at me, Minette."

She did. He had always been handsome, even when racked with sickness, but now the color had returned to his skin, the luster to his dark eyes, and the heavy waves of hair clustered in small ringlets at the temples of his fine-boned face. His thin mustache looked particularly rakish today. Oh, his elegance and breeding were attractive, and even the unmistakable hot light in his eyes was not upsetting.

As if reading her mind, he added gently, "You have no reason to be afraid of me. I shall not force myself upon the woman I love. She must say that she loves me first. Tell me the truth, *mon ange*. Could you love me one day?"

"Are you willing to marry me, knowing that I am not ready for it?"

He laughed. "I am not willing to marry anyone else. Only give me a little encouragement, just a little, and see how I can wait for you. Marry me now, and we will both have a new life."

"Here? In this house?"

"You haven't been listening."

"What is it I haven't understood?"

"This house, all its claims on me, is the life I am try-ing to escape. No, our Eden is elsewhere. Have I men-tioned Sans Pareil to you?"

"You spoke of it in the hospital. It's your family plan-tation, upriver."

"It's another world. There are twenty-five thousand *arpents* of land at Sans Pareil, prime bottom land, and the Mississippi keeps giving us more. You know what the river does? It piles the most fertile soil in the world high on its banks and adds to our boundaries. The river makes me richer each day. Land, more land to grow rice and indigo and perhaps sugarcane, if we can ever manage to undercut the price of sugar from Saint Dominique."

"What is indigo?"

"A bush, my inquisitive lamb. A tall bush with long, disorderly leaves. From it we make dye to color clothes in a whole range of blues."

"Now you sound like a planter. But you never did before!"

"You are very astute. I've never given Sans Pareil the attention it deserves because I had no one with whom to share my enthusiasm. You think any of those Creole belles would willingly leave this little pest pot of a place?"

"Is that what you think of New Orleans?"

"It's a good beginning, that's all. Someday this will be a great city, but for the moment, it's a low-lying plague spot that manages somehow to be twice as expensive as France."

She spoke slowly. "Prosper, you've asked for honesty from me, and now I would like it from you. Have you asked me to marry you because of some misplaced feeling of obligation? When you were ill, I found the doctor for you. But you saved me from the chevalier de Pombiers. You owe me nothing. I owe you my life."

"Don't be so damned humble. Convent teaching! The meek don't inherit the earth—far from it. And they're probably pushed about in heaven, too. Your problem, my Minette, is that you do not see yourself as you are, strong. Who but you could have nursed me back to health and come through that business with the chevalier unscathed?

"I am not unscathed. I have nightmares."

"I will get rid of them for you. And all the more reason to hurry to Sans Pareil."

"Yes, I might feel safer away from New Orleans."

"You'll see how we agree. When I look at you, I behold the most beautiful, honest, and courageous woman I will ever be fortunate enough to meet. Yet you don't even know who you are, what your strengths are. You have yet to develop all the fine instincts and qualities I sense within you. I will be your teacher of life as well as your husband, Minette."

She was silent for a while.

"Ah, accept me, Minette, so I may hurry to tell *Maman*."

Amadée in her life forever. No wonder she was apprehensive. He felt her shrink away from him. "Prosper, you are a good friend—you are a good friend, and I shall probably come to love you sooner rather than later," Minette whispered.

The tears in Amadée's eyes when he broke his news quite astonished Prosper, who did not recognize her heartfelt relief. They would not be staying here with her! Her drinking, gambling, gaming son whose hair-trigger temper made him a terror on the dueling field, this lover of sensation and connoisseur of women of all colors, was willing to leave New Orleans.

Was he so jealous of the girl that he wanted to bury her in the country? For burial it would be! Sans Pareil, with its sweating slaves who worked naked in the steaming fields, covering themselves only when they approached the main house. Sans Pareil, that country fortress of a house, standing in the terrible isolation of its land. The days there were endless. Let this Minette sink into the long, hot silences. Let her grow careless of hats and veils, let the milk-white skin coarsen and redden, the smooth hands wrinkle and bronze. Let her age, dear God, let her age quickly in that daily downpour of sun.

Aloud, her voice trembling with happiness, Amadée congratulated her son and his bride-to-be on their wise decision. So sensible that they leave New Orleans. The chevalier de Pombiers was influential enough here to make trouble for the family. Certainly the authorities would not want to follow Prosper upriver to Sans Pareil. All they had to do was stay there, watch over the de la Fosse investment, and live in the grand manner of the planters. So intelligent on all counts.

Prosper, surfeited with compliments and preoccupied with Minette, didn't question Amadée's preparations for a small wedding. It wasn't easy to find an obscure church in an unfashionable area and to invite the bare minimum of relatives, just enough to prevent him from being insulted. With care, Amadée chose only cousins Celestine and Aurore to represent the family. The haste and semisecrecy of the wedding made plain Amadée's low opinion of Prosper's choice. Minette was to be ignored thereafter.

"You know how wild Prosper has always been," Amadée confided. "Such rages when anyone crossed him! Well, he is now head of the family and has plans to settle down. He has chosen a good strong girl to bear him sons, a girl who will obey without questions because he is giving her a luxurious life she never dared to dream about."

"At least she is beautiful," said Aurore. "She reminds me a little of you when you were younger, Amadée," she added injudiciously.

"Absolute nonsense," declared Celestine. "Amadée is and always was incomparable!"

Amadée promised herself to remember Celestine's next birthday with an expensive gift.

"I am grateful to the girl," she told them, "because she has finally turned Prosper in the right direction. I had almost renounced hope of his marrying at all. And so we are hurrying before he changes his mind!" she laughed.

"Yes, we all know Prosper. You have been a valiant mother, Amadée."

Amadée accepted the compliment with becoming modesty.

For all her forethought, there were still problems during the ceremony. Minette had insisted—insisted!—on inviting the other basket brides and the nuns from the Ursuline convent. What a motley crowd! That plump Celeste with her bearded farmer. One Eulalie, with an impossibly vulgar wagoneer of a husband who had never even heard of the de la Fosse family. And the worst, Berenice something, a sail-fitter's wife dressed in her pathetic best. Of course, Minette chose Berenice for a public show of affection—a great, smacking kiss! The girl had no moderation, which might be an attraction to Prosper in their lovemaking but was thoroughly déclassé here.

As she stood in her shimmering white lace and summer satin gown, hair piled high to accommodate the veil and a discreet coronet of flowers, Minette felt the good wishes of her friends surround her. It was a fairy tale, wasn't it, a Cinderella story come true. And she and Prosper would live happily ever after. She felt so grateful to the man beside her.

When the bridal pair knelt on cushions before the priest, Minette glanced at Prosper. Since he was barely taller than she, he seemed more comfortable when they were kneeling. How handsome was that brocaded waistcoat and the cravat stiff with lace! He caught her look and gave her a conspiratorial wink. At once she felt easier. Couldn't good friends become lovers? She would prove it.

That fool of a priest is carried away by the presence of so many nuns, Amadée thought, he's added words to the Mass just to preen before them! Prosper seemed to endure the priest's vanities with perfect calm. Amadée watched the decisive grip of his usually languid hands as he placed his grandmother's ring of gold and Brazilian emeralds on Minette's finger. Nothing like a reformed rake to make a tyrant of a husband. *Grace à Dieu*, the wench would be pregnant most of the time, providing handsome grandchildren but staying out of New Orleans. Amadée would not have to stand beside her and invite comparisons. And she could teach the children to call her something besides *Grandmère*.

As the wedding ended in the sunshine of a soft New Orleans afternoon, Amadée felt restored to life.

10

The distant clanging of a bell woke Minette. She stretched, raising her legs, flexing her fingers and toes at the mosquito netting, conscious of the fact that she was now alone in the huge, dazzling white bed. The room was still shadowy—morning sun did not enter here—and the large, simply made pieces of plantation furniture reared their bulk around her. Such monstrous armoires and chests, chosen with an eye to capacity and durability. Yes, it was unquestionably a man's bedroom and reflected Prosper in a mood she did not know.

Prosper. The pillows beside her were still dented with the imprint of his head. They had lain down together last night, their first at Sans Pareil, holding hands like children and whispering in the silence. *Here we are, finally. Listen to the wind steal around the house. Can you see the stars through the window?* And then Prosper's voice had taken on a different timbre. A rising heat from his body had crept along their joined hands; she'd felt him quiver and stretch toward her even while remaining in his place. He broke their contact, tossed restlessly for a while and suddenly threw back the mosquito netting to pace the room.

"It will not work. I can't sleep beside you like a tame tabby cat."

"But, Prosper—"

"My promise? Yes, I know, and curse the day I made it! I will honor it, Minette. I want you to accept me joyfully as a lover as well as a husband and friend. Only hurry! How long can it take to erase this other fellow from your mind? He's dead, is he not?" He stopped as he saw the expression on her face. "Ah, sweet, I did not mean to hurt you."

"You do not hurt me, Prosper."

"Ah, Minette, we'll know such happiness! Many women have liked me, and I've satisfied them all. All!"

In sudden confusion she began to rumple the bedclothes to simulate a honeymoon night.

"What can you be doing, *ma chère?*"

She smiled. "I am upholding the family honor. After all, your servants—"

"Who?"

"Prosper"—she was laughing—"you can't make them invisible. How many did I meet last night? Was it twenty?"

"Eighteen. And I have not the slightest interest in what they think. They are not expected to think of anything beyond their jobs. They have a proverb among themselves: Servants see but don't see, hear but don't hear. Quite as it should be!"

"Do you understand them?"

"What, me? Never. It's not required, either. I behave with a certain degree of humanity and expect fidelity and work in return. Those who can't manage the equation I don't keep."

"I don't think it will be easy for me to be so . . . attended to, Prosper. I'm used to taking care of myself."

"Don't you dare. They'll think they're not satisfactory and expect a lashing as punishment."

She shuddered. "Eighteen people!"

"You won't have to deal with them, sweet. Give your orders to Mam'Odile. She's in charge of the house."

"Oh? If she's in charge, what am I?"

"An angel. A lily. A princess who doesn't know where the kitchen is. I didn't marry beauty to have it soil itself with household chores. You are the mistress here, and your job is to amuse and enchant me, that's all. The place runs passably well on the carrot-and-stick principle. Good work means gifts and more meat at Christmas. Thieving, lying, and laziness will put them out in the sun with the field hands. Believe me, these pampered house Negroes won't last long out there. And they know it."

"That sounds very hard."

"It gets their attention, I can tell you. *Que voulez-vous?* These people have been taken out of the jungle. How do you think their own chiefs would have treated them if they didn't work in their own villages? You can't imagine the tortures. Their fate would be much worse."

"Worse than being a slave?"

"Am I to hear such childish cant from my wife? Who would do the work if they weren't here? Would you? You wouldn't last a day. Enough of these pieties, which I'm sure you have learned from the Ursulines. And by the way, how is it that the good sisters employ some slave labor around the convent? How do you explain that?"

Minette couldn't. But she volunteered, "If they have them, they will educate them, teach them to read and write."

"God forbid. It's a dangerous undertaking, and I'm

not at all sure that the Church doesn't forbid it as well as our own law. Don't you know that it's a crime to teach a slave to read and write? Are these nuns above the law?"

How had she made him so angry? She took his hand, and he quieted.

"The Church does not usually interfere with the established order of things, and in that, the Church is right," he said. Kissing the hand she offered him; these little intimacies would skillfully pave the way for their complete union. He was constantly touching her with the lightest of pressures, stroking her hair or her shoulder, trailing his fingers along her arm. She'd begun to enjoy accepting these small caresses from such a very dear friend.

"But now, *chérie*, my work day begins. I'll have Mam'Odile sent to you. She'll tell you which are my favorite foods, and if you are so eager to do something here, you can choose my dinner."

Mam'Odile stood in Minette's room like a sturdy ebon tree, big but not fat, tall as a warrior and strongly proportioned. She radiated a watchful dignity. Her voice was softly civil, yet not servile, as she described Prosper's preferences.

"M'sieu Prosper will eat pork, prefers beef to it and is most fond of chicken."

"Lamb?"

"I cannot say. We have no sheep at Sans Pareil. He will also eat game birds and prefers pheasant. Our dinner, our main meal, is at midday. In the evening, supper is a much lighter meal."

"So he likes chicken. How do you serve it to him?"

"Often in the plainest ways: grilled or broiled on a spit. But he also likes chicken pilau, deviled chicken, and chicken sauté à la Louisiane."

"And what is that, Mam'Odile? Tell me about the chicken sauté à la Louisiane.

"It's just the usual, madame. One makes a roux, to begin with, and cooks the fowl in it."

"A roux? What is that?"

"Do they not use the roux in France, madame?"

Minette was wisely silent. The only thing she had ever done in the kitchen of the Paris convent was to wash down its walls.

"Describe the roux to me, Mam'Odile."

"You begin with the browning of flour in fat. Then you add your other seasonings, onion and garlic, chopped very fine. We also use celery, parsley, bay leaf, and filé powder from New Orleans. The secret is never to use water. Here at Sans Pareil, we cook in beef or chicken bouillon made from boiling the bones. For fish dishes the very best roux is made from the liquor of oysters."

"Oysters here, so far upriver?"

"No, unfortunately, and M'sieu Prosper is very fond of them."

"Why doesn't he send to New Orleans for a barrel?"

"He has tried, but they spoil along the way."

"Surely the river is full of fish."

"The field hands eat it, not M'sieu Prosper."

"I have tried fried catfish in New Orleans. I find it delicious."

Mam'Odile looked at her strangely. Was it the fried catfish? Minette wondered. Or was the mistress of the house attempting to become too friendly?

"Very well, what else does my husband like to eat?" Minette pursued.

"For his second breakfast—"

"Second?"

"Work begins with first light here, and M'sieu Prosper has a soft roll with his coffee. Later on, when he's come in from his tour of the fields, he may take a dish of creole gumbo with rice—that is like the French *bouillabaisse*—or the *chaurises* sausages, or eggs."

"And desserts?"

"We have a good cook and baker who pleases him."

"Show me the kitchen, Mam'Odile. Then I will decide on the menu."

Something like obstinacy set those large features. "Madame, you will soil your gown in the kitchen."

"Why? Is it a dirty place?"

An affronted recoil replaced the obstinacy. "*Mais, non, non, non!* But there is smoke and the odors of food. That's why the kitchen is separate from the house. I do not think that M'sieu Prosper would like you to go there. When Madame Amadée was in residence, she would never—"

Minette cut her off. "I mean to know the kitchen and the house. I am not Madame Amadée. This is another Madame de la Fosse."

Minette hoped that she had produced a tone of authority. Whatever Prosper thought, she must learn the workings of this house, not sit in her room embroidering flowers and being languidly fanned. She would be discreet, she would humor Prosper to his face, but she must learn, and she would. She had a proverb of her own: "Let but the needle pass, and the thread would follow." It had come from the nuns, who disapproved of idle thoughts as much as idle hands. If work began at first light here and she remained idle, then such long, empty days would soon make her a bored and boring companion.

The path to the outbuilding was deeply grooved, and the size of the kitchen suggested much entertaining and many guests. A fireplace completely covered one wall;

hooks and cranes at various heights held pots and trussed cuts of meat and fowl. These turned slowly over the flames, dripping delicious juices into other pots below. Sweet potatoes cooked in the ashes, like chestnuts. There were separate baking ovens, heated with glowing coals, and a pastry table with a long, cool marble top.

"M'sieu Prosper will ask for a charlotte russe from time to time," said Mam'Odile, "though the whipping of the cream takes a while. He also likes sponge cake spread with raspberry jam, and we keep a supply of those little ginger cakes, *les estomacs mulâtres*, that they sell in the market in New Orleans. Of course, we make them here. We make everything here."

Above Minette's head, bunches of dried herbs hanging from the ceiling did constitute something of a fire hazard, as did the numbers of straw gathering baskets piled in one corner, but the kitchen was clean and all its silent workers wore white. None of them looked at her directly, and Mam'Odile seemed to feel that introductions were unnecessary. There was one exception, a small child, who was separating snap beans in the corner. He smiled shyly and ducked his plaited head.

"How old are you, little fellow?" Minette asked him.

There was a winsome show of toothless gum.

"Léon is six. His mother is one of the cooks. With the other children of the household, he gathers fruits and vegetables from the gardens. But I do not know if he gives the master an honest count. What is it, Léon? One bean for the table and two for your own stomach?"

Mam'Odile's ponderous attempt at humor made the child roll his eyes in terror.

"Back to work, Léon." The child bent quickly over his beans.

"How many cooks are there here, Mam'Odile?"

"Three regular and one woman, Fantine, who does only baking. The house staff is fed from this kitchen, as well as guests at all times."

"But there are several hundred workers on Sans Pareil, no?"

"Yes, but they have their own eating places where they live." She made it sound quite far away. "And their church is out there, too."

Bon Dieu, thought Minette, this parish of people, these numbers to be fed and cared for! It was as big as three convents put together, and only a few moments ago she was proposing herself as mother superior! If the thing runs from day to day, perhaps it's best to do as Prosper says: play the grand lady and not interfere. But in the matter of food, she would have her say, she decided. The savory steam in the kitchen was making her stomach grumble.

"I would like to have the chicken sauté à la Louisiane today," she ordered. "And a vegetable."

"We still have some *mirlitons* in the gardens. M'sieu Prosper is fond of stuffed *mirlitons*."

Minette thought she might be too if she knew what they were. And aloud, "Rice?"

"That is our main crop. It's always on the table."

"Biscuits?"

"Always."

"I would like something tender and green." Ah, that sounded better—more assertive.

"*Salade* at the main meal? M'sieu Prosper doesn't like it then."

"But I do."

"Very well, madame."

"Please choose the wine, Mam'Odile. You know what my husband favors. And let's have some sort of egg custard for dessert."

"M'sieu Prosper likes flan."

Does he she wondered. She must ask him what it was. Aloud, she approved the menu with what she hoped was a worldly air. The disconcerting thing about Mam'Odile was the strength of her glance. It was as if incoming rays of light were blocked by the dark obsidian of her eyes and sent back at you, redoubled in power. Minette had the disquieting feeling that the light continued to probe inside her, illuminating her past. Could Mam'Odile sense, somehow, the convent orphan in the work sabots and patched clothes? She might have to play the grand lady, but she would not be too grand. In spite of Prosper's careless disregard of his household slaves, Minette knew that this woman was going to be important to her life here, and it was better to avoid antagonism.

Returning from the kitchen, they walked around the exterior of the main house. Minette was startled by its simplicity, its air of tropical island homeyness. The house stood high on whitewashed brick pillars, yet it comprised only two stories, surrounded by broad verandas. The staircase leading to the second floor was at one end of the front veranda. The house was of whitewashed brick, too, since termites made short work of wood. But the steeply pitched roof, with some narrow windows suggesting an attic of sorts, appeared to be wooden and shingled. Altogether, it was less pretentious than she had expected but very comfortable, and she liked the way that the native trumpet vines and cape jasmine ran right up to the railings, and lilies massed below the verandas. No stiff Parisian formality here.

Then it struck her that the de la Fosse house in New Orleans, that baronial residence so out of keeping with its wooden neighbors, would have looked more appropriate here, while Sans Pareil—Without Equal—was distinctively creole and would have graced that smaller lot in New Orleans. But Amadée had a taste for grandeur, it seemed.

The prospect from the house was pleasing. An avenue of trees ran down toward the river, and the breeze, when there was one, brought scents of flowers and lemon.

"Observe the roof, madame," said Mam'Odile with a pleased air. "Every shingle hand-fitted in white oak. But no nails."

"And why is that?"

"Too costly. We make our own nails here."

So that meant a blacksmith and a forge, too. Minette had been doing some calculating during their walk from the kitchen. There must be hogs and chickens and cattle to be raised for food; hunters to go out and shoot game; fruit; orchards; oats, hay, and fodder to be grown for the horses and mules; vegetable gardens.

Then there had to be a washhouse and a dairy, a smokehouse, and an infirmary. Out there somewhere in the fields were rows of slave cabins, and they had to be repaired, and wells dug. There must be a mill for grinding grain and someplace to process this indigo plant Prosper had told her about. And stables and barns, wagons, a church, storage buildings for the crops. *Bon Dieu*, how much money did it take to *make* money from a plantation? Prosper had told her that Sans Pareil did very well indeed, and so it must! But the responsibility for all this was crushing. Minette's respect for Prosper grew.

"The sun is strong. Shall we go inside?" Mam'Odile suggested.

Yes, she'd hardly had a look at her own house. Again, it was harmonious but not overpowering: six rooms downstairs, four up. It smelled of beeswax polish and flower petals, but for all that, there was a carelessness of arrangement in the furniture, an indifference to the effect, which certainly suggested a bachelor's house. Drapery was at a minimum, the chairs had no charming little cushions, the rosewood piano in the parlor, though gleaming with polish, looked as if no one ever sat down at its bench and caressed its keys. The main room—the salon, she supposed—seemed to combine business and pleasure, with a tall planter's chair and smaller seats set out for those who came to see Prosper on matters pertaining to the running of Sans Pareil. Off the salon was a small office with a high *secrétaire;* that was where he did his endless paperwork. And in the center hall, the family portraits were scattered on the walls.

"Wait!" Minette stared at one pictured face. It might have been a mirror.

"It is Madame Amadée."

"But—"

"Yes, it might well be you."

Amadée, with a long mass of blond curls dangling over her shoulder and a dress with billowing sleeves from an earlier time, looked startlingly like Minette. Oh, not feature for feature, perhaps, but the total impression was overpowering.

"She could be my sister."

"We all noticed the resemblance, madame."

"She was beautiful."

"As you are now." Mam'Odile immediately looked away.

Minette examined the picture more closely. There was a charming little white dog and, in the window view behind the figure, an improbably shimmering sunset.

"The picture was painted at the house in Pointe-à-Pitre, on Saint Dominique."

"You were with the de la Fosse family when they lived on the island?"

JOIN THE
TIMELESS ROMANCE READER SERVICE AND GET FOUR OF TODAY'S MOST EXCITING HISTORICAL ROMANCES FREE, WITHOUT OBLIGATION!

Imagine getting today's very best historical romances sent directly to your home — at a total savings of at least $2.00 a month. Now you can be among the first to be swept away by the latest from Candace Camp, Constance O'Banyon, Patricia Hagan, Parris Afton Bonds or Susan Wiggs. You get all that — and that's just the beginning.

PREVIEW AT HOME WITHOUT OBLIGATION AND SAVE.

Each month, you'll receive four new romances to preview without obligation for 10 days. You'll pay the low subscriber price of just $4.00 per title — a total savings of at least $2.00 a month!

Postage and handling is absolutely free and there is no minimum number of books you must buy. You may cancel your subscription at any time with no obligation.

GET YOUR FOUR FREE BOOKS TODAY ($20.49 VALUE)

FILL IN THE ORDER FORM BELOW NOW!

YES! *I want to join the Timeless Romance Reader Service. Please send me my 4 FREE HarperMonogram historical romances. Then each month send me 4 new historical romances to preview without obligation for 10 days. I'll pay the low subscription price of $4.00 for every book I choose to keep — a total savings of at least $2.00 each month — and home delivery is free! I understand that I may return any title within 10 days without obligation and I may cancel this subscription at any time without obligation. There is no minimum number of books to purchase.*

NAME_____

ADDRESS _____

CITY_____STATE_____ZIP_____

TELEPHONE_____

SIGNATURE _____

(If under 18 parent or guardian must sign. Program, price, terms, and conditions subject to cancellation and change. Orders subject to acceptance by HarperMonogram.)

GET
4
FREE
BOOKS
(A $20.49
VALUE)

TIMELESS ROMANCE
READER SERVICE

120 Brighton Road
P.O. Box 5069
Clifton, NJ 07015-5069

"I was."

"And the others here?"

"No. I am the only one. All the others were … sold when the family left Saint Dominique. They were most particular about that."

"Why? I should think they would want to keep the people they knew."

A discernible shadow crossed the tall woman's eyes. "Not at all. New slaves were bought in New Orleans."

Sold. Bought. There was not a trace of emotion in the black woman's voice. Yet perhaps someone dear to her had been sold away. Minette thought, pray God that I may never do such a thing!

"Mam'Odile, why do you suppose Madame Amadée's portrait is here instead of in her New Orleans house? It's very well done, I think. If it was mine, I'd hang it proudly."

"I couldn't say," Mam'Odile said simply.

"And who is this frowning, insufferable child?"

Mam'Odile's long hand came up to hide her smile. "Your husband, madame."

La! No doubt this story would travel to the others. *Tant pis.* Well, it couldn't be helped.

"Tell me, were you also with the family when Monsieur Prosper was growing up?"

"When all the children were growing up."

"All?"

"He had a brother and sister, twins. Antoine and Aglae. Fever took them both."

Leaving his mother her only precious son, Minette thought. No wonder they were so close. Could it be a habit of indulgence on Amadée's part that had made her accede so rapidly to his marriage? Minette was hardly a catch. Well, if they could unite on their feelings for

Prosper, perhaps there was hope of improving relations with her *belle-mère*, her mother-in-law. At present, the barely masked coldness in the woman's eyes was enough to freeze the bones.

"Do you plan to stay at Sans Pareil, madame?"

"What a curious question."

"It's only that M'sieu Prosper hasn't spent much time here of late. We've hardly seen him."

"Yet Sans Pareil has continued to grow."

"But it's now at the point where it needs more than an overseer. It needs its master."

"I can see that, Mam'Odile. I believe that we are here to stay."

And so do I, thought Mam'Odile, looking from Amadée's portrait to Minette's face. The young mistress seemed to belong here. No lolling Creole belle, she. The girl had worked, worked with her hands. And her curiosity, the way she reverently touched the objects of the house, said she had never seen such things, was not used to money. No grand dowry in the background here; Prosper must have married for love, or something quite like it. Prosper—imagine! Who would have known he even had a heart?

"Are you tired, madame?" she asked. "Would you like to rest on the chaise upstairs, or perhaps on the veranda? I can bring you a cool drink."

"Not yet, Mam'Odile. I still have much to see."

She wandered slowly through the rooms, turning the keys in coffered boxes, trying the piano keyboard, feeling the stuff of the curtains. With each minute adjustment, she was establishing herself as the mistress here.

Mam'Odile watched silently. Would Prosper get her with child soon? But who knew with whites and the games that they played? Indeed, how could Prosper have married someone who looked so much like

Amadée de la Fosse? Or was that the very reason? Better not to question the whys of anything; she was safe here only because she knew a secret and the family had decided not to take the chance of selling her. How unexpected life was. Once, long ago, she had been Oka MnathaKoto, who had urged on her father's warriors and danced—how she had danced! But every day she lived, it became harder to remember.

"Please tell me if you are tired, madame," she said. "This climate is not so easy. One must adjust to it gradually."

"But the wind is fresh and pleasant. Is there as much fog as in New Orleans?"

"During the winter months, madame. Then the fog presses close, and the trees disappear. But only then."

"Is it cold?"

"I have heard that New Orleans can be colder."

"Yes, that surprised us when we came. So far south and yet so raw at times."

"And France?"

"Paris in winter?" Minette was thinking of stone steps, scrub buckets, and icy knees. "I am tired of feeling cold."

"Then you will enjoy most of our year. And the country is beautiful."

"Oh, yes. I should like to ride out beyond that horizon, to go on and on."

"We have horses. What sort do you require?"

"I don't know, Mam'Odile. I have never been on a horse's back. But Prosper has said that he will teach me."

"He is an excellent horseman."

"I hope he is patient with me, then."

Mam'Odile shrugged. That remained to be seen.

11

Their companionable marriage ended three weeks later, with the arrival of the new moon. Just as it sailed clear of the clouds in a midnight sky, Minette turned and found Prosper in their big bed. She tentatively moved closer to him, and their bodies touched, the warmth of her skin glowing against him.

"Yes? Say yes!" he demanded.

By way of assent, she turned to face him, slipped her arms around his back. They held each other, with gentle kisses, until his hands began to stroke the delicate nape of her neck, massaging it until her eyes half closed in contentment. Then he began to whisper of his love, and during the steady flow of endearments his hands moved, gently exploring her arms, her shoulders ... and her breasts. She shivered at the intimacy at first, but he made it seem so smooth, so natural, when he cupped her breasts and circled her stomach with that delicate touch. It was impossibly hypnotic when he teased her breasts with his tongue, and then lightly used its probing on the tender parts of her body. When his hands eased her legs apart, she was floating in acquiescence, and while he played there, rubbing and stroking, whispering love phrases, requiring nothing from her but that dreamy assent, her body and mind opened to him. He entered her slowly and skillfully, so that only a few convulsive shudders marked his passage and the end of her maidenhood. Her body was more ready than she knew, wet and eager, and he dallied, protracting the movement, until she whispered, "More, more!" Even then, there was no sharpness to his thrusts, only a mounting pressure, a warm bluntness that expanded to fill her.

"Help me, my darling. You can help me now," he said, cradling her hips in his hands.

Now she felt the friction, the motion, the edges of hot pleasure, and she crept out of her dream of acceptance to follow his guidance, rising and falling beneath him as he directed. There was a slight stirring of pain, but it hovered between hurt and excitement, and she let it grow until the excitement was everything, and she closed her eyes to hoard it to herself. Now and now and now ... It happened like a flowering, a burst of color behind the eyes, a spattering of diamond leaves of light, and then she sank back, hearing his panting breath at a distance, sinking away from him on bones that had just dissolved to warm water.

"Prosper?" It was the barest whisper.

"Brava. Brava, Minette. You were made for love. I climaxed deep within you. So deep, we may have made a son tonight."

The words did not register. She was floating away into a dazed half-sleep. Her hands fell from his shoulders, and he pulled her nightgown back into place. For a long time he looked at her in the moonlight, the sleeping ivory face, the golden tendrils of hair still damp from his mouth. He smoothed the hollow in her throat where the pulse fluttered and put a parting pressure of his lips there. Finally, his possessive nature had won. Minette was his now, all his, his to awaken to bolder displays of passion as time went on. He had been careful, had reined himself in against the screaming pressure of his own body, and it had been right.

Now he glanced at the moon. May there be something to the old wives' tale of a full moon, a healthy boy. There were maladies in his family, gradually accumulated with that damned Creole habit of marrying cousins. Well, he'd broken the chain with this beautiful, glowing creature who was so much stronger than she realized. Together they would produce the perfect child.

12

In the next months, Minette explored the world around her and invited in the "neighbors." A relative term, since the plantations here were so isolated from one another. Invited guests came with wagons and luggage; their average stay, two weeks. The choices were Prosper's. "Not these two—he's a windbag, and she has a voice like a saw cutting trees." Or, "Not that family—he can't hold his liquor but insists on drinking." Finally, the first couple came overland, the master and mistress in one coach, a wagon carrying their personal servants and baggage behind. Sans Pareil was not big enough to accommodate several such visiting families at a time, as was customary on many plantations.

Their guest, Madame Ladigue, declared, "We never sit down to a meal without ten or twelve at table."

"We have too damn much house," said her tall, bony husband. "It attracts visitors like flies to honey. Prosper here is smarter. Keeps a place just big enough not to interfere with the main thing, the crops." The talk turned inevitably to crops and then to the stubbornness of Monsieur Ladigue's blacks and what he did to curb it. Shuddering at the casual brutality, Minette was glad to leave the table with Thérèse Ladigue.

Yet the puffy, pouting woman bored her. There was nothing in Minette's background of grindingly hard work and strict daily pieties to equip her for inane social chatter. Madame Ladigue was painfully envious of her looks and fearfully curious about her origins; she rattled off the names of a dozen families in France, exploring their genealogies, inviting Minette to establish connections. But Minette was wary of such traps. It wasn't fair to Prosper to provide a feast for the up-country gossips; it was enough to say that they had met in New Orleans, married, and the devil with the rest. *Zut*, such language. Ah, she was borrowing much from Prosper, his words, his point of view, even some of his less cynical opinions. Since they'd become really man and wife, fewer explanations were made.

The Ladigues left earlier than planned, and she offered no protest at seeing them go. Prosper was bored, and Prosper always came first, even over the compulsive rituals of creole hospitality.

He had taught her to ride and pronounced her seat excellent, but at the same time he had warned her not to ride to the boundaries of their estate and never without a groom. The Indian tribes of La Louisiane—Caddo, Arkansas, Atakapa, Natchez, and others—had been bribed with presents and treaties but never completely subdued. They were the real reason for the string of military forts protecting New Orleans and the rest of the system extending up through the northern Illinois country to the French possessions in Canada.

It was true that the French settlers needed to be alert

against incursions from Spain or England, who had adjoining territories, but that kind of war was usually settled by diplomats, not savages with tomahawks. The nearest protective fort to Sans Pareil was Fort Rosalie, built on a high bluff in the territory of the Natchez Indians and named after the wife of a French governor. But it was several days' ride over hard ground to reach the fort, or for the soldiers to come to them. In case of Indian skulkers or raiding parties, they must take matters into their own hands.

Prosper's overseer carried a brace of pistols, and so did he. He'd finally, after much deliberation, decided to teach Minette to shoot. She was cool, he admitted that. And she'd proved to him that she was not likely to let the gun blow up in her face. So he let her practice and complimented her on her progress. For all his inclination to treat her like a decorative china doll, he could also be a realist.

Just how much of a realist she discovered during the visit to Sans Pareil of *la famille* Metoyer. Madame Metoyer was kindly and much interested in discussing the latest fashions from England and France, sent to the colony as miniature outfits on fashion dolls to be copied by skilled local hands. She enthused about the style, with hussar's braiding and a sweeping cape, and predicted it would be sensational on Minette. She even had the name of a skilled seamstress who made the rounds of plantations, staying for lengthy periods and doing all that was needed. Madame Metoyer's warmth cheered Minette and Prosper too, ever the dandy interested in the latest fashion.

But a more troublesome characteristic of the Metoyers was that they had come to La Louisiane very early, and they shared the fervor of its founder, the sieur de

Bienville. Pierre Metoyer extolled the glories of the colony at too much length of an evening when Prosper was in one of his unpredictable gloomy and sarcastic moods. Alone, Minette could soothe him. In company, his reaction was unbridled.

"Have you ever heard of John Law, Pierre?"

"You mean the founder of the Company of the West?"

"I mean the cheat and criminal who, with the king's connivance—"

"Prosper! You speak of His Majesty Louis XV."

"A feeble offshoot of his father. A stupid and greedy man who was taken in by an incredible speculator. Do you think that this huge colony was established for the benefit of France?"

"I think—"

"You think what you're told, Pierre," Prosper cut in. "And it's a lie. La Louisiane was established so that John Law's company could speculate in selling shares to all comers, which is exactly what he did at great profit as the value per share went from five hundred to eight thousand francs."

"I bought at the earlier price, Prosper. I was fortunate."

"What did you buy, Pierre?"

"Shares in the Company of the West, which became the India Company. Why, Law acquired all the fur trading rights and the right to collect all revenues and taxes for France, with commissions for his work. How could one not take an advantage of such an opportunity?"

"I have sold my shares, Pierre. All of them."

"But why?"

"Because there is no substance to them, no more than a soap bubble blown out of a child's pipe. The French treasury is bankrupt and has applied to Law for a loan of 1,600,000 francs, to be raised by the sale of still more shares!"

"I say bravo to that."

"Do you indeed? And what do you suppose will happen when Law's company asks the Crown to be relieved of its charter for Louisiana? And you can be sure that will happen when he's unloaded all the shares he can to still more fools. Then he'll have the money, and the values will tumble. The bubble will burst, ruining everybody and leaving us with a colony that France doesn't want and can't support, filled with the poor who are not even French."

"Not even French—how can you say that?"

"Did you never take note of Law's company seal, Pierre? It's on each of your shares. Take a good look. It shows an old Greek god leaning on a cornucopia, and out of this cornucopia pours a flood of golden coins. Now, that is meant to represent this colony. Do you think it's an accurate picture?"

"No, not yet. Life is not easy, but—"

"Not easy for you, Pierre, and you're one of the privileged. What about the poor devils from every country where Law circulated those damned posters of friendly Indians giving away their furs? The rabble of Europe, with nothing to lose, came here, lured by his false promises of prosperity. John Law needed their bodies to populate the empty spaces so that he could collect more titles and charters to land."

"The colony is large enough to care for them, surely?"

"Surely not. The colony can hardly care for its own, and France has all but disowned us."

"Where is this leading, Prosper? Are you telling me that you will sell your holdings here and go back to Saint Dominique?"

"No, my family will never go back to Saint Dominique." This was said with particular emphasis.

"Then why have you told me all this?"

"Because I want you to believe me, Pierre, before your shares are worth less than the paper they are written on and the colony is saddled with a plentitude of undesirables. Why, Law had the jails opened to find colonists! His ships carried the inmates of France's hospitals and asylums! Of course, many of them have died by now, but the original numbers are there on paper, and paper, in this case, is John Law's weapon in pressing his claims."

"You paint a very gloomy picture, my friend. Your own wife is a recent *émigrée* from France, I believe."

"Ah, Minette is part of the antidote for the plague of speculation and foreign rabble. But it's too little and too late."

In a moment, Prosper was telling her story. It was then that Minette realized her husband was drunk. A thoroughgoing snob, he'd often told her that he loved her in spite of her origins, and she was quite certain the particulars of her background had not been circulated throughout the family. Not that there was anything to be ashamed of, Minette told herself fiercely. Not at all. Not everyone could be born an aristocrat. Come to think of it, Prosper had a low opinion of most aristocrats, too. He cared only for their privileges.

Still, she felt as if she'd been stripped to her shift and stood up for inspection. And the servants were listening too, of course. The servants were always listening. Putting metal pieces over the keyholes of company rooms to prevent spying or eavesdropping had accomplished little. They always knew. It was fortunate that she hadn't tried to play too grand a lady with

Mam'Odile. What would the woman think now?

Madame Metoyer was fascinated, her kindly intent unmistakable. She took Minette aside for a cozy chat, and soon Minette was telling her stories of convent life. But she did not directly answer Madame Metoyer's question about how she in particular had been selected as *une fille à la cassette*. She would never mention the chevalier de Pombiers. What if the Metoyers knew him? For *that* story to become common gossip was both horrible and dangerous!

Though Prosper had argued with Pierre Metoyer, they remained friends, and a few days later their parting was amicable. Minette would miss Madame; she realized that she was growing lonely for the feminine ambiance of her former life. Women could be cruel, true; but they understood things that no man could guess.

Minette suddenly thought of red-haired Berenice with her red-haired Arnaud and who knew how many red-haired little children by now. How she'd love to visit Berenice in New Orleans!

But of course, Prosper would never allow it. He hadn't seemed such quite a snob when he was in the Royal Hospital. But perhaps serious sickness was one place where democracy existed, since all people were on the same footing with Death.

A few weeks after the Metoyers' visit and before that of the next couple, the Duhamels, Minette woke one morning to find the room spinning. She barely made it to the slop jar in time to vomit up the previous night's meal. Her stomach continued to heave, on nothing, refusing to subside. Thank the fates that Prosper was long gone to the fields and would not witness her dishevelment. Finally she lay back, exhausted, wondering what particular bit of rich cuisine had betrayed her.

A knock at the door brought in Mam'Odile with the accustomed breakfast tray: pancakes this morning, swimming in syrup. One look sent Minette to the slop jar again. This time she heaved and brought up some sort of fluid, after which she let Mam'Odile almost carry her across the room and tuck her into bed.

Shortly, she felt better. As her breathing calmed, she felt Mam'Odile fussing over her, wiping her face, testing her forehead for the burn of fever. There was none. The whole unlikely incident was receding and Minette was about to drift back into sleep when Mam'Odile said, "May I speak, madame?"

"Well, then?"

"You may be pregnant, madame. You have a look around the eyes that is quite familiar. If you are sick again tomorrow morning—"

"I won't be," Minette decided.

But she was, and for several mornings following, though with somewhat less severity.

By this time Prosper had to be told, and he could barely suppress his excitement, kissing her hands with a humble devotion quite unlike his masterful lovemaking. But, no guessing—he wanted the opinion of their family doctor in New Orleans. He wrote to his mother and to Dr. Robideaux and sent a courier down to the river to put the mail aboard the nearest passing ship. Meanwhile, he hovered at Minette's elbow, with pillows for her back and instructions and prohibitions for her continued health. At first, she luxuriated in the attention, but then it became too much. She turned cranky, snappish.

In this mood, and with the lassitude that now overtook her, she lost track of the days and was surprised to have the bedroom invaded not only by Dr. Robideaux, with his careful, formal manner, but also by her *belle-mère*, Amadée, and Amadée's shadow, Ti Manou.

They had come to save her work, the women said, to take over her responsibilities for the present, while she, the precious container, rested her way through the first dangerous months of pregnancy. Useless to struggle to a sitting position; she was coaxed down flat again and held there by stories of early miscarriages and the general fragility of ladies in her condition.

But this "help" brought Minette no relief or tranquillity; she didn't want interlopers in the house. Amadée was doubtless rearranging everything, reasserting her iron control over as much of her son's life as she could, including Sans Pareil, which she had professed to be "perfect" for the couple and their exclusive domain. And then there was the strong dislike between Ti Manou and Mam'Odile. It crackled in their meetings, and they were like two cats, fur ruffed high, walking stiff-legged around each other. The tension in the house reached teeth-grinding levels.

Prosper, however, seemed untouched by it, merely highly pleased that Dr. Robideaux had examined her, pronounced her satisfyingly pregnant and healthy and left.

And it was soon a very obvious pregnancy. By the end of the third month, the laces were snapping on Minette's clothes, and, to give Amadée credit, she had come prepared with replacements. The gowns were of the finest quality but shapeless. Minette looked the other way whenever she passed a mirror, but Amadée's solicitude only increased as the mother-to-be continued to swell out of her normal shape.

Still uneasy with her *belle-mère*, Minette complained to Prosper that there was no need for his mother to stay to the full term of her pregnancy. He countered with stories of difficult deliveries in his family; de la Fosse babies were aristocratically fragile.

"But this will be my baby too, and there is nothing fragile about me!"

"It's best to take no chances."

"Is this to happen with every pregnancy, Prosper? You've said that you wanted more children, and that's important to me, too. But am I to be made a prisoner each time?"

He attempted to soothe her with soft praise but was just as determined as her other jailers.

"How can I convince you that I don't need such pampering? I feel perfectly well."

"We don't want to take any chances, Minette."

"You said that before. But there are months to go yet, and what shall I do with myself? Must I wait until I nurse the baby before I can feel useful and take some pleasure in motherhood?"

His face darkened at her persistence.

"What is it, Prosper? I intend to nurse, even if de la Fosse tradition disagrees."

"Much as I should like to protect your lovely breasts, *chérie*, I agree that my son needs his own mother's milk, instead of some ignorant wet-nurse's."

"You're convinced it will be a son?"

"I feel it."

"And when he comes, will you do me the kindness to call him *our* son? I am, after all, your partner in this enterprise."

"Pardon me, my darling. But you have no idea how much this child means to me."

She thought that she did, but somehow, rather than pleasing her, it disturbed her.

For weeks, Minette suffered their solicitude. Amadée's visit lengthened, grating on her nerves, while Ti Manou slipped in and out of the rooms in her enigmatic way, always allegedly on some errand for Amadée. But at odd moments, when she turned suddenly, Minette felt the woman's catlike eyes on her. Ti Manou. A friend or an enemy? She had found and rescued Minette, nurtured her very tenderly when she lay recovering in the de la Fosse house in New Orleans. But here, in the shadow of her mistress, Amadée, she seemed a different person, sly, dangerous. "A witch woman, that Ti Manou," said Mam'Odile. "Me, I keep waiting for her to turn back into a black cat."

Prosper was becoming even more of a problem. He began to drink heavily and made no attempt to hide it. It began as soon as he came in from the fields and continued through his inevitable entries in the plantation ledgers: how much was harvested each day, its weight, its probable price on the market as compared with last year's figures. Not every planter kept his own books, but Prosper would trust no one else. While he covered pages with his fine copperplate, he sipped red wine. There was more wine at dinner, both red and white, plus liqueurs with the coffee. By the time he joined the rest of the family in the salon, he was a sodden presence, content to sit in his special chair and let the candlelight wink off his gold rings as he raised his glass from time to time, sipping leisurely but often.

This had seldom happened before Amadée came. Minette's happiest evenings had been spent alone with Prosper. As part of her social education he put himself out to read to her or tutor her at the piano or play *vingt-et-un*, one of several card games popular among the aristocracy. They often walked in the moonlight and sometimes rode. Out of sight of the servants, Minette unbound her hair and let it float free for the pleasure it brought them both.

None of that was possible now. Amadée had assumed command. She was bright and *au courant* but supremely self-absorbed; she talked at Minette rather than engaging her in conversation. And though she tried to hide it, her disdain for her daughter-in-law was obvious. *Bon Dieu*, Minette thought one night, all that seemed to matter to anyone was the child. And who was to say whether Amadée would go home even after she had counted its fingers and toes? What if she and her shadow remained, taking over the baby as well as her life with Prosper?

Brooding and resentment had been alien to Minette's nature until now. But pregnancy and circumstances had altered her in ways she hardly realized. She was more combative, anxious to defend herself and the child she carried. And the explosion, when it came, was over something relatively trivial.

It centered around the spinet. Prosper had taught her a few simple tunes to play, and she'd practiced them faithfully. Amadée, quite an accomplished pianist, monopolized the rosewood spinet with classics and popular ballads. Minette envied her rippling arpeggios, and when Amadée, one night, began a song that Minette could play, she asked for a chance to demonstrate her own progress. She glanced at Prosper for encouragement, but he was sunk in his usual silence. She was beginning to hate the unsmiling stranger her husband had become.

Surprised, Amadée moved off the bench but stood beside it and watched Minette's hard-learned fingering. The scrutiny unnerved her, and she hit several wrong notes. Amadée's features twisted in exasperation.

"Not that way. Let me show you. Heavens, the arrangement of your fingers. And stop pounding the keys. Who could possibly have taught you so badly?"

And with that, as they say in the taverns, the cork blew out of the bottle. "Your son, madame. My husband. The master of the house, if only he would exercise that privilege."

"What is this nonsense, child?"

"I am not your child. Don't pretend civility. I know how much you look down on me. If I was not carrying the de la Fosse heir, you would not even be here. But let me assure you that you are not needed. You can go back to your *belle* New Orleans. You say you want to make my life easier, but you are suffocating me. If you're truly concerned with the welfare of your grandchild, you would leave!"

Startled, Prosper got to his feet.

"My husband," she cried. "I hold you responsible as well as your mother, and I will tell you why. I did not ask that she come. Had you consulted me, you'd have discovered that I didn't want her here. But you didn't. You decided for me. And it was a wrong decision. It has spoiled everything. I am unhappy, and you—just look at yourself, Prosper. You weren't like this before she came."

"Minette, you forget yourself." This was Amadée's warning.

"On the contrary, madame, I am finally remembering myself. I am free from you at last."

"What sort of talk is that?"

"The truth. I don't want you to take over my life, to bend and twist it to your own shaping. I am no pallid little child to be bullied into inactivity. It's not good for me, not good for the baby—oh!"

Prosper moved to steady her. "What is it, Minette?"

"Just a dizziness. It's gone now. See what this argument is doing to me?"

His arm was suddenly protective around her shoulders.

"I agree with Minette, *Maman*. Let us end this conversation."

"But I have been wronged, my son! And your wife's wild rudeness only proves that she cannot take proper care of herself. She belongs in bed. I advise you to put her there."

"No!" Minette got her breath back. "You will not dispose of me. You will not order me around in my own house. This is my pregnancy, my baby. I know you don't like me, but I am the other Madame de la Fosse, and you will treat me accordingly. Do you hear?"

Amadée did not deign to look at her. It was as if the furniture had stood up on its rear legs and protested. Her eyes were fixed on her son in a contest of wills. "Prosper, I am waiting. You know what is right. Do what must be done."

"I shall." His voice was strong, but he would not meet Amadée's steely eyes. "Mother, I ask you to leave in the morning. I will have the carriage ready."

"How dare you speak to me that way!"

"Sans Pareil is in my name, don't you remember? It is my house, and you are only a guest in it."

"Only a guest? Oh, that I live to hear you speak this way to me! Have you completely forgotten your honor as a de la Fosse?"

"Save the theatrics, Mother. You cannot tell me anything about the de la Fosse family. But I tell you that the damn thing will come to an end if my wife miscarries."

"Not likely. She's as strong as any peasant from the farm."

"Then why are you here? Only to meddle!" That was Minette.

Again Amadée ignored her for Prosper.

"For some low-class tantrum, you would insult your own mother?"

"*Maman*, you have an unfortunate effect on my wife. That has a bad effect on my son, and I won't tolerate it. With all respect, I want you to go. We'll send word when the baby is born."

"Good night, Madame de la Fosse," said Minette. "I may not be able to bid you good-bye in the morning, so shall we take our leave of each other now? I wish you a safe journey to New Orleans."

Amadée inclined her head frostily.

Minette could not wait to be out of the other woman's presence. She leaned heavily on Prosper all the way upstairs.

"I'll send little Lisette to you," said Prosper when they were in the bedroom.

"Please stay a moment, Prosper. Tell me, you are not angry at me?"

"Do I seem so?"

"Ah, Prosper." She put her soft hands on his face. "You're alive again. You've come back to me. After they leave, can we please go out riding? Just around Sans Pareil? Our baby needs the air."

"But the tracks are rough and rutted, Minette."

"I don't expect to gallop. We'll be sedate and careful and roll along as slowly as you like. But let's do it! I'm perfectly well and longing for activity. Your mother is full of fears, and she's given them to you!"

"She lost a son and daughter."

"Yes, the twins. But she did not lose them in childbirth. The fever took them on Saint Dominique, at Pointe-à-Pitre."

"How did you know that?"

"Mam'Odile told me."

Prosper seemed dazed.

Minette was curious. "Is that why your family left the island? I know that you were rich there, so you didn't have to come, like me."

He was short. "We did."

"Prosper, why did you tell the Metoyers that I was *une fille à la cassette?*"

"I said that?"

"The evening when you were arguing with Pierre about the land speculation rush in the colony."

"The fool didn't believe me. He'll be sitting on his shares, and the bubble will burst beneath him. But we're safe, Minette. When they reap the whirlwind, we'll be safe." He returned to himself. "But I don't remember talking about the basket brides. I must have been insufferable. How can I apologize to you?"

"I am not so ashamed as you are. How is a basket bride so different from an aristocratic daughter pushed into marriage with the highest bidder? At least I had a choice."

"And you chose me."

"You made it impossible for me to refuse."

"I was a catch, you know." He smiled.

"You still are."

"I am glad to see your good humor is restored."

She sat on the bed and patted the space beside her invitingly. "Prosper, it's been so long."

"I don't think we should."

"Oh, Prosper, let's celebrate my choice. Let's make love."

"You know how much I want you. . . ."

"I thought perhaps in my condition, you'd not be—"

"You're ten times more beautiful."

"Ah, then hurry. Please."

She took down her hair, and he was out of his breeches like an eel.

"How I need you," he whispered as he pressed against her carefully.

She pulled him closer with impatient arms. "Oh, my love, I am so glad your mother will not come between us any longer."

It wasn't possible. Prosper, a skilled lover who had taught her to enjoy so many pleasures, could not complete the act. He was unmanned. The member, so alive moments before, could not maintain its erection and finally sank limp against his groin. Minette's efforts to coax it were useless.

"I knew I should not have tried to make love to you tonight," Prosper muttered.

"We'll try after your mother leaves tomorrow."

It was the wrong thing to say. "This has nothing to do with my mother, curse it! This is no simple failure on my part. It is a warning, an omen of danger. I will not risk my son's life!"

Turning away, he buttoned himself back into his breeches.

Minette was silent. The more he protested, the more she was sure that Amadée had very much to do with it.

"Good night, my wife. When Lisette is through preparing you for sleep, tell her to make up a bed for me in the sitting room. The couch will do for tonight."

"And tomorrow?"

"No, Minette, no. Don't tempt me. It will be useless."

Alone again, she was surprised to find that the flare of desire faded as quickly as it had come. He hadn't even realized that Amadée—

Lisette entered, a shy mulatto girl Mam'Odile was training as Minette's personal maid. She busied herself undressing the mistress—much simpler these days since the stays and laces had been discarded because of her pregnancy. As she was being eased into a white lawn night garment, Minette realized that Prosper had never answered her question about why *la famille de la Fosse* had left Saint Dominique, apparently in haste. Secrets. He was full of secrets. As were her mother-in-law and Ti Manou. What sort of man had she married?

13

Several months later, an event occurred that would change the course of Minette's life. Two days' hard ride toward New Orleans from Sans Pareil stood Fort Rosalie, part of the chain of the colony's fortifications protecting its capital city. Its prospect from the high bluff above the river was as noble as its command, Monsieur de Chepar, was ignoble and ill advised. His dealings with the Indian tribes were criminal in their arrogance and ignorance. De Chepar's aim in his post was to get rich quick, and to this end, he ordered the Natchez Indian chief of a village called Pomme to move out all his people. Their land would be turned into a plantation, which de Chepar would sell at a handsome profit. The chief explained that the bones of the tribe's ancestors were buried there, and they could not leave, but de Chepar would not change his mind. He threatened to send the chief to New Orleans in chains if he did not obey promptly.

In tribal council, the Natchez decided that they

could not permit themselves to be so tyrannized by the foreigners they had welcomed into their territory. But they needed time to think of a way to get rid of these disagreeable guests, the French. They tempted the greedy de Chepar into a delay of several months, during which time each Indian family in Pomme would pay him a tribute of corn, furs, and wild turkeys. The furs decided de Chepar, who assumed that the Indians were capitulating out of fear. He agreed.

But the Natchez used the delay to carry the peace pipe to other tribes of the many Indian nations in Louisiana and convince them to cooperate in a massacre of the greedy French. The plan was this: The warriors, pretending to go out on a hunt in preparation for a great feast, would borrow ammunition and firearms from the French. A commander who had such complete contempt for the Indians' abilities would likely suspect nothing. Then the Indians would go among the French, apparently peacefully, and thoroughly infiltrate the fort and its town. The signal to set off the massacre would be shots fired in front of de Chepar's residence.

As the shots rang out, the Indians turned on the people around them with guns and with knives for scalping. Panicked, screaming, the French ran for shelter, only to find themselves outnumbered by the Natchez, even though the tribe was without reinforcements. The colonists were slaughtered where they stood. There were a few pockets of determined resistance, where Natchez warriors' bodies piled high, but when the dreadful time was over, the Indians had lost fewer than fifty men, while they had killed more than two thousand French. Women and children and some Negroes were sold to the English as hostages or slaves in the English territories of Carolina.

The insulted chief of the Natchez, "tired of being treated like a dog" and "preferring death to slavery under the French," had his ceremonial chair brought to the fur warehouse of John Law's ubiquitous India Company. From his seat he directed the decapitation of his enemies. De Chepar was saved until the last, at which time the chief, in very passable French, reminded his captive of all the times he had willfully cheated the Indians in the past. "You are unworthy to die at the hands of my warriors," he decreed. "Miche-michequipi, take him!" And he turned him over to the lowest of the common Indian people, who rode on de Chepar's back as if he was a dog and shot him full of arrows before they chopped off his head.

The chief was entertained but not yet completely satisfied. Also, his supposed allies, the Chickasaws and the other tribes had not appeared and he realized that the Natchez had taken a great chance, acting on their own against the French. But they'd succeeded. He praised his warriors lavishly and ordered them to attend to such nuisances as the women with nursing children who cried and screamed. These were promptly killed and tossed on the pile of bodies while the others, destined to be slaves, were treated with every indignity the Indians thought proper in retaliation. The turkey buzzards came in flocks to Fort Rosalie, descending in noisy black clouds. For them it was a grand feast day.

The complex strategy of the attack on the fort frightened the French almost as much as the extent of the massacre, forcing them to reevaluate the Indian danger. Soldiers for a punitive action against the Natchez poured into the territory. Men were brought from as far away as the Indies to help garrison the other forts in New France's protective chain of outposts. The rallying cry of "Fort Rosalie!" had all levels of colonial society sharpening their sword blades and priming their muskets. Soldiers were instructed to ride through the few towns established upriver from New Orleans and to go among the plantations, reassuring the people by their presence and vowing that vengeance would be swift.

And that was how the soldiers came to Sans Pareil.

Prosper played host to a gallant quartet of officers, passing wine around the long mahogany dining table he'd brought from the Indies.

The unaccustomed din downstairs, the growl of masculine voices, awakened Minette from an afternoon slumber. One voice in particular filtered through her consciousness. She knew that voice! She must go downstairs, even chance exhibiting herself to a roomful of men.

Lisette dressed her in a loose but fashionable sacque dress of pale blue with a long pleated fall in back. "Do my hair," she urged the girl. "Tie it back. Just a ribbon will do—anything. I must go down before the soldiers leave."

Downstairs, the men discussed the late de Chepar's failures as a commander.

"He put his own gang in charge. Even the sergeants and corporals were selected for their personal loyalty to him. Anyone who said a word against him was put in chains."

"What stupidity."

"But did not any have the courage to oppose him?" said Prosper.

"Monsieur Dupont," answered a small wiry officer with remarkable pepper-pot mustaches. "He was second in command under de Chepar. He wrote an official letter of complaint."

"What happened?" Prosper asked.

"He was put in irons."

A few heartfelt oaths went around the circle of men.

"That wasn't the end of it," continued Lieutenant Guillaume Cernaux. "This Dupont was stubborn. As soon as they took the irons off his legs, he went to New Orleans to complain to the governor."

"Perrier? Another political hack."

"But he tried, Monsieur de la Fosse. Because of Perrier's efforts, de Chepar was recalled to explain his conduct, and he was supposed to be broken in rank."

"However, he had influential friends?" Prosper guessed.

"High in John Law's India Company. You know the story, sir?"

"I know too many like it. I will wager that de Chepar was reinstated and sent back to Fort Rosalie with nary a black mark on his record."

"*Zut*, that crowd will stick together! They make the mess and we must go in and clean—" The soldier stopped speaking as Minette appeared in the doorway. Her eyes met his, and Cernaux seemed incapable of further speech.

"Good afternoon, Lieutenant—ah, no, I see it is now Captain Cernaux."

"You know this gentleman, Minette?"

"Yes, Prosper, from New Orleans."

"Gentlemen, may I present my wife, Madame de la Fosse." Though clearly uncomfortable with her presence in her condition, he pulled out a chair for her, and she sank into it gratefully. But she never took her eyes off Guillaume Cernaux, who still stared at her, slack-jawed. Why?

"Minette, are you sure that this discussion will not

be tiring for you? We speak of horrors," Prosper said.

"The horrors I might otherwise conjure would perhaps exceed the truth. I would like to hear a fair account of the dreadful thing so that I may reassure the nervous servants."

"Ah, madame, you can tell them it might have been even worse, with other forts overwhelmed. It was nothing less than a plot among the Indian nations to wipe out all the colonists in lower Louisiana." This was from a rosy-cheeked young officer who identified himself as Lieutenant Peyberan. "One of our company knows the whole story, and we are waiting for him to—"

There was the quick sound of booted footsteps in the hall, a long shadow cast into the room by the sun, and in stepped Alain Gerard. Here it was, the face she had never expected to see again this side of heaven!

"I dream," Minette murmured. "I must have fever." No, he lives. He lives!

Alain's eyes swung toward her as a compass point seeks true north. They searched her face, passed over her loose dress with dawning comprehension, and finally came to rest on Prosper. Alain sat down as if his legs had folded beneath him.

He had aged a bit, grown broader of chest and shoulders. His eyes were the same though, brilliant brown, deepset, shaded by long lashes, and seeming to look beyond the here and now to something only he could see. The poetic gaze—how it had enticed her. He was quite tan, bronzed by steady exposure to a hotter sun than Louisiana's, but the black hair still curled gently around his temples, and he still wore no wig but a simple peruke. A thin white line on one cheek marked a recently healed scar, placed in such a way that it accentuated the angle of his strong jaw. A god of the tropics, now, no longer the classic Apollo. Older, wiser, and, at the moment, apparently wretched with regrets.

Minette used her palmetto fan to cover her labored breathing. Prosper saw her difficulty but, fortunately, misinterpreted it, and he suggested that she retire upstairs. She waved him away. As long as Alain was in the room, she'd never move from that chair. Like a spring breaking free of winter's ice, the old feelings were bubbling and rising to the surface of her mind, the old, sweet currents flowing through the vessels of her body.

The others were speaking to Alain, urging him to tell some story, and he stammered a little, trying to bring his world back into focus. While his mind pulsed with Minette's name, and her face swam before his eyes, he forced his voice to normalcy. He could not look at her with her husband there.

"The Natchez . . . the Natchez were foiled in their scheme to kill the whole colony because of . . . of love. Our soldiers did not disdain the Indian women, gentlemen; they were bold and free, and many took them as mistresses. We French were well loved by at least some of the Indian population. In fact, one of the Sun chiefs of the Natchez had a French father."

"Well, we never stop colonizing," joked one of the officers.

Alain stole a glance at Minette. She kept her eyes down. He almost dreaded the moment when they'd flash blue into his, sending the question of *Why? Why didn't you come back for me?*

"It was the mother of this chief, the princess Stung Arm, who saved us from a much larger tragedy."

"What?" Cernaux laughed. "Now there's a romantic name, Stung Arm. How would you like to fashion romantic couplets to that?"

"Please be quiet," said Lieutenant Peyberan severely. "We asked Captain Gerard for this story. I want to hear it."

"Continue," Prosper agreed.

"The princess knew that there was some great plan afoot, some scheme among the Natchez, the Chickasaw, the Choctaw and other tribes, for a grand, coordinated attack on the whites. She tricked her son into telling her how they were all going to act at once, all in a single day. He said that each of the tribes had been given a bundle of twigs, each of the same number. Every morning of the waiting period before the attack, a twig was to be taken from the bundle and thrown into the fire. When there was only one twig left in each bundle, they would know that the time for the slaughter had come. One twig had to be removed every day without fail to make the whole coordinated plan work. And then each tribe would fall on the designated whites in its territory, all along the lower Mississippi."

"*Nom de Dieu*, and these are only savages!" Prosper was shaken. He turned to Minette for confirmation, but she would not look at him.

"And what did the princess do? How did she foil this grand plan because she loved the French?" asked Guillaume Cernaux.

"She sent for Indian girls who had French lovers in the forts nearby and told them to warn their men."

"Did someone try to warn de Chepar at Fort Rosalie?"

"Yes, an ensign named Mace."

"And what happened to him?"

"He was probably thrown into irons as a coward," said Prosper.

"Monsieur de la Fosse, you are correct." Even as he answered, Alain stared at Prosper.

"Come on, Gerard, finish the tale." The other officers were growing impatient.

"Very well. The princess saw that the French did not believe the warning, so she did the only other thing she could do. She went into the temple of the Natchez where their fatal bundle of twigs was kept and took some out, so that the day for attacking the whites would be advanced. And the Natchez, not realizing what had been done, began the massacre according to plan, made fearless by the idea that their other Indian allies were acting at the same moment."

"But they weren't. And yet the Natchez won. So what is the point, Alain?" Cernaux was testy.

"The point is what is happening now. The other nations who were in it with the Natchez thought that *they* had been tricked and that the Natchez didn't want them to share in the glory and the loot. So they are joining with us, the Choctaw and Chickasaw nations, to punish the Natchez and get back our prisoners. Now we overwhelm them in numbers, and, gentlemen, we will win!"

Minette spoke for the first time and directly to Alain.

"The princess must have known it would happen and that her own people would suffer. What a difficult decision for her to make." The others assented.

Alain's mind whirled. Was there a message for him in her remark?

She'd put a slight emphasis on *difficult decision*. Could it mean that she had loved him still when she married de la Fosse, that it had been a difficult decision for her to make?

But no, she'd been told he was dead; Cernaux, in all good faith, had made her believe that.

How beautiful, how tempting she was. This wasn't

the springtime maiden he had left aboard the *Baleine*. Here was a woman in the rich splendor of consummated love, a pregnant goddess of new life, and damn the sharp, piercing jealousy in his own loins! He had no right to it, no right to any claim on her. What had he expected? She was a prize among prizes and had found a rich, well-connected husband. The fact that de la Fosse was also handsome and well built in his dandified way only made Alain ache more sharply.

He forced away the picture of them together, knowing it would return to torture him indefinitely. There was no help for it. He would always love her. But she had chosen a better life than anything he could offer. He was not born a rich planter's son, and he'd never made the money to stake himself to a chance at fortune. Too much imagination and a taste for intrigue had done him in. He'd had an enviable life of adventure, and meanwhile another man had taken Minette from him.

If he'd ever had her. How much importance had she put on their silent Saint Malo romance, their fleeting shipboard idyll? A few short weeks could not balance out against a lifetime of luxurious security. The title of Madame Gerard could not compare in influence with that of Madame de la Fosse. This child she carried would never have to scrabble for a living. Her son would be born into at least two thousand arpents of rich river bottom land, hundreds of slaves, uncounted gold livres, which the de la Fosse family had reportedly taken from Saint Dominique.

Her son. Strange how sure he was that Minette would deliver a son. He imagined the child favoring her completely; he did not want to consider any resemblance to de la Fosse.

Alas, he was being a proper dog in the manger! The

least he could do was congratulate the husband and wife, wish Minette happiness. He would make himself do it and try not to look into her eyes, which might haunt him for the rest of his miserable days.

Prosper detected signs of what seemed to be fatigue in Minette. He would cut this meeting short. Minette's renewal of acquaintance with Captain Cernaux had not made her happy. Ridiculous to suspect a past involvement there, not that little Gascon with the pepper-pot mustaches and the strongly accented French that betrayed his family's provincial origins. Hardly Minette's type of man. But the other one, that quite dashing fellow who had told the story of the princess . . .

Prosper rose to propose a toast. "To Princess Stung Arm, without whose intervention our entire colony might not have had a future."

With general laughter and a chorus of *"Buvez un petit coup"*—drink up, my lads—the toast was celebrated.

Lieutenant Peyberan, his boyish cheeks flushed with wine, rose next. "A toast to the unknown Frenchman who so impressed the princess."

Much laughter, slightly bawdier.

Peyberan couldn't stop. "A toast to his French rapier!"

"Gentlemen, my wife is present! We'll have no tavern humor here."

"Madame, I apologize." Peyberan was shamefaced. "I meant no offense."

"None has been taken," said Minette calmly.

The young soldier bowed clumsily, the effects of the wine all too apparent.

It was also apparent that the visit was over. As the officers buckled on their swords, Prosper beckoned to Guillaume Cernaux.

"I am much interested in this Captain Gerard, your

friend. Where does he get so much information?"

"Alain is our man of mystery, Monsieur de la Fosse."

"And why is that?"

"He . . . has no permanent assignment. He disappears from time to time. He suffered a grievous wound in the Indies, and I must confess I thought him dead." Here, Cernaux, remembering that he was speaking to the man who was Minette's husband, became uncomfortable.

"And yet there he stands, a healthy man. Nine lives, would you say?"

"More than nine." Cernaux felt that he was now on safer ground. "He has certain connections to the government, assignments to gather intelligence, you understand."

"So he is no ordinary soldier."

"Ah, but a man of honor."

"I have no reason to think otherwise, Captain. I only inquired."

"And I have enlightened you."

"Not very much. As you say, a man of mystery."

What was it about the fellow, Prosper wondered, that made the hairs at the nape of his neck prickle in alarm? He watched Captain Gerard approach his wife to make his farewells. It was quite proper and yet . . . what? Minette was unusually pale and diffident. It was more than the strain of the pregnancy, or the strain of her appearance now before a roomful of men, which had rather surprised him. But he was no Oriental pasha to keep his wife in seclusion if she wished to join the company. No matter what his mother would say, he was proud to advertise her condition, to boast of the first of the new de la Fosse dynasty. Let them envy him.

For all his nervous suspicion, Prosper did not see what happened between Minette and Alain Gerard at the last moment of their leavetaking. She extended her hand, offering her fingertips. He was slow to take them, but when he did, bowing over her hand in a formal gesture, the most exquisite pain flashed from her hand to his, a jolt of desire that rocked him to his heels. Her eyes were wide, blazing, and the message unmistakable. The touch of her hand, its vibration along his nerves, the urgency in her eyes . . . and the so-softly whispered words, said with such honesty, "Wait for me, Alain!" He could not believe it. *Wait for me.* He tried to put his happiness into his eyes, he tried to make them say, silently, what every fiber of his body strained to tell her. Wait for you, my Minette? I will wait forever!

14

When she was alone, Minette's reaction set in.

What had she done? How did she dare, all swollen with child, and her husband standing a few feet away, beg Alain to wait for her?

It had crept past her defenses, this forlorn wish that didn't dare to be a hope, much less a dream. It had come back at the sight of him, the sound of his voice—now, when it was much too late. Perhaps it was the voice of her body, which Prosper had awakened?

Prosper. He could not have heard her words, but what if anything, had he seen on their faces? She was so glad that she had never told him the name of the man she was mourning. Otherwise, she'd fear for Alain's life now. She remembered Prosper's violent attempt to kill the chevalier. If he decided that he had any sort of evidence, he'd call Alain out to some hidden place where the gentlemen of New Orleans still defied the law and satisfied their honor. Worse, he could hire readily available assassins to ambush Alain and throw his corpse in with the city's garbage, as happened to the losers in tavern brawls.

But it wasn't Prosper who brought on her deepest anguish. It was the weight and presence that occasionally wriggled and thumped against her belly. The baby was not yet entirely real to her, but already she felt the overpowering love that would bind her to the child forever. There was no escape in life from that bond. And her baby would be the heir of the de la Fosse family. That meant she must remain with Prosper. He might let her go without killing her, but the baby he would never relinquish.

No. There was no place for her to turn, no way out. She could almost hate Alain for reappearing and stirring up all her old longings and anguish. She must let him go; she must deny those foolish words.

Lutie came in to announce dinner and help her mistress downstairs. Lutie had been a surprise, a singing child bought for her pleasure from the auction at New Orleans, a little singing blackbird come to this larger, airier cage. Lutie knew all the Creole ballads, and they charmed Minette, even as she sighed at the unrecognizable French. Now Lutie danced before her, singing of Comper' Lapin, the gossip rabbit and ultimate nosy neighbor.

At dinner, Minette's appetite was feeble, and Prosper remarked on it, urging her to eat for the baby's sake. She tried, but nausea rose in her throat. Only some of the angel cake dessert went down.

"I think your time is growing closer. You have that look."

It's fright, Minette thought. Fright and self-disgust and, *Bon Dieu*, help me, desire. She would almost like the baby to be born now, that the pains of childbirth might distract her from the deeper pain that would not abate. She feared she would be old and withered before she was ever free of it.

"Alain Gerard, that handsome captain," Prosper was saying.

"What?" It was sharper than she intended; shock crept into her voice.

"I agree with his estimate of the Indian campaign. The Choctaw and Chickasaw are coming in on our side, and we'll soon have the prisoners of Fort Rosalie back from the Natchez."

"Is that what he predicted?"

"Apparently you weren't listening, my dear. You seemed preoccupied at the time. I was afraid you were not well."

Was he playing with her, or did he truly suspect nothing? Perhaps Alain was safe from him after all.

"Now the Natchez will be moved off their land," Prosper continued. "I expect those who resist will be sold as slaves in the Indies."

"To Saint Dominique?"

"There is a constant turnover of men. More are always needed."

"They die like flies in the fields, you mean. But I don't think that these proud Natchez will make good slaves, Prosper. They'll kill themselves and cheat the traders of their investment."

"All the Natchez land will be open to settlement, Minette. Think of it—leagues and leagues from Bayou Manchac to the Ohio River. It would take more than a week's ride to cross it."

"Suppose the other Indian tribes decide to claim it?"

"Then there will be another war. But it's all friendliness now. We have our Indian allies where we want them." Prosper yawned and stretched.

"A good time for our baby to be born, a time of peace."

He paused. "I should like to see that Gerard fellow again. He impressed me. He may go far in the military, and it's always good to have a personal friend in that quarter. I'll invite him back, and that peppery little Gascon he travels with—what's his name?"

"Cernaux."

"Ah, you did remember something from the conversation. It is Cernaux. But you didn't recall the handsome Gerard."

Minette shut her eyes in pure terror.

"What is it, my dear? Dr. Robideaux waits at his cousins' plantation for our summons. Shall I—"

"A weakness only, Prosper. I am tired."

"And you've eaten nothing."

"I wanted nothing!" She heard the hysteria in her voice and did not try to check it. "Lutie! Send me Lutie!"

"Let her sing you to sleep, eh?" He saluted Minette with his wineglass. "Your time is fast approaching, *chérie*. I can feel it."

"You can feel it? You, a man?"

"You are weighted with apprehension. That's natural. I am in tune with those feelings of yours."

God prevent it, she thought.

"You are completely at the mercy of your body."

He knows!

"I must confess it gives me a certain pleasure."

She took a breath. "Why?"

"Because, for all that angelic beauty and modest demeanor, you are usually so strong-minded. Any man who thought you a mere frill would be mightily surprised to collide with your resoluteness, your cool, calm will."

"You make me sound more like a statue than a human being, Prosper."

"And you're as lovely as the classical Graces, my dear. I meant no unflattering comparison. But now, in your condition, you are wholly female—difficult, capricious, illogical, turning from smiles to tears in a moment. A new Minette and a thoroughly enchanting one."

"Lutie!" she cried before he could come closer. The child came running in from her post outside the door of the dining room. "Lutie, help me upstairs."

She rose with surprising difficulty as the agile Lutie supported her under the arms. The blue dress dragged at her, or was it the effort of moving her feet?

"Prosper, good night. It has been"—she permitted herself a bit of bravery—"an interesting conversation. I have much to think about at leisure."

"Do so, Minette," said Prosper, lighting a cigar now that she was leaving. "Yes, do so." His face was hidden as the smoke rose around it.

Upstairs, Lutie was doing her best to distract her mistress. The maid, Lisette, had prepared her for bed, and now Lutie fluttered her eyes as she sang love songs and made her tones wistful. "*Cher, Mo' L'aime toi*," she intoned, a lovesick maiden in every particular. It was a droll performance.

"Sing me the one whose melody I like so much. I think you called it 'Salangadou.'"

"Oh, the poor old soul." Lutie's voice rose in a haunting melody that sounded like the wind rushing in the trees . . . Salangadououou . . ."

Minette closed her eyes. What would happen to this delightful little girl in later life? Would that voice be stilled by adult reality? Or, if she continued to live by her talents, would she become another Hera?

Why do I think of Hera? Minette mused as the dancer's luminous black eyes and hair rose again in her memory. The woman was a sensuous animal who lived by attracting men. But could she escape feeling their contempt for her even as they used her body? Prosper's description of the woman she had become tonight had reminded her of Hera. Yet her husband claimed to prefer that sort of behavior. Why? Why did men insist on such false ideas of women? Were only nuns free of such images and demands? Perhaps she had lived with the nuns too long.

Still humming, Lutie eased Minette into a comfortable sleeping position in the big four-poster and unfolded the satin coverlet.

"Is this warm enough, mistress? Or perhaps too warm? Would you like a glass of cool water?"

Minette shook her head.

Very softly, Lutie began to sing "*Fais Do Do*," the lullaby for children. She backed away, still singing, and slipped outside the room to take up her position for the night, stretched across Minette's threshold on a pallet.

Lutie thought the mistress had finally accepted sleep. But in the dark, no comfort came. Minette's unhappy thoughts closed in at once, circling on the same old path, and when she saw Alain's face in her mind, which she could not prevent, slow tears ran down her cheeks.

At last, the moment for which everyone had been waiting was finally here. Hours of labor were behind her. There was a haze of sweat across her eyes, and arms that had gripped the bedposts for hours gave way to the pain of the baby fighting its way out of her body. She could feel its frantic effort. Dr. Robideaux leaned close, shouting, and she gave a mighty heave, riding the back of the pain, thrusting, thrusting, and immediately knew that something had happened, something brand new to the world lay on the bed, touching her inner thighs.

Dr. Robideaux drew it carefully away from her. She heard a feeble wail. Her body was still clenched like a fist, she still vibrated to the pain, but they were soothing her, many hands busy for her comfort while the baby was washed in the pan of warm water beside the bed and bundled into soft wrappings. Dr. Robideaux pried Minette's hands from the bedposts she had clutched so long.

"Don't you want to hold your son?"

Prosper's face swam into focus above her. "Well done, *chérie*. He is perfect."

Braced with pillows, she reached for the precious bundle. But he was covered with soft down like a little animal.

"The vernix," said Dr. Robideaux. "Normal to babies. It will soon disappear."

"But his face . . ." She was bewildered by the head, which seemed flattened, and the features overlarge, like those of a dwarf.

"Have you never seen a newborn child?"

She heard Prosper chuckle. "In a convent?"

"Be assured, he is perfectly normal. You will see."

At that moment, the baby's eyes opened and fixed on her. They were blue, her own in shape and color. She had made this being; there was no question about it. He was hers and the most beautiful baby ever.

"He is Olivier," she murmured. That was the name she had chosen to lead all the other proud syllables that would tie him into the family lineage. She too had been so sure it would be a boy that she had chosen no name for a girl.

Prosper touched the baby's head in blessing. "Olivier de la Fosse." He looked as if he was about to cry with happiness. The baby made a restless, instinctive movement toward her breast.

Bonneted in white, Olivier had all but disappeared in the depths of the beribboned cradle. Minette had rejected the lace-edged sheets sent by Prosper's great-aunt Clotilde. Too scratchy. She'd surrounded him with the softest and lightest of everything. From time to time she leaned close to listen to his breathing, such a soft, thready little sound. The room must be kept very quiet so that Minette could hear him continuing to breathe. She was anxious, couldn't believe that this miracle was hers to keep.

When Olivier found his lungs and cried for hours, Prosper retreated from the bedroom. Minette began to nurse him on demand, deaf to any advice from others. The experience itself was a sweet and private sensuality, an indescribable mix of emotions as the tiny tugs sharpened and grew stronger, the baby finding his natural rhythm. God had given mothers a touch of divinity; from her body, Minette provided life for her son. What was any other emotion to this? As long as she held and suckled Olivier, she was content.

Minette wanted to be alone with the baby, but Prosper hovered over them. He would study Olivier's tiny hands and feet seriously, predicting a tall young man who would tower over his father. Not all Creoles were of short stature, he claimed. Olivier took after his paternal grandfather, who belonged to the cadet branch of a most noble house. A lucky inheritance of blood and breeding would produce long, baronial bones.

Prosper had surprised Minette with his interest at this stage. She had thought he'd be bored by babies and only take cognizance of Olivier when he was old enough to speak. But he was besotted by this baby. When the first silvery blond hairs began to appear, favoring Minette, Prosper was enraptured. A blond prince had come to *la famille* de la Fosse.

But as Olivier flourished, Minette dimmed. The turmoil inside her could not be denied; it made itself evident in her eyes, an increasing pallor, a strained expression, and a habit, when she thought she was unobserved, of drawing short, sharp breaths, as if her heart was being deprived of something necessary to life. Her decline had to be pointed out to Prosper, whose attention was entirely on his son.

Dr. Robideaux was consulted. Due to his long friendship with Prosper's family, he had not yet gone back to New Orleans, but remained within call at his cousins'. He began to visit Minette, drawing her into conversation after his examination was done. He could see that she was laboring under some tremendous pressure, but she did not confide in him, and Prosper provided no clue.

Emile Robideaux was at a loss. His patient was losing ground. She was still devoted to her baby, but an advancing listlessness crept up on her, a dull apathy he could no longer ascribe to the shock of childbirth. A blossom was closing; a woman was fading into something so withdrawn that, at times, he feared for her sanity. Robideaux had seen too many of these sad, dull-eyed females. They sat quietly in the dimmed rooms of family houses, their gaze vacant, fixed on nothing, until they no longer reacted to the world around them, and then it was too late. They were gone beyond recall. In Minette's case, he knew that her trouble was not physical; though it affected her body, it was somewhere beyond the reach of medicine, deep in her mind.

He finally confronted Prosper. "Is all well with you and your wife, sir?"

"In what particular?"

"Have you resumed conjugal relations?"

A pause. "She shows no interest, and I would not force myself upon her."

"Perhaps you should. Your relations were enjoyable before the birth of the baby?"

"Extremely. She was an apt pupil."

Robideaux coughed discreetly. "Prosper, I would advise an attempt to revive that interest. Woo her as you would a new woman. Create a climate of intimacy, startle her with surprises, try to draw her into emotion of any kind. The thing to be avoided is this numb acceptance of everything around her. It is not Minette."

"It was not, in the beginning. But thank *le bon Dieu* the infant thrives."

"Don't you want your wife back, man? You must make the effort!"

"Might it have something to do with the season? There's the melancholy of summer's ending. The damned fogs are beginning to close in, and when I awake in the morning to a sea of mist hiding my fields, I can tell you that I am daunted before I begin."

"Prosper, if you feel that there is some connection between this place and her unnatural lassitude, take her away from it. You have left Sans Pareil in the hands of overseers before."

"And they cheated me, Doctor."

"What? Why did you take no action against them?"

"Why? To advertise my stupidity? I have enemies who would enjoy such a lawsuit; I'd be made ridiculous. No, I believe I've solved that problem by careful management. The place will turn a healthy profit, now, and it's my son's heritage that I must protect."

"Does that mean you do not feel free to take Minette away for a time?"

Prosper shrugged.

"At least, then, make an effort to resume your former closeness."

Prosper could not be sure of his welcome in Minette's bed; he had been away for more than a year. He began his campaign by coming in on Minette at Olivier's bedtime; she still would not permit the cradle to be taken from her room. While caressing the child, he could also stroke her shoulders and laugh companionably at Olivier's natural reluctance to sleep. She did not thrust him away, but neither did she respond and lay her head on his shoulder, as she used to do. Now Prosper caught Robideaux's alarm; this was like communing with a spirit, or trying to hold the husk of a woman. What life she had in her went to Olivier. The rest was nothing but a shadowed sadness that never left her eyes and mouth.

One night Prosper's patience snapped, and the result had him stomping and swearing through the house and out to the stables for a treacherous midnight ride over pitch-black paths. He took a tumble and bruised his wrist, came back covered with mud, and that ended the courting of his wife.

She hadn't wanted him, he thought angrily. He'd forced her. He had slipped the sleeping gown off her shoulders before she could protest, had nipped and nuzzled her breasts. At the same time, his hands were busy beneath her gown, attempting to stimulate her. *Mon Dieu*, the woman hadn't had sex in so long. Had that white flesh turned to marble? Finally there had been some response, but it seemed almost involuntary, from her body alone. She hadn't resisted—far better if she had, giving him some emotion to fan into passion. But emotion was absent. She'd simply acquiesced. She'd done her duty. And the moment he stopped his efforts, she was gone again.

He had hurt her, he knew. There would be bruises on that pale flesh tomorrow. But she wouldn't care because she hadn't been there in the bed with him. He'd been coupling with indifference. What he did no longer mattered.

Well, madame, two can dance to that tune. If the fire's gone out, why should I dally in the ashes?

But he was concerned for her effect on his son. Robideaux was again consulted and advised a change of climate.

"My dear Emile, this isn't France. We live in a wilderness. What do you suggest I do? Send her up north to Saint Louis with the Indians?"

"New Orleans is the only choice, Prosper."

"Are you suggesting that I send her to my mother? Then she will go mad completely."

"I have never said—"

"But you've been hinting, haven't you? Do something about your wife or Olivier will have a mother who has to be in an asylum."

"We have as yet no asylum in Louisiana."

"Unless you consider the whole colony such a place. But you throw the onus back on me, Emile. I am to send her away, yet where? And have her watched. By whom?"

"Prosper, I have a plan. Minette is not in harmony with the world around her. The more we press her, the more she retreats into some pain of her own."

"I take no blame for any of it. I have given her a luxurious life. She's had the finest of everything. You know what she came from."

"I'm only concerned with what happens to her now."

"And I am not? She's my son's mother."

"That brings me to the other essential. Olivier must go with her."

"Never!"

"He is the only thing she loves."

"He is the only thing *I* love, the meaning of my life! You suggest that I put him into exile with a woman who may be going mad?"

"You said *exile*, I did not. I had something much simpler in mind. Take her to New Orleans and—"

"Then we must visit my mother. She has not seen the baby yet."

"I must confess that surprised me, Prosper."

"She and Minette had words here. Mother refused to come to Sans Pareil without a proper apology."

"Well, she can't expect it now. I'm sure she won't insist, if you bring the baby to New Orleans."

"And then?"

"Prosper, your wife needs to be with her son, and only her son, if she is to heal. I propose that you leave her in New Orleans with him. There are some quite charming and comfortable cottages to rent, and if you send her with a carriage and a ménage of servants—"

"For how long?"

"Let me be the judge of that. I will continue to monitor her progress."

"And send me reports?"

"Of course."

"I don't like it, Robideaux."

"It is not the ideal solution. But the illnesses of the spirit do seem to respond to the absence of anxiety."

"Anxiety? Am I to assume that you mean me?"

The doctor looked at him expressively. Prosper, remembering the brutal taking of his wife, did, on reflection, see that a case could be made for temporary separation. But from his son, no.

"Doctor, you mentioned a healthy climate. New Orleans is pestilential."

"Not at this time of year. The winds of oncoming autumn have blown away the summer fevers. Prosper, I warn you. This is no time to temporize. If there's no improvement in her condition, you may well lose your wife. And then where will Olivier find what he needs? For a small child to lose his mother is the most profound tragedy. You may become the most important person in the world to him at a later stage of his life, but it's impossible now."

"It seems that I am the one who must suffer in this."

"Have you had so much experience of suffering?"

"Be careful how you speak to me, Emile."

"She did save your life, Prosper. You would have died at the hands of that crew at the Royal Hospital had she not found me. You were far gone."

"I did her a good turn later with de Pombiers."

"So you did. But was it not also a matter of consequence to you, Prosper? Didn't you also do it because you wanted Minette and carried her off into marriage before she had a chance to think?"

"To think of what? I offered her the world. All the other basket brides married lowly tradesmen."

"A pity there are not enough de la Fosse men to go around."

"Listen, *mon vieux*, I made a marriage that had no advantage to the family whatsoever."

"Ah, such virtue, such unselfishness."

Even Prosper was forced to laugh. And he was forced to agree with Dr. Robideaux. He made plans for Minette and Olivier to stay, for a time, in New Orleans.

15

After so long away, New Orleans burst on Minette like a revelation. After the great night silences of Sans Pareil, the noises of its city streets sang to her senses. In two years, the town had grown in a disorderly fashion. Flat-nosed, half-naked Choctaw, French allies now, were given a wide berth because they were usually drunk. In the coffeehouses frequented by the rich men who had come from Saint Dominique, the ex-planters regretted old times and sipped all day at their special island wines. The motley crowds shuffling through the muddy streets drank gin and rum, went to Mass on Sunday mornings and cockfights on Sunday afternoons, always on the move in search of amusement and pleasure. It was hard to believe in that other New Orleans of hardworking families in wooden tenements or simple cottages. They were there, they kept it running, but the general impression was of endless carnival, with the lord of misrule in charge. Anything was possible in this city of visible sin, and that message was slowly borne into Minette's mind, even as she struggled with problems she thought insoluble.

They stayed, only temporarily, with Amadée. His mother immediately did what Prosper had expected and organized an enormous tea reception to show Olivier to the family. He lay in Prosper's gilded christening cradle, as regal as the king at Versailles giving an audience, a good, quiet, handsome baby with clear blue eyes, occasionally reaching out toward some bauble or bit of lace on the visitors who leaned close to inspect him. He accepted the strangers without fear and won their hearts. The compliments flew to Amadée; how he favored her side of the family! Prosper's wife—something of a curiosity and much discussed—was also in evidence but obviously not well. She sat so silent and demure that the baby, with his high coloring and air of confidence, seemed to be much more Amadée's son than his proper mother's.

Minette was in a curious waking dream. There, in the softly carpeted room, with its many candles, the gleam of tea services, cakes, cookies, and sherbets set out on silver trays, her mind drifted away to the moonlit deck of a ship and the couples making love among whom she and Alain Gerard had stepped so carefully. The entwined amorous figures remained before her eyes when the rest of the scene faded, and she was mildly interested to see them dotting Amadée's draperies and heavy lace-embroidered linen cloths. What it meant she did not know. But they were more real to her than the insubstantial people who filled the room and spoke to her in voices that buzzed like summer flies. If only she could go upstairs and rest. She would, if not for Olivier. But how could she leave him here?

Prosper had noted the signs of detachment, the eyes

that stared, as Dr. Robideaux had warned him, at no fixed point. He was more and more concerned. He'd formed the notion that Minette was playacting, perhaps in revenge for his brutal possession of her, and he'd counted on their return to civilization to bring her to her senses. It hadn't. She was as pliable as a jointed doll and every bit as lifeless. Even now, his mother was signaling him to remove her from the sight of their guests.

Minette protested a little, but Prosper kept reassuring her that Olivier would be brought to her soon, very soon, and with a gentle supporting hand beneath her elbow, he made a smooth exit from the salon and guided her upstairs.

He turned down the spread on the large walnut bed—the first time he had ever done such a thing in his life—and removed her gray velvet slippers.

"Ti Manou will bring you a warm drink, and you must rest."

"Olivier?" the voice was faint.

"Haven't I promised? When you wake, he will be here."

"What do we do tomorrow?"

"We go to Father Peyzac, and there is the small ceremony of Olivier's other names. He will be Olivier la Tour Milhet Garimond Chandeleur Lossage de la Fosse."

There was a phantom giggle. "Poor little baby. Such a heavy burden to bear."

"It is his heritage, after all. When he is aware of it, he will be proud of the connections."

Minette sighed and lost interest in the conversation. She lay at rest, but her eyes were open in that damnable stare, and Prosper left the room quickly. On the stairs, he met Ti Manou carrying a small silver teapot and porcelain cup and saucer.

"What witches' brew is that?"

"Only a *tisane*, an herbal tea. Perfectly harmless."

"I'll hold you accountable if it isn't." He pushed past her, going down to the family.

In consultation, Prosper told Amadée of Dr. Robideaux's advice.

She was at first adamant that Minette should not be trusted with Olivier. After all, the child had an adoring grandmother and aunts who would be delighted to supervise him. Prosper explained that the seclusion of Minette with the baby was part of the cure. "Cure!" Amadée was contemptuous. "She's the luckiest girl in the world and too stupid to appreciate it."

"Nevertheless, I've decided that we shall follow the doctor's regime."

"You've decided for *my* grandson? Suppose she hurts him?"

"She will not hurt him. And I am giving her Lisette and Lutie, with Bella to cook and Dominic to drive her."

"That is hardly secluded."

"What do you mean? They are servants. She need not speak to them. But she will be watched. Robideaux will visit and report any progress."

"I say get rid of her. She has turned out badly. I warned you but you never listen to me. You can always marry again, but can you be sure of getting a son like Olivier? Take him from her, I tell you."

Prosper wore his stubborn look. "Not yet."

"I don't understand that."

"You do not need to, for the moment. I will engage a cottage for her, but I don't think I'll tell you where."

"In a city of this size, I could find her in hours."

"I ask you not to. I want you to promise me to leave

her alone, and not to set your black cat on her, either."

"You refer to Ti Manou?"

"Promise me. Swear, on your honor."

Reluctantly, she did.

True to his word, Prosper found a very pleasant house, furnished, not large but commodious enough, with a small private garden shaded by crepe myrtle trees. The neighborhood was not far from the Place d'Armes and lively enough to banish memories of the awesome solitude of Sans Pareil.

But he did not set Minette down with her household and leave; he lingered for a few days, marking the rooms with his presence: his boots, his reading spectacles, the scent of his tobacco, turned-down pages of the books he wanted Minette to read in the long evenings without him. A male animal marking out his territory, he managed to impress the servants with the extent of their responsibility for Minette and Olivier.

Prosper's misgivings were instinctive; he disapproved of Dr. Robideaux's reasoning but had nothing to substitute for it. As she was, Minette was useless to him now. Yet she was still nursing Olivier, a supremely important factor. Of course, they must not be separated. In these early months, whatever her own mental troubles, she and she alone could give Olivier his health. And as suddenly as this malaise had come upon Minette, it could lift. She might well improve.

At times, however, he wondered uneasily who would emerge in her recovery. She was now a complete stranger to him, her mind as closed to his understanding as if he'd never lain with her or celebrated the little daily rituals of marriage. Sweet biddable lamb no more! Someone else looked out of those startlingly blue eyes.

When he finally made up his mind to do so, he left

quickly, with a kiss for the sleeping Olivier. He did not wish to kiss his wife, for he thought that she looked at him with little recognition and much indifference.

He was correct. Prosper gone? Minette took vague notice. Her days were filled with people bustling around for her comfort, and it was enough to find the energy to answer them when they spoke to her. At first the effort to do that simple thing exhausted her completely, but the concern in their eyes finally reached her consciousness, and she tried to respond. How heavy her head was, how slow-moving her hands! She seemed timed to the ticking of the clock, each heavy, penetrating minute adding to a long, pointless existence.

Olivier was brought to her often during the day, and those were the best times. When he nursed she came alive, the pressure of his mouth brought a tingling awareness into her body. The grasp of his tiny fingers on hers was like a message from the world. The milk appeared without effort, and his vigorous sucking was a phenomenon she watched with amazement. How can it be that my body continues to supply this wonderful substance when I can feel nothing, when I lie here waiting for the baby's next visit as if I were floating above my inert self?

At first, days passed without time, then gradually she became conscious of hours again. The morning sun took on a special meaning. The heavy spray of flowering vines climbing the wall outside her window was something to be appreciated instead of a pink blur before her indifferent eyes. Objects around her grew harder and brighter, each with its corona of morning sunlight. A consciousness of textures returned; the rich grain of the mahogany table invited stroking, the cool roundness of her water carafe was a pleasure to hold. Colors returned to her drained shadow world. Blue came back to vibrate in its richness, then rose and gold. Dr. Robideaux, on his twice-weekly visits, appeared in full color to her now. She tested the scent of his tobacco on her memory; it brought back other recollections. She no longer watched the motion of his jaw without listening to the words as he spoke; now she tried to answer his questions, and he waited patiently for her slow replies.

"What has happened to me, Doctor?" she asked one day when curiosity about herself had gradually returned.

"I have no name for it," he answered. "Let us simply say that you left us for a while, went elsewhere."

"Am I recovered?"

"You are recovering. I would like to see you spend the cool part of the day in the garden, Minette."

"That would be pleasant."

"Pleasant? That word occurs to you? If so, it's good news indeed for Prosper."

"Oh, yes, Prosper." With an effort, she interested herself in Prosper. "How is he?"

"I am in correspondence with him. He misses his wife and child. Would you like to see him?"

She shook her head. There was some reason she did not want to see her husband; perhaps someday it would reveal itself to her.

"Can you ask him not to come, Doctor?"

"Yes. Actually, it would be a hardship for him to leave Sans Pareil just now. He is very busy."

"I am glad that he is busy."

"But I will tell him that the treatment is succeeding. You improve, and Olivier is flourishing."

"Doctor, may I ask you something? Olivier often cries nowadays after he nurses, and no more milk comes to quiet him."

"It's time to try him on other food, my dear. He is a large baby and well developed physically beyond his age. He begins to need more than you can give him."

"But I don't want to stop nursing."

"It will stop of its own accord. There are many soft foods to add to Olivier's diet, little by little. I will speak to your cook."

"But then he won't need me."

"Not need his mother?" Dr. Robideaux was smiling broadly. "That day will never come. Ah, you do care, Minette! You are interested once more."

"Are you going to tell Prosper that?"

"Don't you want me to do so?"

She sighed. "Tell him that Olivier is progressing. It's true, isn't it?"

"Absolutely true. I've rarely seen a healthier baby."

"Oh, yes, tell him that!"

"And what shall I say about you?"

"You can mention that I am sitting in the garden."

First came the sunlight and then, gradually, a little occupation with lace-making, an old skill from convent days, and one day a newspaper was put before her. That was a jolt; the world crowded in, pressing almost physically on her temples, and she flung away the news and ran indoors complaining of a headache. From that day on, she began to dream again, crowded, nightmarish dreams. In the morning Olivier's many new sounds and expressions would divert her and help drive back the memory of those dreams.

She began to be possessed by a dreadful sense of urgency. It lay behind her calm face and tormented her with its senselessness. What? What? She acquired the habit of drumming nervously with her fingertips—Dr. Robideaux frowned nowadays when he took her pulse but prescribed nothing—and she lashed out in impatience at the servants. If I am coming back to life, why is it so painful? she asked herself. Why are my nerves afire?

More weeks of increasing impatience. She'd grown in size, like a giant, she told herself. The cottage was suddenly too small for her. She overflowed its rooms, burst its doors. She knew that she'd made the servants afraid of her, even little Lutie. Yet she could not stop; restlessness drove her along, wanting, wanting. Even Olivier, no longer nursing but still the center of her world, was not enough.

The truth came one morning with such clarity and simplicity that she at last understood how ill she had been. Her body was calling her back to life as a woman. And she did not want Prosper, her husband. She wanted Alain Gerard.

Lisette, carrying up a breakfast tray, heard unaccustomed sounds of movement in the bedroom. Someone was dragging furniture around. Frightened, she hurried in without knocking, to find Minette rummaging through the armoire, having moved the heavy chair to reach the hatboxes stacked on top of it. The room was in disarray. Her usually neat and meticulous mistress had overturned almost every drawer and jewelry box.

"Breakfast?" she quavered.

"Yes, yes, I am hungry. Where is Olivier? Has he eaten?"

"Not yet, Madame."

"Bring him in. We shall breakfast together. No, no, I'll feed him. But afterward, I will want the hip bath. Hot water, towels. Heat the iron. Heat my hair-curling irons, too. Go!"

After the bath and a vigorous toweling, Minette

chose a dress she had never worn before. It was in the newly fashionable dove-gray tone, pannier-skirted and finished with a double row of white ruching for a collar. An hour after that, the transformation was complete. There stood a golden beauty in the cool, pearly color, her hair under a straw *chapeau*, gloved and shod in gray velvet, with more white ruching and lace to be seen trailing from inside each wide sleeve of her gown. Her parasol was white, her earrings, pearls set in slender gold pendants that danced with the toss of her head. Olivier made an immediate grab for the ear bobs. He clearly approved of them and the trailing lace sleeves; the whole new look of his mother produced a contented humming noise of seeming appreciation.

But where was Madame going in such glory? "Out" was the only response. "Have Dominic bring the carriage around for me." Minette was perfectly pleasant and perfectly adamant about going alone, leaving Lutie and Lisette with the baby.

It was only the first of many such drives, and Dominic swore that she never stopped, but they circled and recircled the city streets while she scanned the faces of the passersby. And that was all? All! Whomever she sought, she did not find, but she searched with great determination each day, avoiding only the part of town where Amadée de la Fosse's house was located. They began and ended at the Place d'Armes and timed their excursions, Dominic noticed, to the drill periods of the soldiers stationed in the barracks. And, yes, they attracted great attention. She did not seem to care.

"A man," said Lisette mournfully in the kitchen at night. "Madame is looking for a lover."

"How can she have a lover?" Dominic demanded. "She has been at Sans Pareil all this time."

"Then it is someone from the past, from before her marriage to M'sieu Prosper." They both turned to Lutie, who'd almost sidled to the door before Lisette cut off her escape. "Has she said anything to you, child?"

Lutie's face closed sullenly. "Nothing. I swear, nothing. But even if she had, I wouldn't tell you."

Lisette's slap caught her on the side of the head. "Wake up, dreamer! This is your life we're talking about, and ours. Do you want to be found floating in the river, have some fisherman cast a hook right through your squishy body? He'd do it—don't think he wouldn't."

Lutie's "Who?" was tearful.

"Who? M'sieu Prosper, that's who. Oh, I could tell you stories about things that happened at Sans Pareil, and for much less reason than this. If she finds the man she's looking for, we're gone."

"Poor Madame Minette. She has no happiness."

"Lutie! She has her baby."

"Is that enough?"

"It will have to be. She's not the first white woman who married rich and found disappointment. But the man she married will have no mercy on us if she manages to put the horns on him. We must stop it."

"How?"

That was a question they couldn't answer.

One night Dominic came home with disturbing news. "A man got into her carriage today."

Lisette dropped the pot she was cleaning, and they were still as mice in case the noise should bring Minette. But there was only silence from the bedroom.

"What kind of man, Dominic?"

"Not her kind, not possibly. A funny little fellow

with thick mustaches that turn up at the ends. He must use good wax to—"

"Dominic!"

"They talked for a long time, but I could not follow his French. He's not from here but back there in the old country. So, at any rate, this soldier—"

"A soldier! *Mon Dieu!* Did they seem friendly?"

"I am afraid so. They knew each other from before."

"What did I tell you?"

"And she gave him a note."

"Why didn't you do something?"

"What could I have done?"

"How do I know? Why didn't you run him down with the coach, and while you were helping him up, steal the note?" said Lisette.

"Woman, you are only making noises. You sound like M'sieu Carencro, the buzzard. 'Squawk, squawk, run down a white man and steal his note.' You'll have me killed even before M'sieu Prosper does it."

"This is the nicest mistress I have ever had, but I won't die for her."

"What will you tell M'sieu Prosper? That his wife gave an ugly little soldier a note? And be whipped for angering him? I assure you, Lisette, that's the best that can happen to you then!"

They decided to wait and redouble their watch on Minette. After all, where could she go without the coach and Dominic? How could she contact the mysterious man she sought?

In her room, Minette lay very still. She could sense the agitation in the servants' voices but not make out the subject of the conversation. She was filled with the most extraordinary optimism. Cernaux had said—and how unimaginably lucky to find him—that Alain was upriver at Point Coupée, on one of those mysterious assignments of his. He would be back within the week. But here was the real news: He had been offered a transfer to France and refused it.

Why does a young man refuse a plum posting in Paris? Perhaps because he waits for someone. His eyes had said *Forever* that day at Sans Pareil. He stands fast; he is faithful. And here I am. Nothing else matters except that we come together. I won't be stopped this time. Minette's sickness had been an expression of the clash between her mind and her body, the beliefs she'd been taught and the reality of her longing. But she and Alain were outside society rules; he'd come back to her from the dead. Surely God was granting her a second chance to love—dare she *not* take it? Wasn't it a kind of miracle? So she reasoned. As for Prosper and the others . . . ah, *tant pis!* She summoned up her old standby with a cool recklessness that amazed her. I don't care, I must have him, she thought. We must have each other. There is nothing else that matters in the world. It was time to love.

16

On foot, Minette approached the house. It had been a long, circuitous journey, first in the cart, then riding pillion on a horse with Cernaux, a hooded cape disguising her face. She had not been followed; they'd waited to be sure of that. And now the house of her happiness stood before her. It was most ordinary, even poor, a typical construction of dried mud and bricks. Square-built, it stood high on wooden posts and had a wraparound porch. But the shutters were in disrepair, the thatched roof ill kept, and the tiny garden neglected. No one loved this house anymore.

I will love you, Minette promised. *Only keep my secret.*

Cernaux had rented it. He had done everything to avoid throwing suspicion on Alain. All the long way out from New Orleans, he had itemized his disapproval of the chances they were taking, but the words had blown past Minette like puffs of wind. He might justify his part in this as he wished, but only when he said that he'd had no other choice, that he could stand no more of

Alain's silent suffering, did Minette leap into listening life. Good Cernaux, can't you urge this horse on? I cannot wait!

Now that she stood with her hand on the door of the house, she held back. When you step over that threshold, Minette, you are committing . . . She sighed in distress and confusion.

Suddenly Alain opened the door from within. He stood so very tall, and the poet's face she had seemingly dreamed into life was subtly changed, handsome but harder. Yet she saw in his eyes the same life, the same wild happiness, that she felt.

When he murmured her name, she went into his arms, burrowing deep against him, finding a place where his shirt buttons parted and placing her lips against his burning skin. Then she was lifted—so lightly—and carried into a room where the floor was covered with flowers.

He'd bought everything in bloom, emptied the flower stalls to make a carpet of delicious fragrance for the floor of the bare room. They were down on it in a moment, unable to wait, fumbling at each other's clothes—ties, hooks, buttons, all undone with hasty, trembling fingers. His uniform jacket made a pillow for her head, and she lay down among the flowers to receive him. Their mouths met delicately, then fiercely—lips, tongues, teeth—her face devoured with soft kisses, her eyelids caressed, her throat explored. The healthy scent of his hair was more delightful than the flowers as he nibbled at her skin, lipped her shoulder bones and teased his way down to her breasts. The aching in her nipples exploded into pure, throbbing joy under his touch, and her body arched involuntarily beneath him. They were frantic to lose themselves in each other. His arms were a vise; her legs sought purchase in the muscles of his back. She could not be close enough, could not answer the rhythm of his strokes inside her as savagely as she desired, or she'd burst through his body. Again, again, each thrust building a pure and primitive happiness she had never felt before. The moaning in her ears was her own, as soft and steady as a faraway wind. The rise and fall of her body, exquisitely timed with his, was as natural as the motion of waves at sea, and when the big wave crested over, she fell down and down into welcoming fathoms, into the warm, lapping blackness of complete release.

Years of deprivation, of hunger, of soul-deep loneliness fell away in Alain's embrace. Though in terms of time and familiarity this soldier was a stranger to her, this stranger was her home, the home she had never had. And when their breathing finally slowed and the world stopped spinning in her head, she marveled at this second miracle in her life. Olivier was the first. Alain was the second, a lasting, passionate love born of a long-held girlish dream and a fleeting shipboard flirtation, yet weathering time and trouble to culminate in such perfection.

Minette knew that no other man would fill her as perfectly as Alain had done. If he did not know the little goads Prosper had learned in bordellos, he did not need more than he had, because the moment he touched her she was so hot with desire, so eager to touch his skin, bury her face in him, breathe in the maleness of his body, that there was no need to stimulate a response. They might build desire slowly in days to come, but not now, not till this years-long thirst was temporarily slaked and the frenzy of finally meeting had given way to gentle surfeit of tangled legs, linked hands, and easier breathing.

"It will be years before we can lie peaceably together," said Alain, as if reading her thoughts. "But have I hurt you, my darling?"

"Sweet wounds to be healed by your returning touch."

"Is this my modest little angel?"

"Once, yes. Not now."

"Now you're a whirlwind."

"Ride the whirlwind, then." She stretched out her arms in invitation, then paused. "Alain, you know I married only because they told me you were dead."

"Cernaux has never stopped apologizing. But he believed it. And, in a way, I was dead to the world of men. My body was kind enough to keep me alive, but my mind was benumbed by the shock of collision with another man's sword. I lay in a sort of unnatural sleep for months, I'm told, and then awoke to pain. But the pain, at least, was consciousness."

"Who tended you during this long sleep?"

"A woman of Saint Dominique."

A disagreeable emotion invaded her. "Was she very beautiful?"

"She was old and wrinkled, with ten children, but she was beautiful to me when I opened my eyes at last."

"Yet you are not scarred."

"Credit her healing with that. I've come to think a good deal more of old women than I did. They have a special magic. So when this stream of gold is silver"—his hands touched her hair—"I will love you more deeply still."

"What happened to you then, Alain?"

"After I realized that the troops had left without me, thought me dead, I stayed, recovering, in Saint Dominique for many months. What a beautiful land,

and how unhappy its future will be! The white planters cannot hold on, and they deserve to lose. They were unbelievably cruel to their slaves, until even those demoralized people found the strength to fight back. Futile efforts until now, but something is building there like the pressure in nature's volcanoes. Those shining white beaches will redden with blood. Were it not for what I feel will happen there, I'd return with you to its sea winds and its paradise of fruit and flowers."

"I married a planter from Saint Dominique."

"Yes, de la Fosse. I wanted to kill him that afternoon at Sans Pareil when I saw you standing there, blooming with new life."

"Huge with pregnancy," said Minette.

"Incomparable, like a harvest goddess. And his."

"If I am his, why do you think I am here with you? Why do you think I have dared all?"

"Because God heard my prayers."

"Did you pray often?"

"Enough to satisfy all the nuns in your convent." He arched back to look at her. "My darling, I remember such a shy little convent kitten. Whatever became of her?"

"Do you want her back?"

He groaned with delight and seized her in a mighty hug. "Can I hope that you will come away with me?"

"Oh, Alain, it is not so easy. You have forgotten my son. I cannot leave—"

"Why can't we be a family together?" Alain broke in. "I will love Olivier!"

She smiled. "I like the sound of his name on your lips."

"You have not answered my question, sweet."

"Because I cannot."

"Is it because I am a soldier? My term of enlistment

is up. I serve only in a special capacity that I will explain to you someday. But I am free and only remained in New Orleans because you bade me wait."

"I could not imagine that."

"Why? I'd have waited forever. But now we can leave."

"Without my son?"

"No! I can offer the boy a good life."

"It's impossible. Prosper would never let him go. Olivier is his sole heir, his greatest pride, the mirror of himself."

Alain got to his feet, striding the room, forcing his mind to clarity. "You can't leave your son. I can't ask that. But what of us?"

"Must we know all the answers now? We've just found each other."

"Minette!" He was down beside her again. "I can't lose you again. You aren't saying that this is the only time we'll have together?"

"No, my darling, I haven't the strength for that."

"Thank God, or I would think I'd been brought back to life for nothing."

"Never say that, Alain."

"Then I am paying for my sins, because I am in limbo."

"Can't you accept this arrangement for now?"

"Will there be an end to it one day? And I mean a happy ending, which does not include your husband. I hate the thought of you and Prosper together!"

"We no longer have . . . conjugal relations," she said, suddenly shy. "Prosper's interest lessened with Olivier's birth. But that alone would never have brought me here." Alain's mouth was busy against her throat again.

"Give me time," she whispered. "I cannot think of what to do, especially with you near me."

"Don't think, then. How much time have we left?"

"Only an hour before Cernaux returns."

"Let's make it glorious. Ah, Minette, I don't intend to throw away happiness. But how shall I exist until we meet again?"

She closed her eyes.

"You shall have all that I can give you, Alain! Can that content you for now?"

This time their lovemaking had a tender, reflective quality, a sweeter, deeper idyll as they guarded their paradise, desperately determined not to lose each other again.

Minette arose with crushed flowers in her hair to make herself presentable for Cernaux on the homeward journey. Alain was memorizing her even as he watched; she could see him concentrate on how her hands moved to pin up her hair, how she smoothed her face free of errant petals. He'd carry the image until they met again, as she would cherish her last sight of him, his fingers raised to his lips in a light, farewell salute.

Suspended in time, they stole happiness from a questionable future, meeting as often as could be arranged, hoarding their love against the time of deprivation when Prosper would return to judge the success or failure of his wife's cure. Dr. Robideaux was delighted with her progress. Who knew what encouragement he might be writing to her husband?

Alain's anxiety grew with each parting; he often wanted to shake a promise out of her. His wrenching fear of losing her even drove him to dark thoughts of challenging Prosper. God knows he wanted to kill that dangerous, dandified fool! But he knew that Minette could never countenance the purchase of their long delayed happiness at the price of someone's life. She was already guilty enough over giving in to her emotions and yielding to the demands of her heart and body. He could not rush her and though he loathed passive inaction, he could do nothing to endanger their fragile happiness further.

When the end to their sweet time together came, it was from an unexpected direction. Prosper had not returned to New Orleans, and Minette's bewildered trio of servants had not solved the mystery of their mistress's sudden, unquenchable happiness. The agent of destruction was One-Ear Sen, the peddler who had heard Minette singing in the prison of the chevalier de Pombier's house.

This man made his living by theft as well as legitimate trade. He was not a skillful thief: forays in the wrong locations had earned him that cropped and branded ear. But he had a nose for unprotected places, and this house on a dusty road had a neglected, promising look. If nothing else, he might steal some seasoned wood to patch his own hovel.

Sen was thoroughly startled, as he crept onto the porch, to hear noises within, gasps and sighs of pleasure, the music of lovemaking. The shutters were closed, but he found a hinge eaten away by rust and was able to peek noiselessly inside.

He was stunned to see the white woman he had found for Mambo Ti Manou. What a great harlot she must be—first with the old man, and now with this young, strong one. See them go, wrapped around each other like snakes! Sen's wrinkled member stirred in recalled desire. His breath came short and fast, and he knelt uncomfortably at the window so he could give a complete account of everything to Ti Manou, who would surely want to hear of this. Oh, a very complete account. On the way to see her, he was still so stirred in all his parts that he hoped she'd give him enough money to buy a whore.

Ti Manou cut into his sloppy-mouthed account and handed him money for the information.

"Do you want me to keep watch on them?" he said eagerly. "I could keep close to that house until they come back."

"Why should I pay you to enjoy yourself?" she answered disdainfully. "Once is enough. Are you sure of everything you've told me?"

"Shall I tell you again, from the beginning?"

She sent him quickly on his way.

The problem now for Ti Manou was what, precisely, to do. She must tell Amadée that the trouble in the marriage she had long ago foreseen had come to fruition. But she must not let Amadée interfere in the workings of the Great Mother, the goddess Erzulie. Perhaps Erzulie would want Prosper and the soldier to clash. Perhaps she even wanted Prosper's death. He had always been incipiently evil, a man of great charm but dissolute, and before that a sinister, destructive child who had tormented small animals.

Well, she would simply set the matter in motion. She would present Amadée with the evidence of her, Ti Manou's, powers and suggest she send a messenger up the river to Sans Pareil, with the hope that Prosper would not harm the bearer of such humiliating news. After all, Prosper was a true de la Fosse, and they were all, ultimately, more than a little mad.

That night the servants in Amadée's mansion heard her hysterical laughter, and in the morning one of them had been posted on a very important errand.

Each time she met Alain, Minette prepared for hours; her reward was the slow, glorious, welcoming smile with which he greeted her. Under her cloaked disguise, she wore the finest dresses in her wardrobe. They didn't stay on her long, but they gave such pleasure. Today it was a new fashion, a dress stretched over metal panniers that presented a narrow silhouette from the side but, from the front, an outrageous width of golden apricot taffeta. She had to sidestep through the narrow door and pirouetted for his admiration before he remarked that fashion was folly for lovers.

"I would love you in a palm leaf skirt," he assured her. "And I'd love you a damn sight sooner." The metal panniers were an unbelievable nuisance in his eager hands, and she was just free of them and standing in her petticoats when they heard a scraping noise on the porch outside.

Alain at once picked up his sword and edged toward the door. When he flung it open, he caught a glimpse of dun-shirted One-Ear Sen running away. The old voyeur, usually so stealthy, had gotten careless in his anticipation and excitement.

Minette heard the frightened hammering of her heart as Alain said, "It was only an old man, I think, and poorly dressed. A peddler, a vagrant who picks up trash and sells it. We have nothing to worry about."

"But he was watching us! Perhaps he has watched us from the beginning!"

He caught her in his arms, holding her secure against his chest. "Don't distress yourself, my darling. We'll find another place to meet. Even though a prowling old tomcat like that means nothing."

"Was anyone with him?"

"No."

"Still, I hate the idea of his watching." She shivered, pressing closer.

"He doesn't know who we are, Minette."

"Still, it may mean . . ." She stopped speaking, unwilling to finish the thought.

Alain felt her unspoken fright and despair. But perhaps the best and only way to end this impasse, this trap they were in, was to be somehow found out. The separations were unbearable. He was more than ready to take on de la Fosse the duelist, and the matter of Olivier could be settled if he was lucky in combat. Oh, for a clean solution and an end to this ignoble hiding in corners like scrabbling rats. Minette had never truly belonged to de la Fosse anyway. She had always been his, as he was hers, in this world and the next. Even if there was to be retribution for their sin, he welcomed it. He wanted to fight for them, and his every instinct told him that he would win.

He tried to impart his confidence to Minette, but they did not make love again. He pulled her down gently and held her like a child, fingers twining idly in her hair while they waited for Cernaux. She pressed against him, shuddering occasionally, but accepting the comfort he offered.

For Minette, the way home seemed full of menace. A chilly breeze presaged New Orleans's surprisingly cold and damp winter weather. While no leaves whirled in the wind's gusts, the trees looked gray and dispirited, the riverfront streets of the city ever more of a quagmire, the houses dull and scabrous with the sun gone. Such apprehension seized her that she left Cernaux and his cart even before their usual cautious point of departure and stumbled home alone.

No smoke came from the kitchen chimney, no candlelight winked through the chinks of the shutters. There was no one to welcome her. She struggled with the front door, then ran in, calling the name at the heart of her fear. "Olivier!" No voices answered, not Lutie's, not Lisette's.

Minette ran up the stairs, blundering along the familiar hall in the gathering dark, and into her room. Only a stuffed toy, a ridiculous rabbit, lay where Olivier's cradle had been, but its belly had been slashed and the stuffing had spread on the carpet.

Then she saw the note, written with tremendous force in Prosper's heavy, slanted script. His angry pen had blotched the paper, its pressure had torn a hole in it.

> *To the Queen of Liars: No, I will not kill you, though you richly deserve it. What you do not deserve is to be Olivier's mother, and I am taking him from you. I have no further interest in your fate. Do what you will, live in sin with your lover, beg in the street. Do not come to Sans Pareil to plead with me for mercy; you have forfeited all rights as wife and mother. Olivier is your son no longer. I shall see that he never remembers you. As for the foolish blacks who helped you betray me, don't look to them either. They've been sold as field hands. At your peril, let this be the last communication between us.*
>
> *Prosper de la Fosse*

Olivier! And Lutie, Lisette, Dominic. All her fault. *Bon Dieu!* Where could she turn? Alain would be gone from their cottage. She had no one in this moment of terror but her conscience, and it began to speak to her remorselessly.

17

"The way is finally clear for us, Minette. Make Prosper give you a divorce."

"How, Alain?"

"Darling, we have nothing to lose now, but he does: the respectability of his family name. If he does not agree to grant you your freedom, we can make him look ridiculous by making our situation public. I don't think he'd care for that."

She drew in her breath sharply. She was not sure *she* would care for a brazen display of her adultery either. Maintaining at least the fiction of her own respectability might be crucial to seeing Olivier again.

"Ah, Minette," Alain said, reading her thoughts as ever. "You know we are both damned already by the Church for our sin. We're both cast out. You faced that when you came to me and faced it bravely. Society can make little difference now."

"I would have died without you, Alain. I had to come."

"Then why can't we be happy together?"

"Olivier. I cannot let him go without a fight. Prosper will not give him to me, and the law is on his side."

"What's your answer, then? To cast me away as well?"

"Only for now, only for appearances. I am hoping to make an ally of time. Prosper fully expects me to go away with you, and when he sees that I do not, I am in a stronger position to at least demand that I see Olivier from time to time."

"And break your heart with every visit, Minette."

"But he will know that I am his mother. Prosper intends to cut me out of Olivier's life entirely. I can't let him do that." The tears were very close now.

"Let's take this plan further. If Prosper thinks that we are no longer lovers, then you hope—it's but a hope—that you will be allowed to see Olivier?"

"He has less reason to refuse me. Even the law tells me that."

"So you will be satisfied with occasional visits to your son and live on those?"

"I don't know! But things must change over time. At least the tie to my son is not severed."

"But at our expense, Minette. You're cutting *us* apart."

Now she collapsed in tears. He held her gently, ashamed to be burdening his love at a time when her heart cried out for her child. But it was a necessary cruelty. He was fighting for their future. The present was already lost. Yet for all their passionate love, he knew that she had already decided on her course of action, and all that was left him was to try to forget her, which was impossible, or to go along with this vague plan, which put them both in limbo.

She spoke in a faint voice. "Once, I waited for you on faith alone, Alain. Had I not heard of your death, I would have waited forever."

"And that's what you require from me now?"

"Alain! Don't you see there is no other way? I haven't the means to fight Prosper for my son. So I must try to placate him instead." She saw the sadness in his eyes. "Please forgive me. It's just the way things are."

"I have some money, Minette. It's not the wealth of the de la Fosse treasury, but it exists. It was meant for the three of us to live as a family. No, don't cry again. The money is yours to use."

"I cannot let you do that."

"You cannot refuse me. If you dare, I will know that you mean to cut me out of your life. If this is your way of telling me good-bye, let me hear it from your lips. I will find some way to bear it. But don't soften the news and increase my suffering. Minette, will you let me help you? Is it to be yes or no?"

"If I take your money, what will you do?"

"I will make it easier for your damnable conscience and go away."

"Alain!"

"Did you expect me to stay in New Orleans and not try to see you? If separation is our bargain, I will honor it, but I can only do that if I remove myself from my darling temptation."

"Where will you go? For how long?"

"Are you sure you want to know?"

"*Bon Dieu*, don't do this to me! Please, Alain. I must imagine you to be someplace."

"There is a matter that has been offered to me, Minette. I refused the offer because it would take me beyond the borders of La Louisiane, and you were here.

Fortunately, no one has been fool enough to take it on since I said no. It's mine if I want it. But I will not be able to communicate with you; expect no letters."

"What is this mission?

"Espionage."

"The danger," she whispered. "*Bon Dieu*, the danger!"

"It's not the first time for me, Minette. You see before you an accomplished spy. I've lived by my wits for a long time. And such work is well paid."

"But if you're caught?"

"The usual odds: prison or the gallows."

"I will be afraid the whole time you are gone!"

"Then perhaps your fear will advance your plan of action, if you think of me and tremble and wonder. When we are married, I shall take up some honest trade."

"When we are married ..." Her voice was dreamy.

"Minette," he said desperately, "are you sure this is what you want? I can't forget that your husband practically gave you permission to live with me."

"That was a trap to make it impossible for me ever to get my son."

"Ah, Olivier," he said sadly.

She searched his face. "Don't ever resent him, Alain, or fear he stands between us. You are both in my heart. But don't ask me to make a choice now. I can't."

"I have no choice, either." He smiled without much happiness. "I love you. Body and soul." He held her against him lightly, smoothing her hair.

"Then we must both find courage."

"We already have that, or how could we be here? Luck is what's needed, my darling. *La fortune*. Are you lucky?"

"How can you ask me that question when I'm in your arms?"

"My God, I can't let you go!" But he did, stepping back to a safe distance, as if it could protect him against temptation. "I will make immediate arrangements about the money," he said. "But where will you live?"

"My friend Berenice Robillas will help me, I'm sure of it. I will ask to stay with her. I can pay my way there and be useful as well."

The house of Berenice and Arnaud Robillas, a kind and devoutly practical pair, had seven rooms. Seven rooms sounded quite grand, but the first two were Arnaud's workshop and warehouse, filled with the canvas, rope, and tackle from which he made his living as a sail fitter. The kitchen was in a free-standing shed behind the house, and that left one central room for eating, family activities, and occasional service as a parlor for guests. Up the short flight of rough wooden stairs were the three bedrooms, one for the parents, one for the two young children, Vincent and Cecile, and one for all the accumulated clutter of living. Minette moved in there, displacing the pots, tubs, baskets, flatirons, chests of clothes, and bunches of dried herbs awaiting transfer to the kitchen.

Where did Berenice manage to store these things now? Minette joked that she buried them in the scrap of garden beside the house.

"Dig?" said Berenice. "We'd drown."

It was true that water waited only a few feet down. Even the garden path from the wooden gate to the front door was not pebbled but covered with a fill of crushed oyster shells that crunched underfoot. They were always reminded that theirs was a city practically afloat.

Berenice was a superb household manager. As warmer weather approached, she took down the heavy winter curtains to replace them with yards of cheap, cool, unbleached muslin. She reintroduced her old friend Minette to a world of economies; no more *sabayon* dessert with sugar, eggs and wine, no more pâté or brioche. Those belonged on the de la Fosse table. Here it was red beans and rice with a hambone for flavor, hot gumbo soup with filé powder, stews that stretched scraps into a main dish. Good fresh bread was available. A man who owned a cow provided milk for the children, and from any leavings Berenice made cheese. She hunted the markets for end-of-the-day bargains and bought fabric for clothes from the street peddlers who cried their wares from wagons. Buying secondhand, she fed and clothed her growing family with the aplomb of a general. Berenice was losing her rosy freshness through hard work, but she didn't seem to care. And neither, apparently, did Arnaud. As Minette could tell through the home's thin walls, they took their pleasure nightly in the knotted-rope bed and wondered how many children *le bon Dieu* would see fit to send *chez* Robillas.

The family's contentment touched Minette. How simple and lovely life could be! But after a year, she was no closer to a solution to her own problem, and she was growing desperate. The timid representations made by her lawyer, Monsieur Grandin, to Prosper had produced no results, even as the precious supply of Alain's money dwindled on his services, and he had no more hope to offer her. One morning Minette sat bolt upright in bed after a bad dream and decided to take action. She must go upriver herself and confront Prosper at Sans Pareil. He could hardly set the dogs on her in Olivier's sight. She would surprise him.

The fates set out to make her plan more difficult. The Atakapa Indian tribe to the west of New Orleans went on the warpath to avenge some insult by the French. Rumor had it that these Indians were still cannibals. Soldiers were sent in to subdue them, and regular boat service upriver was discontinued. It was too dangerous to make the run until the army said otherwise.

"This is the perfect time to go!" Minette exclaimed. "If I went on a scheduled boat, Prosper would be more likely to find out I was coming."

"So he would, but you'd be alive," Berenice and Arnaud told her. "Who can guarantee your safety now?"

But Minette was possessed of a wild impatience; something within her insisted that now was the time to go. Olivier would certainly be a toddler by now, and perhaps he even knew a few words. She must make sure that *Maman* was one of them.

"We won't be responsible for your death," Arnaud protested. But she kept at him, and in the end he found a way to put her daring plan into action. The solution involved a riverfront acquaintance of his, a self-proclaimed *voyageur* who hunted fur-bearing animals in the swamps. Louis LeGros was dirty and hard-drinking with scarce cash and expensive habits. He was told that if he took Minette upriver to Sans Pareil in his canoe, he would be paid only on her safe return to New Orleans.

"That way I may save her life," Arnaud told Berenice. "LeGros is one who would push her out of his canoe and claim an accidental drowning. But I've told him she must be alive and in good health if he wants to collect his money."

"He has his revenge on you for that," Berenice answered. "Look at the fantastic sum he is charging Minette."

"LeGros knows that she must be desperate if she even considers this trip now. Unfortunately, it will take most of the money that Alain has left for her."

"She won't care," Berenice replied. She'd often watched Minette hold baby Vincent, walking the floor as he struggled with teething. Clearly she was hungry for the feel of a child in her arms. "She won't care at all."

Thanks to her pirogue journey from the coast to New Orleans, Minette was prepared for traveling with Louis LeGros. The routine was the same, but she'd felt much safer with the Indian paddlers. At night, before the fire, the bearded, long-haired man's pale, wolfish eyes followed her every motion with lustful curiosity. Only the promise of money, she was certain, saved her from rape or worse. She ignored him as much as she could and prayed for the journey to be over, prayed that this wide and frightening river that allowed them to pass with such majestic indifference would soon become the narrow stream between high, silted banks that bordered Sans Pareil.

Almost at her destination, they encountered a flat-boat crowded with soldiers drifting downstream. With hails and hoarse shouting, the men delivered the message that the campaign against the Atakapas was over and the French victorious. That removed at least one fear; even LeGros, for all his boasting about Indians he had slain, seemed easier in his mind, less prone to reach for his musket at every new bend of the river.

In her mind, she managed to cut him down to size. When he put her ashore on land that she knew and asked insolently how many days her business might take her, she was able to reply that it was none of his affair; he was being overpaid to wait and should start his vigil immediately. As she left, she saw him uncork the first of several bottles of wine.

Sans Pareil, drowsing in the sun, was much as she had left it, the faraway figures of field workers seen against the horizon, the solid, almost fortresslike aspect of the house with its attendant buildings commanding the foreground. She had no key—why would the mistress ever need a key?—but Mam'Odile must have seen her approach, for the door opened hurriedly, and she was drawn into the front hall and folded affectionately in the woman's powerful arms. One look told Minette that Mam'Odile knew everything and was her partisan.

Cautioning silence, Mam'Odile pointed to the salon. Minette was suddenly conscious of her stained skirts, evidence of her journey across the plantation. She looked like what she was, a beggar. Prosper, always immaculate, would doubtless enjoy the contrast and would know how to twist the knife by reminding her of what she'd lost and what she'd become. He'd show no mercy to the weak.

Despite her dishevelment, Minette lifted her chin and swept in like a duchess. Prosper was not immaculate today. Slumped in a chair, a half-emptied wine bottle beside him, he did not even turn as the door opened. His eyes were fixed rather vacantly on two little boys at the other end of the room.

One was Olivier. *Bon Dieu*, his baby face had disappeared so soon! How his plump cheeks had lengthened and the little chin formed so solidly. Blond hair curled over his collar. There was a hint of Amadée—yes, Amadée—in the tilt of his nose, and those wide eyes of her own blue had truly focused on the world. She'd missed the transformation.

She turned to Prosper—and found him enjoying her

frustration. He raised his eyebrows with eloquent sarcasm.

Olivier did not know her. He glanced at her briefly, incuriously, and went back to his play. She started toward him, half expecting Prosper to stop her. He didn't.

"Olivier? Would you look at me?" She crouched to his level.

The serious blue eyes turned toward her. A small hand, still chubby, reached out to touch her hair, then mischievously pulled on a curl. It sprang back into place, and Olivier, delighted, lifted both hands toward her.

She knelt and held still; she ached with wanting to pick him up, hold him close. But, no. It must be on his terms. He touched her, wondering, apparently, at the softness of her hair and skin. There was still no recognition in his eyes, but his interest in her held, and she suddenly heard herself repeating the little lullaby she'd used to soothe him into sleep. "*Ron, ron, petit bergeron.* Remember, Olivier, the little shepherd and his sheep?" The tiniest frown produced a wrinkle above his nose. He remembered something—he was going to speak!

"Dirty," said Olivier, pointing to the stains on her dress.

Prosper's mocking laughter rang out. He called Olivier, and the boy hurried to the shelter of his father's arms. The other little one, the companion, stood staring at Minette. She would not turn and give Prosper the satisfaction of the anguish written on her face, so she nodded to the little stranger and asked him his name. Silence. Glowing black eyes stared back at her. Suddenly she realized that this was a mixed-blood child, a *sangmêlé*, one of the many names for those born of white and black parents.

It gave her the strength to face Prosper again. "You told me once that on one of your birthdays, you were given a little slave and a pony as gifts. Is this what you're doing to Olivier, teaching him that owning another human being is right and normal?"

"You think the child is a slave?" Prosper was enjoying himself hugely now, his eyes sparkling with malice. "Tell the lady, Olivier. Does this little boy belong to you?"

Her Olivier shook his head.

"Who is he?"

Olivier looked puzzled. "Pili."

"His name is Philippe," said Prosper. "He's the child of our . . . seamstress."

Was there the slightest hesitation in his voice? Minette felt that she was being excluded from some joke that gave Prosper great satisfaction.

"Philippe, go get your mother."

The child ducked his head obediently and hurried out. Olivier, suddenly impatient of being held, tried to wriggle away from his father, but Prosper wouldn't allow it. "Have you seen what you came for, madame? My son does not know you. Are you satisfied?"

"No, you monster. What have you told him? That I am dead?"

"Precisely. And you *are* dead to him. I promised you that."

"How can you do this, Prosper? You once told me that I saved your life."

"I believe you were repaid at some danger to my own. Or would you rather that I'd left you for the old man to slobber over?"

"I think my service to you was more lasting." She bit off the words. "You'd be out in the cemetery now instead of holding your son."

"Exactly. *My* son. Mine alone."

"No! Never!"

"*Never* is a word I'd used to describe our marriage, Minette. I never had you completely. I never knew why until I discovered your tawdry lover."

"I told you I believed him dead. It's the truth. I thought he was dead or I'd never have married you. You knew that too. We had a bargain!"

"Which you broke."

"No. He was not part of that bargain. How could he be when I thought he was dead?"

Olivier began to cry, no doubt frightened by these angry adults.

"Stop that, Olivier," his father said. "Be a man."

"Can't you show some sympathy? He's only a child. Olivier …" She reached toward him.

"Don't touch him or I'll break your wrist!"

Olivier cried louder.

The door opened, and Philippe came in with his mother. She was dressed in black with a white apron, her hair was smoothly netted into a chignon, but in spite of this domestication, it was still Hera, the dancer. She limped forward. Limped? Hera?

"Take the boys out on the gallery," Prosper ordered.

"Yes, m'sieu." Hera looked humble, deferential, broken, Minette thought with a sudden, unexpected rush of pity.

"Hera came to us after an accident ended her dancing career." Prosper's voice was silky again. "She had trained as a seamstress originally."

Minette bit down hard on her lip to see Hera leading Olivier away with the other child. Her son turned to give her one more curious glance and then apparently forgot her.

"You still want to go on fighting me, Minette? Why not give up a lost cause? Olivier is a de la Fosse. You can have another child with that . . . that soldier of yours."

"I am not with—" she stopped. If Prosper was going to be so intractable, why give him the satisfaction of knowing her sacrifice and sorrow?

"What, has he tired of you already?"

She nearly lunged to scratch his eyes out but stopped herself in time.

"Tiger, tiger." Prosper was vastly amused.

"I won't give up, Prosper!"

"I know you won't. And this new . . . celibacy of yours could be a nuisance if your indefensible case ever stumbled its way into court."

He waited for a reaction. There was a crack in his composure, Minette thought. Something was worrying him. She sensed some kind of an advantage, if she could only find out what it was.

"Now that I see you so dull and drab, Minette—you certainly look like the commoner you are—I'm slightly less inclined to add to your miseries. In fact, I can solve all your problems. I offer you your freedom—a divorce and a cash settlement—enough for you to marry a tradesman as was your original intent, I believe. All you have to do for this largesse is to renounce all claim to Olivier."

"He's my child!"

He saw the fury in her face. "Not ready to listen to reason yet? A pity. Well, another time. I can wait. Can you? You're losing your bloom, Minette. You look stringy and anxious. Better hurry and find someone to marry—after we agree, of course. Would you like some food? I'll have Mam'Odile set out something in the kitchen."

The kitchen, she thought. Prosper, you are crude. But she gave no sign that the barb had stung her.

"What, not hungry after your long trip, Minette? Well, *tant pis*, as you often said. Eat pride."

"I didn't come here to beg."

"That's exactly why you came. And you see by now that it's a failure. But I'm not ungenerous. Why don't you go upstairs to the room you had and see if there are any clothes remaining in the armoire? I think I gave them all away, but I may be mistaken. Anything would be an improvement over what you're wearing. That rag stinks of river mud. What did you do, swim here?" he taunted.

She didn't answer.

"Go on. Take anything you find. And while you're there, you can remember all the luxury you threw away. Other women might have killed for it. Not you, of course. You are above such crass comforts as beautiful clothes and gourmet food and high position in society."

She knew that if she did not react he would lose interest and stop goading her. She clamped her lips tight.

"Well, I believe this rather one-sided conversation is concluded," said Prosper. "You may go whenever you like. But I'll be with Olivier, so don't try to see him."

"Treat him gently, Prosper. Try to remember that he's only a little boy."

"What I do is no concern of yours. Think over my offer, and don't wait too long. I have nothing to lose by waiting, but you have a great deal. Pity. You were so beautiful once."

Upstairs, in front of the long, gilded mirror, Minette assessed herself. It was almost two years since she'd slept in that bed in dimity nightgowns, donning quilted satin robes when, in the morning, Lisette served café au lait in the blue-and-gold set from Paris. Pampered child bride! Lisette would arrange the curtains so that the morning sun could not strike her mistress's eyes.

Lisette. Where was she now? Prosper had as good as killed her, selling her into the fields. How she wanted to avenge Lisette and Dominic and poor little Lutie! Their memories hung thick as dust in the air of the unused bedroom.

No clothes in the armoire: Prosper had been thorough. And the drawers of her chiffonier seemed empty. As she closed the top one, something rattled inside. Quickly she reached in, and her hand closed around a forgotten string of pearls. Sweet triumph shot through her. These were the pearls Prosper had bought her in celebration of her pregnancy; how very apt! They were beautifully matched, of a cream that was faintly rosy, and finished with a fleur-de-lis clasp set with pavé diamonds. That clasp alone would finance the fight her lawyer must make to counter Prosper's offer.

Bon Dieu, thank you. She would go on fighting; she had smelled fear in Prosper. He had shifted ground from "Communicate at your peril" to this humiliating but tangible cash settlement and offer of divorce to renounce her right to Olivier. As if that was possible. Olivier might not remember her, but he'd shown an instinctive liking. She could imagine the clasp of his chubby arms when he was finally returned to her, the sticky kisses and the clear voice piping, *Maman, maman*. Her boy.

She thought of Olivier's companion, that poor little *sang-mêlé* child. She even felt sorry for crippled Hera. But, Prosper! Only searing hate for him, a hot, unpleasant taste in her mouth. He thought she'd already lost

Alain, yet his cunning had made him instinctively offer a choice that *would* separate them unless she could make Alain understand. She could imagine Alain's response: "He has offered you a divorce and a settlement, Minette. Can't you be satisfied? Can't we be happy now, never forgetting Olivier but planning to tell him the truth when he's a man and can understand? Olivier has his whole life before him. We have only now."

Yet Minette had a magical certainty that somehow she'd have both Olivier and Alain. She couldn't be made to choose.

The sun slanted lower through the room, touching on the rush mats that had replaced the Oriental rugs. It was late; Louis LeGros would not want to start downriver tonight. Should she stay here rather than risk another night with him staring at her across the fire? No, Sans Pareil was unbearable with Prosper in it, maliciously keeping Olivier from her. Better the foul-smelling LeGros. But she must hide the pearl necklace well. He'd certainly murder her and tip her body into the Mississippi if he discovered it. The necklace was worth more than the sum she'd promised him for this trip. And sold, pearl by pearl, it guaranteed her future.

18

Berenice and Arnaud welcomed her back to New Orleans with relief. She told them everything. Berenice was delicately sympathetic about Olivier, assuring Minette that even her own Vincent and Cecile went through periods when they seemed to ignore her presence.

"My heart sank to my shoes when my boy turned away from me. I wanted to run after him, to get down on my knees, take him in my arms, but I wasn't even allowed to!"

"*Quelle bête!* That man you married isn't human."

"I wouldn't let him see me suffering. And for all my pain, he made me that despicable offer."

"To give up Olivier for a divorce and some money? Does he really think you would consider it?"

Arnaud, listening, broke into Berenice's indignation. "*Eh bien*, who cares what he thinks? He's offering something. Negotiations have begun. Where there's room to maneuver, there's room to win."

"Maneuver? Arnaud, we are talking about a mother who is separated from her child. You can't imagine how Minette feels."

"Ah, please." Minette was conciliatory. "Don't argue on my account. I won't get Olivier back tomorrow or the week after or for who knows how long. I must control my emotions. If I go about dissolved in tears, does it make the situation any better?"

Minette changed the subject. "Have you heard from the girls, Berenice?"

"Yes, Celeste came here the day after you left. Her husband had some legal business in town, and she coaxed him to bring her along."

"How is she?"

"Pregnant. Round as a barrel and indecently happy. He is teaching her to speak German. You should hear the sounds she makes—*ach, ach!* They would choke me."

"Is Otto trying to improve his French?"

Berenice shook her head, laughing. "But Celeste will see to it that the child's first language is her mother's."

"*Her* mother's?"

"I believe she is carrying a girl."

"Did she say anything about Eulalie?"

"Oh, yes. Still skinny as a post, with a skinny little boy."

"Well, we've all proved fruitful. I think they'd be pleased at the convent."

"You didn't ask about Seraphine."

"I am afraid to, Berenice. I feel it can only be bad news."

"*C'est vrai.* They found her in the river."

There was a long pause. Then Minette said, "I cannot believe that Seraphine would take her own life."

"We'll never know, will we?"

"So beautiful—"

"So poisonous." Berenice was unrelenting. "I'd rather look like me and be happy. Arnaud loves my every freckle."

"True, but the ones that I alone am allowed to see are the ones that I prefer."

"Shame, Arnaud!"

"Why? We are all married here." He stopped, worried that he might have offended Minette.

"You're thinking that I have one man too many, Arnaud? I don't even think of Prosper anymore. It's as if I'd never married him. I belong completely to Alain."

Berenice heard the tremor in her voice and offered immediate reassurance. "He said you would not receive any letters from him. You mustn't worry."

Minette let her control slip. "He is in constant danger, Berenice. He's on a secret mission, and if he's caught, he can be hanged!"

"I didn't know," whispered Berenice.

"He didn't want anyone to know."

"Oh, Minette. First Olivier is stolen from you, and now Alain—"

"Stop clucking over what might happen," Arnaud said firmly. "Alain has come back from the dead once, hasn't he? Minette never expected to see him again but there he was. I have confidence in him. So should you. I believe that Alain and Minette were meant to be together and one day it will happen. We'll find him on our doorstep. Minette, if I were you, I'd pay a visit to your lawyer and get things moving again."

She smiled at him gratefully. "I'll go tomorrow morning. Now that Prosper has indirectly acknowledged my rights by his offer, perhaps we can find a way to get the case before the judges."

"In court?" Berenice's eyes were wide, wondering. "But the expense, Minette. How can you afford the expense?"

Minette touched her hidden pearls. She'd been selfish, yes, hoarding them against the day when she could begin a legal fight for Olivier. But she'd be selfish no longer: her good friends needed so many things! Some of the money from the sale of the pearls should go to them now, the rest would pay the lawyer. She'd take the pearls to a good, reputable jeweler and fight for the best price.

In M'sieur Barre's shop, he held the necklace up to the light. "Oh, exquisitely done. A perfect symmetry of colors. Incredible effect."

Delighted, Minette asked, "How much are they worth?"

"How should I know that, Madame?"

"Is it not your business, sir?"

"I deal in true gems, Madame. I can tell you that a very cunning artificer made this necklace but it has no value except as a curiosity."

"What!"

"You might be able to sell it to some woman who wants to flaunt wealth that she does not possess. Such a woman could go as high as fifty francs."

"Only fifty francs?" Minette gasped.

"They are the finest fakes that I have ever seen but fakes nonetheless. Would that they were real for both your sake and mine." He paused inquisitively. "May I ask where you obtained them?"

Minette could not answer. He put the pearls back into her trembling hands.

"I fear you have been most cruelly disappointed but—"

Minette ran out of the shop.

It couldn't be true but it was. In her haste and humiliation at Sans Pareil, she hadn't stopped to question the incredible coincidence of finding the pearls at the back of an apparently empty drawer. She had hoped too much, thereby providing further entertainment for Prosper.

He had sent her into her former bedroom, hadn't he? Told her to look around at bygone luxury? Prosper had staged the whole thing . . . why? It was mad, but mad in such a patient, calculating way that it was doubly frightening. For how many months had he known she would come, sharpening his hatred on passing time? He might still be laughing now as he thought of her visiting a jeweler with these "pearls."

Had he given her real pearls at Olivier's christening? Minette had never thought to question the worth of what she received. But no, it would not have been then because Prosper still valued her, was still infatuated with the miracle of a healthy son. Later, when he began to hate her, he had planned this piece of theatre. Perhaps he'd even explained it to Hera, laughing at her gullibility. Buy the false pearls, bait the trap with hope and let her think . . . for such a little while . . . that she could fight him back.

So many hints and insinuations of madness had escaped her. Her servants had gossiped about the dark disorder in the de la Fosse family. All along, there'd been too many secrets about whatever had happened in Saint Dominique. And Prosper's total vengeance on her servants, even little Lutie, should have warned her. There was the spectacle of Olivier's toy rabbit with its stomach wantonly slashed . . . what kind of man stooped to such macabre details? A madman, a long-sighted madman who could plan vengeance that was still so far in the future. That was Olivier's father.

Bon Dieu, Olivier! No, Prosper would never hurt his son but what if Olivier had inherited anything from the sickness in Prosper's mind? She fought off despair by remembering her son's level blue gaze. *Pas possible!* Her boy was healthy and normal.

But what to do now? She'd hoped to deal with Prosper in rational, legal ways but that was laughable now. How could she fight a madman?

Sunk in her own misery, Minette plodded home. At least her selfish instincts about the pearls had shielded Berenice and Arnaud from crushing disappointment. A share of the "pearls" could have solved all their problems. She would never tell them about the existence of the necklace; she owed them that.

19

The months went on with Olivier far away. The months became a year with still no word from Alain. And then it was the time of year for storms, but the one which humbled New Orleans had nothing to do with the whims of nature. This was a calamity fashioned by man. It had begun as a dark and threatening cloud of rumors in Europe, then it crossed the ocean on whirlwinds of scandal and finally showered a deluge of financial ruin on the New World as all the shares in John Law's India Company became sodden shreds of paper. All the wealth of furs and fees, farmlands and fine properties disappeared. The ever-expanding Mississippi Bubble, that giant shimmering illusion of prosperity burst with the sound of breaking hearts. The overextended company with more shares than cash had, over a period of years, paupered all classes of society. The shell of the company lingered on for a while—John Law escaped the consequences by dying—but what he had set in motion could not be stopped and continued to depress the economy for a long time afterward. There was no financial recourse for the bilked thousands. Notices of forced sales and bankruptcies appeared on the lampposts of New Orleans, in cozy proximity to the usual black-bordered notices of citizens' deaths. In fact, the gigantic bankruptcy created a new class of walking dead. They could be seen everywhere on the streets: morose or drunk, feverishly gay or unnaturally casual, but always pathetic simulations of their former selves.

Prosper had predicted this when the Metoyers visited Sans Pareil. Minette remembered the evening well, and she could recall the look of skepticism on Pierre Metoyer's face. The poor Metoyers. But the de la Fosse family was safe because Prosper had seen the danger and sold off early. Olivier was safe, his inheritance of Sans Pareil intact.

But Arnaud Robillas, even though he hated gambling or speculating himself, was badly hurt in the crash: his customers couldn't finance the building of new ships. He was forced to fall back on the patching of sails for the fishing fleet, an activity that barely put food on the table. Berenice, at first without his knowledge and then with his tacit consent, began to take on fine-sewing jobs. She repaired priests' vestments and altar cloths. She sewed for ladies who would not come to her neighborhood; she went to them. Minette took care of Vincent and Cecile, who had made her their honorary *tante*, and she assisted Berenice as much as she could. But even in the convent her skills in embroidery and drawn work had been far below average and lack of practice since had made her positively clumsy. She preferred housework instead, freeing Berenice to sew. When Arnaud saw Minette carrying water or boiling clothes, he could not look her in the eye. This had been the mistress of Sans Pareil! But the mind-numbing physical work freed her from the futile circle of her thoughts. Each night she dreamed of Sans Pareil, by day she schemed to bring Olivier away from Prosper, back to her. But she could not see the way.

Minette grew thin and her hair lost its sheen. She developed a kind of black gallows-humor utterly unlike her former personality. And so she could look up with a smile when Berenice came home one night gaily waving a notice, saying:

"Guess who is ruined now!"

"I can't wait to find out."

"You'll enjoy this, Minette. It's the chevalier de Pombiers. They are selling that house of his, auctioning it off for debts. So there is some justice in the world, eh?"

"You've asked that question of the wrong person."

"Cheer up, Minette. You'll never have to worry about him again."

"Fate is strange. If he hadn't kidnapped me I would not have married Prosper."

"But you would not have had Olivier."

"True. How little control we have over our own lives. It's as if we were pieces on a chessboard in some unknown power's employ."

"An *unknown* power?" Berenice shook her head. "That's a long way from what we were taught in the convent."

"So am I," said Minette sadly. "I hardly recognize myself."

When the long day's work failed to tire her, she took aimless walks. New Orleans was as gray as her constant mood; bereft of its street musicians and vendors since people had no coins to spare. And today's weather was peculiarly unpleasant. The sky had a brassy, sulphurous tinge like early sunset and the wind veered constantly, ruffling the undersides of the leaves. In between puffs of air, there was dead calm. Moving or still, the air was oppressive and Minette turned, walking quickly back toward the house.

At home, Berenice had just returned. Arnaud was swearing in his workroom, and the children were fighting. Minette had unusual trouble in quieting Vincent and Cecile; the girl was set on bullying her baby brother, and he struck out at her with whatever he could seize. The devil was in the air.

Berenice, disdaining any help, went out to the kitchen to prepare the gumbo rice for their evening meal. It was the fourth time this week for the gumbo; today there were a few small fish to add to it. Stale bread could be heated up in the sauce. Hungry though she was, even the prospect of food failed to cheer Minette.

A blast of wind sent her scurrying to close the shutters. The sky was now a solid gray with black clouds piling up like cairns of rocks. The wind had settled on a direction and was blowing with steadily mounting power. There was a high keening noise to it, a faraway whistling she'd not heard before, like a giant drawing his breath. A spatter of rain hit the roof and was whirled onward.

At first she thought it was a church bell ringing, but Minette knew the church bells of their neighborhood, and the hour did not correspond to any of the public services. Besides, this was deeper, mournful, tolling steadily. She was listening in puzzlement when Arnaud burst in.

"I'm going upstairs for my ledgers—my God, where's Berenice?"

"In the kitchen."

"Get her! No, I will. You stay with the children. Get them some warm cloaks. And water, we'll have to take water, fill all the flasks. Do we have any dry biscuits? Berenice will know. Put on your sturdiest shoes, Minette. Take a cloak for yourself. And what else? Sulphur matches. We will need sulphur matches. Maybe bandages, too."

"Arnaud, what do you mean, where are we going?"

"To higher ground, Minette. The church of Saint Gregory, that's the best we can do around here."

"But—"

"Don't just stand there. Get started! Get everything together. Don't you hear the hurricane bell?"

20

The bell kept tolling for hours, even after they'd struggled against rising wind to the safety of the church. Inside, darkness assaulted them. The church's interior was so fiercely swept by draughts that each time someone attempted to light a candle to a saint, the wind whistled it out. The altar was a dark, shrouded shape, and they huddled as close to it as they could, shifting, rustling, murmuring, as they tried to sift rumors from possible facts. Outside, New Orleans crouched like a blind beast, houses shuttered tight, candles extinguished. Had the river already topped the levees? Was there a wall of water forced up to monstrous size by the hurricane and bearing down on the city? So went the questions. The sound to listen for was not the roar of wind but the lapping of water advancing stealthily in the streets. That was the silent enemy who could slip in beneath the doorsills. That was death.

They could feel the building resist the wind, feel it shake and strain in the dark. The windows must have been trembling under the changing pressure for some time, for now the one stained-glass window, pride of the church, flew inward to disintegrate against a stone wall, sending out showers of color followed by cries of pain as the glass shards found human targets. A child let out a piercing scream. The wind came through like a cannon-ball, smashing its way across the room, tearing at the far wall until a loose stone tumbled and gave it room to exit. People's small possessions rose in spirals to follow the stream of wind. To save themselves, they clutched each other and lay down on the floor, a solid, inert mass to set against the wind's power. So much rain was being driven in through the broken window that they soon were drenched.

Minette clutched Berenice and Arnaud, who held their children. The world had been reduced to a very small compass: lie on the floor or be smashed against a wall; hold tight while the wind rose to demonic shriek-ing that filled the ears and made the heart thrum and vibrate; pray if you could; keep your eyes closed.

How long were they there on the stone floor, soaking in rain and fear? How long before the noises in the heav-ens ended? At long last the roaring stopped and the eye of the storm sailed over New Orleans. It was morning.

The light and the silence were unimaginable. Move-ment was tentative. Those who could find their balance after a night on the stones struggled to rise. A sudden whispering and a cry announced the discovery of death among them. Two elderly citizens and a baby had died during the night. Their neighbors had felt the life heat leave the bodies, but what was to be done in that pro-tective tangle, pressed flat by the force of the wind? Two priests who'd been alongside their parishioners on the floor all night attempted to comfort the mourners.

Hurricanes were, after all, acts of God, however incomprehensible.

The survivors of the long night wandered about, testing their cramped limbs, trying with whispers and broken conversation to recover themselves. The banks of candles burned steadily now, and more than a few people knelt on the cold stones, this time in gratitude for survival.

When they ventured outside there was no wind at all. The sky, a mild blue, presided benignly over a scene of wreckage. Houses sagged as if swiped by a giant fist. Fences had been torn apart, sometimes piled in heaps of unbelievably neat kindling. The streets were rivers, carrying pots, boots, and dead animals along in the current.

Holding the children, who'd whimpered through most of the night, Minette and Berenice summoned resolve to begin again. Arnaud reminded them that he had braced the house with heavy ship's timbering. If it were still standing with the storm having done its worst, they could go home and weather whatever blew through once the eye had passed.

The house was standing, but the kitchen at the back had been sheared off cleanly, the garden was under water, and chickens perched on the nearly submerged shed roof. Still, they'd done far better than many of their neighbors. In spite of the warning hurricane bell, their neighborhood appeared to have been caught unprepared. There was more than debris in the swift-running waters of the streets; there were human corpses.

Berenice hurried by them, pushing Minette and the children ahead of her. Arnaud wanted to pull the poor dead devils out of the wet, at least, but Berenice urged him to worry about his family first. After all, the remainder of the storm was coming back.

The second part was less damaging than the first. Heavy sheets of rain obscured the street, but there was not such a fury of wind. When it had passed, people came out to assess their personal disasters. The bodies floating in the streets had gone, washed down toward the levee, presumably.

Eventually there was news. The city had taken a full-clawed swipe from the hurricane and had survived. That elemental force had gathered itself and turned upriver, where it was now rampaging, and the sky to the north churned with lurid, ugly clouds. Upriver, there were no protective levees, only the crumbling banks of the Mississippi, and houses built perilously close to the water. Upriver was Sans Pareil and Olivier. And then the city began to hear that upriver was also plague.

The Mississippi, driven by the fierce winds, had risen and spilled over its banks, invading the fields and contaminating the sources of drinking water. There was plague water in every well. People were dying, choking on their own congested lungs. Their tongues swelled, their faces went darkly ruddy. Barely able to speak, they called constantly for liquid, but it was never enough. Red as demons, they became delirious and died faster than the coffin-makers could build boxes for them.

A call went out for doctors, but there were enough sick and dying in New Orleans to occupy the physicians there. Or so it was said. The men of medicine decided this plague resembled the sort of typhus that had decimated armies; in other words, a hopeless situation. *Sauve qui peut*, save yourself, was the watchword of sensible citizens. A plague line was declared, separating the upriver communities from the city, and none would cross it.

"The nuns will go," declared Minette. "I know they will. And I'll go with them."

"And die?" Berenice was blunt.

"Your children are with you, *ma chère*. I have only Olivier, and I don't know what's happening to him."

"But you can have other children! You and Alain can have a whole family!"

"Does that mean I should desert Olivier? Let us not speak of this anymore, Berenice. I don't want us to quarrel."

Berenice stumbled away from her friend, looking for the comfort of her husband, who would scold her with the same loving helplessness she felt now. If there was a way to get upriver, even if it meant putting herself in danger of a dreadful death, Minette would find it.

Minette had less trouble than she had imagined in persuading Sister Immaculata to take her upriver with the Ursulines' mercy party.

"You are a good nurse. You did not contract malaria, which argues a certain natural immunity. And you know the treatment?"

"Cold sponge baths when possible, large amounts of liquid to keep them from choking to death on their dryness, and medicinal herbs regularly to thin out the heavy congestion of blood." Since Minette would be tending whoever might be sick at Sans Pareil, she needed to know all procedures.

"If ever bleeding was needed to remove their diseased blood!" Sister Immaculata lamented. "But we can't do it ourselves. I wish we had surgeons to go with us."

"It's a scandal that they won't."

"They don't have our protection," said Sister. "They are not armored with faith in the Lord."

"I wonder if I have enough faith, Sister."

"You are going to rescue your child, Minette. The Lord understands that."

Minette went home to say good-bye to her friends.

"No water," Arnaud warned her. "Drink no water."

"Not even boiled?"

"I don't trust it, Minette."

"What shall I drink, then? Champagne?"

Arnaud managed a laugh. "I imagine that your hus— that Prosper de la Fosse has a fine wine cellar at Sans Pareil."

"Of course he has."

"Then your problem is solved."

"And what do you recommend for cleansing my teeth, Arnaud? Shall that too be champagne?"

"No, no, sauterne is good enough there."

It was good to laugh together and to coddle her two godchildren, Vincent and Cecile. For who knew what the future would bring?

"I did not tell her about the body," Berenice confessed to Arnaud as they were climbing into bed that night, perhaps their last with their friend Minette under their roof.

"Are you sure it was he?"

"Sure? I almost stepped on his hand! It was the same hand with that signet ring that chucked me under the chin at the convent. He told me I had hair the color of rowan berries and that I would make a fine brood mare.

A woman doesn't forget a compliment like that."

"Made to make babies, eh?" He lunged at her playfully.

"Arnaud, be serious."

"Well, the chevalier de Pombiers, the old bastard, finally got what he deserved. And Minette probably didn't need to be reminded of him now, what with her other troubles."

Berenice shuddered in agreement. "Ugh, that big red face, half in and half out of the water. Thank the Lord his eyes were closed."

"How did you keep Minette from seeing him?"

"I pushed her into the house with the children. And after the storm came again, he was gone. What do you suppose the chevalier de Pombiers was doing in our neighborhood? Still looking for Minette? She shivered again. "He must have tracked her to our house!"

"Still on the hunt? Perhaps," Arnaud ventured. "He was a madman."

"My poor friend attracts madmen. Prosper de la Fosse appeared to be such a fine gentleman for Minette, and yet these noble families who keep marrying their cousins because no one else is good enough for them turn out their own sort of monsters. Imagine denying a mother her own son!"

Arnaud gave his wife's waist a squeeze. "Thank *le bon Dieu* that you and I, sweet, have no such problems."

"We will have if we make another baby tonight," Berenice observed. "Remember, I'm a fine brood mare."

"The more the merrier, eh?"

"Not till you get your business back on its feet!"

"I will tell you a secret, my sweet. The hurricane wind has blown me good fortune. So many ships were destroyed that new fleets must be built. I'll be busier than I've been in years."

"First build me a new kitchen if you want to eat."

Arnaud sighed. Berenice could be relentlessly practical.

"How long," he ventured, "has it been since Alain Gerard left?"

"Perhaps two years."

"I liked him, you know. But . . . do you think he will come back?"

"If he can."

"Exactly. *If* he can. In his line of work, many unexpected things can happen."

"Don't say it."

"Why not? We are both thinking it."

"Don't say it," Berenice insisted. "It's unlucky."

"Poor Minette needs luck, doesn't she? First she's involved against her will with the madman de Pombiers, and then with a vengeful husband, and now the man she does love turns out to be a professional spy who keeps disappearing. Who can she count on?"

"Herself, I expect."

"A woman, alone?"

"What 'alone'? Aren't we her friends?"

"Don't you wonder, Berenice, if Minette has occasion to envy us? Wouldn't she have been just as happy with an honest fellow like me, who is there at the table every night . . . and a comfort in bed later on?"

Berenice found that her "honest fellow" had cunningly enmeshed her in his arms and was affectionately squeezing whatever came to hand.

"Kiss me good night, Arnaud."

21

At Sans Pareil, a grayness pervaded everything after the hurricane. The sky was leaden, the air opaque with a dispiriting sheen, the fields obliterated by tons of silt. Turkey buzzards drifted above the bleached, featureless landscape.

Minette almost lost her bearings. This broken, flattened land—could it be Sans Pareil? Should she turn back to the river, where the nuns had promised to wait one hour for her before moving upstream? But then she smelled kitchen smoke and knew she hadn't been wrong. It was Sans Pareil after all. The straps of the pack she carried on her shoulders were painful, but she quickened her pace, grateful for the stout convent boots that were getting her through the mud.

The brick kitchen house stood starkly alone, its sheds gone, the chimney in a heap of rubble, and greasy, pungent smoke pouring out of a hole in the roof. Two slave children playing outside stared at her in consternation and ran into the building, reappearing with the familiar form of Mam'Odile.

At least this general of the household troops was still alive!

"Mistress, mistress! Can you be real?" she called.

"As you see me, Mam'Odile. And Olivier? Tell me of Olivier."

"He was spared. He is well."

Minette's legs went weak in her relief. Mam'Odile, more gaunt and ashen than before, shooed the children away and helped Minette into the kitchen, where she placed her on a rush-bottomed chair.

Minette looked around, bewildered. The hooks and cranes for holding meat and trussed fowl were empty. The pastry table stood forlorn. Only the dried herbs still hung from the ceiling.

"What is in your pack, mistress?" Mam'Odile asked.

"I've brought medicines."

The older woman sighed. "For a moment, I hoped it was food."

"I thought you would have more need of medicines."

"The plague has done its worst with us and passed on. We are left"—she gestured at two scruffy black heaps on a table—"with what we can find."

"Crows! *Bon Dieu,* you eat crows?"

"Anything we can catch in our snares."

"And what's that boiling in the pot over there?"

Mam'Odile looked ashamed. "Corn husks. I am trying to make a soup."

"The cattle, the sheep, the poultry? All gone?"

"Long gone. What we could find after the hurricane we butchered or smoked."

"The cows, too? Couldn't you spare one cow for Olivier's milk?"

"Lord bless you, mistress. Olivier eats regular food. He's a big boy now."

"I must see him. I can't wait. What kind of an excuse would bring him down here?"

"Excuse?" Mam'Odile was puzzled. "Why is one needed?"

"I cannot go up to the main house. My husband is there, isn't he?"

"Mistress . . ."

"What's happened?"

"Come. I will show you."

Only the wind accompanied them between the kitchen and the main house. The desolation was complete. The arbor was gone, and the cape jasmine bushes, and all the lovely, flowering vines.

"The Mississippi came rolling in on us, with the wind lashing it higher and higher. See the marks on the house," Mam'Odile explained.

Lines of mud just below window height showed how the flood waters had risen around the plantation house. How terrible for Olivier! And she had not been here to comfort him.

"This way, mistress." Mam'Odile was walking past the house to what had been the back lawn sloping toward the river. The few remaining trees were twisted and almost leafless.

"Where are we going, Mam'Odile?" She followed to a knoll where she'd often taken the baby. Something else stood on the knoll now, a rectangular structure of new brick, long and low.

"We lined it in lead, mistress. We took the lead off the roof gutters on the house because there was nothing else. But the water won't get in at him if the flood comes again."

Prosper's tomb.

Minette felt a sharp icicle pierce her heart. "When . . . when did it happen?" she whispered.

"When the plague was at its worst. He was very brave for once. I give him credit for that. Kept to himself, away from Olivier and Philippe, even though he longed to see them."

"And what of Hera?" Minette thought suddenly.

"She died too."

"God must love orphans, Mam'Odile, for He makes so many of them! How many of our Sans Pareil people died, do you think?"

"At least half."

Three hundred souls worked here, Minette thought. And half are gone?

"Where are the survivors?"

"Looking for food," answered Mam'Odile. "They roam up and down the river, sometimes gone for days. There are no fences between the plantations anymore."

"How soon can next year's crop be planted?"

"There is no money to buy seed, mistress." She paused. "I am sorry to intrude on your grief, but I must ask you . . ."

"I do not grieve," Minette said quietly. "Ask what you will."

"Who now owns Sans Pareil?" asked Mam'Odile.

"Why, Olivier, of course. It is part of his inheritance."

Mam'Odile looked strangely relieved. "And you, as his mother, are his guardian until he comes of age."

"Why, why, yes, I am. . . ." In all the shock, her new position of power had not yet even occurred to her. Under the bombardment of so many emotions in so short a time, she felt near collapse. She almost wished she could fling herself on Mam'Odile, like a child seeking comfort. But she couldn't. She was mistress now, looking out for the interest of her son.

"Well." She sought practical ground. "Have you written to the de la Fosse family to tell them of Prosper's death?"

"Written? No one here can do that."

Minette suddenly recalled that teaching slaves to read and write was against the law.

"We were hoping that you would come, mistress. Or someone."

"You are behind a plague line here, Mam'Odile. No one will visit."

"But you came."

"I came for my son. Please, take me to him."

Turning her back on that brick tomb, she had the strangest sense that Prosper was staring at her all the while that she walked toward the house.

A child's laughter was heard through a bedroom door, and Minette hurried toward it, clumsy with the latch in her eagerness. As the door swung open, she saw two little boys wrestling with each other on the floor. Olivier turned and saw her first. He was unmistakable—but he was not the baby who'd been so indifferent to her anguish on her last visit. His blue eyes were more alert; he had more understanding.

"*Maman?* Are you my *maman?*"

She held her arms open.

Like a little whirlwind he threw himself against her, burying his face in the instinctively remembered scent of her. They rocked together in an ecstasy of recognition while her hands stroked his head, felt the shapeliness of his bones, pressed the blond curls so much like her own. Olivier, her son!

Above his head, she met the eyes of the other little boy, who was watching from the corner to which he'd retreated. Huge, suffering eyes in a swarthy olive face. For Hera's child, *Maman* would never come again.

She spoke to Olivier gently. "Is that your friend Pili?"

"Pili?" He began to laugh.

"You used to call him that."

"I did?"

"When you were a baby."

"He is Philippe, *Maman*. My cousin." Suddenly his eyes filmed, and the tears rolled. "*Maman*, Papa is gone, he's gone!"

"He's . . . he's not gone, Olivier. He is resting in his little house in the garden."

"That means he's dead. He left me. Don't you leave me, will you? Say you won't leave me!"

"I will never leave you again."

Olivier clutched her, tears still falling. The little boy in the corner was crying too, silently, almost secretively.

Minette extended a hand. "Come here, Philippe. Come to me." He moved tentatively; she beckoned again. "It's all right. We'll have a good cry together."

Soon she had them both burrowing into her sides, nestling for comfort. Such loss, and at such a tender age. Her own parents, whoever they were, had been only ideas to her. She could not dream of them, miss them specifically. But the girls in the convent who did remember their families would cry at night as she lay there dry-eyed, wondering what it must be like to miss someone.

The door opened. Mam'Odile, on the threshold, gasped to see Minette embracing both the boys. "Mistress!"

"Well, it's been raining in here, Mam'Odile, but soon the sun will shine again." Both the little boys now pulled away from her with a show of manliness, wiped their eyes, and retreated.

"You have a good heart, mistress." Mam'Odile's tone was wondering. "A very good heart. Who would have thought that—"

"Ah, let's not make so much of this," Minette cut in. "I know he's Hera's child, and she was no friend of mine. But he's lost his mother—"

"And his father."

"He knew his father?"

"Mistress, haven't you guessed? I know he doesn't have the look of M'sieu Prosper, but—"

"Prosper's child? With her?" She swung around for another look at Philippe. "I don't believe you!" And yet, there was something, now that she had been alerted, something that recalled her husband, perhaps in the modeling of his cheeks and lips.

Philippe looked frightened by the intensity of her stare. He sensed her anger, and his lips quivered.

"Outside!" Minette pulled Mam'Odile into the hall.

With the door firmly shut behind them, she turned on the older woman. "You knew. You knew all the time, and you never told me!"

"M'sieu Prosper would not allow it."

"It would have been only common decency!"

"I am still a slave, mistress. I must obey orders."

Minette sighed. "But how is it that Philippe seems to be the same age as Olivier, when Hera only came to Sans Pareil after I left?"

Mam'Odile's eyebrows lifted. She was waiting for Minette to make her own connections.

"Oh. Yes, now I see. When I was pregnant with Olivier, and he was too considerate to bother me . . . Oh, damn him, damn him! Where did he keep her?"

"In the slave quarters. You never went there."

"I never went anywhere. He kept me in the house

with books and the spinet and Lutie—" At the memory of that singing child and her fate at Prosper's hands, Minette swore, harsh sailor's oaths she'd heard Arnaud use.

Mam'Odile's face lightened in something like amusement.

"Oh, yes, I know bad language and I've known bad men, but never a duplicitous liar like this Prosper de la Fosse! He went from her to me, did he?"

"No, mistress, that might have endangered Olivier. He did not return to you until after he tired of her."

"But she had his child."

"That was why he did not send her away."

"Wasn't one family enough for him?"

"M'sieu Prosper . . . liked to collect sons."

"You mean—you mean he has done this before? Oh, I can't believe it!"

"I've grown old with the de la Fosse family, mistress. I know their secrets."

"No, no, I can't take anymore! I feel as if I never knew my husband at all!"

"You knew the best part of him."

"And how long did that last? Until I was pregnant, and his attention wandered? I feel so . . . so dirty . . ." She covered her face with her hands for a moment. "No, that cannot be so," she continued. "I have my own behavior to answer for. But at least, the guilt is not mine alone."

"Guilt? Over your soldier?"

"How did you know about him?" Minette was amazed.

"I saw it the day he came to Sans Pareil with the others, mistress. The joy shone from your face."

"Am I so transparent?"

"That day you were. You could not possibly hide it."

"And M'sieu Prosper saw?"

"He saw something, but I doubt he understood what. He did not know the soldier was your lover."

"The soldier was not my lover! We had loved each other, but I had thought him dead before I married."

This time, without further consideration, she laid her head on Mam'Odile's shoulder for comfort.

"And now he is gone again." Her voice was not quite steady. "He does dangerous work, and I have not heard from him in so long."

"I will pray that he returns," said Mam'Odile. "You deserve some happiness."

"Thank you."

"What will you do about Philippe, mistress?"

She sighed. What *would* she do? Philippe was not her son, but he was Prosper's. "I suppose I should write of him to his grandmother, Madame Amadée."

"And do you expect that woman to take Philippe?"

"He is her grandchild, and an orphan now. Besides, you just told me that Prosper has done this before."

Mam'Odile's face was shadowed. "But neither Monsieur Prosper nor Madame Amadée was required to act in those cases. The children did not live."

There was a chill finality about the remark, which aroused Minette's old suspicions about Amadée and Ti Manou. *The children did not live.* Were they assisted from life by voodoo magic?

"Mam'Odile, you have known Madame Amadée for years. Do you understand her?"

"I am afraid of her."

"And Ti Manou?"

Mam'Odile shuddered.

"Well, perhaps they need not know about Philippe.

But I must write and tell them of Prosper's death. They may want to claim his body."

"Pardon, mistress, but I don't think so. It's considered very bad luck to be buried with a victim of a plague."

"And you think that the de la Fosses who are already in the family mausoleum will object?"

Mam'Odile shrugged, and Minette laughed. "*Bon Dieu*, it's hard to be a de la Fosse. My poor Olivier. He will be the heir to all of that."

"Mistress, I think you should prepare for a battle with that family. They won't want your son to have Sans Pareil now."

"I'd like to see them stop him!"

"They are many; you are one and only a woman."

"Madame Amadée is only a woman, too."

"She has the help of Ti Manou."

Mam'Odile appeared to be convinced that in the battle between good and evil, Minette was far outmatched.

After putting Olivier and Philippe to bed, Minette roamed the house. It was unnaturally quiet, and the ticking of the mahogany grandfather clock in the lower hall sounded very loud. On the stairway she turned, thinking of that hall filled with guests. When Prosper was feeling lordly, he had set a fine table and invited everyone to a party. The Metoyers stood there again; the Duhamels, the Trenets, all that country society with its constant gossip and determined flirtatiousness.

She'd never been fully at ease with any of them, always too self-conscious to enjoy her guests and too afraid of making a mistake in the social code they all shared. The long and elaborate dinners were planned by Prosper, and to her they were a wilderness of cutlery, where she covertly followed Prosper's use of fruit knives and sherbet spoons.

So much crested family silver! It now belonged to her son, whose fortunes she would have to protect and insure. Could she send the silver to Amadée de la Fosse as a security for the money needed to bring Sans Pareil back to life? She had to convince her that the plantation would continue to turn a profit that would benefit her as well as her grandson.

A new Minette sat down to breakfast in the morning. She drank her sassafras tea and ate the hoecakes made in ashes while Mam'Odile apologized for the poor fare.

"Remember our company breakfast? Pancakes and waffles, smoked ham and biscuits, buttermilk and fresh corn cakes—"

"One day, we'll eat that way again, but for now, Mam'Odile, I want you to listen to a few ideas."

She explained the plans that had kept her up half the night. First, she would write to New Orleans with all the news of Prosper's death and suggest the use of the family silver as security for a loan.

"But—"

"Let's not use that word, Mam'Odile. The de la Fosse family is nothing if not practical. They will mourn and do business both. They know they're losing income from this place even as we speak."

The solution for Sans Pareil might be sugarcane, Minette had decided. The river soil now inches deep on the property was extremely fertile, and she had heard that if you planted sugarcane in such rich ground you might bring in as many as three or four crops a year.

"We have never planted sugarcane," Mam'Odile said.

"Find out many of our people have worked in sugarcane fields elsewhere. They'll know how," said Minette. "And that brings me to what you must do for me."

The housekeeper looked wary.

"I want you to talk to all the workers who are left, Mam'Odile. We must have at least one hundred and twenty, am I correct?"

"Yes, mistress."

"And they've been doing all sorts of jobs, like carpentering and making bricks and building wells?"

Mam'Odile nodded. "Everything on Sans Pareil was made here."

"Better and better. Tell them I want to meet them and hear their ideas. If they've been doing the jobs all along, they'll know what's needed to rebuild."

The other woman looked at her with an odd expression.

"I don't know anything about running Sans Pareil," Minette explained patiently. "I lived here like a princess, playing with all the shiny, beautiful things my husband gave me. I believe he wanted it that way. But now it will have to be different."

"What do I hear, mistress? You are going to consult your slaves?"

Minette looked at her sharply. "I take good advice from anyone who has it. But it must be good advice. You can't let me make stupid mistakes."

Still the other woman would not commit herself.

"Come on, Mam'Odile. It's the only way. We will run this place together, all of us, and run it like good French housewives, wasting nothing!"

Was the housekeeper going to laugh or cry? "Mistress, we will do our very best, oh, yes. And, I think you will be much surprised."

22

Brave words to Mam'Odile aside, Minette was frightened. The big meeting last night, the meeting she had asked for, had unnerved her.

All those faces turned in her direction. Children, too, she was glad to see; quite a number of them had survived the plague. But even they were waiting for her decisions, hoping that somehow they'd find enough to eat and life could continue. And that mute dependency was the heaviest burden she had ever felt.

Mam'Odile was the interpreter, speaking pidgin French and some African language full of clicking sounds. It hadn't occurred to Minette that she couldn't understand her people. How had they managed to live in this alien land? A sense of their pain stole over her.

A tall man rose to make a long speech in which she discerned the word *sucre*, sugar. He had worked in a mash house, boiling the cane syrup, Mam'Odile said. Holding up his fingers, he tried to show Minette how much machinery would be needed to produce a crop. It seemed a lot. Then a woman, heavily pregnant, opened her mouth and pointed to her gums.

"She has scurvy," Mam'Odile had said. "She needs green things for the health of her child."

"Green things?"

It seemed that a certain sort of green, like watercress, grew in the beds of small streams hereabouts.

"Why haven't they gone and gathered it?" Minette demanded.

"No one told them that they could. They are slaves."

"Then I shall send them! In the convent the work was apportioned to those who could do it best. We'll do that here. Let the women gather the plants." Her glance settled on two elderly women, wrinkled and stoic. "And let these two take care of the mothers' young children while they are away."

"Well enough," muttered Mam'Odile. "Their useful work in the fields is over."

"And the old men, where are the old men?" Minette was suddenly full of energy.

"Hiding behind the younger ones, hoping you will not see them."

"I want to see them. Mam'Odile, there was never an old man who didn't love to fish. I remember them along the Seine. Tell them, Mam'Odile, that we will never starve as long as the river flows by. I want a fishing army, a cadre of old men who will go down to the river and fish to their hearts' content for all of us!"

With the translation, the impassive faces split into startling smiles, and she heard a deep chuckling run through the crowd.

Minette gathered information that day and promised to visit the workers' quarters with medicine for their children.

Her newfound enthusiasm, however, was severely battered by the first evening spent with Prosper's ledgers. He had disciplined his usual elaborate scrawl to a tiny but legible script for these books, but the plenitude of arithmetical figures was daunting. She had no aptitude for figures, but she persisted, and finally, after much study, she gained some basic understanding of how much Sans Pareil produced when it was running normally. She found the de la Fosse family's original investment one evening when her eyes were about to go dim. They'd put in a great many livres, but they'd taken out much, much more. In the future, some negotiations about percentages Prosper had set might be called for.

What? Listen to me! Am I to negotiate? Minette laughed at her absurd thoughts and went on working. Sans Pareill had had a dip in profits while the two overseers were in charge, but after Prosper fired them and took over himself, the accounts once more balanced. Now she was responsible for Olivier's inheritance, and she feared that if she had to hire an overseer, most would not hesitate to take advantage of her inexperience.

It was obvious that she must make allies of her in-laws, she decided. They needed each other. She needed money to rebuild and run Sans Pareil, and Amadée needed her share of the plantation's profits to maintain her home in New Orleans. There was seed to buy, and horses, cows, and mules. There were chickens and fabric for clothes and basic supplies and, worst of all, the machinery for processing sugarcane. Maybe later they could try tobacco, as one of the workers had suggested.

Any way she turned, she needed the de la Fosse name for backing and financial credit. But she must not appear too eager. Perhaps the lack of income from Sans

Pareil would pinch Amadée's pockets enough that she and the family would make the first move.

Amadée, when she arrived, was at first simply a grieving mother, the hard, brilliant edge of her appearance and conversation blurred and softened. She had little to say to Minette but spent a great deal of time with Olivier and professed herself to be delighted with him.

What must she make of Olivier's conversation about his cousin Philippe, Minette wondered. She probably thinks he has an imaginary playmate. Minette had managed to separate the two boys and keep Philippe out of sight.

For a while, the visit seemed almost ordinary, a family gathering in the face of grief, a normal period of condolence. Ti Manou slipped about the house like a shadow. Cousin Aurore and Attorney Barsalou, the other members of Amadée's party, did seem to be assessing and appraising the contents of the house. But perhaps that was their way.

She could afford to wait a little while, Minette concluded, and not precipitate events.

So Minette was not prepared for the family's first move. After several days of muted condolence and cordiality, Amadée rose at the dinner table to announce her intent to buy out Olivier's share in Sans Pareil.

"Buy him out, madame?" Minette stood up. "If I had the money, I would buy out *your* shares for him. He is the de la Fosse heir."

"Hear this, then," Amadée said, gesturing imperiously at the lawyer.

"Show her the document, sir!"

"It appears to be a certificate of marriage," said Barsalou in his dry little voice. "A contract between Minette Marsan, spinster, and the chevalier Hector de Pombiers. They were joined in holy matrimony at the residence of the chevalier by a certain priest of the Jesuit order, Père François—"

Minette, trembling with agitation and anger, accidentally swept her wineglass to the floor. This was it, the countermove? With this they hoped to drive her out of Sans Pareil? The fools.

"You are wasting your time, Lawyer Barsalou," she said.

"I disagree, madame. It appears that you have committed bigamy."

"And your marriage to my son was invalid!" Amadée was triumphant.

"It only appears that in your haste to claim what was not yours, you have been deceived. Where did you find that paper? It was in among Prosper's things, wasn't it? I gave it to him. We both knew that it was a forgery."

"Easily claimed. But Prosper cannot speak for himself," the lawyer commented.

"And can the chevalier de Pombiers?" Minette allowed herself sarcasm. "Produce the old man. I challenge you!" She knew the old man had died in New Orleans during the hurricane. The paper-thin walls of the Robillas house had seen to that.

"The document speaks for itself," the lawyer insisted.

"I disagree," Minette challenged. "And I am alive to oppose it. To disprove my word, you would need to find witnesses to such a marriage, and none exist, because the marriage did not exist!"

She sat down to a suddenly discomfited silence and, though her heart was pounding so violently that she thought they must surely see it knocking against her chest, she coolly signaled Mam'Odile to bring in the dessert, which was some carefully gathered wild strawberries.

An uneasy truce set in, and after dinner Cousin Aurore and Lawyer Barsalou played piquet in the salon, slapping down the cards with much animation just as if they had not been seriously embarrassed.

Amadée appraised Minette silently until Minette said, "Sans Pareil has provided a good income for the de la Fosse family and can do so again, with the family's help. But I am holding this place for Olivier, and any more attempts to dislodge me—"

Amadée waved the notion away. "You cannot blame me for trying."

"Let us not discuss it further," said Minette dryly. "Since we are yoked together by Olivier and the need for income, we must see to it that Sans Pareil recovers. I will need your help with the banks in New Orleans, and my ledgers will be open to you. I will be happy to have good financial advice and need some local man to keep me aware of market conditions. Sans Pareil is going to switch to growing sugarcane. I had thought of using the family silver as security for a bank loan, but if you have other suggestions ..." She stopped.

Amadée was peering closely at her. "Can this be the same silly, helpless creature my son Prosper brought home?"

"Yes, madame. But I profit by experience."

Minette had the sensation of being covertly watched. She turned slightly to see Philippe crouching in the hall. *Mon Dieu!* how he looked like Prosper now, Prosper in a rage!

"Go back to bed," she warned him quietly.

He ignored her and advanced into the room, wearing his nightgown but holding himself like a prince.

"I want to meet the guests," he announced. "Is that my *grandmère?* I want to greet her. She has spent all her time with Olivier, and I was not allowed to see her."

They were all looking at him now as he set himself before Amadée and made a childish attempt at a bow.

"What an amusing little black monkey," said Amadée. "But he is very impudent. If I were you, Minette, I'd have him whipped."

The child raised his huge black eyes to her and continued, "Aren't you my *grandmère?* You must be. Papa described you very well to me. He said that you were golden-haired and beautiful—"

"Take him away!" Amadée would not look at Philippe.

"*Psst!* Cousin!"

Olivier, his fair hair tousled, barefoot and wearing his cambric nightgown, was edging around the doorway of the salon. "Come on, come on." He gestured at Philippe.

"Go with him, Philippe," said Minette in a voice he could not ignore. "This was not well done. You shall be punished tomorrow."

He gave her a hot, defiant look and ran to the shelter of Olivier. They could hear Olivier scolding him as the boys hurried upstairs.

"Cousin?" Amadée's face was crinkled in distaste. She caught sight of herself in a mirror and instantly relaxed her facial muscles into smoothness.

"I found them together," Minette said flatly. "Prosper wanted Olivier to have company of his own age."

Amadée managed to shrug it off. "I gave Prosper a little black servant of his own when he was seven years old. It was very droll. Prosper was reading about the customs of the royal English court and found that the prince had a whipping boy whose job was to take his punishments. So he used little what's-his-name in that role.

How the lad would bellow when he was beaten for Prosper's misdeeds! Yes, very droll, very clever of Prosper."

Cousine Aurore laughed heartily. "I remember. A noisy little boy, I thought. Whatever became of him?"

"After Prosper outgrew him? The fields, I expect. They all went to the fields in the end."

"They didn't last long in that climate," put in Lawyer Barsalou. "Strange that they didn't last in the Indies when they came from places just as hot."

Minette did not let her disgust show, but she could not get over the deliberate cruelty she had just seen. Surely as Philippe had looked at her with an expression identical to Prosper's, Amadée had known who he truly was. But the word *grandson* would never grace this child.

23

In the following months, Minette devoted herself to the sugarcane plant. It swayed in her dreams at night, with brushlike flowers atop stalks fifteen feet or higher. By day she watched the wind ripple the acres of stalks on Sans Pareil land, waiting for the right time of tasseling to cut. In her mind she already saw it harvested, the cutters moving up and down the rows, stripping off the leaves with the hooks on the backs of their large steel knives, slashing the joints of the stalks with surgical precision, gathering the stalks into heaps called windrows for their trip to the sugar mill.

Sans Pareil had a sugar mill now, a round stone building. It had a crusher to extract the sweet juice from the canes. It had vats in which the water content would evaporate and the juice become thick and syrupy, other vats for boiling the syrup until it became molasses, still other devices for extracting the crystals of raw sugar that formed in the molasses at the right time and temperature. Sugar was whitened in earthenware block forms.

Molasses that had not formed crystals went back through the process again, and from the last brown sugar was made, and tafia, a kind of rum.

Nothing was wasted. In the fields, what remained of the stalks after the harvesting was buried in the furrows to sprout new young cane plants. The rich river soil that had poured over her fields during the hurricane was the equal of anything in the Indies and could support, she was assured by neighbors, three crops a year.

But her success with sugarcane did not mean that Sans Pareil had solved all its troubles. Half of its land was still not in use, half of its working force gone, and there was no money to get more slaves. The de la Fosse family kept her on a short financial tether. Her neighbors were baffled by the fact that she did not hire an overseer and scandalized by the system of work groups, or cadres, she had organized among her slaves. Each group was led by the most experienced man and had a quota to meet. She had hoped that the spirit of competition would set in among the cadres, and it did.

One of her fellow plantation owners, an elderly man from a most distinguished family, did become a friend. Raymond Iberville, a cousin of the sieur de Bienville, was charmed by the pretty widow but appalled by the work schedule she set for herself.

During the long days, she lived on horseback, inspecting the construction of the buildings gradually being replaced, checking on planting and harvesting, hearing complaints and dispensing justice. She was out from first light until the fields grew dim, and in the evening, the plantation's ledgers waited. It was important, she felt, to project leadership, authority, even authority that wore a skirt and rode sidesaddle. But this precious authority was paid for by inroads on her strength. In the evenings it was all she could do to drag herself to bed, and in the morning she was startled at her own hollow-cheeked reflection in the mirror.

The boys were another problem. Perhaps because of the early loss of both parents and his exclusion from legitimacy, now or ever, due to the circumstances of his birth, Philippe was becoming a real little devil. He made constant mischief, lured Olivier into trouble, and tormented the house servants with his misguided, destructive bids for attention. They hated him. Feeling vaguely guilty and doubly helpless, Minette could not seem to find the time for the problem of Philippe. Sans Pareil was nearly consuming her; there was precious little left over.

That was what Raymond Iberville warned her about on his frequent visits. He always had some logical reason to call; it might be helpful advice on her frustrating encounters with the banks, or the advisability of her growing indigo again, or the possibility of his renting some of her idle bottom land to grow rice. His own soil was so dry that what grew best was cotton—too time- and labor-consuming ever to turn a profit in this coming new decade of the 1740s. She slowly began to understand that he was courting her. It was a sobering discovery. Raymond Iberville? Never! He was decent, honorable, rich, and—boring. She did not want to think of how much help his wealth could be.

Especially, she did not want to think of him at night. She was usually too tired for the stirring of any feeling, but when a wave of warmth did wash over her and memory made her breasts tingle, she was always back in the shabby little house in New Orleans, lying deep in flowers with Alain Gerard. On those nights, no matter how exhausted she might be, she remained wakeful, prone to sudden starts into the darkness, grasping at fragments of half-remembered dreams. Against all logic—for obviously he was dead, or had no intention of returning to her—her body rebelliously recalled Alain. Her breath came faster even as she tried to relax. The bed was lonely; her life was passing without pleasure. Name of God, what could she do? Raymond Iberville was not the answer.

But he persisted. He would settle her problems with the banks; he would tame Philippe and set Olivier on the right path. Only consider it, Minette! As Christmas approached, she felt extremely lonely and accepted an invitation to a party at his plantation, Beau Rêve. He was overjoyed.

For the party, she wore a gown she had found in the attic—one of Prosper's old selections for her. It was lilac with a draped overskirt and rose satin sash.

"It's loose. I've gotten thinner," she observed to Mam'Odile.

"Tie the sash tighter, mistress."

"My hair." Minette lifted the mass of it. "How is hair worn these days?"

"Powdered, I have heard."

"What? Here?" She laughed. "In Paris, yes, but in this climate? It would be torment. Do something with it, Mam'Odile. I put myself in your hands."

She closed her eyes, and the older woman kneaded her neck and shoulders. In blissful relaxation she felt the slow brush strokes in her hair. The result was an intricate, coiling coiffure, finished with lilac ribbons that matched the gown.

It deserved a compliment. "You are very skilled, Mam'Odile. I had no idea."

"I have coiffed Madame Amadée," she said. "She has hair much like yours."

Minette stared into the mirror. "These days, she probably looks better than I do."

"Who knows what her face is really like these days? The witch woman keeps her looking so youthful."

"How, I wonder?"

"Mistress, please don't even think about it. Stay far away from that!"

It was November but only pleasantly cool. Minette wore a warm cloak and drove to the party in a wooden calèche. The body of the carriage could be raised or lowered to accommodate more or fewer people. Ungainly but practically untippable, the calèche lumbered along with Minette in solitary splendor behind the driver.

Of the others gathered at Raymond Iberville's Beau Rêve, some had come from great distances to partake of his overnight hospitality. Older women carried little sacks of silver coins for their favorite gambling games; younger girls looked for cavaliers and practiced flirtation with their fans.

Raymond's house was soft, rose-colored brick enclosed on three sides, two of which boasted upper and lower galleries. Brick paving extended to the front door and served as decorative trim around the plantings. By some miracle the hurricane that had fallen in full force on Sans Pareil had spared the much grander Beau Rêve, and the ballroom festooned with holiday wreaths was lively with dancing when Minette arrived. The music was supplied by some of Raymond's house servants on fiddle, banjo, and concertina. Beyond the ballroom, she could see the dining table laden with huge, candle-warmed bowls of gumbo and Louisiana pilaf, shining silver and porcelain, cakes, eclairs, and marzipan. Raymond was rich, and she could be mistress of

Beau Rêve with only the slightest encouragement, Minette thought wistfully. If only she wanted it.

On the dance floor the young people were twined together. The older women were gossiping and gambling at *vingt-et-un*. The men clustered in the long hall, drinking too much wine, muttering about weather and market futures and their untrustworthy government, bemoaning their taxes and the rising price of slaves.

To which group did Minette belong? She was twenty-four, a settled matron's age. But she didn't gamble and was disinclined to talk about children with the other mothers. What could she say about Philippe, for example? My husband's bastard has inherited his father's difficult temperament and who-knows-what from his mother? That would put a pause to the jollity.

Sighing, she walked up to the closest group of men, anxious for any useful information she could glean from them. They ceased conversation immediately as she approached, which was maddening. There was an awkward silence until Raymond Iberville came forward, introducing her as the mistress—and manager—of Sans Pareil. Men who had known Prosper looked at her doubtfully, but when Raymond put a proprietary hand on her shoulder, tension eased and the financial talk began again.

It was barely an hour later when Minette broke away from the group, stiff with fury. She had just enough manners left to keep assuring Raymond that she had enjoyed the evening but could not stay for supper because of a sudden indisposition. She felt his reproachful eyes on her as she climbed into the calèche; she'd make more apologies later. Of course, it was not Raymond's fault that his plantation had been spared by the capricious hurricane, but some of the other men had been hit as badly as she, and every single one of them had been able to negotiate far more advantageous loans with the banks than she could manage. While they'd had virtual debt forgiveness, she'd had the interest on her loans raised. To consolidate her notes, the only possible next step was a mortgage on Sans Pareil itself!

How could this happen with the de la Fosse credit behind her? Aha, she had finally seen the light. The de la Fosse family itself was behind her troubles. She'd succeeded in bringing Sans Pareil back from the dead, and they'd decided to steal it from her.

Oh, she could recognize Amadée's hand in the matter. She'd let Minette get into a position from which she could not retreat because of permanent expenses taken on with the improvements she'd made and then, oh, then, she'd conspire with the banks to choke off her credit. She'd squeeze and squeeze, thought Minette, and finally offer to buy Olivier's share for a much lower price than it was worth. *Voila!* She would have to leave Sans Pareil, and her son would be cheated of his heritage.

How dare the de la Fosse clan? How had she been so stupid? How could she stop them?

When she reached Sans Pareil, she stormed into the house. Mam'Odile met her in the hall, fairly trembling with urgency.

"What? What is it, Mam'Odile?"

"In the salon, mistress—please!"

"I don't want to see—"

"Yes, you do!"

She let herself be led. And there, in the salon, a ghost was waiting.

Alain, dusty and weary, was finishing a glass of Mam'Odile's citron punch. When he saw Minette, he replaced the glass on a wooden taboret but for a moment said nothing.

He'd come. He'd just appeared. Alain!

Her throat was suddenly dry. "Welcome," she managed. The voice was hardly her own.

"Am I, Minette? Am I really?"

His voice broke the spell, and she hurled herself into his arms. He was astonished, and then his body acted for him, as hers had.

Everything was swept away—his long disappearance, doubts, regrets, questions. Whatever had happened to him, her body was clamoring that this was the only man that she would ever love.

Wordlessly, she led him upstairs, and at the door of the small bedroom where Minette now slept, Alain lifted her into his arms like any bridegroom.

"Shall we begin again, everything new? I take thee, Minette—"

"Yes! Hurry!" was her answer.

But he would not hurry. He undressed her as if he had never seen her before, discovering the hollows of her arms, the dazzling curve of shoulder, the slowly revealed breasts. It was delicious torture. With complete concentration, he slid the clothes away from her body, here a bit of leg showing, there the firm waist. He took off her shoes and caressed her feet, teasing her insteps with the pressure of his thumbs.

"Alain!" She trembled in her petticoat, and he undid its buttons with the same deliberation. Her own hands, feverish and desiring, felt his muscles glide beneath her palms, helping him out of the cocoon of clothes. Her fingers passed along the edges of his ribs, caught in the short down curls on his chest. Smooth and rough, pulsing soft and hard. They breathed and shivered in unison, prolonging the moment until finally he stood naked before her, fully erect. He lifted her onto his body. Her legs clasped his back, and he carried her like an ivory goddess to the altar of the bed.

Love flowed in and out of them as they murmured to each other. She opened to him, and he sank himself into her, growing again and again with an intense concentration of desire that moved them to shuddering glory, over and over. They were pearled with sweat, scented with each other. They clung, inventing new caresses, changing positions with the unison of a dream.

When they finally let go of each other, when the whispers and soft sounds of passion gave way to the even breathing of contentment, it was out of simple exhaustion. They had come so far together.

Alain licked and tasted each of her fingers slowly, sealing her into him, making her essence his. "You are mine," he whispered.

"Tomorrow," Minette murmured, her eyelids dreamily closed.

"Tomorrow?"

"Tomorrow we can go to the priest, Alain."

"Ah, what a catch I am." His fingers retrieved a lilac ribbon from the ruins of her coiffure. "I have no money. Can you afford to marry me, Minette?"

"Mmm . . ."

"Just imagine your neighbors." He nuzzled her neck, blowing warm currents of air onto the places he delighted. "Isn't there some rich gallant who'd choke with laughter at your choice?"

"Raymond Iberville, perhaps."

"My rival?"

Her delicate shiver told him all he wanted to know. "He was a friend. He wanted more." She shrugged.

"You haven't even asked me where I've been all this time."

"Do I want to know?"

"Oh, yes." He was grim. "I've been in prison for espionage. The Spaniards caught me in their territory."

"Prison . . . That explains your leanness, my poor darling."

"You take it better than I had imagined."

"No, Alain, I don't. It makes no difference to you and me. I have found that good men are often sent to prison."

"My darling Minette, I see that becoming rich has not affected your natural benevolence."

"Rich? I am close to losing Sans Pareil!"

Her troubles came out in a rush of confession. She told him how the de la Fosse family, conniving with the banks, had forced her into a corner. The responsibility of holding Sans Pareil for Olivier was almost more than she could bear. And Olivier, she sobbed, was growing away from her, changing before her eyes, perhaps because of Philippe's unfortunate influence.

"And who is Philippe?"

She told him; she could not stop speaking until she had laid everything before him. He listened soberly, cursing once that, while they had suffered their painful separation in New Orleans, Prosper himself had been living with Hera and produced Philippe.

"But our pain is over now. Nothing can hurt us any more."

"Do you truly believe that, Alain?"

"I intend to prove it to you. You've been carrying such heavy burdens for so long. But I am here now."

24

Minette's second wedding was a small affair. She invited her neighbors to a short ceremony in the plantation chapel, even the reproachful Raymond Iberville. She wore a gown of cornflower-blue watered silk and carried a white and gold prayer book in place of flowers.

"The boys aren't dressed," Mam'Odile had reported breathlessly just before the ceremony. "They say they aren't coming out of respect to their father."

"Philippe's idea!" Minette was upset.

"Their presence is required," Alain said calmly. "Let me manage this."

At the last moment, Olivier and Philippe had appeared, scrubbed and irreproachable, and taken their places in the pews.

"What did you say?" Minette whispered, for the chapel was filling with guests.

"I reminded Olivier of his duty to his mother, and I pretended complete indifference to Philippe's presence at the wedding, so of course he came."

"Well, it worked this time, but—"

"I see the problems, my darling, and we'll overcome them in time." Alain reached his own conclusion about the boys.

"They are growing up like little animals without education," he told Minette. "I can begin teaching them the basics for now."

Schooling was not compulsory at first. Alain made himself available for all kinds of instruction and waited for the boys to come to him. Olivier came first, drawn in by the masculine skills of horsemanship and tests of strength, then fascinated by the arithmetic needed in constructing new buildings on the plantation. Next it was carpentry, a skill of Alain's. Thus Olivier was led gently into regular lessons without quite realizing it.

Philippe had stayed away from the classroom, but finally Olivier's progress, his slate filled with neat letters and rows of numbers, made him so envious that he joined the daily lessons. He proved to be bright, though erratic. Philippe continued to hate Alain, who understood it quite well, but he did learn to dissimulate. The real battle they fought was not to achieve results in the schoolroom; it was over Olivier. Because he could see that his destiny was less fortunate than Olivier's, Philippe was determined to rule in Olivier's heart. He began playing the tempter with a hundred little tricks, embroiling Olivier in so many petty disobediences and resulting in punishment that Olivier too felt a hardening in his heart against the stepfather he'd at first admired.

Minette was distressed to see Olivier grow away from his parents. He no longer wished to have his blond hair affectionately tousled by his *maman*, he did not bring her any more little wonders for inspection, leaves, mushrooms, and pretty stones. There was little she could do but trust Alain to solve the problem.

Alain was no more eager than Minette to repopulate the plantation with the numbers of slaves it had formerly boasted; he relied more on the technical expertise of the day. But machinery cost money, which the bank refused to lend. Slowly, Alain came around to Minette's opinion. They were not being dealt with fairly. Their credit was good, production was increasing, and still they were blocked.

"Someone does not want us to succeed, Minette."

She repeated her suspicions about the de la Fosse interference behind the scenes. There had to be a way to deflect them.

Alain, one evening, asked for a talk with Mam'Odile.

"You have been with the de la Fosse family since Prosper was a child."

"It's true, M'sieu Alain."

"I heard a certain story on Saint Dominique . . ." Alain watched Mam'Odile grow apprehensive. "I only want you to tell me if it's true. Don't be afraid."

"It was a long time ago."

"I know that, Mam'Odile. But think back. This story concerns a group of slaves on the de la Fosse plantation at Pointe-à-Pitre, led by one man," Alain continued, "They started an insurrection because of the cruel treatment, and they thought that all the slaves on the plantation would rise with them?"

"Most were too beaten down," muttered Mam'Odile. "Only a few, like Aristide, had courage left." Her voice was unsteady.

"So those who wanted to revolt were betrayed?"

She looked away. "It was like Judas, M'sieu." For

money, someone betrayed them to the overseer, their enemy. They were captured. "Aristide," said Mam' Odile. "He led the revolt."

"One of the young slaves with Aristide had just given birth to a son. Am I right?"

"You are, M'sieu Alain." She continued now to tell the story. "When the de la Fosse family captured the rebellious group they put them in a cattle barn. The family did call on the police, but before the police came, the barn somehow caught fire, and all inside it burned to death, including the slave girl and her little son."

"So I have heard." His voice grew very soft. "Who was the baby's father, Mam'Odile?"

The housekeeper looked into his eyes. "M'sieu Prosper."

Listening, Minette drew in her breath sharply.

"Where was Prosper when the barn burned?" Alain pursued.

"On the plantation."

"What did he do?"

"To save them? Nothing. You could hear the screams and smell their bodies burning. Ah, God!"

"And Prosper?" Alain persisted.

"Went into town, hid in a brothel, and stayed there three days getting drunk. Madame Amadée finally sent the overseer to get him."

"And then?" asked Alain.

"There were questions from the police. Even on Saint Dominique, this was too much. But there was nothing to see. They were not even buried in graves! They were shovelled into a pit. Madame Amadée said the remains could not be identified."

"What a horrible accident," whispered Minette.

Mam' Odile's face went very still. "Can you really be

so innocent, mistress? They had to die, and so they were burned. The men had to go because they planned a revolt—you can't sell such a slave to another planter, mistress. Young Idélie had to die because of her son. You think that Philippe looks like M'sieu Prosper? You should have seen the baby Léonce. Black like his mother but otherwise a perfect image."

"Prosper's son," Minette murmured.

"Murdered by his family," Alain said. "Whom do you suspect, Mam'Odile?" he asked.

The woman still looked apprehensive but resigned, as if having said so much, there was no going back now. "All of them. His father. Certainly, Madame Amadée. And Prosper himself for letting it happen and running away."

Involuntarily, Minette glanced out at the garden and Prosper's tomb. Now she understood his fear and excessive solicitude until Olivier was safely born. His one legitimate son and heir. But why couldn't he have held back from creating Philippe? Or was that boy a replacement for baby Léonce? How many disdained little boys had Prosper for a father? She began to pity Philippe.

"These are the secrets you mentioned, Mam'Odile, that day you spoke to me of your past?"

"Yes, mistress. They paid well to keep it quiet in Saint Dominique."

"And they left out of shame?" Minette asked.

"Bless you, mistress, they had no shame. They were told to leave. The authorities felt that if they stayed, it might cause more slave revolts. Those rich planters are always afraid of being killed in their beds."

"Do they still have money there, Mam'Odile?"

"I believe they have overseers for their interests there."

"A stake, something to be lost," Alain said thoughtfully. "This may be our salvation, our one chance to save Sans Pareil for Olivier." He rose confidently. "I am leaving for New Orleans in the morning."

There was no use arguing with Alain. Minette had already discovered both his impulsive temperament and the rock-solid determination that must have helped him to endure his term in the Spanish prison. He would use whatever means he could to force the de la Fosse family to stop interfering with the banks that supplied Sans Pareil with credit. If that was blackmail, then Minette would do penance until he came back.

His absence was a penance itself, Minette found. She felt profoundly alone, not only in bed but during her every waking moment. Partners and lovers, they worked so closely together that she could not shake the habit of turning to consult him. The boys were different when he was not there, more blatant in their disobedience, and she realized how much she had come to depend on Alain to manage them. A hundred things she had ceded to him, a hundred responsibilities had been removed from her shoulders.

Could he succeed now in New Orleans? He could be forceful as well as loving. The man who kissed the arches of her feet each night as he removed her shoes was the same man who had endured bloody battles, secret missions, degradation in a Spanish prison. Surely he would fight his way to victory for them.

On the shaded gallery of Amadée de la Fosse's house, Alain sighted over his thin china coffee cup as if it was the barrel of a gun. He had just exploded the charges in front of Amadée, and she, in a mauve sacque gown with a great deal of lace, had not bothered to deny them.

"I suppose the old black woman told you," she murmured. "You realize that the word of a slave is not evidence."

He inclined his head. "I have other friends on Saint Dominique, white and well placed. But why speak of evidence, madame? There is no intention of taking this matter to court. I had in mind a simple trade."

He told her what he meant. She denied any conspiracy with the banks. He pulled out a portfolio of figures, adding that several neighbors of Minette's could testify about their more fortunate experiences with the same banks. For good measure, he threw in the illustrious name of Raymond Iberville. The man, however personally disappointed, was too much of a gentleman to want Minette to fail at Sans Pareil.

Amadée listened with little change of expression, but Alain knew that he'd struck home. Without ever admitting her activities, she implicitly promised to stop doing them.

"Favorable loans?" Alain pressed. "Nonfluctuating interest? No pressure to consolidate old notes into a mortgage? Status as a good account recognized?"

She nodded, apparently bored with the subject.

"I want no surprises, madame," said Alain. "We will continue to make money for you at Sans Pareil and to hold the plantation for Olivier."

At last she showed some animation. "Tell me of my grandson."

He suppressed an impulse to ask her which grandson she meant and launched into a glowing account of Olivier's progress.

"A true de la Fosse," Amadée said.

God forbid, Alain thought. It's as if Olivier hadn't a drop of the crazy de la Fosse heritage in him. It had all gone to Philippe.

"I shall never see my grandson," said Amadée, rather pathetically.

"You can see him at Sans Pareil."

She dismissed that. "I hate the place. And my health does not permit much traveling." She thought for a moment. "Send me the little black monkey. I will do you a favor by taking him off your hands for a time."

"The little black—"

"Philippe. Oh, I know who he is, Monsieur Gerard. I choose to ignore such unpleasantness. But he is diverting and reminds me of . . ." Her voice trailed off.

"You would not be . . . unkind to him?"

"Since when has a good Creole household offered less than the best of everything to any guest?"

That much was true, Alain reflected. And Philippe would be wild to come, out of his mind with joy at the possibility of any crumb of recognition from his *grand-mère*. The more he thought about it, the better the idea seemed. Time alone with Olivier might also re-strengthen the boy's attachment to Minette and himself. Alain wanted to deepen his relationship with the boy. Someday Olivier might call him Papa. That would be a wonderful day.

He rose, saying that he would have to consult Minette.

But Amadée had read his expression and saw that the thing was already done. She smiled coquettishly. "You are a man of decision, Monsieur Gerard. And I shall keep my part of the bargain."

"I warn you, madame. No tricks."

Lace rustled as she rose, tall as his Minette. "Shall we declare a truce?"

* * *

"A two-month visit for Philippe? Did she really say that?"

Back at Sans Pareil, Alain was giving Minette an account of his meeting with Amadée. But she did not share his enthusiasm.

"She hates Philippe. You had only to see her face when he called her *grandmère*. We can't send him."

"He'd want to go."

"Of course. He's a child. But she'll only hurt him again."

"Minette—"

"We are being selfish, Alain. We're looking for a peaceful time for ourselves. But what about him?"

"I don't think she would dare to hurt him now, even if that had been her original intent. We bested her in this business of interfering with our bank, and she does not want us to spread the Saint Dominique story in New Orleans. And because she is Amadée, she probably knows you would be afraid to send Philippe. She gets a little of her own back by daring you to do it. Your worry would be a pleasure to her."

Minette smiled. "That does sound like Amadée."

It all sounded very safe and logical. Still, her feeling of unease persisted.

Predictably, Olivier protested the separation from his playmate, but Philippe chose to lord it over his half brother and sailed downriver quite happily. An undeniable shadow lifted when he went; the house servants breathed more freely when their small tormentor had gone.

Alain tested Amadée's word and found it binding, for their credit problems seemed to evaporate. They were able to reinstitute the planting and processing of indigo at Sans Pareil, and since there was war in Europe again and the armies of certain nations were brave in military blues, their new project found a ready market.

But war unease was spreading to the New World too. Their territorial neighbors, Spain to the west, England in the eastern Carolinas, began to make competing noises. Relations between England and its colony of American settlers were slipping as well. In fact, Alain confided to Minette that one of his espionage assignments had been to scout French territory for a group of American colonist investors who wanted to move and do business there. And even the local Indians, apparently pacified, began to stir and rumble, protesting government policies toward them. The remnants of the sun-worshiping Natchez tribe, long thought in exile, appeared among the other tribes under their protection, and made threatening preparations for attack against the whites who had almost wiped them out.

Were they safe at Sans Pareil? Minette wondered. The heavy shutters of the house folded inward like protective wings, and when the gunports beside the upstairs windows were supplied with rifles, the isolated house was like a fort. But Alain assured her that attacking plantations was a tactic the Indians had abandoned because it brought too-swift reprisal from soldiers. Their small numbers now confined them to surprise attacks on lines of transport.

"Philippe should stay in New Orleans and not try to come home," Minette declared at once. "We must write to Amadée to keep him there until this uprising is over."

The letter was answered with surprising speed. Philippe was no longer in New Orleans. Because of the danger on the river, Amadée had arranged to have him sent back overland by stagecoach.

Alain swore. The mad bitch! The Indians were not going to stop river traffic. The overland routes were precisely where they would hit.

Minette knew now what her stomach and brain had been trying to tell her for weeks. This was deliberate. Amadée had simply found another way to revenge herself for her humiliation by Alain. And getting rid of a bastard grandson would be an extra bonus for her.

The God-cursed de la Fosses! Whatever Philippe was, whatever trial he might be, he was a child, alone, and might be in the hands of Indians. No stagecoach had arrived. It was past due.

At dawn, Alain left for New Orleans, riding the stage route with gun and knife at the ready. Where the lowland silt gave way to the higher banks of the Mississippi upstream, he found the coach, lying on its side in dense brush. The wheels had been taken away, the upholstery hacked with knives. An arrow, a Natchez arrow, remained like a calling card in a splintered doorframe. There were no bodies inside the coach; what had become of the passengers? Dead or alive, the Natchez Indians had Philippe.

Pushing his horse hard, Alain rode into New Orleans and confronted Amadée. The catlike gleam of amusement in her eyes—"Returned so soon, Captain Gerard?"—confirmed Minette's worst suspicions.

He headed for the soldier's barracks at the Place d'Armes. There he found his old friend Guillaume Cernaux, who was now in charge of a company of Choctaw Indians, France's newest allies.

The records of the stagecoach line for that journey showed three passengers, one of whom was Philippe.

"Light candles for the older two," said Cernaux. "Middle-aged whites? No chance. But the boy is another matter. The Natchez may well keep him."

"Can you help me, Guillaume?"

"Of course. That's why my company is stationed here. We avenge such raids."

"I have never ridden with Indians," said Alain. "Do they obey your orders?"

"Now they do."

"Guillaume, could your Choctaws sneak up on a Natchez encampment?"

Cernaux laughed. "They'd rather do that than eat or make love. Have you ever seen the Choctaw way of stalking an enemy? Superb! They walk in single file through the woods, and the last man covers the tracks of the others by brushing back the leaves and earth where they've stepped. There's no trail—it's like a spirit passing! And then they attack a sleeping enemy at daybreak, yelling like demons."

"You can't let them do that this time, Guillaume. They can't attack unless it's necessary to help me get out with the boy."

Rapidly, Alain explained the situation and his plan to go alone, unarmed, into the Natchez camp to bargain for Philippe.

"Who is this Philippe for whom you risk your life?"

"He's the bastard son of Prosper de la Fosse and the dancer Hera. Surely you remember Hera?"

"Too well. I'd let the Indians keep him."

"You don't understand. Minette would never forgive me if harm came to the boy. It's my fault that they have him, Guillaume. My own stupid pride let me think that

I understood the situation, but I was wrong."

"Minette was always kind, but I am surprised her generosity includes the raising of her husband's bastard by Hera as a brother to her legal son. That goes too far!" He tapped his forehead to indicate what he thought of Minette's judgment.

"Guillaume, you must help me."

"It's certainly within my authority to punish the Natchez for attacking the stagecoach."

"And killing the driver, I'm sure. I saw dried blood," said Alain.

"The driver and probably the passengers. As for your little bastard"—Cernaux shrugged—"who knows?"

Alain looked wretchedly unhappy. Late that night he wrote a letter to Minette, telling her how to continue the projects he had started at Sans Pareil if he were not there to share them. It broke his heart to think that his own wrongheaded self-confidence had put them into this position.

He swore to love her beyond death and predicted that their souls would find each other in the afterlife. In an irrepressible burst of optimism, he added, "I hope to reach you before this letter does, and then we may tear it into pieces together. When you next see me, God willing, I shall have Philippe with me."

He blew out the candle and stared wide-eyed into the dark, remembering Cernaux's last entreaties.

"Why, Alain? Why do it?"

"I've told you. For Minette."

"She'll be in agony if you die."

"You won't let me die, Guillaume. You'll come rushing in to save me."

"Yes? Have you ever seen how fast a Natchez warrior can swing his ax and take your head off?"

"I won't be standing still waiting for it, you may count on that."

"God help you, Alain."

"For Minette's sake, I think He will."

25

Chief Atalan, the leader, or Sun, of the remnants of his Natchez tribe, sat before a dying fire. His mood was melancholy. In the muted flames he saw the end of the Natchez nation's past glories. If only they had not gone alone to war against the French. Gone now were the fields and forests of the plateau land whose very name was Natchez. Gone their neat cabins, gardens of melons and squash, hunting, harvests . . . all gone since the disaster at Fort Rosalie. They had won a glorious victory but lost the war. Now they were hunted, banished from their land. The other tribes could no longer be trusted; former friends as well as enemies had sold out to the French. What was left of the proud Natchez withdrew to places no other tribe desired and lived as outlaws, searching still for undisturbed territory.

But where would it end? Would they be driven into the sunset land at the edge of the world? Atalan wondered if he could hold his band of Natchez together. He was most sad at holy times, like tonight, when the oak-bark flame that symbolized their god, the Sun, was allowed to die. It would be relit at dawn by the priests, but during these hours "between," the Natchez without their guardian sun-flame scarcely seemed to exist.

As he stared into his own fire and thought of the sacred flame, a white man stepped out of the shadows and made a gesture of respect. On any other night Atalan would have killed him immediately and beheaded the guards for allowing an enemy to creep in too close. But of course the guards had not challenged this stranger during the hours "between." Any man, even a white one, might enter the camp in peace then, and safe passage out would be given until the lighting of the new sacred flame at dawn. But how had this white barbarian known that? A traitor from the other tribes might have told him. He listened resignedly to the greeting in French. He understood the language and could speak it well enough, but he had hoped never to hear the sound of it again.

Alain could not believe his luck. The Indians guarding the camp had seen him but let him approach, merely closing ranks behind him as he went toward the chief. No one had so much as touched him or the goods he carried. And now the chief, Atalan, seemed ready to listen.

Alain told his story plainly. He was here to offer knives and woven cloth and many useful things for the exchange of one little boy.

What made the white man think that the Natchez had this boy? the chief demanded.

Alain answered carefully that the boy was missing from a stagecoach that had been attacked. In case the chief denied the attack, Alain had brought the Natchez arrow that had pierced the coach, and now he laid it silently at the chief's feet. He was not here to avenge the matter of the coach, Alain repeated. He was here because he knew that the Natchez seldom killed boy children and he wanted to trade.

"Describe the boy," the chief commanded.

Alain did so. "And he is called Philippe."

"I have seen this child," said Atalan. "But he is not mine to trade."

Alain laid out his trade goods, holding the knives high so that their blades flashed in the firelight. He was prepared to wait and settled comfortably on his heels.

"We have had many dealings with the whites," said the chief. "Our ancestors came from the south and west, in an empire called Anajuac in Mexico. The whites came to our shores in the floating villages you call ships. We traded with them. We were a great people in those times."

"The Natchez can be great again," Alain said politely.

The chief nodded without conviction.

"Who has the boy?" Alain asked.

"One of my nobles. He is called Quecho."

"I would like to show him my trade goods," Alain said.

"I cannot tell if he would be interested," answered the chief.

But this was only part of the negotiation. Alain could see that Chief Atalan coveted the knives.

Quecho was summoned. He was a tall, arrogant-looking man, almost totally naked, his body heavily tattooed, and pendants with bone plugs dangled at his earlobes. Quecho was as imperious as any French lord at Versailles. Indeed he was part of a social structure that could give lessons in protocol to the French court. Natchez society was divided into three classes: the suns, who were chiefs; the nobles, and the commoners, called stinkards. Stinkards might be elevated by marriage into a noble family but no noble could ever be brought down in caste. Noble descent proceeded through the mother's line, and mothers were particularly honored.

Quecho examined the goods without any expression of interest or pleasure, but he barked out a short command, and soon Alain saw Philippe standing at a little distance from them. The boy was dressed as an Indian.

"This is not much for a healthy male child," said Quecho disparagingly, as Chief Atalan translated for Alain. "Tell the white man," said Quecho to Atalan, "that I am raising this boy to be my son and support me in my old age. I am teaching him now to hunt the wild turkey."

"We are more successful than your hunters," Atalan boasted to Alain. "We use the skins of dead turkeys as our disguises. We creep up on the birds and imitate their calls. Our arrows do not fail."

Alain held up a length of red cloth from his pack of goods and waved it in the firelight. "This would help in the hunting of the turkeys," he observed. "It is the color of their wattles."

Both Atalan and Quecho looked at the cloth with interest. Alain knew he had scored an important point.

Quecho continued. "I am also teaching this boy to hunt deer and how to spear fish in the water. I do not think that these things you have brought are worth the time I have spent on him."

Alain waited, but nothing more was forthcoming. The silence deepened, but he did not feel that the negotiations were over.

Finally Atalan spoke in a voice that barely disguised a peculiar satisfaction. "There is something else you can offer for the boy, and I think that Quecho would agree.

It is an ordeal, a test of bravery, and on this night, when the sun-flame dies and is reborn, the gods would be pleased to witness it."

"What is the ordeal, Chief Atalan?"

"We shall light three rows of fires and let them burn into walls of flame. You must run through them. If you are successful, we will take your goods, and you may have the boy."

"And if I fail, you will keep the goods and the boy," said Alain.

The chief smiled pleasantly. "That is so."

Alain was careful to show no anger.

Chief Atalan continued. "This night is a time of holy truce. That was why you were allowed into the camp."

Alain said, "If I die during this ordeal of flame, isn't my death a violation of the truce?"

"That is an excellent question," approved Atalan. "But it does not apply because you do not have to undergo the ordeal. You are free to leave."

"Without the boy?"

"Of course. But if you try to reenter to get the boy after the truce is over, we shall kill you. Your head"—he pointed to a long pole some distance from the fires— "would be put there. It is our custom."

The Indians politely looked away to allow Alain to think. Philippe was still standing where Quecho had indicated. Alain had never seen him stay in one place for such a long period of time. He thought wistfully, was the boy better off with these cunning savages? Would they succeed in making a decent person of him? A moment later this hope was eradicated. A vision of Minette's face and Olivier's tears for the loss of Philippe entered Alain's mind. The boy's presence had eroded the happiness of his marriage and his attempts to be a father to Olivier; now it seemed that his absence would make matters even worse. But could he survive three walls of flame? He would have to try.

"*Courage, mon vieux,*" Alain murmured to himself. The impulsiveness that had gotten him into this impossible situation was rising again like a fever in his blood. He had a sudden conviction of success, an intimation of invulnerability. His life must be charmed, he thought. How many times had he come back from the dead? There must be some luck still left.

And then he was standing up and nodding to the chief.

The waiting Natchez began heaping brush for the fires.

Alain remembered the sweet odor of burning sugarcane. That was it, he told himself. He would picture a fire in the sugarcane at Sans Pareil, threatening the house, threatening Minette and Olivier. He must rescue them. Keeping the image like a charm in his mind, he raced toward the roaring crackle of the Indian fires.

Pain. Smoke. Choking. He wanted to scream but dared not open his mouth to the thick black smoke. He could not see. He could feel—my God, he could feel the flames crawling on his legs—but he kept them moving. Run. Run. Hurry. Hurry if you want to save Minette.

And then he was through, rolling on the ground to put out the fires on his back and legs. In agony he rose and stood before the chief, smoke still rising from his clothing, burned and ashy but triumphant.

"I claim the boy," he said through clenched teeth. "Put him on my horse."

The chief nodded assent. Alain dreaded swinging his seared legs over the saddle and settling himself into its hard contours, but he did what had to be done, and a silent, stunned Philippe, still as a stone, put his arms around his waist. Alain spurred the horse, and without a backward glance they left the encampment of the Natchez. Through watering, smoke-seared eyes, Alain discerned the lightening sky. It was dawn, the end of the truce time, and had he lingered in camp the Natchez would have killed him, ordeal or no ordeal.

An unholy screeching burst out behind them as Cernaux's Choctaws came out of the woods and fell upon the Natchez. He had almost forgotten their existence. As the shouts faded behind them, Alain felt Philippe's arms begin to tremble and heard the boy's gulping sobs. Did he cry for the Natchez? Slowing the horse, Alain took them into the early-morning cool of a grove of trees. He climbed down stiffly, and reached for Philippe. The boy hit him a hard crack on the nose.

"You little devil!" Then Alain saw Philippe's face. What a mask of tragedy and desolation, old far beyond his tender years. A suffering spirit looked out of the huge black eyes.

"You betrayed them!" Philippe whispered hoarsely. "You betrayed the Natchez warriors!"

"Does it mean nothing that I've just risked my life to get you back?"

"You should not have done it!"

"Now you tell me that, after I nearly roasted alive! It's a good thing I rescued you, Philippe, or you'd be dead back there in the Choctaw attack."

"At least I would die with my people."

"Your people?"

"They accepted me," Philippe wailed, "when no one else would. They told me I could be one of them, a Natchez warrior, when I grew up."

"But you are not an Indian, Philippe."

"What am I, then? Not all black, not all white, the son of the worst woman in the world."

"Who told you that?"

"Madame Amadée. I can't even call her *Grandmère*. She explained to me what my mother did. I am so ashamed."

"Hera was your mother," Alain said quietly. "That's all you have to remember."

"But Madame Amadée said—"

"You need not listen to your grandmother. Your own mother was far wiser."

"You knew my mother?"

"Yes."

"Were you one of her—"

"No, and never say or think that again. Your mother died trying to save you, and so did your father. Remember when they wouldn't let you come to them? It was because they were dying and didn't want you to catch the plague. Don't you call that caring for you?"

Philippe sniffled into silence.

"Look, my boy," Alain began. "I know that your life is not easy. I know that you envy Olivier's future. But don't do what you were doing. Don't try to take Olivier away from us. We can be a family, and you will be protected, but you must accept us and our ways if the arrangement is to work. Do you want it to work?"

The boy barely nodded.

"Think about it. Sans Pareil can always be your home if you will make it possible."

The boy looked down, his heavy black eyelashes, a legacy from both Prosper and Hera, veiling the expression in his eyes.

"Call it a truce between us," Alain continued. "Like the Natchez truce. Only it will go on and on. When you are older, if you stick to the truce, we will have long conversations about the world and your place in it. I will try to answer all your questions. But for now, we must put our faith in the truce. Agreed?"

Philippe let out a sigh and nodded.

"And I will see you in the schoolroom every day. We need you. Really, you are better than Olivier in arithmetic. He will need your help."

A ghost of a smile appeared on Philippe's face. It was enough for now, Alain decided.

The pain had set in deeply, and Alain discovered that he could not sit his horse. He put Philippe in the saddle and led the animal, leaning heavily on it for strength. Many times he staggered and nearly fell. On trembling sinews and screaming nerve ends, he finally led them into a traveled road and waylaid a passing hay cart. Seeing that his horse and Philippe were secured, Alain closed his eyes and drifted into unconsciousness.

He had a memory of leaving the cart, of being carried to a big, deep bed. He awoke to Minette crying over his wounds, kissing his poor scorched hands, and declaring her love over and over. Then there were cooling unguents and the winding of bandages while Minette and Mam'Odile conversed in low tones. More sleep, so close to the sleep of death. At one time, Olivier was there, crying. At another time, there was Philippe, the dark incarnation of Prosper and Hera, gazing at him with an expression he had never seen on that face before. Then he was gone again as consciousness floated away.

How long was it before he woke to find himself alone with Minette? He could not say. But he could bend his knees and elbows without much pain. He could smile. And he noticed a smile of her own, a charming, secretive smile, that was quite new.

"What is it, my love?" he asked.

"What is it? A girl, I think, though Mam'Odile says it is too early to tell. But I would like a sister for Olivier, wouldn't you?"

A happy man fell asleep again on her words.

26

The months of pregnancy passed swiftly this time. And Alain, while every bit as solicitous as Prosper had been, managed not to make Minette feel like an invalid, praising her strength and looks and disposition. He was full of a quiet joy, evident in the way he moved, in the enthusiasm with which he rose shortly after dawn and headed for the fields. All the responsibilities were on his shoulders now, and she was content in her warm bed mornings, still flushed from the caresses with which he left her.

She knew by now that she was not living with some romantic demigod, but a man of mettlesome temperament who was often stern with the two boys and who was bent on instilling a soldierly efficiency in the workers at Sans Pareil. Yet he was well liked because he was more than fair in his dealings. To her he was still a miracle, dearly loved. His personal scent, which combined pressed linen with the heat of his skin, always aroused her desire.

For his birthday, she had ordered a good broadcloth riding coat with stiffened slits for more ease in the saddle, and though he laughed at her insistence on a smart cut, he abandoned his customary rolled shirtsleeves and wore the coat whenever the weather permitted. She thought it looked quite as dashing as his army uniform and would sometimes rise as early as he did in order to see him leave, watching the proud set of his shoulders as he swung into the saddle and urged his big bay gelding into a trot.

Alain, her love. They were not alike, but her caution balanced his impulsiveness nicely. They settled into each other and reveled in their differences. They agreed on the name of Arielle for the baby to come.

Arielle. The name was perfect for the delicate little sprite who arrived on schedule and with a minimum of fuss. Arielle was a delightful combination of them both. Olivier was mesmerized by his new sister, fascinated by her tiny fingers and toes.

The situation had improved in Alain's improvised schoolroom, too. He drilled the boys hard on the basics but warned Minette that the time was soon coming when they must either find a schoolmaster to teach Latin and other advanced subjects or send the boys away to school. Yet no school for young white gentlemen would accept Philippe.

Alain searched constantly for a solution, but without success. Schoolmasters were hard to come by, upriver. And even if he and Minette could organize some arrangement with the children of neighboring planters, whereby there would be continuous school for several months out of the year, what would happen when the children told their parents they were sharing lessons with Philippe?

Then the tragedy occurred. It was summer, when the afternoons were often shaded by thunderclouds on the horizon. For the most part, the clouds moved on, taking the flash and rumble of their storms elsewhere, but occasionally they burst like ripe grapes over Sans Pareil, sending sheets of rain over the fields, sluicing gullies through the fertile land. If such showers came at midday, the land steamed for hours as the strong sun sent the vapors back into already heavy air.

On one such afternoon Olivier and Philippe, not required in the schoolroom, were playing in a patch of woods near one of the creeks that emptied through the plantation land to the river. Though Olivier was much taller than Philippe, the other boy maintained his advantage by constantly boasting about the time he'd spent with the Natchez Indians, and what he had learned from the noble warriors. Grudgingly, he parcelled out bits of information to an eager Olivier. Today the lesson was fishing.

"The Natchez use reeds. They cut them and dry them over a fire or in the sun," said Philippe.

"We have no dry reeds," Olivier complained. "You might have cut some a few days ago if you knew you were going to show me this."

"I didn't know if you were ready to learn," said Philippe loftily. "Sometimes you don't want to pay attention."

"Well, I'm ready now," Olivier countered. "If we don't have reeds, how about thin twigs? There are plenty on the bushes."

"Gather them," Philippe directed. "I'll do what comes next." Elaborately casual, he took a small knife out of his pocket.

Olivier gasped. "You're not supposed to have that!"

"Well I have it," Philippe smirked. "And we need it."

He sharpened the ends of the twigs Olivier collected, pointing them like darts. Then he frowned. "I forgot the cords."

"The what?"

"The Natchez use cords made of bark strips or something, and they tie them to the reeds and throw the reeds like spears into the water."

"You can't throw these twigs."

"We'll use them like spears," Philippe decided. "We'll stand in the creek and spear the fish."

"Are you sure?"

"Watch this, Olivier." He stepped into the water, waited until the ripples had subsided, and studied the shallow bottom.

"There's a shadow moving," offered Olivier.

"Be quiet, will you!"

Philippe leaned forward again, intent, then plunged his stick into the water. But a moment later he dropped it, and his mouth opened in a soundless scream.

"What?"

"Snakes!" Philippe whimpered. "They bit me. There's another one—oh!"

"Come out of there, Philippe!" But the boy seemed paralyzed, and Olivier charged into the creek, dragging him out. Before he left the water, he felt a tiny, sharp sensation on his own left heel. What had appeared to be shadows of fishes were snakes, gliding beneath the surface, heading downstream in V-shaped ripples. They looked like long and leaden gray water . . . moccasins!

Philippe was gasping on the bank. "A lot of them bit me!"

"One bit me too, I think."

Philippe had his knife out. "Cut me where they bit me. Let the blood out. Hurry, hurry!"

Trembling, Olivier slashed at the spots Philippe showed him. The boy squealed as the blade bit into him, and Olivier shook even harder. Soon Philippe's legs were flowing with blood.

"We've got to run home!" he whispered. "Olivier, I mustn't stand still. Must move to get rid of the poison."

He started off, staggering a little. Olivier turned and nicked his own heel where he'd felt that sharp little sting. Blood appeared. Bleeding must be right; doctors did it all the time.

Hours later, Philippe's fever climbed beyond belief. Minette tried everything she had learned at the Royal Hospital—and saw it fail. The boy went into convulsions before her, his body snapping into stiff angles, jerking and flailing as she tried to hold him down. She shouted for Alain, who was tending Olivier in another room. The boy, thanks be to God, was not nearly so affected as Philippe. Olivier had fallen asleep, his limbs still, not convulsing.

Minette began to pray rapidly, convinced that Philippe's end was near. She threw herself across the bed to keep him from falling to the floor. When she felt Alain's hands bracing her, there was momentary hope, but then the boy's eyes rolled back into his head, showing only whites, and foamlike spittle appeared on his lips. The convulsions increased in severity until she thought the poor little body would be racked apart; so strong were they that she and Alain combined could hardly hold him. Minette kept calling his name, hoping to rouse the boy, but there was only the tortured hissing of his breath. Then, just as the chimes of the hall clock struck midnight, Philippe's eyes flew open, shining like black jewels now, staring straight at Minette. His lips parted as he tried to form some word and failed. The breath ebbed from him, and he was gone.

Minette turned to Alain. There was something sadly symbolic, she felt, in poor Philippe's dying at midnight, the point of balance when it is neither day nor night but between two worlds, as Philippe had been in his life. Apt, but no comfort in it. As she wept in Alain's arms, her next thought of Olivier. How could they tell him?

Olivier slept on, his body refreshing itself after the fever. In the morning they were still undecided about how to tell him. Philippe had been washed, wrapped, and prepared for burial in the garden beside Prosper. There would be a short service, and work would be suspended for the pitiful child, dead at the age of seven.

All morning, as she waited for Olivier to awake, Minette was thinking of Amadée de la Fosse, whose spite had set in motion the tragic conclusion of Philippe's life. Had she sent him north in the stagecoach *hoping* that some accident would overtake him and prevent him from reaching Sans Pareil? Was she capable of that? Evidently.

When Olivier's eyes flickered open, he was silent for so long that Minette began to wonder if the snake's poison had robbed him of speech. She began to coax him softly to answer her when he stopped her with an upraised palm.

"I know," he said simply.

"What do you know, *mon cher?*"

"The snakes killed Philippe. I can see it on your face, *Maman*. You do not have to pretend. I know."

Looking into her son's eyes, she could suddenly see the man he would become someday, and the vision was oddly comforting. She could count on him; he would not fail her.

"You don't have to stay with me now," Olivier continued. "I would rather be by myself and think about Philippe. He was my brother. I want to remember everything about him."

Again he lapsed into silence, and as he wished, she left him.

The day promised to be sultry, and Minette decided to hold the service during the coolest part of the afternoon. The bell summoning the workers of Sans Pareil would begin tolling an hour in advance to give them time to make themselves ready. Minette had changed into her only black dress, fed the baby Arielle her lunch, and taken out her Bible to prepare for the simple burial when she was interrupted by an agitated Mam'Odile.

"The witch woman is here. Yes, her, all by herself, just like a black carencro buzzard!"

"Did you tell her that Philippe is dead?"

"You don't have to tell a witch," mumbled Mam'Odile. "She knew it. And she wants to see him."

Ti Manou was as composed as ever, but her eyes glittered with an emotion Minette could not identify.

Alain came swiftly to Minette's side and greeted Ti Manou with sarcasm. "Have you brought Madame Amadée's condolences?"

"No."

"I thought not."

"She does not know that the boy is dead."

"And how is it that you do? Oh, I had forgotten your magical powers. But couldn't you have come earlier and saved Philippe?"

"No, M'sieu Gerard. I can only look into the future. I knew that he would die but not the hour."

"Still, you came very close. He died last night."

"Less than twelve hours. Good." She nodded to herself.

"I know that you liked Philippe," said Minette. "But why have you come all this way, Ti Manou?"

"I have come to save his soul," was the answer.

"What nonsense is this?" Alain reddened angrily. "The boy is dead."

"Dead to you. Dead to your world. But not to mine. And his soul, for which you Christians are also concerned, is in danger. It is *dessunin*."

"Enough!" Alain sputtered.

But Minette stopped him. "Explain," she said. "We will listen."

Ti Manou nodded. "*Dessunin* is what we call the separation of the soul from the body."

"We also believe—"

"I know what you believe, Mistress Minette. But voodoo followers know that the body has two souls. One is the *gros bon ange*, the personal soul—that is the one you hope to send to heaven with your prayers. The other is the *loa mait-tête*. This is the spirit-soul that enters a person the first time he is possessed by a voodoo god."

"You are saying Philippe was possessed?" Alain asked.

"Of course. He inherited it from his mother, Hera, a voodoo believer."

"What happens to this *loa mait-tête* now?" Alain demanded.

"If it is properly exorcised, it will return to its home in the waters under the earth. If not, there is danger to those closest in blood. And who is the closest living kin to Philippe?"

"Olivier," Minette whispered.

"Exactly."

There was a silence.

"Do you see the danger now?" Ti Manou persisted.

Alain shook his head. "I cannot believe—"

"Do it, do it at once," Minette burst out.

"Take me to Philippe," Ti Manou said quietly.

Ti Manou lifted the sheet with which the boy was covered, moved under it, and lay on Philippe. She took a small beaded rattle from her pocket, kissed it, and called on the *loa* to leave Philippe. She spoke into his unheeding ear in a continuing stream of whispers, calling his name. She moved the body so that Philippe seemed to half rise from the bed.

Minette choked back an exclamation of fright, and Ti Manou, her concentration interrupted, motioned that they should leave the room. As they walked down the hall, holding each other tightly, they could hear her low chanting behind them.

"We do not have to believe, Alain. Only for our peace of mind," Minette pleaded. In her imagination rose the figures of Mother Catherine and Sister Immaculata, stern and uncomprehending. She forced them back.

Olivier's voice sounded suddenly; he'd crept up on them. "What are you talking about? What is happening to Philippe?"

Alain and Minette looked at each other. She decided to brave it. "Ti Manou has come to give him a voodoo burial ceremony, Olivier."

"That is a good thing," Olivier said, "because he believed."

"Olivier!" Alain was astounded. "How do you know he believed in voodoo?"

"We used to talk about it," Olivier replied. "He said it reminded him of his mother because she believed. Now he will be closer to her."

"Ti Manou was right," Minette admitted.

"It seems so. But I don't accept—"

"Alain." Olivier cut into his stepfather's musing. "I would like to see Philippe now."

"We'll all go," said Alain gently.

Philippe, son of Prosper de la Fosse and Hera, dressed in a little black suit, lay in his newly made coffin. On his forehead Ti Manou had outlined a cross in white powder. His hands and feet had been washed again in water sweetened with herbs and leaves and then dried. His nose and ears were plugged with cotton wool, his mouth tied closed by a cord knotted atop his head. His big toes were also tied together.

"So he won't get up and walk," Olivier whispered, matter of fact. "And shouldn't you burn all his things?"

Ti Manou looked at Olivier with appreciation. "The true knowledge creeps in everywhere," she commented. "Don't cry for your brother, Minette's son. He is well protected, and now, so are you."

They watched her drop a rosary into the coffin, together with the finger- and toenail parings she had collected from Philippe. The last to be added was a handkerchief, a small, pathetic touch that made Olivier cry for the first time. To the sound of his sobs, Alain hammered the coffin shut.

The funeral was not held until the sun had gone down, again on Ti Manou's advice. All the Catholic prayers were said and hymns sung, with Minette leading the singing. At the same time, a bonfire of all Philippe's possessions was burning in a nearby field. The men and women of Sans Pareil kept watching the blaze restively, whispering together.

"Do they know?" Minette asked.

"Of course they know," said Ti Manou calmly. "And they will respect you for taking the precautions you did, laying him to rest in the old way."

Gradually the blaze in the field died down, and something seemed to pass with it. They returned to the house.

"I am so proud of Olivier," said Alain. "He was so strong."

"There will be more tears in private," Minette told him. "They grew up together."

"How shall we help Olivier's new loneliness?" Alain wondered.

"You spoke of a school for the children of this parish. Let's make it happen."

"I will advertise again for a schoolmaster—this time in all the New Orleans papers," Alain said. "Suppose we hold classes for several months a year here at Sans Pareil. Would you be disturbed by so many children?"

"I grew up without the slightest privacy." Minette laughed. "The more, the merrier. Especially children."

"Are you suggesting, in a roundabout manner, that Arielle needs a younger sibling?"

"*Eh bien*, m'sieu. As you like." Minette was finally smiling, and her hand slipped into his.

27

In the morning, Ti Manou prepared to leave.

"Do you go back to New Orleans?" Minette asked.

"No. I have left Madame Amadée."

Both Minette and Alain were startled. Ti Manou, Amadée's shadow for so many years!

Minette's expression silently asked why.

"For Philippe and a number of other reasons," answered Ti Manou as if Minette had spoken.

"But who is with her now?"

Something like a smile elongated the voodoo woman's lips. "Her mirror and her fear of growing old. Boon companions, eh?"

Alain nodded grimly. "It's still not justice for what she has done."

"She will not outlive you," said Ti Manou. "Her time is not far away."

"Please don't tell me anymore."

"What will you do now, Ti Manou?"

"I will begin a business of my own. I will be an herbalist."

An audible sniff told her that Mam'Odile had entered the room.

"Can I do anything to help you?" Minette volunteered.

"Yes, you can pay me for the success of my protection."

"What protection is that?"

Ti Manou chuckled. "You have been living with my charm in your house. I hid it here before Olivier was born. I knew you would have need of them. I am afraid that M'sieu Alain's ordeal with the Indians used up most of the magic, but—"

"Charm? What kind of charm? Some mess of shells and leaves and chicken feet?" Mam'Odile broke in.

"It was hidden," said Ti Manou coolly.

"You think I never clean this house? I find what is hidden."

"But you have not found this."

"We'll see!" Mam'Odile marched toward the bedroom with the others following. Ti Manou, on hands and knees, ran her fingers over the cypress paneling. The clever hands explored each minute crack and came away empty.

"What did it look like?" asked Minette.

"Very small. A thin sliver of wood—special wood—with a red thread looped around one end and a half a coin turned sideways."

"That bit of nonsense?" Mam'Odile was smiling widely now. "I thought it was something the children brought in here to play. I threw it away."

"When?" Ti Manou was sharp.

"When? Now let me see . . ." Mam'Odile was tantalizingly vague. "A long time ago, say before Philippe was taken by the Indians. So what you want us to pay you for, conjure-woman?"

"Your time, your thought," Minette hastily interceded. "I want to give you money to start in your new profession."

"I owe you much," she added tactfully. "Without your help I'd still be with—"

"Yes, that old chevalier was truly possessed, and not even a believer," recalled Ti Manou. "Yet there are many forms of his madness. I do not regret withdrawing my powers from Madame Amadée."

"What will happen to her now, Ti Manou?"

"She will die a little every day until her time comes."

"We all do that," Alain interjected.

"You cannot understand the savage torments of vanity, M'sieu Gerard. But Philippe and all the other victims of her cruelty will be avenged." She looked at Minette again. "I want to give you something." She reached into the bag she carried and drew out a slender dark green flask.

Alain stretched out his hand for it, but she placed the bottle squarely in Minette's palm.

"Guard this well."

"What is it?"

"It's what Madame Amadée would kill to have. This is the secret of her marvelous complexion."

"My wife needs no such help," said Alain quickly.

"Not now of course, m'sieu. But there are years to come."

"What do you see of the years to come?" Alain asked with unwilling curiosity.

"France will give Louisiana to Spain, and you will be ruled by the Spanish dons. There will be rioting and bloodshed in New Orleans. But then—"

"Please don't tell me the future if it is horrible!" Minette begged.

"You will not feel pain. There will always be a market for your crops. The French will settle down with the Spanish but still remain French. Live your life in peace, and one day, when your mirror tells you that it is time, Madame Minette, you may open the bottle."

Ti Manou left, accepting only a token offering and food for her journey.

As soon as she had gone, Alain began protesting, urging Minette to throw the bottle away. Nothing could convince him of the magic in beauty potions. He took somewhat more stock in Ti Manou's predictions about Spain's rule in Louisiana—the knowledge he'd gained during his time in Spanish prison made that more credible. That was power politics, the chicanery of kings, but this was nonsense, and quite possibly dangerous. He was half afraid of Ti Manou. She might be a charlatan and faker . . . or perhaps her charm *had* helped him with the Indians. . . .

"She's like a sudden chill of air on the back of my neck," said Alain. "It makes me shudder."

"I think she is well disposed toward me," Minette answered.

"Think what you like. But throw away the bottle, please."

Minette promised to consider it but procrastinated. She placed the bottle among a row of other flasks on the dressing table, dusted it from time to time and gradually forgot about its mystery.

The months went on, and then a year. Arielle, her baby, was now a true personality. Minette admitted spoiling her, as did Alain, and surprisingly, Olivier.

Arielle ruled her brother with a tiny fist. He was her willing horse in play, her champion in accusations of misdeeds. She made impossible demands on his time, which he accepted with great good nature. Mam'Odile warned Olivier that he was spoiling his sister for any possible husband—husband!—by setting standards of niceness no one else could equal. Olivier laughed. In her unexpected way, the tiny, perfect little girl, who had Minette's face and Alain's coloring, eased the emptiness left by Philippe. He adored her pert charm and was ever protective, and even when Alain's plans for a school class came to fruition and Sans Pareil played host to a timorous French *maître* for three months a year, Olivier continued to spend time with his little sister.

Alain, with ever more ambitious plans for the plantation, worked long days and into the nights. Minette, released from the tyranny of the saddle by day and ledgers at night, found herself confronted with the endless tasks of a plantation mistress. She picked medicinal plants in the woods as she had done with Sister Immaculata so long ago and brewed them into teas for dosing the sick. She visited her workers' quarters, learned their patois and their superstitions, mediated small quarrels, and oversaw the running of the house, the spinning of yarn, the making of clothes, the birthing of babies. She did proud the standards of the hardworking Ursuline nuns. And she always made time for her family.

One afternoon, however, Arielle, half walking, half crawling, escaped from Olivier, who was deep in a schoolbook, and made her way into Minette and Alain's bedroom, where she began to investigate the curious things she saw. Olivier heard a cry and the sound of glass breaking and hurried to Arielle, shouting for help as he ran.

Arielle had swept all the bottles off Minette's dressing table and stood in a circle of broken glass. But in her hand she still clutched what she had reached for, the slender dark green flask given by Ti Manou. She'd managed to pry out the stopper, upend it, and pour the sweet-smelling liquid over her face and arms.

Mam'Odile's cries of horror reached Minette's ears as she came on a scene of frenzied activity: Arielle being scrubbed with strong soap until she cried, vigorously rubbed down with toweling and soaped again. Minette's fearful glance showed no change in her daughter. The redness was friction-induced, and she finally persuaded Mam'Odile to stop scrubbing. The fretful little girl was taken into her mother's lap, where she finally whimpered herself into content. A sweet odor like lilacs and tuberoses clung to her skin, but there was absolutely no change in Arielle. Minette held her for a long time.

So much for illusion, so much for eternal beauty? At least there had been nothing in the potion that could hurt a baby. Had it been all talk and promises? But no, wait, what about Amadée? Despite her age, her complexion had been magnificent, unlined and flawless. Perhaps the potion could do nothing where there existed no need for improvement—such as a baby's perfect, rose-petal skin? Minette preferred to think so. She felt a gentle disappointment that she'd pass into old age unaided. Ah, well—she reached back for an old favorite—*tant pis*, so much the worse. But perhaps in years to come, Arielle . . .

That night, in their bedroom, Alain expressed his relief. "I'm glad the potion is gone as long as the baby wasn't hurt. I've never been comfortable having its witchcraft in the house. Each time I pass Philippe's grave and think of how we buried him—"

"I would do it again."

"These *loa mait-têtes!* Who knows if they really exist?"

"Remember that Philippe was also buried with a rosary. Does that count for nothing, Alain?"

"One against the other, eh? Well, I am on the side of the angels. Where is that confounded flask Ti Manou gave you? Do you still have it?"

She gave it to him. He opened the window and casually tossed it out into the yard.

"Done," he said briskly. He seized Minette in an amorous grip. "Let my eyes be your mirror, sweet. Look in them. What do you see?"

She permitted herself a little coyness. "That I am beautiful?"

"Always use this mirror," he said, "always," and he sank to the bed, tugging her into a flurry of arms and legs and then suddenly exchanged the deep drinking kisses of gratified, married lovers. Out of their clothes with practiced ease, they sported in the moonlight slanting through the windows.

At last Minette curled sleepily against Alain. Satisfaction brought relaxed, untroubled breathing and soon after, sleep.

The moon's rays lighting their room fell also on the yard below, where a sleek black cat approached the empty green flask Alain had tossed out so lightly. The cat grasped the flask in its mouth, eyed the window from which it had been thrown, lashed its tail in farewell, and moved off smartly, disappearing into the darkness. The faintest odor of lilac and tuberoses was all that remained.

COMING NEXT MONTH

THE MIST AND THE MAGIC by Susan Wiggs

A spellbinding romance set in 17th century Ireland. On a cliff high above the sea, John Wesley Hawkins meets Caitlin MacBride. With true Irish whimsey, Caitlin has just grasped a white and blush-colored rose and wished for her true love. Hawkins walks into her life, but danger and adventure lie ahead before these magnificent lovers can find a happy ending.

SILENA by Terri Herrington

A powerful romance set in Nebraska in the late 1800s. Silena Rivers is on a quest to discover her true identity, with the help of handsome Wild West showman Sam Hawkins. But along the way, they find that love is the only thing that really matters.

THE ANXIOUS HEART by Denise Robertson

An enchanting contemporary novel set in London about a courageous and feisty young woman who pulls herself out of a low-income tenement building to discover the amazing world outside.

THE MAGIC TOUCH by Christina Hamlett

Beth Hudson's husband, Edward, was a magician obsessed with the occult. He had always promised her that he would be able to communicate with her from beyond the grave; and two years after his death, his prophecy seems to be coming true. With the help of Lt. Jack Brassfield, Beth reopens the investigation of her husband's death and gets more than she bargains for.

AMAZING GRACE by Janet Quin-Harkin

An engaging romance set in Australia just after World War I. Grace Pritchard, a beautiful young Englishwoman, is forced to choose between two men . . . or face a difficult future alone in the male-dominated and untamed Australian outback.

EMBRACE THE DAY by Susan Wiggs

A Susan Wiggs classic. An enthralling and romantic family saga of spirited Genevieve Elliot and handsome Roarke Adair, who set out for the blue-green blaze of Kentucky to stake their claim on love.

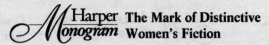 **Harper Monogram**   **The Mark of Distinctive Women's Fiction**

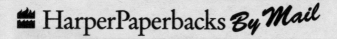

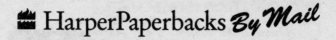
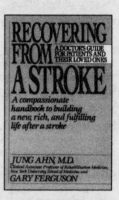
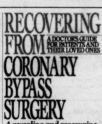